Potluck

by Jack Rudloe

ISBN 1-892590-37-9

Published by Out Your Backdoor Press
Jeff Potter, publisher

Disclaimer: This is purely a work of fiction. Any similarity to individuals, living or dead, or other legal entity is coincidental. It is intended for entertainment only.

Library of Congress Control Number: 2002116763

Copies of this book are available directly for $14.95, plus $2.05 shipping and handling, from:

Out Your Backdoor Press
4686 Meridian Rd.
Williamston MI 48895

or:

OutYourBackdoor.com
info@outyourbackdoor.com

Contact info for Gulf Specimen:
gulfspecimen.org
PO Box 237
Panacea, FL 32346
(850) 984-5297
gspecimen@sprintmail.com

cover design by Owen Neils
copyediting by Joey Harrison

Contents

Acknowledgements 5

Author Biography 7

1 / The Freighter 1

2 / The Burning of the Night Shadow 11

3 / Opportunity Knocks 19

4 / Lupino's Plan 31

5 / Bales, Bales, Bales! 41

6 / The Baptism 51

7 / Above Suspicion 60

8 / Shrimper's Dreams 68

9 / The Engine Blows 78

10 / Lawton's Fish House 88

11 / The Hopper Run 99

12 / The Conspiracy 106

13 / April 117

14 / The Tampa Connection 131

15 / Voyage to Colombia 140

16 / The Guajira Peninsula 157

17 / Packing Out 172

18 / Storm at Sea 187

19 / The Coast Guard Cometh 201

20 / The Return of Lupino 214

21 / The Off-Loaders 225

22 / The Fight 233

23 / The Marine Patrol 242

24 / Reunion 251

25 / Blessing of the Fleet 262

In memory of Captain Edward Keith, a shrimper and good friend, who went down at sea, trying to provide people with good things to eat.

Acknowledgements

In the mid 70's I was writing a non-fiction book about the shrimping industry, called "Shrimper's Log." It would've been the first overview of this way of life. However, it didn't take long for a very different story to emerge, which I called "Potluck."

I want to thank the many people who helped me with the work. Some are in prison, others are dead, and some will remain anonymous. I would love to acknowledge the key advisors who made this book possible, spending long hours telling their tales, but I cannot.

However, to friends like Lucy Shepard and Jack Silverstein, David and Mary Ann Frisby and Pam Lycett, who helped with the research, technical advice and preparation of the manuscript, I wish to express my gratitude. My wife Anne and son Sky, and Gulf Specimen Marine Lab volunteers, Ed Gartner, Dave Norris and Ed Komarek read the manuscript and offered their suggestions. Tom Baker, Mary Ellen Chastain, Barbara Hogan and Jim Prescott helped with proofing. Victor Nunez and E. Stuart Gregg III provided a voice of encouragement; and my neighbor, the Reverend Charles E. Barwick, provided me with the regional spiritual backgrounding that my characters might have felt. Martha Beidler, with her deep knowledge of mythology, helped me put Preston Barfield's quest into the context of the great human experience. And her husband Richard's friendship, advice and support has been a cornerstone in my life. Carl Metcalf and Nicolas Cotes have also been helpful. To all these, and the people of Gulf Specimen Marine Laboratory—Doug Gleeson, Debbie Clifford, Ken Corbett, Victor Spencer and Torres LeBrun—I shall be forever grateful.

1

The Freighter

Captain Preston Barfield was trying to keep awake. With heavy-lidded eyes he looked out over the distant lights of other shrimp boats working in the Gulf of Mexico. He wiggled his shoulders and stretched his legs. The clock on the wheelhouse wall of the *Lady Mary* read 2 a.m. In another fifteen minutes it would be time to wake up Charlie, his deckhand, and get the nets on board.

Preston was a bear of a man. At more than six foot four inches, his head almost touched the cabin's ceiling. His stubble-rugged face was weathered by sun and sea far beyond that of a forty-year-old man. Listening to the north wind moaning and rattling the windows, he flipped on the radar, which started the T-shaped beacon on the cabin roof revolving. Three white electronic blips flashed back at him, leaving comet-like tracings on the luminous green radar screen. They faded away until the revolving line picked them up and they flashed again.

Each blip within the concentric circles represented another shrimp boat, roughly sixty-eight feet long, the size of his own *Lady Mary*. The captain's callused fingers adjusted the knob, extending the range to sixteen miles. He wondered if there were any more fools besides himself out there in the wintry off-season trying to scrape up enough shrimp to pay for fuel and groceries.

Suddenly, there was a large flash at the edge of the screen. Strange, he thought. It looked like a tug pushing a string of barges, but they were outside their normal shipping routes. Again it flashed, and this time he was certain it was a ship, roughly three hundred feet long. And in that remote North Florida coastal area, where there was no commerce, that was even stranger.

Then he understood. His eyes grew wide. Another blip about the size of a shrimp boat appeared on the screen. He watched the small blip closing rapidly until it merged with the ship's and became one big blip.

Preston stepped down into the cabin and regarded his lanky deckhand, peacefully asleep in the fetal position beneath a heavy, brown army blanket. He was a deceptive picture of innocence, with his soft, youthful skin, and his shock of blond hair. Although he was twenty-three, he had a slender face with the start of a thin, scraggly beard that made him look more like a teenager. Charlie Hansen's mouth was open, issuing tired snores, while his eyelids twitched occasionally.

Preston shook him lightly. "Come on, Charlie," he said gently, "it's about time to wind 'em up. I want to show you something on the radar." He went back to the wheelhouse. The deckhand groaned, rolled over and mumbled something unintelligible. He lay there for a minute, finally thrust himself up from his world of private darkness, and in one motion, slid into his salt-stained blue jeans and jerked the worn leather belt with a tarnished brass buckle around his narrow waist. Then he crammed on his fish-scale-covered boots, stretched hard, and groggily made his way to the coffee pot.

"How long I been asleep?" Charlie yawned, swallowing down the strong black coffee.

"About an hour," Preston replied, staring down at the radar screen with more than casual interest. "This will wake you up. Come take a look!"

Yawning long and loudly, Charlie pressed his face against the rubber gasket that ringed the radar screen to shield out background light. He studied it for a moment with dull, uncomprehending eyes, then cried, "Damn, Preston! That's a freighter. Looks to me like they're hauling a load of pure old mary-wanna! Lordy, Lordy, I wish that was us out there, instead of them. One little run and a man could be fixed for life. I'm so broke I can't fix the transmission on my truck and I gotta walk."

"Yeah," Preston quipped, "fixed for life all right, right in the jailhouse. I've about got a mind to call the Coast Guard, no tellin' what kind of cutthroats are out here..."

"Don't do that!" Charlie warned. "We'll have them crawling all over our boats! We won't never get no sleep tomorrow, and it will come back on us. Remember last month they wrote you a ticket 'cause the fire extinguisher was out of date? Cost you a hundred dollars, didn't it?"

"Yeah, that's true. They got Willie the same day 'cause his turtle shooter was four inches too short."

"They sure did. They arrested him, made him quit fishing, run to the dock, confiscated the net and wrote him a two-thousand-dollar fine. Screw them bastards, I wouldn't call 'em for nothing!" grumbled the deckhand.

Then he looked wistfully, " 'Sides..." he went on, "maybe they'll spill some, and we'll pick up a bale or two."

"If they do, you ain't puttin' it on my boat, Charlie. I don't want nothing to do with it. Dope's the ruination of the world!"

"Ah, come on, Preston. That's easy money. One night's work and you've got it made in the shade. Wouldn't you like to have a new boat? One of those super trawlers that could take the weather—like the ones advertised in *National Fisherman* magazine for three hundred thousand dollars?"

"You know I would. I've dreamed about it, but that ain't the way to get it, Charlie," the captain replied looking down at his deckhand. "And damned if I want to end up in the State's Hotel, like that sorry brother-in-law of mine did! By the way, you heard from Lupino? He said he was gonna try dragging down at West Pass."

"No, I ain't heard him on the radio," scoffed Charlie. "You know yourself if he was out here like he's supposed to be, he'd be driving us nuts bragging, telling lies about how many shrimp he's caught. He's layed up at the dock, and got some scrawny whore on board. I saw his sorry-assed deckhand Peabob just before we left, and he was drunk as a skunk. Didn't look to me like they were going nowhere."

Preston grunted. Why had he ever listened to his wife, begging him to co-sign the note for her brother after he got out of prison? Buying the *Night Shadow* was supposed to help him go straight. The little pisswad swore he'd stay out here and shrimp round the clock, regardless of the weather, do what Preston told him, and pay the bank note. Lupino was already three payments behind.

Charlie was still focused on the radar screen. "You know they're catching hell out there tonight in this sea!" His blue eyes were wide-awake now, and he drawled with admiration, "Rough as it is, they'll beat all the rigging off their boat."

"They don't care nothing about the boat," Preston shot back contemptuously. "It's just the wrapper for their dope. They don't care if it gets beat all to hell as long as they can haul a load. Probably some sorry deckhand stole someone's boat for the night."

"Well then, he's a *rich* sorry deckhand. I heard they pay a hundred thousand dollars for a load, maybe more."

"That ain't any of our business," Preston snapped, putting on his faded yellow slicker suit. "It's all theirs. And if they end up in the State's Hotel that's their business, too. I'm a shrimper, Charlie, not a damn dope smuggler. I'm proud of what I do, and I love this way of life—even when it's hard like it is now. Now, let's get the nets up."

He threw open the door and stepped out into the night air. Charlie followed, his wool cap pressed down over his big ears and blond side-burns. "Man, it's colder than a well-digger's ass in Alaska," he shuddered. Then he took a deep breath, to drive the last of the sleep out of his body.

Rubbing his hands, Preston put on his heavy leather gloves and engaged the winches. The *Lady Mary* shook and grumbled loudly above the steady chatter of the engine, as the great spools began reeling in six hundred feet of cable. His breath steamed in the frigid air as he spoke, "If it don't get any better this tow, we'll anchor and call it a night." With his greasy gloved hand, he snatched the moving cable to keep it from piling up on one end of the drum.

"Hell, I wouldn't care if we went into the dock right now, we been out here what, a week now? And I'll bet we ain't made expenses. I'd just as soon go home and hunt me some cooter," Charlie tested, watching the captain's reaction, hoping he'd relent.

Preston grabbed another handful of cable, "Can't do it, Charlie. Those shrimp might show any time. Hell, they may show tonight. The water's still cold, but I've seen it happen before. The first boat on the scene is the one that makes the money. And I need to make some money bad. Mary's gonna have that baby in a couple of months, and the doctor said there's complications. What little insurance we got won't cover the half of it."

His deckhand nodded glumly. He knew Preston was three payments behind on his truck with the finance company, and two payments behind on his own boat, all due to doctor bills. But he also knew that he'd be lucky if he shared a hundred dollars this trip after deducting expenses, and that was a week's work.

Charlie offered testily, his teeth starting to chatter from the biting north wind, "Those boys packing out that freighter don't have them kinda problems. They're rolling in money. I think we ought to make a dope run down to Colombia and get in on some of this easy money. At least we wouldn't be freezing to death down there, that warm tropical weather, and those good-looking women. I know one boy who made the run, said he about screwed himself to death down there."

Preston gave him a hard look, so he dropped the subject. To say Charlie Hansen was proud to be Preston's deckhand for the past five years was an understatement. He not only respected and admired his captain, he practically worshipped him. He knew all about his worries and wished that somehow he could help fix them. Nothing tickled him more than sitting around the bar bragging to the other deckhands how they dragged bottoms that other captains were afraid to go near for fear of losing their nets. When the other boats came in empty-handed, Preston often managed to find shrimp. But lately, no one could find any.

The winches turned around and around, fattening with cable. All at once, the two sets of otter doors rose out of the sea, and the iron shoes slammed together with a loud crash. Quickly they locked off their winches. The ironclad otter doors that weighted and spread the two large funnel-shaped trawls dangled from the outstretched steel outriggers on either side of the boat, their tickler chains covered with festive yellow and orange sea whips and white strings of accordion-like whelk eggs.

Preston moved quickly back to the wheelhouse, shoving the throttle in the corner, and the engine responded with a loud scream. The *Lady Mary* surged ahead washing down the catch. The first bloated bag was hoisted out of the sea, showering icy water on deck and swinging like a gigantic medicine bag. With the caution of a bullfighter, Preston approached it. With each roll of the boat, the great webbed prison, gorged with a half ton of fish, protruding stingray tails, and catfish spines, swung past him. He grabbed the dangling release ropes at the bottom on the next pass and it dragged him a couple of feet. Then, throwing all his two hundred and fifty pounds against the slipknots, he snatched back and forth until the bag opened.

An avalanche of life came squashing down on deck. Big cow-nosed rays pounded their wings, croakers grunted, and bright yellow loggerhead sponges tumbled and rolled like boulders. Crabs went everywhere, and octopuses blushing with rage and spurting black ink, slithered across the deck. Then they dumped the next bag on top of it. Preston's booted foot pushed through the mound of life, churning up sea robins, sticky brown sea cucumbers, and exposing yellow finger sponges, but his eyes were only for the shrimp. The deck lights made their stalked eyeballs glow like hot red coals, but they were few and far between.

Patiently, Charlie waited, holding the whip line, wondering if he was going to make another strike or be reasonable and join the rest of the fleet anchored down behind the barrier islands. Preston was wondering the same thing.

When the captain re-tied the tail bags and jerked his thumb toward the water, Charlie had his answer. He nodded with acceptance, having learned to respect Preston's hunches. He jerked the pelican hooks loose and the two nets slithered across the deck and slid over the side like two green, webbed scaly serpents. The otter doors splashed down into the sea dragging the nets behind them.

Charlie crouched over the pile and started culling. They called him "Popcorn Charlie" because he could make the shrimp fly through the air as he culled. Few deckhands along the Gulf Coast could beat him, and he was proud of it.

His fingers working in a blur of motion, he grabbed shrimp out of the catch and threw them into his basket. Before him, the pile grew smaller and smaller; behind, a shrimpless pile was spewed out like tailings from a mining operation.

In an hour, the decks were clear. When the last shovel of trash fish splattered into the sea to the screeching delight of hovering seagulls, Charlie washed down the fantail. White foamy saltwater blasted away the fish slime, hog chokers, bits of parchment worm casings and scattered the crabs that hid in the corners. They scrubbed the deck with a broom until it gleamed wetly under the deck lights. The sooner the catch was off the deck, the sooner he could get back into that warm cabin. When the last shovel-load splattered into the sea, Preston helped him ice the shrimp and stowed them in the hold.

They went inside, feeling the comfortable, warm heat that emanated from the galley stove where the burners gave forth eerie blue flames. Then Charlie remembered the radar screen, and went over eagerly to see the progress of the smugglers. He was disappointed to see that the freighter had moved out of sight, and only the small blip of the shrimp boat remained.

Two hours passed. Charlie boiled up a pot of fresh shrimp for a midnight snack. He and the captain had settled down to enjoy them, when suddenly a familiar voice broke the radio silence. "Calling the *Lady Mary*, calling the *Lady Mary*! Come in Preston."

Well, at long last, here he is, Preston thought, hearing that familiar whiny voice. Only, Lupino sounded agitated; that meant something was wrong and it could be anything. Lupino was good at running aground, getting his wheel caught in the net, or having mechanical problems, often from his own doing.

"Where you at?" the captain demanded.

"I know where he's at, the sorry bastard," Charlie said jealously, as he mopped his shrimp in cocktail sauce. "He's at the dock and got some whore on board with him. And he's calling just to bug me."

"Listen, I've got trouble, Preston. That number six spray valve broke on me again. She's spraying diesel all over the engine, I'm afraid she's fixing to blow."

Preston was exasperated. "I swear, Lupino. I thought you fixed that damn thing. You're liable to catch fire and burn up..."

"Stand by," his brother-in-law said. His voice was tense and definitely not his usual bantering, happy self. "Just stand by," he repeated a little hysterically. In the background was a strange roaring sound. The engine was going *voom...voom...voom...* And then there was only static.

Charlie got to his feet. "That don't sound so sporty. Something's bad wrong."

"Sounds like his motor's fixing to blow up." Preston's voice was worried. "Lupino!" he shouted into the mike. "Shut her down quick!"

"I can't!" the voice wailed back. "She won't shut off!"

A few minutes went by in silence. Again Preston called him on the radio, but there was no reply. Just empty, eerie static.

Then, suddenly, a hysterical Spanish-accented voice blurted out, "Help! We're on fire. This boat is going to blow up..." then the voice was drowned by static.

Preston and Charlie looked at each other in frightened confusion. They didn't recognize the voice. Uncertainly, Preston grabbed the mike.

"Come back, there. Where are you?"

"That didn't sound like Lupino," Charlie said, puzzled. "It didn't sound like old Peabob, neither."

Suddenly the familiar but panicked voice of his brother-in-law burst back on the air. "Preston, we're on fire! Calling the *Lady Mary*! Anybody..." He was breathing heavily between words. "We done used up all our fire extinguishers...we're going to jump."

In the *Lady Mary*'s wheelhouse they could feel the fear bursting over the radio box. Before Preston could get his position, Lupino's voice was cut off as if it had been severed with a knife.

This time the silence was permanent. No amount of calling did any good. The captain took a deep breath to calm himself, so he could think. "Charlie, get those nets up quick! We better go look for him."

The deckhand jammed into his boots, grabbed a slicker and bolted out the door. Preston switched his radio over to the Coast Guard channel and raised them. He related what just happened, and the dispatcher began asking regimented questions in a monotone calm, controlled manner. "What is the name of the vessel in distress? Who is the Master?" —What was Preston's name, what was the name of his vessel, what was the Master's name.

"Look, it's the *Night Shadow*, and my brother-in-law, Lupino Talagera, is the captain." Preston then snapped, "Now, why the hell don't you quit asking me all these questions and send a plane to look for him."

"We can't send a spotter out before daylight," the voice came back, "and there are no cutters in your area. We'll try to contact other vessels to assist. And sir, it's illegal to use profanity on the airways. Now again, what is the name of their vessel, who is the Master and what is their position?"

"I don't know. He didn't say," he said evenly, controlling his anger at their ineptness. "He was too busy putting out the fire. Look, you know everything I do. You'd better get a chopper or a boat out here now! I can't waste any more time. I've got to get the nets up. Stand by!"

He rushed out to help Charlie. The boat began to rattle and shake noisily as the winches were engaged. As soon as the nets were decked and emptied, Preston shoved the throttle forward, and the *Lady Mary* surged ahead. Charlie then threw all his energy into culling to get his mind off his tension, hurling big sponges over the railings, and kicking fish out of his way. Lupino was a pain in the ass, but after all his annoyance, he was still Charlie's best friend, and they'd grown up together. The deckhand was frantically picking out shrimp, when Preston grabbed the shovel and started scooping the un-culled catch overboard, shrimp and all.

"Hey, what are you doing?" cried Charlie in surprise. "There's still shrimp in all this—more than we got in the last three tows."

"Let's get everything off the deck now. We may only be a few miles away, but if we keep dribbling out trash, we could have sharks following us. I know its cold, but there might be some big ones in that deep water." As Charlie shoved all the life through the scuppers with the push pole, he noted that Preston was right, the shrimp were picking up. After he called the Coast Guard back, and told them everything he could, Preston felt helpless. They could call all the boats they wanted, but he knew he was the only shrimp boat out there, except for the smugglers.

Time was working against him. The words, "We're going to jump," rang in his ears. He winced when he thought of Lupino and his crew hanging onto a life jacket, floating in those bitterly cold seas, being swept along in the currents.

Preston pushed the throttle forward and looked out at the dark sea through the salt-sprayed cabin windows, hoping to see a glow or a light, but all he saw was darkness. Lupino didn't say where he was, didn't give them a clue. Then suddenly the image of that marijuana-hauling freighter and the smaller boat marrying up to it on the radar screen popped into his mind. "That's not Lupino. It better not be!" he cried aloud. Then added angrily, "He wouldn't dare, not after all the trouble he got into—not after going to jail. Not with me co-signing on his note!"

Then he remembered getting a notice from the insurance company just before he left to go shrimping, and a sinking realization came over him. Lupino had failed to make any payments at all on the insurance, and coverage was cancelled. That meant Preston was probably about to lose everything. Then there was that Spanish voice on the same frequency, which was even more suspicious. It wouldn't be the first time Lupino fell in with bad company. Ever since his brother-in-law ran that first load of dope, he went from being a passable fisherman to a lazy bum. Three years in jail didn't straighten him out. It only made him sorrier.

Yet, in spite of all the trouble Lupino managed to get into, everyone around the coast liked him—in small doses. His impish grin and mischievous black eyes appeared before Preston.

Lupino wasn't cut out to be a shrimper. It wasn't so much that he wasn't built for it—being skinny, weak and much too short. He lacked patience and he hated being at sea for more than a week. As much as he loved to bullshit and talk, Preston thought, he should have bought himself a party boat and become a fishing guide for rich balls. Now he might die for his mistake.

Running wide open, the *Lady Mary* fought the wind and seas. Preston stood at the helm, gazing at the darkness, looking for some sign of light. Charlie nervously paced the small wheelhouse, glancing at the radar now and then, and going out on deck to look around. But only the black sea and cold stars looked back.

Preston glanced down at the temperature gauge, and throttled down a notch when he saw it climb to 183° F. "Won't do a bit of good if I blow this old engine all to hell pushing her too hard," he said grimly, and slowed down.

Charlie extended the radar screen and picked up a blip. "Got something!" he cried.

Preston studied it carefully and nodded, "That could be him." He took the boat off automatic pilot, turned southeast and reset the course.

A half hour later they saw a yellow glow on the horizon to the east. He swung the *Lady Mary* toward it. Soon they could see fire, and as they approached, Preston drew back the throttle to half speed. To Charlie's questioning look, he replied, "If they're overboard, the way this wind and tide are running, they could be anywhere out here. I damn sure don't want to chop them to pieces in the prop wash." He beamed his spotlight over the empty, dark waters, looking for survivors.

2

The Burning of the Night Shadow

If Lupino Talagera hadn't been so jittery, he would have been proud of himself as he bucked the seas heading away from the freighter. But with twelve tons of marijuana on board, and a crew of Cuban smugglers, his hands trembled with fear and exhaustion as they gripped the spoke handles on the wheel. Anxiously, he glanced over his shoulder at the men lying on bunks in the cramped cabin. They were smoking joints and trying to relax. The Cubans all had mustaches, were loaded with gold jewelry, and could have easily played banditos in spaghetti westerns. All they needed were shoulder belts full of bullets and sombreros. From the moment they came on board in Carrabelle the previous night, he was fearful of them.

A tall American they called Rick, the one with a blond crew cut who was built like a varsity wrestler, carried a machine gun pistol with a silencer on the barrel. He was sleeping with it on the top bunk, hugging it close like a teddy bear. The Cubans carried .45-caliber automatic pistols. Only the other American, Blake, a youthful man with a ponytail, who jumped off the freighter with great agility at the last minute, wasn't blatantly armed.

Right on schedule, Lupino and his brooding crew had met the three-hundred-foot rust bucket out in the Gulf of Mexico, fifty miles south of Apalachicola. During the trip out, Raul, the meanest and biggest, exchanged codes with the captain in Spanish over the radio. Through the darkness it came, with only enough running lights to keep them from colliding.

The swells lifted the *Night Shadow* up and sent her battering into the steel bulkhead which towered above them, blow after blow. When the boats were finally lashed together, with only two rubber truck tires between them, down the rusty ladder scampered twenty or more small-boned, dark-skinned Indians in khaki rags. They swarmed over the *Night Shadow* and made room for the avalanche of burlap-wrapped bales that thundered down on the deck. The Indians were professional. In less than an hour they would cram 300 eighty-pound bales into the hold.

They stuffed them into the bow, the engine room, the lazarette—any place that had space. More bales rained down from twenty feet up, shaking the small shrimp boat.

Lupino was down in the hold with them, feverishly helping stack. He was so nervous from looking at the big machetes strapped to their sides that he almost vomited from fear. And still the bales kept coming. These emaciated, dark-skinned wrecks of humanity would be paid five hundred dollars to make the trip, and all they had to eat on the month-long voyage was two live cows and a couple hundred pounds of rice.

All of a sudden, a great rolling swell threw the shrimp boat hard against the steel bulkhead. Metal bent, stay cables popped, timber shattered, and Lupino looked up to see boards and crash bumpers flying off and floating away.

"My boat, my boat! We're gonna sink, cut her loose, quick!"

He ran forward, drawing out his pocketknife, but Raul pushed him back. "Not before we're loaded!" More bales rained down. The Indians jammed the remaining fifty into the cabin—then bedlam broke loose. They grabbed anything that wasn't nailed down, they begged for money, food and demanded cigarettes. What's more, the transom was a wreck, the ribs were exposed, the boards were shattered, and nails were sticking out.

Rick, the steely-eyed American, fired a blast into the air with his sub-machine gun. Still chattering, and not at all subdued, the Indians scurried back up the ladder, carrying off most of Lupino's underwear, shirts, knives, forks, plates, and all his canned goods.

They were just about to cut loose when a blond-headed American stranger hurried down the ladder and jumped six feet to the deck, carrying a duffel-bag and a .45 automatic. With a wide grin showing lots of good white teeth he said "Hi-ya" cheerfully to Lupino and introduced himself as Blake. Lupino thought his accent was funny—it wasn't southern, it wasn't northern exactly. It was polished and educated. Lupino noticed that his clothing was surprisingly clean, and so was his hair—an amazing feat for anyone living on that grubby barge.

Then the man waved adios to the Indians, strode forward and shook hands with Raul. As they moved away, Lupino learned from snatches of their conversation that this fellow had ridden the freighter all the way up from Colombia. They had made two other drops along the south Florida coast, recovering all their expenses. Now, he said, this last and final one was pure profit.

A few more hours and they'd be at the dock to unload the bales into a tractor trailer. It was a cinch, Raul said. In a few more hours Lupino's money troubles would be over.

The longer they ran, the worse the smell of diesel fuel permeated the air, mixing with the pungent odors of marijuana. Lupino felt someone jabbing a finger into his back, and turned around to see Raul's fierce black eyes boring into him. "Hey, you got a fuel leak or something. It stinks of gas in here."

"Naw, it's nothing to worry about," Lupino tossed off reassuringly, "I been running this way for a month now. If it gets much worse, I'll go down and fix it, but we can make it to the dock." He turned back to the wheel, frowning. He had a rag tightly wrapped around the injector to keep it from spraying, but it must have worked loose.

One of the Cubans started to light a joint, and Raul shouted for him to stop. Lupino laughed nervously, "It won't hurt, you can't ignite diesel fuel with a damn cigarette. It takes a hell of a fire to get it going."

Raul repeated something to the others in choppy, guttural Spanish, and they laughed. There was something ugly about him, something mean that made Lupino's skin crawl. It was hard to decide who was more dangerous, Raul, with his sudden fits of rage when anything went wrong, or the superior-acting Cubans who spoke no English. They were very blasé, smiling a lot, stuffing cocaine up their noses and acting like they hauled more pot than an airport porter carried suitcases. Then there was Rick, Raul's silent bodyguard, with his machine gun, who had the chill of death about him. Out of the whole bunch, the only tolerable one was the new man, Blake, who had jumped aboard out of nowhere. No one had said anything about picking up a passenger.

The smell of diesel fuel was getting worse. Suddenly the lights flickered, dimmed and flickered again. Permeating its way through the smell of marijuana was the stench of burning electrical wiring.

Lupino's narrow features twisted, his eyes became wide as he licked his lips anxiously. Then a noise from the very guts of the engine began to shake the vessel. *Voom...voom...voom!* it roared, as it labored.

"Hey, something's burning," yelped Raul, jumping to his feet. "The goddamn boat's on fire!" Lupino cast around for the fire extinguisher, snatched it off the wall, and ran out into the night air followed by Raul.

Flames were licking up from the engine room. "Holy shit!" yelled the Cuban, his black eyes popping from his round, scarred face. "We're gonna burn up. Where's the life boat?"

Lupino cleared his throat. "There ain't nothing to worry about. This has happened before. It's that fuel injector, it's just some grease on the engine burning. Don't worry," he said confidently, "I'll put it out."

"This happened before?" shrilled the Cuban in a rage, above the panicky yells of Spanish of his crew. "What kind of shit outfit did we hire?!" But Lupino didn't hear him. Grabbing the radio, he made contact with Preston and told him to stand by. Then he made his way, hand over hand down into the smoke-filled engine room and pushed his way through the narrow corridor lined with bales of marijuana, stacked from floor to ceiling, to reach the burning engine.

Voom...voom...vooooommm. The noise was deafening, out of control. The whole boat was shaking. Instead of the spray valve jetting diesel into the fuel injector and the cylinders, it was blasting an aerosol mist of fuel into the supercharger. This ignited it into a fiery vapor, and flames were beginning to eat into the grease-soaked wooden bulkhead, peeling the burlap off the bales.

Holding his breath, Lupino frantically emptied the fire extinguisher, but it only quelled the flames for a moment before new orange tongues sprang up. All the while, the deafening pinging roar of hot pistons rang in his ears.

Defeated, he scurried up the ladder with the empty cylinder in hand. "I can't put the son of a bitch out from here," he yelled hoarsely. "We've got to get those bales out of the forepeak so I can get to the front of the engine."

Just then Lupino slipped on the ladder and caught himself on a rung, wrenching his shoulder. He yelled with pain. Raul grabbed him by the arm and jerked him up with incredible strength. He looked at him with cold hatred and slapped him savagely across the face. "I ought to throw you into the goddamn fire!"

"We've got to stop the fuel," Lupino cried, backing away. "We've got to shut the engine off or she'll blow sky high!"

Raul dove for the wheelhouse, snatched the microphone off the hook, yelling, "Fire! We're on freaking fire!" Then he yanked the throttle back and switched the key back and forth trying to shut it off. But the cables were melted and the engine wouldn't stop—it continued roaring louder and louder as the pistons madly pounded in their cylinders. By now smoke and sparks were coming up into the cabin. The crew was frantic, the smell of fear mingled with the smoke.

His black eyes snapping with rage, Raul jerked the throttle back again so hard that it broke off in his hand. Amidst the frightened cries of the other crewmen scrambling around looking for life jackets, he stared down at it in dumbfounded shock. With a cry of inarticulate rage, sent it hurtling through the glass window.

Lupino came choking and panting into the cabin, "She's a goner," he cried above the deafening scream of machinery and panic. "I can't get to the front of the engine on account of all that pot. There's nothing we can do."

He reached for the microphone, "Calling *Lady Mary*...calling *Lady Mary*...anybody...Preston...we're on fire. We're going to jump. Help us!"

The lights flickered on and off for the last time and the radio went dead. Amidst the confusion of the other men scrambling around, yelling and grabbing their possessions, Lupino stood squeezing the microphone button, as if he could make it come to life. Suddenly someone was shaking him.

It was Blake, the new man that had jumped off the freighter. "Where are the life jackets? We can't find them!"

"Under the bunks, I think," Lupino replied in a daze, dropping the microphone. They were ahead of him, madly rummaging through the drawers, throwing off mattresses. Only four life jackets were found.

Lupino tried to reach for one and Raul viciously elbowed him in the stomach. "The captain goes down with the ship, my friend." His golden teeth reflected the growing firelight. With a demonic grin, he reached for his knife. Lupino backed away trembling. There was death in the man's eyes.

The north wind gave a sudden gust, fanning the flames and sending up a shower of hot sparks. Lupino ducked and bolted past Raul and ran back to the stern.

He was terrified; he had heard fearsome stories about Raul. A Cuban refugee, he had worked for the CIA. Years ago, after he was caught in the Bay of Pigs invasion, he was taken back to his village in Cuba. He had come as the great liberator and to his amazement, Raul heard his fellow villagers drawing straws and arguing over who was going to have the privilege of shooting him.

He managed to escape, carrying a perpetual bitterness and rage into the jungle. Twenty years later he found a use for his talents in the warfare of drug-running.

He would enjoy killing Lupino. "You garbage," he hissed, following him. "Six million dollars worth of reefer is going up in smoke." Desperately, the men burst into the frigid night air, some barefooted or in their undershirts, clutching their wallets and gold charms. The big, blond American had his machine gun and an armload of clips. Blake looked fatalistic. Choking from the noxious fumes and billowing smoke, Raul stopped long enough to grab his attaché case.

"The lifeboat—where's the life boat?!" Raul bellowed over the dying roar of the engine. He cast around wildly, looking up at the wheelhouse roof where it should have been.

"We ain't got no lifeboat," groaned Lupino miserably, watching the fire eat into the charred wood until it looked like the hide of an alligator.

Raul's fist slammed into Lupino's face, sending him sprawling on deck. Spluttering with hatred, the Cuban jerked out a long, silver knife that gleamed against the flames.

Blake, the Anglo, jumped between them. "Raul, there's no sense in this. We may need this man before it's over. Besides, if you cut him, you'll draw sharks."

"That's right," said Lupino thickly through a cut lip, as he rose to his feet. "You got no call to do that. My brother-in-law, Preston, is coming. He probably called the Coast Guard. You won't get away with killing me. It'll get out!"

Suddenly, with a great popping and groaning, the cabin roof caved in, the flames whipped into a frenzy by the wind. They backed up further against the stern, hanging onto the stay cables and ladder that angled up to the mast. All the while, the engine kept running, the pistons madly pounding. Then abruptly the high-pitched scream stopped. And there was silence, save for the crackling of flames.

"Look!" cried Lupino, "the butane tanks!" The flames licked at the silver gas cylinders that stood beside the burned wheelhouse, turning them sooty black.

"Holy Mother of God!" breathed Raul, crossing himself. He was mesmerized by the flames, watching the boat becoming undone bit by bit until he saw little fingers of hell caressing the butane tanks. "If they go off, we're goners."

"Screw this shit," cried Rick, clutching his machine gun tighter, as if it would protect him. Orange flames reflected off the metallic black barrel. "I'll take my chances in the sea. With all that diesel, she'll go off like an A-bomb."

Just then a loud *whoosh* came from beside the boat. Several black dorsal fins laced around in the flame-illuminated surface.

"Shark!" cried Raul, terrified. He pointed a trembling finger. "Look, there's another one. We're surrounded by sharks!" The other Cubans joined in screaming, "*El tiburon! El tiburon!*" dropping to their knees and crossing themselves.

Raul laughed hysterically. "What a way to die. You got a choice of being cooked or eaten." He turned, smiling evilly at Lupino, "We'll give them a little something to eat, so they won't be so hungry."

Lupino cried, "That's porpoises, you damn fool. They'll protect us from the sharks!"

Raul began cackling. "This asshole cracks me up." His mouth formed a big white toothy grin, showing lots of gold. "Come on, my little Lupino, let's see if that is so. Rick, shoot off his knees, and we will see if the porpoises protect the rest of him from the sharks!" Rick obediently raised his machine gun.

Blake cried, "Hey, look, there's a light out there—I see it! A boat's coming! Don't shoot him!"

Lupino began yelling at the top of his lungs, "Help, help, save me, help!"

The butane tanks were starting to glow a cherry red. Rick waved his machine gun. "Hey, come on, man, help us! Why is he coming so slow?"

"Put the gun down," ordered Blake. "Keep all your guns out of sight. Would you pick up a bunch of guys with weapons?"

One by one they dropped their arms to the deck, save for hidden pistols.

Off in the distance, they saw a shrimp boat casting its spotlight on the water, crawling slowly toward them while the gas tanks grew hotter still.

3

Opportunity Knocks

Cautiously, Preston steered *Lady Mary* into the perimeter of light. When he came within sight of the burning vessel, he slowed to an idle. The wheelhouse and bow of the *Night Shadow* were an inferno. Flames were shooting out the anchor-room hatch. The only place that wasn't on fire was the stern, and there six men stood, silhouetted against the fire. All but two had life jackets on.

"It looks wrong," Preston muttered. "I don't like this a'tall."

Charlie made his way to the bow to get a line ready. "Damn, there's six of 'em, Preston," he called through the open window. "What in hell is Lupino doing with a crew like that?"

Preston looked at his brother-in-law and the strangers through the window, feeling the full force of the heat in his face. The radar screen with the freighter and the shrimp boat popped into his mind.

"Damn, he *is* hauling dope!" cried Charlie excitedly, turning to his skipper. "I can smell it from here."

Preston's knuckles whitened as he clenched the spokes of the steering wheel. "I ought to let the little jerk burn up," he growled, "I'm not getting in the middle of this!"

Visions of pirates taking over his boat and killing him flashed in his mind. He thought of ordering them to jump overboard and swim to him, but the sea was too cold. Instead he reached for his flare gun—a murderous weapon at close range—and shoved it under the cushion beneath him.

Preston eased the bow of his trawler up to the stern of the burning *Night Shadow*, and Charlie made ready to grab the men, who were shouting and preparing to board. The waves lifted the boats up and set them down again with a crash. Wood splintered, and Preston grimaced at the damage as he worked the shift lever back and forth, spinning the steering wheel. Lupino made a flying leap off the stern and landed on the bow with an ungainly thump. Frantically, he pushed past Charlie, who looked at him with open-mouthed surprise, and bolted into the wheelhouse door, slamming it behind him.

When Preston saw the next man quickly reach down and grab a submachine gun just before he leaped, his hand frantically jumped to the shift lever. But he was too late.

With a surprising burst of speed and agility, the tall blond man bolted over the bow, shoved his gun through the open window, and shouted, "Stay put, mister. Let everyone get on first!"

Preston looked down at the barrel with a silencer on the end, and his frightened eyes took in the clip of ugly, pointed machine gun bullets. Then he stared up at the owner, leaning in the wheelhouse window, grinning at him with a lot of well-dentured teeth—he had the look of a Mafia hit man. To him all life was equal: a cockroach's, a fish's, a man's.

Reluctantly, Preston withdrew his hand, as he watched the next man leap aboard, and the next, each reaching for a hidden weapon. Last was a short, dark Latino with a mustache who was hesitating, shouting in Spanish, afraid to take the leap.

"Help him!" the tall thug ordered Charlie. With wide, frightened eyes, the deckhand saw the gun being held on his captain. Trembling, he obeyed, reached forward and grabbed the imploring hand and jerked the little Cuban on board. He came on chattering, "*Gracias*, my friend. Thank God you saved us."

Then one of the others screamed, "Get away, get away! Those tanks are going to blow!"

When Preston saw the cherry red butane tanks amidst the charred and burning wreckage, a new fear overtook his others. He pulled the throttle lever back and threw all the power *Lady Mary* possessed into the engine. The diesel let out a long, throaty scream. The propeller roared, cavitated as it caught air, and waves broke over the stern as the trawler sped backwards.

Lupino was beside him in the wheelhouse, breathing heavily, "Preston, you gotta listen to me…I didn't mean it…I got bad trouble…"

In a rage, Preston grabbed him by the shirt, practically lifting him off the ground, and shook him. "What the hell have you got me into?" he snarled over the screaming engine. He dropped him with disgust and continued backing away from the flaming *Night Shadow*. "Look at the garbage you got on my boat!" He jutted his chin toward the men standing shivering on the bow in front of them.

"Look, Preston, I'm sorry but…"

"You promised Mary you'd never do this again. You put us through hell with your goddamn dope crap."

"Preston," Lupino screamed, "there's no time for that, goddamn it. Please. Listen, that Cuban fella out there, he's gonna kill me. He thinks it's my fault the dope burned up."

"You ain't worth killing, Lupino." Preston spat out contemptuously, looking down on him. He drew a breath, exhaled and dismissed Lupino from his mind, forcing himself to think about what to do next.

Speaking in Spanish, the men were coming in. Raul stepped through the wheelhouse door, thrust his hand forward, "*Cap-i-tan*, I want to thank you. You save my life and the lives of my compatriots." He gave Preston a big, toothy grin.

The others nodded. Preston looked at these foreigners with their gold medallions and jewelry with disdain. He resented the foreigners, especially the Latinos, who were more and more coming into North Florida. "Well, I didn't know there was a party going on out here," he said guardedly. "I just came out to save my brother-in-law. He ain't much, but he's family," Preston added defensively. Then clearing his throat, trying to keep his anxiety under control, he continued. "Out here us shrimpers stick together. Right now there's at least a dozen boats looking for Lupino, and they know I was just picking him up," he lied. "We also been talking back and forth to the Coast Guard."

Raul grinned appreciatively, "Well, *Senior Capitan* Preston, we are glad you came." Preston glanced at the wrestler, who was now standing there blankly, holding his machine gun, waiting for someone to tell him whether or not to shoot. This one-man execution force looked like he would have a black belt in karate, too. The man with the long, blond ponytail stepped forward. "Relax, fella, no one's going to hurt Lupino, you or anyone else," he said reassuringly to Preston. His eyes looked fixedly at the dark, stocky Cuban who appeared to be in charge. "Isn't that right, Raul." It was more of a command than a question, and the Cuban nodded in affirmation. The thug loosened his grip on the machine gun.

The ponytailed man extended his hand. "My name's Blake…" but his voice was lost in an incredible roar of white flames shooting from the burning tanks on the *Night Shadow*. A stifling wave of heat reached over the distance.

"Holy Cow!" yelled Charlie, watching outside the doorway, "There went them butane tanks!"

By now *Lady Mary* had backed to safety, a good couple-hundred yards away, and was still going, but they could see the starboard outrigger of the *Night Shadow* get so hot the heavy steel framing glowed a cherry red. The steel arm that stretched out above the burning tanks wilted in the heat and sagged into the sea.

Then with a terrifying explosion, the diesel tanks went off, shaking the windows of the *Lady Mary*. Three thousand gallons of diesel fuel exploded, and the *Night Shadow* lit up like a falling star. Flaming boards were hurled high into the sky, sparks showered a quarter-mile away.

Then it was over. The fire settled down to a steady burn.

The men stood there, watching it in silence, lost in thoughts of their own mortality. "Well," Blake pronounced with finality, "if you came just ten minutes later, we would all be on our way to Heaven or Hell, or wherever we're supposed to go."

A concerned, worried voice came on the radio. "Preston, where you at?" His brother Justin's voice brought life back to Preston's frightened body. "What's happening? You got them off that boat yet?"

There was silence in the cabin. Lupino looked worriedly at Raul, who seemed to be ignoring him, and then turned to Preston for reassurance. Everyone's eyes were focused on the radio, as if something might come out of the speaker other than sound. When Preston didn't answer, another voice came on. "Justin, I heard him a while ago, talking to the Coast Guard. He was at the fourteen-hundred line, and said he saw something burning. That was about an hour ago."

The talking continued, the air crackling with excitement and concern. Preston turned to Raul. "Like I said, our boys stick together out here." His hand hung close to the hidden flare gun.

Raul smiled at him, unsnapped his attaché case, pulled out a big

wad of bills and slapped it down on the dash next to the big illuminated compass. "*Capitan* Preston, please accept this as a token of our
gratitude. This money, it's for your extra trouble, you understand.
Just tell them you saved your brother-in-law and that he was
shrimping." Raul spoke with a friendly smile, but his dark eyes bore
into Preston with command.

"And if you do say anything else," added the big bodyguard,
"well...let's just say it wouldn't be healthy."

Blake put up his hand and cut him off. "No threats. He saved our
lives and he's been a friend. Why don't we show our gratitude by
putting our guns away?"

"Finest kind," agreed Preston. "You can lay them on the bunks
back there."

The other smugglers looked at each other. Finally Raul agreed,
and half trembling in fear they'd shoot him in the back, Charlie led
the way.

All except Blake, the youthful, blond-haired man with the ponytail. As soon as they placed their guns on the bunk, in one fast move
he reached under the cushion where Preston had been sitting and jerked
out the wide-barrel flare gun, laying it out of his reach. He looked at
Preston with a grin that went from ear to ear. "Just to make things
equal," he said winking.

Preston stared at him open-mouthed. How could he have possibly
known it was there? For the first time he took a close look at this
younger fellow. He was a North American, and unlike the Cubans,
who looked and acted like they just got off the banana boat and were
glad to reach the shore, this fellow moved with ease. He exuded confidence and had a good-natured manner that impressed Preston in
spite of himself. He couldn't quite figure his age. He looked young
but seemed too savvy for youth. Blake was clean-shaven for a sea-
farer. Amazingly, even aboard that vile freighter crammed with people
and pot, he had managed to keep his clothing clean. His accent wasn't
Southern. It might have had a touch of New England—but really he
could come from anywhere.

Raul returned. "Good, now we are all friends. The *Capitan* is a
reasonable man, a man of understanding."

"Oh yeah, I'm just all kinds of reasonable," snapped Preston, jabbing his finger at his brother-in-law cowering in the corner. "If I were
to say anything, this little bastard would go to jail where he belongs.

But, he's family. I can't do that. What you're doing out here ain't none of my business, and I'd just as soon keep it that way."

"See," cried Raul triumphantly. "I knew it, he is a man of understanding."

"And I don't want your money either." Preston jutted his chin toward the big wad of twenties, fifties and hundreds that were scattered over the dash.

Raul looked insulted. The fact that anybody could turn down money was incomprehensible to him. To have it was to have power; you could buy anything or bribe yourself out of any trouble.

Charlie pushed in through the doorway and caught the last of this conversation. His eyes grew wide with greed as he looked at the cash. "Preston, this could solve all our problems." But when he saw the captain's stony face, he pleaded, "Well, if you don't want it, I'll damn sure take it. Man, I didn't see nothing and I don't know nothing!"

Raul grinned appreciatively. "That's what I like! —A man who likes money. We can do business with such a man. What is your name, my friend?"

"Charlie."

"Ah, Charlie—a good name. I'll bet you like to smoke, too? We have some of Colombia's finest."

"All right, cut the shit," snapped Preston. He reached for the microphone. "*Lady Mary* calling the Coast Guard. We have three men on board, they're all safe, but their boat is burning, over."

As usual, the Coast Guard wanted all kinds of details—the names of the captain and crew, the exact position of the burning boat, and more. Doing his best to hide his discomfort at lying, Preston gave them fictitious names for the crew members, and changed the location to twenty miles west of their true position. Then the Coast Guard officer ordered them to remain with the burning boat until it sank and to radio its position so they could mark it on the charts. There would be forms for Lupino to fill out when he came ashore.

When Preston finished satisfying them that he would carry out their requests, he snapped angrily at Lupino, "I really appreciate your sucking me into your bullshit, Lupino. Now if they find out, and I gave them false information, I'll go to jail for conspiracy."

"Not to worry," said Raul reassuringly. "How are they going to find out? It's a big ocean."

"I don't know," worried Preston. "What if she drifts up on the beach somehow? We've got to stay here and see that she sinks."

"You've got a point there, Captain," said Blake, "loaded with reefer like she is."

Preston shifted into forward and started toward the hulk that now burned with a low, steady orange flame.

As they moved closer, they came upon three burning bales of marijuana bobbing on the surface. "There goes sixty thousand dollars," said Blake wistfully, fingering his medallion.

"They must have come out of the wheelhouse," said Lupino. "It don't look like the hull broke open yet. The stern is still in good shape." Despite the massive explosions, the hull remained pretty much intact, even though the charred wood was now only a few inches above the waterline. The cabin was completely burned away, the engine visible and solid amidst the flaming wood.

Preston loosened the grip on his pilot's wheel, his fingers ached, and he wiggled them. "That *Night Shadow* was a good solid boat," he said sadly, looking at the mast lying on her deck like a tree felled by an axe. "What a hell of an end she had to come to. She had a lot of good years left in her." He turned on Lupino accusingly, "Tell me the truth, did you pay your insurance on her like you said or not!"

"I was going to after this run," moaned his brother-in-law. "Honest, Preston, I was. I didn't have the money."

Preston felt numb, he spoke dazedly, as the realization sank in, "So I'm on your sixty-thousand-dollar note."

"I'll pay it," Lupino squeaked. "Honestly I will, Preston."

"And the banks will come after me for it." He looked down at his brother-in-law. "You little son-of-a-bitch," he said quietly. Cursing didn't come easy to Preston, he forced the words out.

Raul had been in the shadows behind them, listening intently to their every word. "Maybe all is not lost, my friends. Maybe we can still salvage something out of this. Look, the stern hasn't burned very much yet. That reefer is packed so tight, it isn't even burning. Hell, it takes the cops half a day to burn it in an incinerator." He turned to Preston and asked thoughtfully, "You sure that boat won't blow up no more?"

"What else is there to blow? Everything that is going to blow has blown."

An avaricious gleam came into the Cuban's eyes. "*Capitan*, how'd you like to make a deal?" Raul gestured contemptuously at the stack of bills on the dash as if a dog had left droppings. "This is chicken money. What have you got here, two, three thousand dollars? It's nothing! How'd you like to make some *real* money?"

"Oh no," said the captain backing away shaking his head, "you're not going to put one ounce of pot on my boat. Hauling you and your..." He couldn't think of a name for them that he could repeat without being insulting, so he cut himself off. "...is one thing. Hauling this shit is another."

"Fifty thousand dollars!" Raul cajoled.

Charlie's head turned, "Hey, Skipper!"

"Shove it," Preston snapped, ignoring him. He detested the way this greasy Cuban with his shiny black, shoe-polished hair was flaunting money around, using it as power, trying to tempt them and succeeding with Charlie.

"All right then, I see we have a hard man, a reasonable man. A man who has the foresight to take advantage of a situation. Seventy-five thousand dollars cash!"

"Jesus, Preston," stammered Charlie, "that ain't bad! Let's go for it."

"And of course we would never forget our compatriot Charlie," said Raul warmly, clapping him on the back. "Twenty thousand dollars for him! And for our little friend Lupino, who lost his boat and now has nothing," the Cuban said with honeyed sympathy, "I'm sure we can find him something to ease his pain."

Lupino looked beseechingly at his brother-in-law as if he were the last hope in the world. "Please, Preston. We could get the pot off my boat, and be gone from here in a couple of hours. Who'd know? I'll give you my share. You could pay your boat off at the bank and I could pay off my loan."

"And I could fix the tranny on my truck. I'd be set!" Charlie put in.

"Don't talk to me," Preston snapped. He turned to Raul, "Forget it," he said with finality. "I'll take you in to the dock and forget I ever saw you and the rest of your garbage."

Charlie pleaded, "For Chrissakes, Skipper, we're starving out here! This is a once-in-a-lifetime opportunity!"

His words struck home—Preston felt guilty. With his reputation for speed, Charlie Hansen could make twice the money working on one of those modern super trawlers. At twenty-three he had spent almost half his life on the back of one boat or another. If he wasn't a drunk, he'd be a captain by now.

But his drinking would have stopped him from ever getting a job on a fancy steel slab with central heating and air conditioning where he could lay around and watch color TV in a spacious, comfortable cabin. So even though the work was harder and the boat was cramped, he stuck with the man who had practically raised him.

"Charlie," Preston said despairingly, "we can make it without it. You can't play in shit without getting some up your nose. Any day now those shrimp are going to run and we'll be in the fat again."

While Preston spoke, Charlie's eyes wandered down to the galley where the Cubans were puffing on two enormous joints, trying to calm their nerves. Impassive as ever, the tall, blond wrestler was polishing his machine gun with a dish towel.

"*Any day now?!*" Charlie echoed incredulously, "Any day now. Preston, your wife's fixing to have a baby, you got all kinds of doctor bills coming up, you're three payments behind on the *Lady Mary*, and you're on Lupino's note. When the bank finds out about this, they're gonna come after you. You got no choice!"

"We'll make it honest," Preston said tightly. "It ain't worth the risk."

"Risk, what risk?" chimed in Raul. "Everything is set up to unload her at the dock. And even if the cops were to catch you, you could say we made you do it. We didn't give you no choice."

"Yeah, no choice," said Rick, coming up the steps gesturing with his Uzi. For the first time, a cruel smile formed on his otherwise bland face.

"Hey! Hey!" cried Lupino, "The boat's going down!"

Waves flooded over the burning bulkheads. Steam and vapor boiled upwards as the cold sea overcame scorching wood. Her burning bow raised upward. They could see her big red belly caked with barnacles. In a moment there was a great hissing, crackling explosion. Sparks flew, the sea closed in, and she disappeared beneath the waves. Preston breathed a sigh of relief.

"*Ai,*" said Raul shrugging, "that's that. I guess we don't have to worry about what happens to the dope."

Then two twenty-foot steel fuel tanks surfaced. They bobbed and floated away. "Look!" cried Preston, "the goddamn thing is coming back up!"

When the *Night Shadow* sank, it broke in two. With a giant eruption, the stern rocketed to the top, and still smoldering and burning, it bobbed darkly above the waves. Buoyancy from three hundred bales of marijuana had ripped the deck off, and bales began spewing out and drifting about like croutons in soup.

"Come now, my friend," the Cuban said impatiently, tapping the deck with his shoe. "We still have a chance to get them. But we're running out of time."

"Look, even if I wanted to," Preston said reasonably, watching the dark, cubed shapes riding up and down on the waves, "it'll be daylight in a couple of hours. It's too risky."

Lupino looked up at him beseechingly; his narrow, blue eyes grew wide and pleading. "Please, Preston, for my sister's sake and the baby that's coming, for Charlie and me. Let's do it. If we go after those bales now, we can save most of them. Even if we get caught," he implored, "they wouldn't put you in jail, not with your reputation in town. The law knows you never even got a speeding ticket!"

"Go to hell, Lupino!" Preston spat out. "I'm not gonna do it. It's too damn risky."

Raul's years as an undercover guerilla fighter had taught him to be calm and give no expression, but he felt hot anger rising over him as he watched the bales floating away. He considered whipping out his pistol and forcing this fishy-smelling bastard to salvage them. His patience was at an end. "That's $6 million worth of reefer wholesale!" he bellowed. "To hell with him. Lupino, you can run this boat can't you? And you too, my friend Charlie—if he don't want to cooperate..."

"Hold on," Charlie stormed back, stepping in front of him with clenched fists. "Touch him and I'll stick those guns up your ass."

In a flash, Rick jammed the machine gun muzzle into Charlie's face, finger ready to squeeze. Charlie froze.

"Now just calm down," Blake said impatiently as if he'd grown weary of listening to a bunch of quarreling school children. "No one is going to shoot anybody. Raul, this man saved our lives. We'd be swimming now if it weren't for him—if we weren't already cooked."

Raul looked through the window despairingly at the dispersing bales. They kept popping up from the rapidly sinking stern section, one right after the other. Then he put his attaché case on the bunk, unsnapped and opened it, exposing stacks of hundred dollar bills.

"This is my final offer," he said through gritted teeth. "I'll pay you a thousand dollars for every bale we put on deck. There is three hundred thousand dollars here. You hear me, you stupid redneck, three hundred thousand dollars!"

"It's not the money, damn it, it's the risk," Preston blurted out, staring back hard into the Cuban's angry eyes. "Use your head, mister. Those bales are going all over the place. There's no way to get them all. No telling how many burned ones are going to wash up on the beach. The Coast Guard and everyone in the fleet knows the *Night Shadow* burned, it'll come back on us. It's going to be daylight in a few hours. We'd have to shovel all the ice and shrimp out of the hold before we could put them below. The Coast Guard's going to send a spotter plane to check it out, you can bet on that. They'll probably have someone waiting at the dock for us, to get a report on how much fuel got spilled, where it went down, that sort of thing. If we're loaded with bales, we'll get caught. It's not going to work!" he said with finality.

Blake sighed heavily. "He's right, Raul. As soon as the first burned bale hits the beach, the cops will be all over Preston like flies on shit. Maybe he could talk his way out of it, but I know they'd be happy to see me, and you too."

Preston looked at him appreciatively, glad of the support, but wondering why the police would be happy to see them. Raul started to protest, but Blake cut him off. "No one's lost more money on this deal than myself. I've got three months setting this up, and put up a million dollars, and I say let's split."

"A boat's coming," cried Lupino, who was looking through the open door. They all turned to see a beam of light sweeping far over the horizon.

"That could be the Coast Guard cutter. They said they had a cutter in the area," Preston lied. "Or it could be some of our buddies coming out."

Raul looked longingly at the smoldering stern of the *Night Shadow* sinking down beneath the waves, and watched the last of the bales boiling up. "All right, it's too risky," he agreed. He looked hatefully at Lupino and spat, "Let's get the hell out of here."

Disappointed, Charlie switched off the deck and running lights, plunging *Lady Mary* into darkness, and with a roar of the throttle, they turned and headed for home.

Preston leaned back in his pilot's chair, gazing in exhaustion at the black ocean, the diamond stars flickering down through the cold night sky. What have I done? he demanded of himself. Have I blown the opportunity of a lifetime?

Grimly, he remembered Mary sitting at the kitchen table sorting bills, wearing her faded pink housedress, tired, pregnant, her feet swelling. "We've bottomed out this time," she had told Preston before he left on the trip. "I'm tired of running from the bill collectors, tired of telling lies. Just once I'd like to pay the light bill in the middle of the month, instead of waiting to the last minute to keep from having them shut off. Every penny we get goes into that damn boat. And then we gotta pay income tax! Why does life have to be so hard?" Now her words haunted him.

Preston Barfield looked resolutely out into the night and tried hard to believe he had made the right decision.

4

Lupino's Plan

"Hey, fella," Lupino whispered urgently, timidly shaking the shoulder of the man with the blond ponytail who was propped up in the corner asleep. "Can I talk to you?" It was dark in the galley; men were asleep in the bunks or sitting around the crowded cabin. Marijuana and tobacco smoke permeated the air.

Blake opened one eye, looked at the nervous Lupino standing before him, with his bushy hair and his worn, salt-frayed shirt. "I'm listening. Talk," he said tersely.

Lupino cast a glance at Preston and Charlie up in the wheelhouse, and whispered, "I got an idea how we can save some of the load. Can we talk about it outside?"

Yawning, Blake got to his feet, stretched, and jerked his head toward the door. They stepped into the chilly night air that bit their faces and refreshed them after being in the stagnant cabin.

The engine throbbed and clattered noisily through the exhaust pipe, and the air had a faint reek of diesel drifting up from the engine room. It was dark on deck, but the moon shown down on the rolling black seas that were breaking into white caps.

Blake looked at Lupino wearily, the exhaustion of the days at sea aboard the freighter and the night's trauma etched into his rugged, handsome face. He waited for Lupino to begin.

"I didn't want to say this in front of my brother-in-law, and those

Cuban fellas are too mad at me, but I think we can salvage about fifty bales."

"Go on," said Blake with guarded interest.

"I got this fiberglass crab boat with a 200-horsepower Johnson motor on it. She'll shit and git—it'll do fifty miles an hour empty. I've had her loaded with oysters before and she'll still get up and plane. I figure we can be back out here in two hours after we leave the dock, load her down with bales, and get on back by dark. I got the Loran coordinates right here," he said tapping his forehead with his index finger, looking wise. "I looked at the readings just before we left."

"Numbers are one thing," said Blake cautiously, "winds and currents are another. That pot will be scattered from hell to breakfast."

"No, it won't," Lupino insisted once again full of enthusiasm, like a bright-eyed squirrel that just uncovered a choice nut, "not the way this north wind is blowing steady. They'll stay off the beach, and there's no other boats out here."

"Except the one that was headed out there when we left."

"You saw he moved off the radar screen. Probably that was some shrimper crossing the Gulf from Texas, maybe headed to Key West. We just spooked, that's all!"

"We'd have to find a new hole to shoot the load into," Blake said thoughtfully. "Our off-loading crew's scattered by now, once they heard it was a bust."

"I think I got that covered," Lupino countered. "We can go up the Ochlockonee River. There's so many creeks and bayous there, no one would find us. Believe me, I know that river like the back of my hand. I've catfished there all my life, and I know places we could stash the load that no one would ever find."

Blake's silence was unnerving. Lupino read the doubt in his eyes. "Look," he insisted, "I know you think I'm a screw-up, that I lost the load and almost got us all killed. But that was just an accident, honest."

"Damn right, I'm thinking that," the man with the ponytail snapped, "and I'm thinking that if you've got the boat and know where to go, why are you telling me this?"

" 'Cause I know that Raul will kill my ass, and somehow I got to make it up to him. I need the money bad to pay off my note at the bank and make it right with my brother-in-law." Desperation was creeping into his voice. "Just make me the same deal that Raul was gonna make Preston, Blake. A thousand dollars a bale and we got a deal."

Blake walked to the stern and stared down into the sea, watching the prop churn up the phytoplankton into an eerie blue glow. Now and then a wave broke over the bow, leaving cold, blue embers scattered on deck like fallen stars.

This was to be his last big load. After that he could buy his ranch and retire in Ecuador. He was so weary of the game. Years ago, when he was a happy hippie, it was high adventure and he became a legend in the drug trade. Now he was a road-worn fugitive. "All right," Blake sighed at last, "I'll talk to Raul. I can't see what we have to lose. But you stay away from him!"

Lupino nodded glumly. "I'll need someone to go with me. I'll run the boat and they'll pick up the bales. Can you go?"

"I'll be the one, if we do it, but we'll have to work fast. Those bales are wrapped in plastic and should be okay. They were riding high in the water. But if they stay out here too long they'll leak and lose value."

Preston was at the wheel, well aware that Lupino had been outside with the hippie for the past hour. When his brother-in-law came in, he growled, "I don't know what you're planning, Lupino, but if you're thinking of coming back here and picking up those bales when we get back to the dock, you're out of your mind."

Lupino lied, "Not me. I've learned my lesson."

"Sure you have," the captain's voice bit with sarcasm. "Just get out of my sight before I kick your lying ass all over this boat, Lupino. I don't want to look at you."

It was almost dawn. The first streaks of cold, hidden sun were glowing in the eastern sea. Through the frigid air came the *Lady Mary*, chugging into Carrabelle Bay six hours after the rescue. They passed half a dozen trawlers anchored down on the sound, their crews asleep. Preston studied the radar screen and saw a small blip moving toward them.

"Uh-oh, we may have trouble," he breathed tensely. "There's a boat headed right toward us. That could be the Marine Patrol."

"I doubt that's them," said Charlie. "Those sorry hammer-knockers don't go out in this kind of weather, it's too damn cold."

"Don't count on it. That could be Ted Miller. He used to be a commercial fishermen before he became a Marine Patrol, and he don't mind running at night, and he ain't afraid of the weather." The captain stared into the darkness. "Whoever he is, he's running without lights like we are."

Moments later, the whining, straining noise of an old, tired outboard motor grew louder as it cavitated, caught air, growled and ran over the chop. The ghostly form of a fisherman bundled up in a slicker suit, riding in a small boat, appeared. He was standing at the bow of his twenty-four-foot open tunnel boat with a piled-up nylon net on the stern. The boats passed in the dawn light.

Raul's voice came from behind them. "Whew, man, that's a rough way to make a living, no? A man can freeze to death out there."

"That's some poor old mullet fisherman sneaking around trying to make a living. If they catch him with a gill net and boatload of mullet, he's headed for the jailhouse. They just put in a bunch of laws that don't make no sense. And it makes everything these people have done all their lives illegal," Preston said grimly. "Those net-banners won't quit until they got the last commercial man off the water."

The captain exhaled with relief when the fishing boat moved by. His stomach felt as if it were full of jumping shrimp. "Still, I'm a shrimper. I ain't cut out to be a smuggler." He said to Charlie in a low voice, "Hell, nervous as I feel running empty, what if we had a load of dope on board?"

Ahead of them were the lights of the shoreline, looming larger by the minute. "All right," said Preston tensely, breaking back the throttle, "Let's get the outriggers up so we can go into the dock."

Charlie and Lupino slipped out into the wind and engaged the winches. The boat shook and rattled as the drums turned around, hoisting the heavy otter doors on board. With squeaking groans the outriggers were hoisted up until they pointed toward Heaven so the boat could squeeze into the dock. Then Preston turned to the strangers, who had been lumping around despondently in the cabin, and pacing around the deck, smoking cigarettes. "I don't want any of you on deck. Until we hit the dock, I want you completely out of sight, understand?"

"Not to worry," said Raul, looking up from the galley bench where he had been talking with Blake. "We're pros, you just go ahead. Can you drive us to my car? It's a couple of miles away at a gas station."

"Yeah, I suppose. It's better than having a bunch of Cubans wandering round the dock. Harold, the town cop, would spot you sure as hell and might ask questions."

Raul grinned appreciatively. "Good thinking, my friend."

When they tied up to the dock in front of Lawton's Fish House, there were several trawlers next to them, but they were all dark, their crews asleep. When Preston switched off the engine, there was a deafening silence. Only the sounds of the breeze blowing through the trees and the barnacles and oysters bubbling and clicking on the wharf pilings could be heard. A car cruised down the highway. Suddenly, there was a loud crash, and a squall, as something tumbled and everyone jumped in fright.

"Goddamn fish-house cats," Charlie's shrill, nervous laughter rang out. "Never thought I'd see the day when a cat would make me jump out of my skin."

Preston pulled his truck down to the wharf, and the smugglers piled in. He drove them to the closed-up service station where they waited until a new, but nondescript white van pulled in. The woman driving it remained at the wheel. Even in the shadows, Preston couldn't help but notice her striking beauty.

Raul said, getting out of the truck, "I won't forget this, my friend. You saved our life. And you've been cool. There's a future for a man like you in our organization. I'll make you one hell of a deal if you want to take your boat down to Colombia. We'll have it all set up for you. One good load and you can retire. You won't have to worry about making dollars as long as you live."

"No, thanks," Preston replied, starting to move down the road, "I'm just a shrimper, not a doper."

"We shall see, my friend."

Preston was about to drive off, when he heard the men hurriedly explaining what happened. "Who hired that imbecile?" the woman's cultured, southern voice rose sharply. When Raul tried to explain, she broke off into a rapid stream of Spanish. Preston couldn't understand the words, but the tone and delivery were humiliating and contemptuous. The tires squalled as she sped away.

When he got back to the *Lady Mary*, he found Charlie pacing back and forth in the wheelhouse. "I was worried about you, Captain. I should have gone with you."

"No problem." Preston looked around. "Where's Lupino and that Blake fella?"

"They took off. I don't know where they went." Then, with a big grin, Charlie handed him a greasy, brown paper bag. Preston looked at it uncomprehendingly. "What's this?"

"Open it," suggested his deckhand.

It was stuffed with money, twenties, fifties and a few hundreds. "Blake left it for you," he said happily, "Five thousand in cold green cash. And look," he pulled out his billfold, "they gave me a thousand! Now I can get my transmission fixed!"

"It's dope money," Preston snapped, throwing it down on the galley table.

"So what, it spends just as good as regular money. Better. You don't have to pay no income tax on it."

Preston sat down wearily on the bench, "If I didn't need it so bad, I'd throw it overboard, Charlie. It's Devil's money. No good can come of it."

"Well, I wish I had a pile of that Devil's money. Preston, don't you realize, we coulda been rich tonight? I mean filthy-ass rich! This is just a tip. Look around you. We could have unloaded right here. No one's around."

"Right here at Sam Lawton's dock, huh?" Preston said dryly, nervously scratching his salt-stiffened hair. The money made him jittery.

"I've heard it's been done before," Charlie whispered. "I've heard that Sam's in the business."

"That's a bunch of crap," the captain retorted angrily. "That's just rumors. He don't need to fool with this crap. He's got a good business already." Changing the subject, he said, "Charlie, why don't you put on a fresh pot of coffee? Damned if I can go to sleep after all we been through, and I'm too nervous to go home. Sam will be open in a couple of hours. We'll unload our shrimp, share up, and go home."

Preston sat down wearily on his bunk, picked up an old *National Geographic* and tried to read it, but the shrimp were jackknifing in his stomach again. He threw it down. "Damn!" he muttered. "Damn! I could kick Lupino's ass. Where did the little rat-faced jerk go?"

At 6 a.m. he and Charlie unloaded their six hundred pounds of shrimp at Lawton's Fish House, which hardly paid the fuel bill. Then Preston gathered his laundry and stuffed it into his brown duffel bag for Mary to wash. Wadded up in his underwear and slime-stiffened denims was the paper bag and the five thousand dollars in cash. As he drove home Preston watched his rearview mirror to see if a cop was following him.

By the time he pulled up into the yard of their modest wood frame house with his contraband laundry shoved under his seat, he was exhausted. He decided he was probably taking just as much risk as if he had picked up the load of pot and brought it in.

It wasn't much of a house, he thought. Most of the paint was peeling, and the roof needed fixing, but Mary kept one of the prettiest gardens on the block, and always had flowers blooming. They had plans to fix the old shack up one day. But all their investment money and spare cash had gone into both boats. With the thought of all the money he could have made, the smallness and plainness around him stood out.

When he pushed in, Mary was looking through a stack of books on childbearing that she checked out of the library. "Oh good, you're home," she said happily. "I'm glad you remembered that we were going to the Lamaze class tomorrow." Her words trailed off and her smile faded when she saw him. "My God, what's wrong, Preston?" she asked in a hushed whisper.

"Your stupid brother managed to burn up *Night Shadow*," he said hotly. "She's gone...history now."

Mary's face paled, her brown eyes grew wide, and she put her hand to her lips. "Oh my God, was anyone hurt? Is Lupino..." She left the word hanging."

"Unfortunately he's fine. We got everyone off just before she went down."

Preston watched her exhale with relief, "Oh, thank the Lord." He looked into her soft, brown eyes, and looked at her great, pregnant belly and wondered, as he had several times before in the last few hours: How much should I tell her? Maybe, with the baby coming, the less she knows the better. But those were some ugly characters and, if there's any danger, she ought to know it.

He compromised, telling her the story of Lupino's dramatic rescue, omitting the details of Raul and the rest of the cutthroats.

Mary listened intently, drawing excited little breaths. She wasn't pretty in the Hollywood sense; she had freckles and soft, brown hair that curled into whirls. Usually she kept it covered with a kerchief to keep it out of the way while she headed shrimp or shucked oysters at her father's oyster house.

"Oh, this is terrible," she moaned, "terrible for all of us. Lupino let the insurance lapse at the bank, and that means they're gonna come after us, Preston, 'cause our names are still on that note. And

Lord, what is Eloise and those young'uns gonna do now? What little bit of money he gives them came from that boat. Now we'll have to take those young'uns to raise. You know yourself Preston, there's been many a night when they wouldn't have no dinner if we didn't give them any."

"Well, we got our own young'uns to raise," he said, giving her a significant look. "Mary, I'm going to bed."

Sleeping at home during the daytime was hard for Preston. Neighbors and kinfolk dropped in wanting to borrow something, or there was traffic noise. Even though he was exhausted, it was late afternoon before he dropped off. Normally, when he came in from a week's shrimping he would slumber for eighteen hours and nothing could wake him.

But that night his wife watched him tossing and turning, mumbling in his sleep. Dreams haunted him; he saw Latinos leering, pointing machine guns in his face amidst the burning hell of the *Night Shadow*. Around four o'clock in the morning, he woke up, dripping with sweat, panting heavily.

Mary moved closer to cuddle him, sensing his tension. "What is it, Preston?" she asked softly, pressing her lips against his shoulder. "You been talking in your sleep. What is the matter?" she asked with concern.

"Mary, what if I could have made a bunch of money quick. I mean a bunch—enough to change our lives, put all our money worries behind us," he ventured theoretically, "but I didn't do it."

Mary raised up on one elbow and looked at him intently. "I don't know, why wouldn't you have done it?"

" 'Cause it didn't feel right. I used to think messing with pot was wrong, but now I ain't so sure."

He took a deep breath, and began the story of how he picked up the five smugglers from the burning *Night Shadow*. They lay there side by side, staring into the darkness while he calmly related the harrowing events. He finished with the boat blowing up and sinking. Mary got up, switched on the lamp beside him, smoothing her green flannel nightgown over her swollen belly. Her wide-eyed expression of shock turned to fury after a moment. "Why that no-good, rotten little..." she groped for an expression befitting her brother and dropped it. "Wait until Daddy gets a hold of him!" She felt betrayed. "He promised Mama and Daddy, everyone of us, that he'd never have another thing to do with hauling dope as long as he lived. That's why we agreed to sign the note on the *Night Shadow*. But ever since he come out of jail he ain't done nothing but run around with every whore in the county. He won't get out and work like he's supposed to; he lets his young'uns and wife starve."

Preston cut her off. "Mary, listen. They said I could make some easy money. This is no lie. They offered me up to three hundred thousand dollars in cold cash money. All I had to do was pick up the bales and bring them in."

"What did you tell them?" she asked in a hushed quiet voice, looking at him with her penetrating brown eyes.

"I told 'em no."

"Well, you done right then," but Preston felt her voice lacked conviction. "There ain't no such a thing as easy money. Even if you didn't get caught, we'd spend our whole lives looking over our shoulders to see if the police were coming. And we got a young'un to raise. Still," she gave a nervous laugh, "I don't know what all I'd do if you came home with three hundred thousand dollars. I've never seen that much money in my life, not all at one time. We ain't seen a run of shrimp in three years. And every year we go deeper into debt. I sure get tired to paying the electric bill and telephone the day before they're ready to cut it off. It sure do tempt a body."

He swung his long legs out of the bed, and shoved himself up stiffly. "Listen, I've got something that'll help."

He went out to the truck and returned with his fishy, bound-up clothes.

"You don't have to show me your nasty, old shrimp clothes," she chided. "I can smell them from here. I'll wash them when I do the laundry in the morning."

He looked down at her and grinned. Mary snapped, "Preston, don't put that nasty mess on the bed!" But she froze as he started scooping out wads of twenty dollar bills, fifties and hundreds. She looked up at him with trepidation. "I thought you said you didn't..."

"This was just a tip for running them in," he said defensively. "They told me to take it for my trouble—insisted on it."

"How much is here?" she asked, fingering the bills as if they were a little dangerous, and yet seduced in spite of herself.

"Five thousand dollars," Preston answered uneasily, as he watched her jump up eyes ablaze. He knew a storm was coming.

"You goddamn stupid idiot!" she yelled, warming into a tirade. "Let me see if I have this straight, Preston. Lupino burns up the boat we still have a mortgage on, about sixty thousand dollars worth. And he doesn't have a dime's worth of insurance. Then you rescue his miserable ass, and some men offer you three hundred thousand dollars to salvage the load. But you refuse because you say it wasn't right.

"Then," she spluttered, her anger welling up, "you sneak them back to the dock, harboring fugitives. I think it's called aiding and abetting in a crime and…and…" she groped for words, "…conspiracy. And then you accept a lousy five-thousand-dollar tip from them. Have I left anything out, Preston? Tell me."

He said nothing.

"Well, have I?" she demanded.

"No," he admitted sullenly, feeling incredibly stupid and inadequate, "except that Charlie accepted it, I didn't. They left it while I was gone."

"Oh, that'll hold up in court, you bet it will!" she said sarcastically. Then tears came into Mary's eyes. "So now we're ruined. The banks are after us because Lupino let the insurance lapse. Wait until they hear that their security is sitting in eighty feet of water. We'll be out on the street. They'll take this house. Only they'll do it while you're in jail for conspiracy."

Preston thought, maybe I really did screw up and missed a once-in-a-lifetime opportunity. I really could have picked up those bales, slipped back to the dock and gotten away with it.

Mary pointed an accusing finger at him. "I'm not going to have this baby in a manger, and I'm not going to go back to Daddy's. You'd better catch some shrimp, rob a bank, run a load of dope, or do something, and I mean it!" she cried. She put her hands over her face and wept. Preston sat beside her, miserable, thinking about getting drunk, thinking this was probably the lowest point in his life.

5

Bales, Bales, Bales!

The wild night Preston Barfield rescued the crew of the *Night Shadow*, the north wind had been blowing in gusts up to thirty knots, and the seas ran ten to twelve feet. Most of the bales that popped out of the sinking vessel were carried offshore and swept out to sea. Bobbing along the waves, they scattered out over a fifty-mile area. Seagulls hovered around the square, burlap-covered packages excitedly pecking away until the plastic wrapper beneath was torn open, then they whittled away at the grass. Seagulls love grass. They get stoned on it and fly in woozy circles.

Who knows what effect marijuana has on the creatures of the sea when it gets waterlogged and sinks. Perhaps, like leaves washed down from the river swamps, it decays and gets incorporated into the food chain. Wave action and sand eventually break vegetable material down into small, soggy particles. Perhaps this potent detritus is acted upon by bacteria, yeast and fungi, which are in turn devoured by minute worms, nematodes, and flea-like copepods, forming an interesting basis for the food chain.

Does it make the minnows that feed on it giddy and more apt to be eaten by larger fish? Or perhaps it affects the reproduction of brittlestars as they sit in the mud and reach up their snaky legs to partake of Colombian Gold.

The bales from the *Night Shadow* that came shoreward were greeted by the local populace with joy. It was the biggest economic boom since the big shrimp run three years before. On the morning of March 16, bales from the *Night Shadow* floated by the twenty-odd shrimp boats anchored inside the sound, and vanished as if they had never been seen. Bales, bales, bales, floating in the sea, washing up on the beaches.

To Captain Tommy Mac of the *Windward Seas* from Bon Secour, Alabama, it was manna from Heaven, a gift from Neptune. He was standing at the rail contributing his own stream of nutrients to the system when a mysterious compact shape came bobbing along. Then another, and another, and another! At first he thought they were bales of hay, then he realized what they were and yelled his sleeping crew awake.

They didn't even have to lift the anchor to get all fifteen on board. Tommy Mac quit shrimping that season, and burned the mortgage on his boat after presenting the bank with sixty thousand dollars in cold cash.

In the little port of Carrabelle, the docks were awash with rumors. Captains and crews struggling to survive the past few years of bad shrimping wailed that riches were at their fingers and passed them by. Everyone believed that everyone else had made a fortune, and those who did make a fortune wailed their pretended disappointment at the rest just the same.

Word spread to the surrounding communities. Canoes patrolled creeks and marshes. Boats that had been sitting in carports gathering dust for years were suddenly launched. People called in sick on their job and went out in the cold and got sick. Men and women stood on the bows of their pleasure boats bounding over the waves, gazing into the shimmering sea with hands shading their eyes, searching for solid, dark objects that might spell riches.

Prices paid varied from fifteen thousand a bale for good quality, dry pot to only a thousand or less for the soggy. Time worked against the seekers—the longer a bale floated around, the less value it had. In garages, basements, old barns, and up in the woods, seaweed pot was carefully opened and spread out on sunny decks to dry. Not all of it was sold. With the whole coast flooded, it was given away for birthday presents and wedding gifts and used in barter. It was smoked at parties, smoked on the shrimp docks and filtered down to high school locker rooms.

Not everyone was glad it arrived. Mr. and Mrs. Murray Johnson, at their weekend cottage on Dog Island, were outraged when six bales washed up on their shore. Huffing and puffing with dedication and indignation, they dragged the soggy bales from the beach. Mr. Johnson stood guard with his shotgun to protect them from beach-combing hippies while Mrs. Johnson called the law. He was a little disappointed when the police arrived, took the bales away and didn't leave him a receipt he could show off.

When word of the bales washing ashore reached the authorities, they rushed in to remove temptation. U.S. Customs officers in blue uniforms, Highway Patrol in tan, and undercover narcotics agents in blue jeans sealed off coastal roads. Customs officers stopped traffic driving back across island bridges and checked car trunks for contraband. Even little old ladies had their buckets of seashells scrutinized.

They stopped one girl with her pick-up truck piled high with sea grass. It was mulch for her garden, she said, but the cops climbed in and dug through it with her pitchfork before letting her go. To her surprise a week later, thousands of little pot plants began bursting up from the sandy soil of her garden. With much paranoia, she weeded them out and burned them.

But twelve hours before the first bale showed up, Lupino and Blake were out there bucking the seas and the north wind, loading up his oyster boat. Lupino's "few hours" to run out and get them turned into the entire day and half the night.

Even with its two-hundred horsepower, the twenty-four-foot Aquasport was having a hard time moving through the water, laden as it was with five thousand pounds of marijuana hidden beneath a tarpaulin. It was three o'clock in the morning as they ran into the Ochlockonee Bay, miles down the coast, and only the stars were shining above.

Then, the whining outboard motor screamed, the foot jumped out of the water with its propeller churning and the boat bucked to a stop. They were hard aground. Blake, who was crouched down beneath a windscreen of soggy burlap covered bales, rolled himself into a ball as the cargo tumbled on top of him.

He jumped up, looking wild, then forced a bit of control over his uncontrollably clicking teeth. He hugged himself, trying to warm his wet body. "What the hell! I thought you knew every sandbar and spoil bank around here, Lupino."

Lupino smiled apologetically. "I thought we could slide over that hump and cut off a half a mile. I forgot about this here crook in the channel, and how dang heavy she is. We got to get out and push her off."

Blake nodded philosophically, then let out a battle yell as he jumped overboard into the water. To his surprise, it was much warmer than the bone-chilling air, and suddenly he felt great. He thrived on adventure, and the discomfort added to it. He threw his weight against the boat, shoving it backward. Running aground wasn't new to him. He was a sailor, he loved the sea. His skin was bronze from lounging on the deck of a pleasure craft, trolling for marlin in the Gulf Stream and lying on Caribbean beaches with his girlfriends.

Three hours later the tide rose high enough for them to push the boat through knee-deep water, then abruptly it was up to their necks. "We done reached the channel. Let's go!" said Lupino, grabbing the side of the boat and hoisting himself up.

Onward they sped, past channel marker after channel marker, until the highway bridge that spanned the river lay ahead.

"Well, we're here," Lupino announced proudly, after slowing down.

"Where's here?" demanded Blake, shivering and looking up at a big tractor trailer speeding overhead.

"At the head of the bay. From here on it's about twenty miles upriver to Molly's place where we'll take out. Say, how's the gas? Check the tank, it's under the bales in front of you."

Blake excavated the first can; it rose light and empty in his hand. Then he found the second; it too was empty. So was the third and the fourth.

"Damn, we're out of gas!" he exclaimed.

Lupino shook his head. "That's the only-est thing I don't like about these big motors. They just naturally drink the gas, 'specially when we're loaded like this. We gotta fill up and maybe buy a couple extra tanks."

"Fill up?" cried Blake in disbelief and outrage. "How in the hell are we going to do that with a boat load of dope?" You said you had enough gas to make this run."

"The seas made us use a lot more gas, and I didn't figure on how heavy this pot was. Don't worry, I used to work for old Sid Parker. He owns the marina, so we won't have no problem. We'll act like we're going up the river catfishing."

"This is too damn dangerous," Blake protested. "Can't we stop a half mile away and lug the gas up or something?"

"Shoot, no. We just can't go toting gas tanks through people's yards. That would be even more suspicious. You gotta trust me. We got to get up into them swamps and creeks and things, and no one will find us. This is the best way. Now give me the money."

Blake fished two one hundred dollar bills out of his money belt and passed them over to Lupino. He closed his bloodshot eyes and disgustedly rested his head in his hands. Christ, how did I get such an idiot? he thought. And what am I doing at his mercy? First the boat burning, now this!

The sun was peeking above the marsh as Lupino motored his pot-laden boat into the dredged-out basin. There were thirty or forty boats there, including sailboats, cabin cruisers and weekend fishing boats moored in the floating stalls. He tied off at the fuel dock, behind two other boats that were already gassing up. Blake was nervously enthroned upon the tarpaulin-covered load like a cross-legged Buddha. Impassive now—resigned to the new difficulties and lack of choice—he closed his eyes and made himself comfortable, trying to forget that their tarp-covered cargo looked like some kind of distorted lumpish creature.

Carrying two empty, red gas cans, Lupino trotted up to the gas pumps at the edge of the floating dock and set them down. Then he went back and got two more. He hurried past the great aluminum warehouse, where sport boats were hoisted and stacked on shelves by forklifts, and pushed into the tackle shop.

Sid, the owner and manager, a thin-framed man in his fifties, looked up from his busy, almost frantic, transactions with customers anxious to get their bait, groceries and gas and be on their way. The trout were running, and when word got out, business boomed. He was an angular, nervous man who bounced around the shop doing everything, happily overworked.

"Hello Lupino," he called out as he rang up the sale for two red-and-yellow, bushy fishing lures. "Haven't seen you in a while. What brings you up to this neck of the woods?" He turned to the lady holding two packages of Coca-Cola. "Yes ma'am, anything else?"

"Oh, just come up here to do a little catfishing and camping up the river," Lupino lied cheerfully. "We need some gas and supplies. Is the pump turned on?"

"Yeah, I'll be with you in a minute."

"That's okay, I'll gas her myself. I got a fella with me that's hot to do some fishing."

The old man sighed, "Ever see one who isn't? Help yourself," the store owner called back from the register, turning to his next customer.

When the pump was clear, Lupino filled the cans, came back in and indiscriminately raided the grocery shelf, grabbing canned sardines, beanie weenies, crackers, Cokes, beer, and potato chips. When he had it all loaded into the dock cart, he waited behind three more people at the register.

"You must be going to do a lot of fishing," said the marina owner with surprise after he rang it up.

"Sure plan to," Lupino replied. And then went into a big rap of how he had this busy executive, who wanted to get away from it all and go up the river for a few days and camp. As he wound his tale, he wondered if Sid was suspicious, or just interested. Then shrugged it off, thinking, they ain't caught me 'til they put the cuffs on.

Blake was sitting on top of the covered bales, trying to meditate and stifle his nervousness. Two middle-aged men and their wives, carrying rods and tackle boxes, ambled down the floating docks in his direction.

Oh my God, he thought, this is too suspicious. They can't help but smell this reefer. Why did I put myself in the hands of that idiot redneck? We're caught for sure. He strained his ears to hear what the couples were saying, at the same time looking up and down the docks, trying to figure out an escape.

"If some people hadn't overslept this morning," the old man was accusing his wife, "we'd be out there right now fishing. You messed around when we should be after those trout. They bite the best when the sun comes up."

"Now, Steven, a few minutes won't make any difference," replied his wife. "I needed to get some breakfast."

Blake breathed a sigh of relief, then froze when he heard the other gray-haired lady sneeze twice in a row, and say, "What is that smell?" She rubbed her nose. "It smells like marigolds," and sneezed again. "You know how allergic I am to marigolds."

The men looked around and sniffed. "I smell it too. But I don't see any."

The lady's eyes watered and she sneezed again. "Let's get out of here. I can't stand it."

"You'll feel better dear," her husband consoled her, "once you get out on the water. You always do."

The two couples passed Lupino and nodded hello as he seized the heavy gas cans and waddled back to the boat as fast as he could go. With his heart pounding, Blake jumped up and helped him load.

Oblivious of the fishermen around him, Lupino hooked up the gasoline and pumped the rubber bulb, forcing fuel into the carbure-tor. Then he turned the key. *Rrrrr...Rrrrr...Rrrrr.* The engine turned over but wouldn't start.

"Oh, shoot," he groaned, shaking his head. "She's flooded now. That's one thing I got off on these Johnson motors. You can give me a Mercury anytime. Lots of fishermen don't like 'em, but I..."

"Will you crank the freaking boat!" Blake said in a low, savage voice between gritted teeth. At last it started. They puttered out of the marina and picked up speed. When they came upon a cluster of boats where sportsmen were casting their lines into the water and reeling up speckled trout and redfish, Blake ordered Lupino to stop. They pulled out their fishing rods—brought along solely for camouflage—made a few casts, and then slowly crept on, pretending to fish until they were out of sight. The boat took off with a roar. As the miles passed, the scenery changed from spiny, brown needlerush growing in brackish water to freshwater broad-leafed saw grass. Soon the river narrowed; luxurious palm and bay trees sprouted from small islands amidst the saw grass.

Black-shelled turtles with yellow markings crawled up on logs to bask. But as the boat sped by, its heavy wake rushed to the shoreline and the turtles slid off. Snowy white egrets and blue herons, in their endless search for minnows and frogs, flapped away disdainfully.

Two hours later, as they sped up the river, navigation became more difficult. They ran at half throttle to avoid logs and snags and slowed for the winding bends. Gnarled, twisted cypress trees towered over the banks, their broad-buttressed bases and prop roots rising from the mud.

"How far is it to the landing from here?" Blake inquired.

"It's still a pretty good piece. Trouble is, we got a bunch of houses coming up in a couple of miles. A little riverfront community called

Caldwell Creek."

"So?"

"So we got to sneak past 'em," Lupino explained. "A big old crab boat like this with a big motor don't belong this far up the river. Most people use ten-horsepower outboards up here. They see us coming through with this big tarpaulin, someone might figure it ain't right and call the law. We ought to find us a hole and lay up 'til dark."

"That's good thinking," agreed Blake, "We were pressing our luck back there at the marina. I don't want any more of that. I've been through a lot, but that really made me nervous."

Lupino pulled back the throttle and the big motor slowed to a rough idle. They moved slowly now, watching for an inlet in the riverbank.

Just then, they heard the loud, droning hum of an aircraft, distant but growing rapidly louder. "That sounds like a plane coming," said Lupino breathlessly. "It could be the law." He looked around widely. "Yonder's a creek," he cried, pointing to an indentation in the river bank. "It ain't much, but we can get in. Hang on."

He rammed the throttle down and the boat lunged forward. With a desperate twist, Lupino drove the big boat into a little side creek that fed into the main river channel, and vanished from sight. The canopy of water oaks closed overhead. Branches slapped them in the face. Blake was thrown on top of the tarp as they rammed into the shallows. The motor revved and balked. Using the power trim, Lupino raised the motor to maximum tilt and powered the boat forward.

When they could go no farther, he leaped out of the boat and ran into the swamp. Blake followed behind, crouching low. The saw grass tore at their hands, and devil's walking stick, a study in thorny protection for an insignificant weed, snagged their clothing. But they hurried on, panting, covered with mud.

The plane's engines droned loudly and steadily over the treetops. It seemed to be some sort of reconnaissance, slowly flying up the river. Lupino caught a glimpse of it through the trees. It was white, with a green star on the tail rudder. "It's the Sheriff's plane, all right," he whispered.

Involuntarily Blake hunched down on the soggy ground like a rabbit about to be swooped upon by a bird of prey. But the plane kept going.

"You think they were after us?" Lupino worried, watching the plane moving out of sight. "Some of those burned bales could be turning up by now. Some of the shrimpers out there will turn them in. Others will get rich."

"I doubt it. There hasn't been time for that. If anything, it was your stunt at the marina back there."

Blake listened to the plane fading off into the distance. "If they saw us and were after us, they'd be turning around right now. You've got to watch it—you get paranoid in this business. They wouldn't know anything unless..." he frowned "...unless your brother-in-law rolled over. You think he'll keep his mouth shut?"

"One thing about Captain Preston, if he gives you his word, it's good. I'll say that for him." He happened to glance down near Blake's feet and froze. "Snake! Don't move! There's a goddamn moccasin, big as your leg, behind you!"

Blake whipped around, and found himself looking into the black, stony eyes of a huge snake. It was camouflaged against the leaves of the swamp floor, its head rising from its coils, tongue flickering, tasting. Blake jumped away as the snake opened its white maw, exposing its fangs. He watched Lupino draw out his pistol and aim. "Don't shoot, someone might hear..."

The pistol went off. Lupino's hand jumped from the recoil and the brown scales of the large, triangular head exploded into blood and pink flesh. It jerked into a tight coil, a writhing heap. Lupino fired again and again, the shots echoing loudly through the woods. "I hate them sons-a-bitches," he shuddered. "Lord, I can't stand a snake."

Blake was angry, "That was pretty stupid. Someone might have heard the shots. One thing I learned in Vietnam, you don't make any more noise than you have to."

"Well, yeah, but I couldn't help it," admitted Lupino. "I hate a goddamn snake."

"We'd better stay right here until dark, cut some of these willow brushes to cover up the boat good. That plane *was* flying pretty low."

A soft breeze stirred the waxy leaves of the red bay tree near them, turning over their white undersides. Lupino reeled around and begin sniffing like a bloodhound, "You smell that?"

"What?"

He drew a deep breath, "You don't smell that? It's pot, green pot. I'll bet that's what the sheriff's plane was after. Someone's growing it around here. Come on."

He bolted off through the slash pines. Not wanting to be left, Blake hurried along to catch up, watching the ground for more snakes.

About two hundred yards away Lupino stopped, walked a grid pattern, still sniffing. "It's stronger here..." He took a few more steps off into the palmetto and shouted happily, "Here it is!"

Blake stood in bemused amazement at the small, hidden crop of *Cannabis sativa*, with its delicately-pointed green leaves. There were ten plants about eight feet tall, each with a thick coat of buds.

The irony of it made him laugh. "They've got it hidden all right."

"Hell, it's all over the woods and the wildlife refuges," said Lupino wisely. "You can't make it honest on this coast, so you gotta grow a little pot or starve to death. I bet I know who this belongs to."

"Come on, let's get the hell out of here," Blake ordered, stepping back. "The last thing we need is to get shot by someone who thinks we're stealing their reefer." He smashed a mosquito on his neck and a big glob of blood smeared on his fingers. "Let's get back to the boat and get some sleep."

"Good idea," agreed Lupino. "I ain't slept in three days."

They returned to the fiberglass crab boat. Loaded with brown bags of marijuana, it looked starkly out of place in the green foliage. "We better cut some brush and cover us up, in case they come looking again."

By the time they were finished, they heard the distant, churning hum of an outboard motor. Anxiously they listened to it drawing closer, slowing down to get over snags. "This sucks," Blake complained. "I don't like this. It could be just a fisherman, but after that sheriff's plane..."

Lupino crept out to the edge of the creek, crouching to get a better look. When the boat passed, he beat a hasty retreat, looking scared and breathing heavily. "That was the mother-loving game warden! He could be looking for us."

"He's probably looking for whoever fired those shots, you asshole. Come on, let's try and get some rest. We'll have to wait until it's good and dark before we take out."

Blake climbed into the boat and tried to make himself comfortable among the wet bales. "I haven't had so much fun since Vietnam," he said wearily, and closed his eyes.

6

The Baptism

The afternoon sun lay low and golden above the horizon, sending shafts of light across the river and down through the canopy of trees. Propped on his elbow, resting on the bales, Blake had given up trying to sleep. He wanted a joint and wanted it bad, but all his cigarette papers were soaked. With a certain amount of disgust, he studied Lupino's sleeping, almost angelic face. The mosquitoes hovered above him, but they didn't land. They delighted in drinking Blake's blood instead.

There hadn't been another boat all day, and he was tempted to awaken Lupino and get started. But smugglers rightly work at night; and discomfort or not, you don't take unnecessary chances. The sun was beginning to set when Lupino awoke. He crawled to the edge of the boat, dipped some black water and washed his face. Then he took a leak off the bow. He turned and contemplated Blake, who was look-ing red-eyed, unkempt and scratched. There were bits of leaves in his normally groomed hair. It amazed Lupino how he had managed to stay as neat as he had, after all they'd been through. "You sure are a mess," he chortled. "You look like you been sorting wildcats."

"You don't look so lovely yourself," Blake said in a tired voice, wishing he could nod off as easily as Lupino had.

A squirrel chattered in an oak tree up on the bank, sparring with another squirrel as they chased each other from branch to branch.

"Look at them two old boar squirrels yonder, fighting over that pussy," observed Lupino, pointing to the branches. "I wish I had my .22 rifle. We'd get us some fine eating."

"You've done enough shooting, and I'd just as soon eat a rat." replied Blake sourly. "Where I come from, no one eats squirrel."

"Son, you don't know what's good. That's the finest eating there is! Me, Justin, Preston and our families used to come camping up here and shoot five or six before breakfast."

"Well, you can have them. How about some of those groceries you bought? I'm starved."

Lupino reached for a can of Vienna sausage and began working off the lid with his pocketknife. "I'll tell you something. There ain't no better way to live than up in the woods. I was gonna take my money from the run, if things didn't go sour, and buy some land up here, put up a double-wide and just live. Maybe I'd make a few dollars catfishing now and then, and grow some pot, but I wouldn't need much to live on. Then I could go to Nashville and become a country western singer. But now, when I get my share, I gotta give it to Preston 'cause of my boat burning up. He signed the note for me at the bank."

"Well, I wouldn't screw him then," Blake observed. "Preston seems like a good fellow."

"He's one of the best," replied Lupino proudly. "They don't get no better. And there's no better shrimper along this coast. He loves his work. He's the last of a dying breed. He knows commercial fishing is coming to an end in a few years, and he's gonna be the last one out there, but he don't care."

The golden light reflected off the black waters and peeked out from the trees in a spectacular sunset.

When darkness approached they threw off the cover of willow branches and pushed the crab boat back down the creek, grunting and straining until they found water deep enough to back out. Against the darkening sky, the heavy outline of the trees made a looming wall along the river. As they slowly traveled north, the shoreline changed and the river became less swampy. It cut through sand hills, oak and pine forests until the bends became still narrower. In the darkness they passed by the little riverside community of Hog Wallow Creek. They could see the blue glow of the television sets as they sped by. Two obnoxious dogs ran down to the riverbank and barked at them, and an owner yelled at them to shut up.

An hour later the bends became shallower, and there were more snags and overhanging branches. Lupino frequently had to use his power tilt to lift the motor's foot and move ahead. Soon they crept along at scarcely an idle, Lupino beaming his flashlight along the banks and in front of them looking for submerged logs. Finally the boat ran aground.

"Guess we'd better get out and start pushing. This is just a sand bar. They'll be deep water on the other side." The beam of Blake's flashlight caught two ruby-red lights the size of quarters that looked up from a nearby bank. "Alligator!" whispered Lupino excitedly, "Look at that sucker. He must be twelve feet long!"

"Oh good, now we'll get eaten alive? How far *is* it to the landing?"

"It couldn't be over another four miles," returned Lupino. "We've come a long way already."

The hard white stars shown coldly down upon them in the open corridor of the river. The shoreline was now a weave of tangled willow, and, where the bends narrowed, it slapped and scratched their faces. Things splashed and rustled unnervingly in the forest. And even Lupino, who loved the river, felt trapped by it. Here, it turned unfriendly and unforgiving. And it grew worse, and shallower, until they finally stuck again on a sand bar. "We've got to get some of this pot off," said Lupino in defeat. "We're just too heavily loaded. We'll be fighting this all night. The river's running down all the time."

"Oh no, we're not. Not after I got it this far. Everything I own is tied up in this pot, and I'm not going to abandon it. We'll set off enough to float, then go back and get it, and keep moving, if it takes all night!"

Blake snatched back the cover and started heaving the eighty-pound bales over the side. Eventually the boat popped up, and they moved on, waded back and retrieved them. Twice more during the night they did the same thing. Finally, Lupino shined his flashlight around the shoreline until he spotted a dark indentation, a creek that fed out from the side of the river. "We might as well give it up and see where we are in the morning. We couldn't be far from Buck's Landing now.

"You sure there's a pay phone there?" the hippie asked wearily. The tension of the past few days, the trip on the barge, the burning of the *Night Shadow*, and now the river—all were coming together, and exhaustion was setting in.

"There was last time I was up there," Lupino reassured him. "But it ain't exactly at the Landing. Molly's Place is four miles up the road."

After they pushed the boat into the creek, Blake collapsed wearily on top of a bale. "I'm tired. Roll us a joint, Lupino. I'm ready to get stoned. Maybe the smoke will drive off the mosquitoes."

"Good idea!" Lupino agreed. He poked around the bales until he found a hole, and pinched out enough marijuana to roll a bomber. Gratefully, he found that the cigarette papers he had stashed away in the bow were still dry.

"This is good stuff, I can tell by the feel of it—the buds are all sticky. I'll fix you a good one," he said to his co-conspirator, but only exhausted snores answered him. Blake lay face down on the tarp.

Lupino puffed away, listening to the croaking of frogs and the songs of cicadas. Soon he was feeling good, as the marijuana had its effects. He thought about going to Nashville. He'd use all his dope money to promote himself to stardom. Before long he dropped off to sleep and dreamed of playing a glittering guitar in a country and western band under blazing stage lights.

But the dream changed, and the drummer turned into an enormous, corpulent alligator, and the scene shifted back to the river. The alligator was sitting on the back of the boat, eating the pot. Lupino watched it swallowing the burlap-covered bales, one after the other, growing bigger and bigger until they were gone. Meanwhile, he was surrounded by smaller alligators, all beating drums to the rhythm of their eating, slapping tails in unison and gobbling scraps.

Blake also dreamed of drums and chanting. Hazy, glowing witches swam before him, spirits of the swamps crossed his path. All about him were devils and demons. All the while the drums beat, *boom...boom...boom...* Would they never stop? He was running now through the woods, and the law was after him with a pack of howling, barking bloodhounds. *Boom...boom...* He was running with a bale of pot on his back. *Boom...boom...* The dogs were closing in on him.

He opened his eyes, still with a feeling of being chased, and saw it was daylight. High overhead the mid-morning sun shown through the foliage. He closed his eyes; it was just a bad dream. And then he sprang to his feet. From around the bend of the river came the sound of drums, pounding resonantly and rhythmically, *boom...boom...boom.*

"Get up! Get up!" cried Blake, shaking Lupino.

Sleepily, Lupino rubbed his eyes, and rose from the tarp, yawning. "I'm glad you woke me. I was having the awfullest dream."

Boom...boom...boom! Then they heard singing and chanting. Lupino wrinkled his narrow face in perplexity, jumped to his feet, trying to figure it out. "Come on, let's see what the hell this is all about."

He leaped from the boat and landed in the mud with a splat. He slogged through a floating mat of purple flowering-arrowheads and bolted into the forest. Following behind, Blake marveled at the ease with which Lupino blended into the woods. He found himself stumbling along, cracking twigs and uncertain of foot, his feet squishing on lizard weed that wrapped his toes like hanks of soggy human hair.

"Out of practice," he accused himself, breathing heavily. It was a long time since the war, when he was in the jungles of Vietnam. But his noise was drowned out by the mysterious drumming.

They cut across the oxbow in the river, and came to a clearing on the riverbank. Squatting down in the bushes they heard the drums beating even louder. Lupino motioned for Blake to stay back and crawled forward on his belly. He returned in a minute, laughing. "It's a bunch of jungle bunnies having a baptism. I didn't know what the hell it was. Scared me half to death! I told you we were close to the landing, we couldn't have been a quarter of a mile away," he said triumphantly.

Blake crept closer, looking at the big wooden bridge that spanned the river, and the flattened, clay road that led down to the water. Before them was a Negro congregation, with all ages of men and women dressed in white, singing, *"Meet you by the River...the beautiful, beautiful Jordan..."*

The smugglers watched in awe as the preacher walked a sinner out into the water, assisted by eight singing ladies. Their gaze was heavenward and joy heightened their faces as they led a young girl into the dark waters. The preacher held her stiffly and slowly arched her backward. The waters of the river closed over her head. She was immersed for a second and then lifted out and she stood upright, trembling, eyes closed. Blake watched with fascination; he had never seen a baptism before. He noted in the instant after the young woman was submerged that something had changed. Her whole body shook with what he, an agnostic, could only call spirit. Then the women led her back to the bank, singing their praises to Heaven. The girl was "saved," whatever that was.

Lupino elbowed Blake in the ribs, grinned and winked. "Bunch of crazy damn coons, ain't they? That gal ain't bad-looking. You know what they say," and then he started chanting a racist little jingle, "Suck a duck. Screw a guinea..."

Blake shot him a look of revulsion and moved away from him. Then, he spied again upon this young woman, seeing her contentment and bliss. Suddenly a great weariness overcame him; it wasn't from running, or lack of sleep, it was his whole life. He was tired of the war, first blowing up people in Vietnam, watching his friends get slaughtered. And then the drug trade. He used to get a thrill out of taking off from a jungle runway in the middle of the night with no lights and a plane full of marijuana. He was as addicted to the adventure as he was to stuffing fifty thousand dollars worth of cocaine up his nose each year. And now he was a fugitive, having escaped from prison, running, running away from the law, and away from himself.

He wished he could join these simple people, and wash his sins away—whatever sins were. Blake watched a maple leaf drifting toward a whirling eddy. Maybe sins were absorbed into the natural system like the dead leaves washed into rivers and down to the sea. Maybe those creatures he'd seen on shrimp boats with segmented bodies, spiny claws, and slimy skins ate the sins. Perhaps that's why they were warty, ugly little things: because they ate greed, sloth, and hatred. Maybe someday, when it was all over, there would be hope for him.

The baptism ended with a resounding, melodious hymn that rang through the forests, and then the faithful, dripping wet, started filing up the landing toward a decrepit school bus parked on the shoulder of the bridge.

"Come on, let's see if we can catch a ride with them. It's a good four miles up the road to Molly's from here, and we got to get to a phone, don't we?"

"You're crazy," whispered Blake incredulously. "We'll look suspicious as hell coming out of the woods like this. It's too risky; we'll walk."

"Naw, we'll just tell 'em some kinda bullshit. They'll believe anything. Just give 'em a couple of bucks." He popped out of the bushes and strode forward.

"Morning, Preacher," Lupino began boldly, approaching the stooped-over little man who was wearing a thoroughly soaked suit jacket, white shirt and tie. His feet were bare and his pants were soaked.

The preacher smiled back uncertainly and nodded. "Morning, Brother."

"Me and my buddy here been catfishing down the river a ways, and our motor quit. I got to call my old lady. Can we catch a ride with you up to Molly's?"

"Yessir!" said the preacher smiling. "Always glad to help folks out. Y'all hop on. We'll carry you there, or into town if you want."

"No," said Blake hastily, coming up to them, "just to the telephone, but thank you."

The driver pulled the door shut, and the wheezing old church bus started down the road, going through an agony of shifting gears. Almost immediately Blake became aware of one of the sisters sitting across the aisle regarding them with far more than the casual interest of the others. Except when she was appraising them, her eyes boring into their souls, she was a big, jolly woman, whose laughter rang out over the bus, as she talked with the congregation about the spirit and glory. Then, her eyes laughed, but as she took in the muddy shoes, bites, and scratches of the white strangers her lips pursed but said nothing.

Lupino whispered to Blake, "Look at that witch. She's giving us the evil eye. I hope she ain't onto us." Blake said nothing, wishing fervently they'd walked the four miles to Molly's.

Finally, she heaved herself up, strode to the front of the bus, and sat down next to them. "You boys sure look like you been having a bad time in de woods with all dat catfishing." Then she added emphatically, "A mighty bad time!"

"Sure did," agreed Lupino nervously. "Our motor broke down, you see..."

She silenced him with a withering look she had cultivated for dealing with rambunctious seven-year-olds in Sunday School classes. She continued, "You been out in de woods a long, long time from de looks of you. You ain't by chance seen none of dem no good dope smugglers they looking for, did you?"

Blake found himself trembling, something he never did, even when the cops were interrogating him. "No ma'am, we sure didn't," he stuttered, turning pale. "We've just been catfishing." Lupino's done it to us this time, he thought savagely. His eyes searched desperately up and down the bus, looking for an escape door. His hand moved closer to his pistol.

"Oh, dat's good!" Sister Arial went on sarcastically, pretending not to see his discomfort. " 'Cause I wouldn't like to come up on none of dem neither, ruining young'uns, selling the devil's weed in de schools, breaking up families and such as dat!"

Lupino started, "You're right, Auntie. I know exactly what you mean. My sister's son got messed up with..."

"Not with all de Lord's work we got to do fixing de church's roof," she said raising her voice, cutting him off, while the others in the bus stopped talking and listened. "Why it leaks so bad, we can't hardly stand it no mo! And somewhere we got to find de money, but Lawd, things cost so much. Ah knows," she added, giving them a penetrating stare, " 'cause ah's de treasurer."

A flood of relief came over Blake. Thank God, he breathed to himself, this was something he could deal with: a payoff. He looked at this lady with her short gray hair pulled back in a bun and her big bosom pushing against her white dress. "How much is it going to take to fix the roof?"

The bus jostled over a washed-out rut in the dirt road, and the driver slowed, shifting through a cacophony of gears before anyone could hear themselves talk. "Oh, we figure about four thousand dollars," the sister returned. "That's a heap of money for honest folks to come by. The brothers in de church gonna do de work, but them building materials sho' come high. They's got plum out of sight!"

Blake nodded and smiled warmly. "Perhaps we can make a contribution to your good works, Sister."

When the bus approached an old shack on the highway with a blue sign reading "Molly's Beer Garden," Blake beckoned the preacher to stop and step out of the bus with them. He said he had something important to tell him. Sister Arial followed, watching suspiciously.

A minute later the preacher was back on the bus clutching a wad of cash, shouting, "Praise de Lawd! Good God Almighty, de Lawd works in mysterious ways. We gonna get our roof fixed!"

Their arms still quivering from the preacher's vigorous handshaking, Blake and Lupino watched the congregation waving excitedly and gratefully as the school bus disappeared down the road.

Blake chuckled, "I should feel ripped off, but somehow I don't."

"Now that's a bunch of shit!" cried Lupino indignantly. "That old witch blackmailing us like that. What a rip-off. If she doesn't call the cops, she'll probably put a voodoo on us anyway."

"And give up that money?" chortled Blake. "Forget it."

"I don't know. You can't never trust them people," Lupino said all-knowingly.

"Lupino," Blake stormed, "take your racism and shove it. I know blacks that could buy and sell you ten times over. They're better educated, better dressed, better-looking, and hell of a lot better company than you are."

"Well, you can kiss my ass!" Lupino retorted for want of something better to say. Then he added, "I ain't got nothing against black people. Some of my best friends are..."

"Spare me, please," Blake said wearily. Then he looked at the dusty phone booth outside Molly's Beer Garden, which was closed. "I hope to God it works." The phone booth was filled with cobwebs, beer cans and dirt. When he lifted the receiver and heard a dial tone, it was bliss. Lupino helped with directions. Now all they had to do was to collect the bales. They left the boat tied to the bank of the placid, dark-water Ochlockonee River and waited for the fish truck to arrive.

7

Above Suspicion

For nine months out of the year, Carrabelle remained a sleepy fishing village. A few local shrimp boats came and went and scraped out a meager living. People oystered, crabbed or fished mullet. But in the cold months fish houses were seldom open. The riverfront was quiet, almost desolate. Blue herons walked on the empty wharves and pelicans begged for scraps.

The pot brought an unexpected economic boom to the town. New trucks appeared on the highway, appliances were replaced, vacations taken. And none of it went unnoticed by Mary or Preston Barfield. "Hank Spivey just put a new addition on his house," she berated him, "and I know for sure that he found two of them bales."

She saw Spivey driving by in a new truck—that was one bale. And, suddenly, Billy Williams was putting a new addition on his house. Connie Lou bought a whole kitchen of new appliances, and Roland Smith tied his boat up and took his family on vacation, trout fishing in the mountains. Preston's five thousand dollars from the smugglers allowed him to catch up his boat payments but nothing more. And Charlie blew his loot partying and was broke in a week.

But it was March, the weather was warming, and everyone prayed that in a few weeks the hopper shrimp would run and breathe new life into the dying economy. In anticipation of the bonanza, boats came from Alabama and Louisiana, and some from Texas. Tired of the dreary cold, they came down from North and South Carolina into the somewhat warmer Gulf of Mexico to wait the run of shrimp. Every day, new families of the captains and crews moved into town and took over every little hotel, motel and rooming house.

To Preston Barfield, time was precious. There was always something to fix on his boat. The sea and salt worked relentlessly on metal and paint. Electrical wires became encrusted with green copper salts, corroded, and failed to conduct current. Worn, rusted brakes on the winches had to be replaced, and old cables spliced or new ones put on.

While he waited for Charlie to come down to the boat to get ready for their next trip, he helped Randy Williams splice his cables and set the bridles on his net. *Sometimes I wish I hadn't learned how to do this*, he thought to himself as he helped drag a hundred feet of cable down the dock. All the shrimpers were after him to help. With six powerful blows, his sharp chisel cut through the flawed section of Randy's cable, liberating tightly twisted wire strands so they popped out in an explosion of sharp jagged wire. Even with gloves and thick calluses, it made his hands sore.

Randy held the severed ends up so Preston could braid them with his marlin spike. "If I wasn't so doggone broke," the slender man of twenty-five complained, "I'd take all this rotten cable off and haul it to the dump. I'll tell you, I wished it was me found some of that pot floating around out here. The other day when that load came in, I hunted it so bad I thought my eyeballs was gonna fall out. Every time I seen something floating along, I run up to it and it turned out to be some doggone old fish box or piece of trash. I know this old boy who'd buy every bit of it."

Harlin "Hank" Spivey, a gruff, unshaven shrimper, was sitting on a fish box drinking a beer, observing them working. "Some of them boys got rich, that's for sure. But one thing it's done, it's brought the Grouper Troopers and Coast Guard down on everybody. They got so many running around they're arresting each other." Hank chuckled, flipping his beer can in the water. "Why, I'll bet they spend a billion dollars to collect a thousand.

"And you know what happens when those crookedy bastards find pot?" Hank went on. "They say they haul it off to the incinerator and burn it, but you better believe it don't all get burned. That's why the sheriff's the richest man in the county. Ain't no telling how much land

and businesses he owns."

Suddenly a gray and black Florida Marine Patrol car pulled up, and they all watched as a stocky, uniformed patrolman walked slowly down to the dock. He was a pleasant fellow, his red hair cut short, almost a crew cut, his face freckled. The heels on the officer's polished black shoes clicked over the silvery boards of the wharf as he approached. They watched him with mild curiosity. "Hi ya, Teddy," Hank called, saluting him with his beer.

"Boys, y'all look real busy," he teased. "The only one who appears to be loafing is Captain Preston here."

"We're waiting for the shrimp to come out of the mud," Randy returned with a grin. "They're all buried up. Waiting's mighty hard work."

Officer Ted Miller wore his gray uniform casually. While it was pressed and clean, it didn't bristle with authority. He even managed to keep his .38 and bullet-lined patent-leather belt from being too obtrusive. The fishermen bore him none of the hostility they felt for the out-of-town cops who stormed up and down the docks like modern day Gestapos, puffed-up with their power. Ted Miller had earned their respect because he was once one of them. But when he could no longer feed his wife and three children by mullet fishing and oystering, he took a job as a deputy sheriff, then later joined the Florida Marine Patrol.

"What you up to, Ted?" Hank asked. "You out looking for square grouper?"

"Got any?" the officer grinned back at him. He was studied Preston, who was splicing the ends of the frayed cable and saying nothing.

"Lots and lots of it," Randy joked. "A million dollars worth. I'm just getting old Preston here to splice this rotten cable 'cause I want to put it in a museum. Reckon I'd tell you if I had any, Ted?"

"You might," the officer shrugged. "There's been some that has. Sam Grover was shrimping over in Liberty Cove the other night and found six bales and called us."

After some small talk, Miller turned to Preston, "You gonna be much longer doing that?"

"Me?" Preston's big head jerked up with surprise. "No, I'm just about finished." A surge of adrenaline shot through him.

"Good. If you don't mind, I'd like to talk to you, private-like."

"Oh-oh!" hooted Randy with a grin. "It's leg-irons, bars and stripes for Captain Barfield now."

"Don't worry," joined in Hank, "we'll bring you a cake with a saw in it."

Preston grinned weakly at them. He felt his hands tremble inside the heavy welding gloves he used to grip the cable, and took a breath, calming himself. Then slowly, deliberately, he pulled off the gloves and turned to the officer nonchalantly, "Come on, Ted. Let's go over to my boat. If you don't mind, I got some net patching to do before we get gone from here tonight. That is, if Charlie gets his sorry behind out of the bar."

The marine patrolman followed him across the decks of several other trawlers to the *Lady Mary*. All up and down the waterfront, boats were tied up four and even five abreast. Preston sat on the gunnel, picked up a section of net lying on deck, made himself comfortable on the railing and began weaving in new webbing. "What's going on, Ted?" His tone was casual but fear made his throat dry.

"I guess you know there's been bales of pot washing all up and down this coast for the past couple of days," the marine patrolman opened.

"Yeah, I know. People ain't talking about nothing else. It's the biggest thing to hit this coast since Hurricane Agnes."

Miller paced around the deck. "We picked up a couple of boats this morning. One had eight bales, the other twelve," he said, his eyes darting around the *Lady Mary*, checking out the wheelhouse roof and trying to peek into the cabin. "They said they were just rushing in to turn them in to us."

Preston winked, "Maybe they were, Ted." He thrust his six-inch needle, wound with white nylon thread, through the webbing, building new mesh. The new white string made a sharp contrast to the old, faded green webbing.

Officer Miller chuckled, "Hell, I don't know that I blame them. If I were out there starving, trying to make a living this shrimp season, and I found bale or two worth five or ten thousand come floating by, I might be tempted to keep my mouth shut and say nothing."

"Not you, you're too honest, Ted," Preston grinned mischievously at him. "You make a case against 'em?"

"No, we just took the pot. The state's not much interested in prosecuting a man who finds a bale floating out there." His eyes quit wandering around the boat and he looked Preston in the eye, "But we sure want to know where it's coming from."

"I imagine you do!" Preston replied. He put down the net for a moment and looked at the marine patrolman in his gray uniform with a level stare. "What's on your mind, Ted?" he asked flatly, ready to put an end to small talk.

"We heard about Lupino's boat burning up, and how you saved him."

He looked back down at the net, grateful for it being there, knowing that if he could keep his hands busy, he'd be less nervous and less likely to say anything wrong. "Yeah, sure did," he grunted with disgust. "Lupino ain't got no sense. Would you believe he had a leaky injector line and wrapped a rag around it to get by until he could get around to fixing it? It sprayed into the turbo charger, caught fire and got away from him. He's just lucky we weren't all that far away from him when it happened."

"When you picked them up," the patrolman said, pacing the deck again, a shade predatory, "did you see anything unusual?"

"It's pretty unusual to come up on a boat burning like hell and fuel tanks fixing to blow!"

Ted Miller grinned, appreciating the reply. He changed the subject, asking a few casual questions about shrimping, Mary, and when the baby was due. He only lived a few blocks away from them in the village. He liked Preston. He'd known him all his life to be hardworking and honest, and he knew Lupino, who was always in trouble. When Ted was a deputy sheriff, he often had to deal with rowdy and intoxicated shrimpers back from the sea, pent up with energy and desire. Preston's deckhand, Charlie Hansen was a problem from time to time, getting hauled up on drunk and disorderly charges, but he was a decent sort. It was a fair bet that Lying Lupino, as they called him, had roped Preston into something.

Life in the sheriff's office was simpler than the marine patrol. If a man broke the law by speeding up and down the highway, drunk, risking the lives of children, he'd arrest him for doing wrong. If he resisted, he'd try to reason with him, and if that failed, he'd bust him in the head and still haul him in.

But as a marine patrolman, when he arrested fishermen like Preston Barfield for catching undersized shrimp or fishing with improper nets or harvesting small oysters, the lines of authority became less clear. When you dragged a man like that into court and made him pay a stiff fine, you were hurting his family. No one knew better than Ted what it was like to be out there in the cold wind and seas day after day to scrape up enough money to pay a doctor's bill for a child's broken arm. He didn't like arresting men trying to make a living, catching fish to feed people. But that was his job.

Preston saw the patrolman's eyes wandering around the boat and staring at the sealed-up hold as they made small talk, and figured he'd better lead him around the boat to avoid suspicion. He put the net down and rose a trifle stiffly. "Ted, I'm damn sure dying for a beer. Would you mind helping me get this hatch cover open?"

"Be glad to," the officer replied gratefully. He was trying to think of a way to look down there without having to make a heavy-handed official inspection.

Together, they slid off the heavy hatch cover that led down into the cavernous dark belly of the shrimp trawler. Preston crawled down the ladder, and Ted looked down at the melting ice on the concrete floor in the dark hole. There wasn't a hint of pot, just the smell of fish-soaked boards used to partition off ice bins. The smell of even one bale, closed up in the hull even for a few hours would linger for days. Even with vacuum cleaners and scrubbing with Lysol, it would be hard to hide.

"You want a beer?" Preston called up from the ice hold.

"No, thank you. I'm on duty."

The shrimper emerged with beer in hand, and as Ted helped him slide the heavy hatch cover back into place, he said, "Hell of a job you got there, Ted. You used to be able to have a cold one when you fished for a living."

The patrolman tossed it aside. "It's a trade-off. We eat regular now. Listen, Preston, I'm not gonna play cat and mouse with you. Six bales washed up on the east end of St. George's Island and two of them were burned." He watched the fisherman intently for a reaction, but saw none.

"So?" Preston said, noticing Ted studying his face for a reaction. He popped the can and took a swallow. The icy beer felt good going down his dry nervous throat.

"So they didn't burn up out there by themselves."

"Oh, I see," he nodded slowly, as if he had achieved some great understanding. "That's the connection. You found burned up bales, and Lupino's boat burned up. I picked him up, and that's why you're here."

All the while Preston kept repeating to himself, *Keep calm, just act natural, you don't know anything.* Again, he picked up the net and began cutting off the frayed ends with his pocketknife and forced himself to relax. "Well, I didn't see any bales of pot when I got him off the boat."

The lie made him feel like his stomach had those jumping shrimp in it again, but he went on. "Hell, you know Lupino. I reckon it's possible he might have picked up a bale or two like some of these other boys did, but he didn't tell me about it. But he'd have to be plum crazy to mess with dope after all the trouble he got into awhile back."

Preston took another swallow of beer and shook his head in wonderment. "Maybe some airplane coming up from Colombia with a load crashed and burned." His explanation sounded hollow, empty and false to him.

"We don't think so, they weren't floating out there long. The centers were dry. So...do you know where Lupino is?" His voice assumed an investigative tone. "We've been looking all over for him."

"Can't say as I do," Preston replied brusquely. "When he hit the dock he hauled ass." Then he let conversation hang, trying now to hide his growing anger at Lupino for getting him into this fix. It made him feel cheap inside. Lying wasn't his nature.

The officer gazed across the river at the brown needlerush marshes and the big white spoil banks that had been dredged out of the channel. Preston probably wasn't telling the truth. Here, right or wrong, families stuck together. At last he broke the silence. "Well, I'd better get on. If you see him, tell him we'd like to ask him some questions. You know, one thing boys like Lupino don't realize. They shouldn't play in the big leagues when they belong in the little leagues."

"What do you mean?" Preston asked quietly, weaving in more webbing.

The officer's jaw tightened and he became angry. "It means these goddamn dope smugglers are dirt. They're trash. A man who hauls the dope is just as disposable to them as airplanes or shrimp boats. Once these people get their hooks into you, they don't let go." Preston got the distinct impression that Miller wasn't talking about him or Lupino. He was talking about himself. "And I'll tell you another thing, they don't think anything about buying a law officer. Several patrol officers have gone to jail for smuggling, and two directors of the whole big Department of Natural Resources did time for influence peddling and helping their buddies launder dope money. It corrupts a lot of people. Hell, I could get fifty thousand dollars tomorrow, if I'd turn my back."

"Ever think about doing it?" Preston asked curiously. "I mean, didn't it ever cross your mind, even once, Ted?"

"Hell, yes, it's crossed my mind," he snapped. "I got bills like everyone else, Preston, but I got to look myself in the mirror when I get up every morning. I got to look at my two little girls and my wife. It's not worth it! Well...I'll be seeing you."

With a sick feeling, he watched Miller walk down the dock, thinking Mary was a hundred percent right. Now he was involved in covering up a crime, and a conspiracy. Preston wondered if maybe he should've brought in the load after all. "Ah, screw it," he said miserably, "I'm going shrimping!"

8

Shrimper's Dreams

Preston pumped eleven hundred gallons of diesel fuel into the *Lady Mary*, signed the ticket for a thousand dollars, and slowly chugged down to Lawton's ice dock, taking his place behind two waiting trawlers. At last they filled up, cast off and headed down the river, and the *Lady Mary* moved into place. Two muscular dockworkers strained to drag the eight-inch-diameter black hose across the wharf and helped Charlie thrust it down into the trawler's cold, dark belly.

"Okay, turn her on!" shouted Charlie from below, gripping the hose in anticipation. His favorite grease-stained 'CATERPILLAR DIESEL' cap was mashed over his unkempt, shaggy blond hair. He'd been up most of the night with some deckhand friends, riding around from bar to bar looking for girls, drinking beer and playing pinball and blowing the last of his tip from the *Night Shadow*. Charlie honestly meant to fix his transmission, but like the great sages he believed in living in the present. "What the heck," he told his buddies, "easy come, easy go. Let the good times roll. The hoppers are bound to show up soon."

Preston relayed the message to a dockworker who tossed the first of many fifty-pound blocks into the crusher behind the hose. A throaty roar, building to an ear-splitting scream began as the great blower cranked up. The noise rang out across the Carrabelle River and up and down the waterfront. Frigid white mists hissed out of the nozzle, and then, all of a sudden, the one-hundred-foot hose came alive like a giant anaconda, thrashing around as it spewed out white crystals of ice.

When the din of the ice machine ceased, he heard a familiar voice shouting his name, a voice that put his nerves on edge. He'd managed to put Lupino and the whole incident out of his mind. He looked up wearily and saw his brother-in-law trying to look sorrowful, but his black eyes darted with amusement.

Long, curly black hair exploded from under his yellow cap. Keeping still was an impossibility; his feet moved about under their own power while his fingers impatiently tapped on his blue jeans. "Preston! Gotta talk to you!" he shouted over the din.

"Ted Miller was here a while ago, and he wants to talk to *you*! And so does the Coast Guard," Preston shouted back. "Unless you want to answer a lot of questions, I'd make myself scarce."

"That's why I gotta get out of town!"

The noise and vibration of the hose began to wind down, the ice stopped coming, and the blower groaned down to a whine, until finally there was silence. Lupino jumped down onto the deck and came over, smiling.

Preston's deep voice rose in anger. "If you've got any sense, you'll be gone from here, Lupino. You're in grave danger. It's everything I can do to keep from kicking your ass!"

"Please, Preston. Let's talk in the cabin. I don't want to be seen around here too much."

Seeing that bulldog, "I'm-not-moving" look on his face, and knowing that no matter how many insults and threats he heaped upon him, there was no getting rid of Lupino when he wanted something, Preston wearily gestured toward the cabin.

"Preston. Listen, I tried to make it up to you," Lupino said dramatically, breathing heavily. "I really did, so help me God! But they ripped me off! They stole all my money!"

"What the hell are you talking about?"

"After you took us back to the dock, that hippie boy Blake and me went back out there. I know you said not to, but I didn't see no other way I could pay the bank off and get you out from under that note. We took my crab boat, loaded up fifty bales and went up the river, and unloaded at Molly's bar. Then a fella came in a fish truck, picked them all up at the boat landing, but we got stuck at the boat ramp and had to call a wrecker. Then we drove to Jacksonville. Blake paid me fifty thousand dollars for them bales, and I swear to Jesus, I was gonna give it all to you."

Preston stared at him in open-mouthed disbelief, shaking his head. "*You...went...back!*" Anger flashed in his gray eyes.

"We sure did!" he said proudly, "and we got away with it, slick as glass. But when I come back to my apartment in Tallahassee and hid the money..."

"What apartment?" demanded Preston trying to follow Lupino's rapid-fire speech.

Lupino looked embarrassed. "Ahh...oh...I got this apartment where I been keeping this redheaded gal," he said hastily, and turned away from Preston's piercing eyes. "Anyway we went out to get dinner, and when we came back, the place was a wreck, the beds were overturned, couches ripped up. They found my dope money. They stole my stereo, my TV, tape deck, everything."

Oblivious of Preston's growing exasperation, he continued. "I don't know who did it. It could have been that truck driver, Blake, or the Cubans, or maybe that American guy, Rick, who was on the boat with us, although I didn't see none of 'em."

"Or maybe it was your two-bit whore you're running around with in your love nest," Preston interjected nastily, working up to a tirade.

"No, Susie Mae wouldn't do that to me," defended Lupino. " 'Sides, she didn't know nothing about it."

"Well, I guess you can't go to the police, can you?" Preston said maliciously. Then he looked at him levelly and said, "Lupino, why in the hell don't you get out of my life?"

"I will, Preston. I'll hit the road and you won't see me no more. If you can just loan me five hundred, I swear I'll pay it back in two weeks." He cringed, waiting for the explosion.

"*What!?*" the captain cried in outrage. "Lupino, you'd better get away from me, and I mean it. After you burnt my goddamn boat... Lupino, you sorry son-of-a-bitch! We're already feeding Eloise and your young'uns. She lives in a goddamn rat hole of a house trailer with no heat half the time, and you tell me you got a goddamn pad in town with thousands of dollars and some two-bit whore waiting on you. And now you want to borrow money from me! Not *no*, but *HELL NO!*"

Lupino weathered the storm, looking at Preston with the pained eyes of a whipped dog. When the captain paused to come up for breath, Lupino hung his head in contrition, "I know I done wrong, Preston," he said choking with emotion. "I got to living too high and running with the wrong kind of people. Dope money does that to you. The heat's on. I gotta get out of town or out on the water until this blows over. If those Cubans catch me on the street, ain't no telling what can happen. They may try to kill me next!"

"That would be nice."

"Can't you give me a job as deckhand? You know I can do the work."

Preston paced the deck, trying to fight down his frustration. "Please, I'm serious," the young man begged, "I'm in trouble."

Preston wanted to throw Lupino into the river, but he was family. Kin was kin; he was Mary's brother. And, oh, how trapped he felt by her family and his, and by the intricate web of mutual dependence that existed in that small fishing village. And Lupino's arguments weren't lost on him. If and when the cops picked him up, there was a good chance he and Charlie would be dragged into it.

Finally he took a deep breath and conceded, "All right. Hopper season ought to start any day now, and then we'll have to pick up some drag-ass deckhand somewhere. If it's okay with Charlie, I'll go along with it."

Lupino gave him one of his wide, monkey-like grins, with an impressive show of teeth that made Preston want to laugh in spite of himself.

Charlie emerged from the ice bin. "Captain Lu-penis!" he cried joyfully. "What brings you to low-rent city? I thought you were in jail!"

"Don't call me that, you piss-wad!"

Preston grinned maliciously. "You'd better watch what you call my senior deckhand, Lupino. He's got a big say in whether you get hired or not. Charlie, he wants a job."

"Excuse me," Lupino corrected, bowing respectfully, "*Mister* Piss-Wad."

Charlie looked at him smugly, then winked at Preston. "Sure, hire him. I could use a fish-boy back there. We'll pay him ten cents a pound for all the shrimp he culls—which won't be much—and give him half the fish money."

Lupino began to huff with offense. Fish-boy indeed! That was an insult. It was starting at bottom of the barrel in fishermen hierarchy. He was after all, until a few days ago, the owner and captain of his own trawler. Watching him splutter, Charlie went on sadistically, "I expect you to cook three meals a day, wash dishes, scrub down the decks after each tow, and when we anchor down, scrub the grease off the engine with kerosene while I catch up on my sleep and..."

"And you can kiss my ass, you piss-wad!" Lupino laughed, his eyes gleaming.

"Damned if I will," Charlie whooped happily, "but I'll be glad to drive my boot square up the middle of it."

Preston knew from years of experience that he'd better cut it off now, or they'd be rolling around in the galley in a good-natured brawl, breaking dishes and making a mess.

"Both of you cut the crap. All right, Lupino, you got a job. You'll draw a full share like the rest of us, but if you come on my boat, they'll be no dragging ass and no smoking pot, or so help me, I'll set you off on the nearest buoy."

Preston jabbed his big index finger in Lupino's chest. "One other thing. I'm gonna keep back two-thirds of your money and pay it to Eloise to support your young'uns. I been feeding 'em long enough."

Lupino looked mortified. "*What?!*" he shrilled.

"Take it or leave it. I ought to keep the rest and make you pay me something on the boat, but until the shrimp shows up good, and you can pay me something, I'll let you keep a little."

Lupino was about to argue, but decided against it. "Preston, I promise I will pay you back one day." Lupino's black eyes burned with sincerity. "Honest to God I will."

Preston rolled his eyes, shook his head with disbelief, then turned to Charlie. "Let's cast off and get going. Lupino, keep your ass in the pilot house until we're offshore. The less people see you, the better."

Three nights later Preston and the rest of the shrimp fleet were roaming the Gulf, looking for shrimp, waiting for the hopper run to start. The nets came up and the nets went down, and each time there was another blurry mountain of fish, squid, scrawny mantis shrimp, silver eels with toothy jaws and glazed eyes, lying dying on the deck. Meanwhile the young men worked like machines under the lights as they crouched over the pile for hours, hands steadily grasping the few shrimp they found, tossing them in baskets, pushing the discards through the scupper holes. There was a running competition between them as to who could cull the most shrimp, but it was no contest. "Popcorn" Charlie always won.

When the deck was clear, the deckhands came into the warm cabin and huddled around the gas stove. "Didn't get but half a basket of them little pee-wee shrimp smaller than my peter on a cold day," Charlie reported, peeling out of his yellow slicker suit. "You know Sam Lawton ain't gonna pay nothing for them. I wish the shrimp would show."

"They will," said Preston optimistically, "they will. And when they do, knock on wood, we'll be there to catch them, providing these other boats don't scoop them up first." He leaned back and glanced at the panorama of deck lights. The boats were so close together, they looked like a city of lights far out at sea. You could almost hop from deck to deck. "Looks like every boat from Key West to Brownsville is over here, and some from North Carolina."

Lupino lit a cigarette and pulled deeply. "A shrimp ain't bright," he declared wisely, "but he knows if he sticks his eyeballs and whiskers out of the mud he'll get 'em chopped off by all these boats. There ain't no way to win at this business. If you ask me, the shrimper's a dying breed. I'm glad I'm out of it myself. I wish I were bringing in a load of pot right into the middle of these boats," he said wistfully. "They'd never find me."

Preston choked on his black coffee. "I don't understand you, Lupino. I really don't. You went to jail for three years, you almost got burned alive, and you're still talking about messing with dope."

Preston cut him off before he could explain. "Go check the try net—it's been fifteen minutes. Count the shrimp this time, and let me know how many are in it."

He watched Lupino jam his wool cap down over the curly black hair that radiated from the top of his head like the spines of a sea urchin.

Preston had to admit there was an edge to this smuggling that could be infectious. Year after year the nets come up, the nets go down, another load of shrimp and fish hit the deck to pay the bills: fuel bills, ice bills, repair bills. Now in his forties, the backbreaking work in rough seas, broiling sun, and freezing winds wasn't as easy for Preston as it used to be. Crouching over piles of squirming life, helping his deckhands pick out shrimp and getting catfish spines in his fingers was taking its toll.

But the real toll was boredom. Ever since he'd come back from the war in Vietnam, Preston had been dragging the same old bottoms off Apalachicola, drinking gallons of coffee trying to stay awake all night during hopper season, listening to the same old talk of shrimpers on the radio. He knew what they were going to say before they ever keyed the mike.

Although he did his best to stifle it, sometimes his soul cried out for change. Some called it a mid-life crisis. Wasn't that why he had put on a big winch, ten thousand dollars worth of cable, and steamed a hundred and fifty miles out to the edge of the continental shelf to drag for royal reds? Three years ago, on one trip, he made a twenty-thousand-dollar catch of big red shrimp, but from there on it was all downhill. After burning out two clutches, blowing an engine, and snagging six thousand dollars worth of cable on what he thought was a submerged airplane wreck, Preston gave up on the royal reds.

With a feeling of frustration and defeat he came in and re-joined the rest of the working fleet, acknowledging that his thirty-year-old boat wasn't built to take the pounding of the blue water, winding in a mile of cable, and fishing two hundred fathoms.

Some nights while dragging his nets in the shallows he dreamed about owning one of those three-hundred-thousand-dollar steel-hull super-trawlers with solid ribs, new rigging and electronics, and a lot more power. A man could make the payments on a boat like that easy if he worked hard, he thought, but he didn't know how to get fifty thousand dollars together at one time for a down payment.

But another voice in his brain blurted out, *Oh yes you do, and in a New York minute. One trip with my brother-in-law's sleazy buddies is all it would take.* But he stifled it.

Lupino pushed into the wheelhouse complaining, "Got one scrawny-assed hopper that time, Preston. They damn sure ain't gonna run tonight, you can bet on that. I ain't saying that dope smuggling and running from the law and getting ripped-off is the answer, but this damn sure ain't. It's slow starvation."

Preston leaned back in his pilot's chair shifting from one buttock to the next on his cushion, stretching his long legs. Slowly he rotated the worn leather seat on the silvery pivot pole to watch the fathometer etching the bottom contour. "It ain't a bad living out here," he defended, stifling a yawn, "if you stick at it, Lupino. Besides, what other *honest* way is there. Working for an hourly wage? Damned if I want some boss-man standing over me telling me when I can use the bathroom!"

Charlie chimed in, obviously offended at Lupino's attack, "Shoot, you don't know nothin'! You show me a job on the hill where someone like me can make seven, eight hundred dollars a week with no education! Lu-penis, you ain't got bat shit for brains!"

Lupino jeered, "When's the last time you made that, Charlie-boy? Tell me what you shared last trip without the Cuban's little contribution? No sir, I ain't gonna be no poor-assed shrimper all my life if I can help it!" He puffed up. "Soon as I get a few dollars together again, I'm going to Nashville. I'm gonna be a big country western music star. Get me one of them fancy jackets with the diamonds a-glittering, and make so goddamn much money I'll leave all your asses smoking in the dust," he announced.

Charlie whooped with laughter and Preston yanked the window down, filling the wheelhouse with fresh cold air and breathed deeply and with great exaggeration. "Lord, I need air. The horse manure's getting so thick in here I can hardly breathe.

"Now, get out there and pull the try net. We'll get gone from here and hunt us some new bottom and maybe find something we can work on."

"Yes sir, Skipper," Charlie chortled. "I could use some fresh air." He thrust back the sliding door and bowed before Lupino with the sweeping gesture of a courtier ushering out the king. "After you, Mr. Johnny Cash."

Then Preston thought to himself, *Who am I to throw off on Lupino's dreams?* I've got my own crazy ones that are just about as practical. Then he laughed aloud. Maybe I'll get my big boat when Lupino gets to be a big country music star and backs me.

He was still chuckling when his crew came back into the wheelhouse, arguing about something. Suddenly there was an unfamiliar metallic pinging amidst the rhythmic clatter of the diesel. He thrust his palm up to shut his brother-in-law off. "Hush. You hear that noise?"

Charlie locked his head and listened for a minute, then shrugged. "Maybe. I can't really tell." They sat there listening for the rattle and looked at the gauges. Everything appeared to be normal.

"Ain't nothing to it, Captain," Charlie concluded, yawning loudly.

"Maybe a skip or two."

Preston stood up, braced himself against the rolling sea, and listened to the exhaust pipe spluttering outside.

"She was mighty hard to crank up this morning," Lupino worried. "I thought we'd never get her started when it was cold."

"She's getting old," Preston admitted tiredly. "Just like me. Wore out. I'm just praying we can make the season with her. A damn overhaul will cost over ten thousand dollars."

Charlie went down into the galley, came back with three steaming cups of coffee and passed them around. He looked wearily at the clock, it was three a.m.

Onward they went, running, running through the night, dropping the try net out, and sampling. But nowhere were there any shrimp. Two or three here...none...five or six there. Finally, they found a dozen, and Preston told them to set the big rigs. It was nearing daylight when they hauled them up, loaded with croakers and thirty pounds of shrimp, hardly enough to pay the cost of fuel.

Numb with exhaustion, Charlie and Lupino sat on the transom out of Preston's sight, smoking a joint, passing it between them. Lupino had managed to salvage ten pounds of weed from his disaster on the Ochlockonee River, but most of it had been stolen. It numbed the pain of catfish spines and aching backs.

"I sure hope I make some money," Charlie ventured. "When I get back I got a date with Vonceil, that gal who works at the fish house."

"The one whose old man works on the tug boat? You crazy, Charlie. He'll kill you! I seen him stomp a man half to death over in Mississippi for just talking to her."

"*She-it*, I ain't worried about it. Besides, he stays gone a month at a time. Plenty of time to get all the snatch I need. She sure got a pretty smile."

As they talked, they kept an eye out for Preston. He raised hell when he caught them smoking marijuana, and didn't allow it on his boat. As Preston ran through the night to get behind the reef and anchor, they watched for the cabin door, ready to pitch their joints if it opened.

When dawn broke with its purplish band of light, they sent the anchor splashing over the side, shut off the engine, and fell into their bunks. The wind blew, rattling the windowpanes, and the *Lady Mary* pitched to and fro against her anchor lines. Wood groaned, metal clanged, and the outriggers jangled. Outside the ocean sizzled, as the eternal small blue mountains were pushed by wind, rising in an explosion of foaming whitecaps marching away as far as the eye could see.

9

The Engine Blows

As the morning sun rose all three men were asleep in their bunks, their snores mingling with the swishing waves against the hull and the forlorn whistling of the north wind rattling the window panes. The creak of the outriggers and block and tackle, as the boat tugged against its anchor, sounded like lonesome frogs in a forgotten swamp.

Into the darkness of their deathlike sleep came the wail of a persistent siren and a voice commanding over and over again, "*Attention. Attention.* This is the United States Coast Guard calling the fishing vessel *Lady Mary.* Calling the fishing vessel the *Lady Mary.* We request permission to come aboard."

At first Preston thought it was a dream, then he awakened and propped himself up on one arm and looked out the porthole. Several hundred feet away was a ninety-foot white steel-hulled vessel with a big, red racing stripe across its bow.

Groggily he swung out of bed and shook Charlie and Lupino awake. He made his way to the open doorway, squinting in the bright afternoon sunlight. "*Attention.* Have your crew assemble on the fantail," a voice barked out. Preston looked up at a dozen Coast Guardsmen standing at their battle stations on the cutter. Three-inch cannons were pointed at them, and the covers of the .50-caliber machine gun had been ripped off.

The cutter came closer, and the officer in charge, dressed in blue, stepped out on the flying bridge and shouted through the loud-hailer. "Stand by for boarding in accordance with U.S. laws."

Onto the deck came Charlie yawning and blinking, followed by Lupino looking rather sleepy and unconcerned. Preston said to him in a low whisper, "I hope to hell you ain't got nothing on you, Lupino, or we're all screwed."

"Not me!" Lupino said in all innocence, and proceeded to sit on the rail on the opposite side of the vessel from the ninety-foot white cutter. His hand dangled below the gunnel, emptying the contents of a plastic bag into the sea. Green flakes drifted off in the current.

Preston spotted the baggy floating off. "You little son-of-a-bitch..." he said under his breath. Then he told himself, *Just keep calm, they don't have anything on us.* But he was jittery. His mouth was dry and his body tense; his stomach knotted up. He drew in a deep breath, held it, and slowly exhaled. "Now take a deep cleansing breath," he ordered himself. He had learned to do that at the Lamaze classes when he sat beside Mary practicing for the big day. What a sight it was with all those pregnant women lying on mats, huffing and puffing with their men beside them. At first he thought it ridiculous. Now he was amazed how it helped ease his tension.

Into the dory scurried the boarding party of six enlisted men and one officer, each wearing a riot helmet, life jacket and light blue shirt with their name imprinted over their pocket. All had side-arms, one carried a shotgun. They had a terrible time boarding in the big, choppy seas. The waves lifted them up and set them down again, and their little boat banged into the crash bumpers. A young, black enlisted man tried to grab ahold of the stay cable with his free hand while in the other he clenched a sawed-off shotgun raised into the air.

After three awkward and unsuccessful attempts, Charlie reached down and grabbed the gun barrel, "Here, let me hold that for you."

"Uh, thanks," the seaman said, confused, and started to release it. Then he realized what he was doing and became flustered. "Uh, oh no. I'll keep this." He yanked it back. But just then the sea went down, and Charlie clutched onto the gun. "Let go!" the seaman yelped.

"Just trying to help," Charlie said releasing and grinned down at them. "Well, give me your hand, then."

The ensign who stood at the rear of the dory behind his men grew furious and bellowed, "Come on. Get aboard!"

There was no dignified way to do it. They scrambled up on their bellies, and quickly righted themselves. Their dignity wasn't helped any by Preston laughing aloud, in spite of his efforts not to.

Brushing himself off, the ensign stormed forward. "Stand on the fantail and don't move!" he ordered the shrimpers. The seamen in their denim uniforms stood at attention, their hands near their .45-caliber pistols.

"Are you the master of this vessel?" the ensign demanded of Preston.

"Yes, I am," Preston replied, coming forward from the back of the boat to ward off trouble before it started.

"Stay where you are!" the ensign commanded sharply, possibly alarmed at Preston's large frame. The top of the officer's crew-cut head barely came up to Preston's chest. One of the seamen rushed forward and stood between Preston and his officer nervously, his hand poised tensely on the butt of his pistol.

The captain put his hands up apprehensively, "Hey, take it easy, Sonny. Don't shoot anybody. We're peaceful, honest."

"Are there any firearms on board?" the ensign demanded.

Preston's good humor began to fade. "Yes, I've got a rifle, and I use it to shoot sharks. Don't tell me that's illegal," he said sarcastically. "I got the right to bear arms, the Constitution says so. Leastways that's the way I heard it." Preston felt strongly about freedom. He considered himself to be a good and patriotic American. He had served his country in war. He believed that cops had their role in society, and he respected it, but lately the Coast Guard was like an occupying army.

The ensign ignored his sarcasm, holding a tight military stance. He looked the big fisherman up and down, noting his fish-scale caked pants, the big greasy hands, the dark stubble on his face, and not liking his disrespectful attitude. "We ask that you display your firearms, sir. Unload them and lay them on the deck."

"How about it, fella," Preston said, after he complied, and they wrote down the serial numbers and called them in. "We've been up for the past three nights nonstop, working our goddamn asses off hunting shrimp. Why don't you save us both some time and let us go back to sleep? We don't have any dope on board."

"It's the law, sir," the ensign said with authority. "It's our duty to perform an inspection."

"Well, then do what you're gonna do," Preston said coldly. A man's boat, like his home, was his castle. His tone and body language made it clear that this was nothing but an invasion of his privacy. Everything had to be done according to the book, according to a checklist. The officer found the documentation and boat registration papers in order. He checked his fishing licenses and permits, and inspected their nets to see that they had Turtle Excluder Devices installed and that the opening did not exceed forty-one inches. Ignoring his caustic remarks, the ensign made Preston turn on all the required lights to see if they were working.

One of the seamen who stood by looking bored was ordered to accompany Lupino down into the engine room to check for fire extinguishers. The expiration dates had to be checked. They examined the life preservers and inspected the bilge for excess oil to see if there were pollution violations.

At the stern, the black guardsman with the shotgun accompanied Charlie down into the ice hold to inspect the vessel's main beam number. This had to be checked against the documentation papers. The enlisted man glanced at the ice bins and the layers of shrimp. He looked a little embarrassed at having to put them through the drill. "I don't guess you got any pot on this boat, do you?"

"I wish," Charlie grinned back at him. "I could use a joint so bad. We ain't been one of the lucky ones that found it."

The guardsman laughed and looked in another ice bin. He spotted a cold six-pack of Miller that Charlie had sitting on ice. There was moisture forming on the bottle, and he licked his lips. The cutter had been checking vessels from Cedar Key to Apalachicola for the past week. Charlie saw him looking and pulled out a bottle. "Here, quick, chug this. They can't see."

The other glanced up nervously to the light above and when he saw no one was watching he grabbed it. It was the best beer he ever tasted. When it was gone he reached into his back pocket and pulled out a little plastic bag of crushed and shredded leaves. "Here, you look like a good guy," he said, shoving it into his hand.

"That from some of the seaweed?"

The enlisted man winked at him, climbed the ladder back onto the deck, and stood by while the ensign completed his check.

Finally the inspection was completed. "You happy now?" Preston asked sarcastically.

"Captain Barfield," the officer replied pompously looking up at the big man, "you must realize that we are doing this for your own protection. There are drug smugglers out here, and they've been known to steal boats and kill the crews. Please excuse the inconvenience."

Preston grunted an acceptance and watched the men get back into the dory. "Stand off!" shouted the ensign, and away they went, back to the big white cutter with the red racing stripe that hovered six hundred feet away.

It took awhile for the shrimpers to get back to sleep. "They ain't so bad," Charlie said, yawning as he crawled up into his bunk. "I mean the guys are just doing their job. Most of them smoke reefer like we do. They know it's all bullshit, but the officer's a prick."

Mary's right, Preston thought. I'll never feel right around police any more. I'll always be on the run. He tried to banish his thoughts and went back to re-reading the thumb-worn magazines and paperback novels on the boat—stories of Spanish galleons, sunken treasures, and Westerns, which usually offered relief from the boredom of being at sea. He liked to read about other people's adventures—they helped him forget his troubles. Charlie had his own library. Stacks of pornographic magazines—but he had looked through them so often the lascivious girls had turned to familiar old wives. He had never learned to read more than a few words, so he went back to his old habit of twiddling his thumbs, ten revolutions forward, then ten backward. The next time he did twenty, then thirty, and so on.

He looked irritably at Lupino, peacefully curled up in his bunk snoring obnoxiously, and grumbled, "The son-of-a bitch! Nothing bothers him."

Eventually they all dropped off to sleep. Late in the afternoon, when the golden light of the setting sun gleamed on the rolling waves, they awoke. Preston mashed the starter button, and the engine groaned, rumbled, and complained a long time before it cranked. They doused the breather with ether until it exploded, died again, and finally the big engine caught, belched black smoke, and began to clatter. "Sure took it's time cranking. It don't sound good. I hope this hammer knocker doesn't leave us stranded out here," commented Charlie.

After they pulled anchor and were under way, Lupino began preparing dinner. "Put on the steaks tonight, Lupino" suggested Charlie. "We're gonna need our strength."

"Hell, we needed it last night!"

Lupino had three steaks frying on the stove, along with a big, greasy pan of french fries. As the seas grew steadily rougher, the grease swilled back and forth in the black frying pan, mimicking the waves. An hour later, singing, *"Please release me, let me go..."* he put the plates on the table, poured the grease overboard and dished out the steaks and potatoes.

Preston joined them at the galley, and they bowed their heads in prayer. Speedily he mumbled through the blessing. It was something he had done for so many years he never thought twice about it. It would have gladdened the heart of any good Baptist to see these rough, rugged men saying their prayers.

As they ate, the seas continued brewing up, and the dishes slid over the table. "Sure is getting choppy," Lupino complained, holding onto his plate.

"Sure is," agreed Preston, sawing vigorously through the steak. "But that's what's kicking these shrimp out of the ground. God, this steak is tough." He gave Charlie a dirty look.

"Well, hell, don't blame me. You were in such an all-fired hurry to get gone, I grabbed the first thing I could get my hands on. It ain't like I had time to shop, you know."

By the time dinner was finished, *Lady Mary* had churned her way four miles over to the Pumpkin Patch on automatic pilot. While Lupino and Charlie were clearing the dishes, Preston seated himself in the pilot chair and looked at the horizon. There were no boats in sight. "I guess I'm the only fool out here in these rocks," he said aloud.

When they arrived, the captain was in no hurry to put the nets out. For a long time he studied the depth recorder, watching the bumps and shapes of the bottom, indicated by the black line etched on the moving sheet of graph paper. It was called the Pumpkin Patch because of the big, round loggerhead sponges lying eighty feet below that resembled pumpkins. If he missed the edge and strayed into the middle of them, the sheer weight of the sponges and rocks would rip his net to pieces.

"All right, drop the try net," Preston ordered when he found the right spot. "Maybe we won't lose it."

Fifteen minutes later, Lupino ambled out on deck whistling, wound in the cable, and grabbed the try net's lazy line with the hook pole. He tried to pull the net up, but it was too loaded.

"Damn idiot," he muttered, "making us drag this rough bottom." He bellowed so they could hear him in the wheelhouse, "Hey Preston, y'all come help me get this thing on deck. We sponged down."

Looking chagrined, the captain and senior deckhand trotted out to help. Together, all three threw their weight backwards against the webbing, and the bloated try net was hoisted up and plopped on deck.

Shining through the green webbing were the unmistakable orange gleaming eyes of the shrimp. No fish, or squid, or mantis shrimp, but commercial shrimp, their eyeballs reflecting off the deck lights and glowing like hot little coals.

Charlie let out a whoop of delight and madly snatched at the release ropes, until the tail bag opened. They lifted the swollen bag, and the deck exploded with shrimp—medium-sized shrimp, roughly forty to a pound, flouncing and kicking and twitching their long antennae and synchronously kicking slender, delicate legs.

Preston laughed delightedly, dropped to his knees and grabbed up a double handful. He looked at their translucent pinkish bodies, and their beating swimmerets, flaming red. "These are run shrimp!" he cried. "We're gonna tear up a shrimp's ass tonight. Charlie, get the rigs overboard. Make sure the tail bags are tied. Lupino, move your sorry ass!"

Down splashed the otter doors pulling their nets behind them as Charlie and Lupino simultaneously released the locks on the big winches. The two sixty-foot long trawls sank down into the waves, and the spools of cable spun madly as the wire snaked through the outstretched davit arms, spinning through blocks. When six hundred feet of cable had spun off each of the drums, they locked down. In five minutes they were fishing hard.

Suddenly the rhythmic, dependable tempo of the engine changed. It went into a heavy, labored clattering, rising in tempo, then falling, then rising again. Everyone froze and looked around in shock. A vibration shuddered through the boat, and then a loud, unmistakable metallic pinging.

"Holy Moses!" exclaimed Charlie, "Sounds like the engine's fixing to blow!"

The wheezing vibration seemed directly connected to the captain's nervous system. He bolted upright, practically jumped over his brother-in-law and raced for the wheelhouse. In three bounds he was at the control panel. His horrified eyes fixed on the temperature needle leaning completely over on the right-hand corner at 240°F. It couldn't be hotter. The wheelhouse shook as the machinery strained under its hard labor, roaring, dragging itself down, overloading, and rattling.

Preston yanked the throttle back hard to an idle and hurried back out to the deck. A hazy cloud of black smoke poured out of the stack pipe. The air had taken on a burned metallic smell, a smell of scorched grease. White steam boiled up from the engine room, hissing like a teakettle. When Preston threw open the companionway door, it blasted him back. "Son-of-a-bitch!" he wailed. "She must've blown a water line."

Desperately, he unscrewed the round threaded cap of the day tank—the water reservoir that cooled the engine. It was hot to the touch. And not only was it empty, but hot white steam and the smell of rust boiled out of it. He had to make decisions and make them fast. "Hurry, get the rigs up!" he shouted. "Get the rigs up quick. If she shuts down with the nets out, we'll be in big trouble!" But as the drums wound, the spluttering was becoming feebler and feebler. Just as the bridle rose up from the dark, whitecapped waves, the engine seized with a sickening squealing sound as the bearing galled on the crankshaft. There was a splutter, then a dead silence, and then just steam whistling out of the vents.

"That's done it," Preston announced with finality. "I had a feeling everything was going too good. I swear, God hates me. But he didn't have to do it the minute we got into shrimp!"

Charlie and Lupino looked at him sorrowfully, not knowing what to say. They watched him take a deep breath, and then get control over himself. "Charlie, go find the pipe wrench," he said gruffly. "We've got to finish getting the nets on board."

The immediacy of that problem drove off thoughts of the long-range consequences and the terrible costs that lay ahead. Right now the nets were dragging behind the boat, soon to become a big tangle of webbing, cable and ropes. Without power to keep the nets stretched out, they were helpless, at the whim of nature.

Charlie lay on his back in the oily bilge, next to the hot engine, turning the winch with a Stilton wrench, bite by bite, winding the cable inch-by-inch. "This is a bitch!" he groaned.

"When you can't do any more, I'll spell you. Then Lupino will take a turn."

An hour later, an exhausted, hot, and greasy Lupino crawled out of the cramped, greasy engine room. He told Preston, "This is for the birds. If I were you, I'd see Raul about a trip to Colombia. I bet he'd slap a brand new engine in this mother and send us down there so fast you wouldn't know what happened. Two, three weeks later we'd be back with a couple of hundred thousand in your pocket. In cash."

Preston ignored him. Exhausted and sweating, he leaned on the transom and looked down into the water to inspect the progress of the slowly emerging net. Something else caught his eye: dark forms were moving in formation. Sharks. The largest one was about ten feet long, and there were untold smaller ones. The phosphorescent plankton in the water illuminated their dark shapes with an eerie, fearsome beauty as they swept their tails back and forth with broad pectoral fins spread apart.

By the time the first light of dawn broke, they hoisted what was left of the nets on deck. They were empty. Sharks had ripped gaping holes in the webbing, gorging themselves until there were only a few pounds of shrimp and fish left. "I hate a damn shark," Charlie growled. "Maybe these environmentalists love 'em, but they don't have to live with 'em. They think they're so endangered and fished out, I wish they'd go swimming with these!"

After they dropped the anchor, they sat in the galley in silent exhaustion. Charlie reached into his back pocket and pulled out a plastic baggy of crushed green buds and held it up.

Lupino's eyes went wide. "Where did you get that?'

"Shit, Charlie," Preston said angrily. "You had that on the boat— what if the Coast Guard searched you? We'd all be going to prison. They'll make a case on that little bit."

"Hell, it *came* from the Coast Guard! That sailor I helped up on deck gave it to me. I traded him for a beer—pretty good deal. This must be worth thirty dollars."

Preston looked at him in disgust. Seeing that Charlie was indecisive, he growled, "Go ahead, smoke it if you want to. I don't care anymore."

"Why not? This is America. Everyone smokes," declared Lupino righteously. "Half the cops do. They own half the real estate in this area. Most of the sheriffs in these little counties got rich overnight."

Eagerly he took the plastic bag from Charlie and sprinkled the marijuana into a sheet of cigarette paper and twisted both ends carefully. He drew deeply, holding the smoke in his lungs until that familiar numbing feeling came over him. Soon the cabin was permeated with pungent smoke.

"Hell, there ain't nothing wrong with it," Charlie said with pleasure. "It comes from nature. The Lord made this plant just like he did all the others, and it sure makes me feel better. Try some, Preston, this is good shit!"

The captain shook his head, "Not me! The jails are filled with losers that smoke it. Besides, that crap hurts my lungs, makes me cough, and doesn't do a damn thing for me. I'm a boozer, not a doper. And I wish I had a bottle of bourbon right now, even though I don't allow it on the boat." Wearily he stepped into the wheelhouse, collapsed in his chair, and raised Justin on the radio. "We're broke down," he told him. "You'd better come get us before we go to the bottom, bad as this bitch is leaking."

10

Lawton's Fish House

As the *Neptune* dragged the crippled *Lady Mary* up the river, Preston grimly surveyed the waterfront. The two trawlers were lashed side by side, like one wounded soldier being half carried and half dragged out of battle by a comrade. Past the ice house docks they went—now empty of boats—past Paramour's Fish House, and Wilson's, and then the fuel docks. Fishermen unloading trout or bags of oysters at the docks stared at them with the sympathetic and curious expression of passersby at the scene of an accident. A small crowd of dockworkers and shrimp headers from inside the big corrugated tin building assembled on the wharf to watch the boats struggle to dock in the swift current. Sam Lawton, owner of Lawton Fisheries came blustering out on the dock, looking chagrined at the crippled boat. He was in his sixties, his belly protruded over his belt, and his double chin and thick jowls made him look a bulldog. He was annoyed. A boat that was down wasn't producing shrimp. One that owed him six thousand dollars for fuel, ice and repairs, like Preston did, and was down, was even worse.

"Damn, Preston," he yelled out loudly, as they were tying up at his dock, "you'd better do something to change your luck. I hope this ain't too serious. You got motor trouble?"

"Yeah, I got motor trouble all right, it's blown all to hell," Preston called back. "It's gonna take a tee-total overhaul."

The captain watched the fish house owner's little pig eyes narrow in anger, his furious fat lips pursed together as he paced around the dock. "Y'all need to get unloaded and move. I got two boats that called in this morning with a hundred boxes each." Then he hurried inside.

A hundred boxes, Preston thought—they must have come up from Key West and been out there for a month. If he hadn't broken down when the run started last night, he could have caught that many in a few hours. Wearily he watched Charlie and Lupino slide the hatch cover off, opening the great cold, dark belly of *Lady Mary* with its bins of ice and shrimp, and climb down the ladder. As he watched them shovel shrimp and ice into the big steel bucket that was hoisted up and dumped into a vat for washing, the full implications of the blown motor sank in. He was going to miss the run, and there was nothing he could do about it. By the time he scratched up twelve to fourteen thousand dollars and got the engine overhauled, the shrimp would vanish like fairy gold. He watched his meager eight boxes of shrimp being carried into the fish house on a squeaking, rolling conveyor belt.

While they were being off-loaded, one of the barebacked dockworkers jumped down on deck of the crippled *Lady Mary*. "Hey Lupino, I got to talk to you, quick."

Down the ladder into the ice hold, he said excitedly, "The law's been looking for you. They've had the Big Bend Narcotics Task Force here. They been here three times.

Lupino blanched. "Did they have a warrant?" When he was at sea, all the problems of the land had vanished from his mind, and now they were all here waiting for him.

"Damned if I know," the youth shrugged, "But that ain't all. Those Cubans have been looking for you, too. You're hot, son, if I was you, I'd get the hell out of town 'til this crap blows over. Susie-Mae said they were watching your place in Tallahassee. You got any place to go?"

The news jolted his composure. "I don't know... I have to think." Lupino forgot all about shoveling.

"Move it, Lupino! Get back to work." Preston snapped angrily. "John Henry, you can talk to him later. We gotta get this boat unloaded." He knew the young man was a dope dealer, and didn't like having him on his boat.

The dockworker whispered a few more words to Lupino, then scrambled up the wharf leaving the deckhands to finish unloading. Then, wearily, Preston climbed up on the dock and found a strange shrimper he'd never seen before waiting for him. He had a bottle in his hand and two glasses.

When Preston got to his feet, the stranger offered him one of the plastic cups filled with ice and whiskey. "Here, Skipper. You look like a man who could use a drink. I know I could if I were in your fix. I've had 'em blow on me before."

"Appreciate it," said Preston, taking the glass and taking a big swallow. "You ain't just joking. My name's Preston Barfield," he said, extending his greasy hand.

"Al Johnson." The big gruff man with a beer belly that hung out bare from under his shirt shook Preston's hand vigorously. "I'm on the *Judy C.*" He jerked his thumb toward a rusty steel hull boat tied up ahead of the *Lady Mary*. "I been there myself plenty of times. Looks like you're gonna be down for awhile."

"Looks like it," Preston agreed, looking at him without expression. "The Caterpillar diesel place can't touch it for a week; they got plenty of other business. So, yeah, we'll be down."

"Fella said you might have a deckhand wanting a job. We got caught shorthanded. I got one man on the boat, and he stays drunk half the time. And there's more trash out there than we can handle. We need to find someone else." Preston looked at this rough, unkempt fellow. He had a coarse Texas accent, but seemed jovial and friendly enough, but you never knew what kind of cutthroats were out there.

When a man signed up someone to work on the back of his boat, there were no questions asked except, "Can you work?" and "Do you get seasick?"

Knowing the fix Lupino was in he said, "I'll talk to my boys. One of them might be interested."

"It ain't easy to get help," Captain Al went on. Then he added wistfully, "I wish I had my old striker back. This big-tiddied broad we picked up in Key West. She was the best deckhand I ever had. She made the trip with us up to Tampa. God, she loved to fuck! When I come into port, I was so wore out, I could hardly go. I was walking bowlegged," he bragged.

Several other shrimpers who were standing around the docks overheard him and laughed. "But when those nets hit the deck, she'd cull off in forty-five minutes, scrub the deck down good, then she'd break shrimp, and do the cooking and the dishes. I ain't never seen such a gal!" he cackled and then broke off into tubercular coughing.

"Well, I can't fix you up with nothing like that," said Preston, repelled at the man's crudity. "You gonna be working around here for awhile?"

"Naw. I imagine we'll make a trip or two here until these hoppers play out, then we're going on to Mississippi for the brownie run and back home to Texas."

A big grin spread over Preston's face. *Yes, yes!* he cried to himself. For once I can give him what he deserves. Working on that garbage scow is a fate only slightly better than death. He pointed to a worried looking young man who was standing in the fish hold shoveling out shrimp. "That dark-haired fella—he's my brother-in-law. He'll be hunting a job for sure, and a little trip over to Texas will do him good. His name's Lupino."

The big captain looked at him. "He don't get seasick, does he?"

"No," said Preston walking off, "just homesick."

An hour later Lupino left on the *Judy C*, and it was months before Preston saw him again. Watching that garbage scow head down the river with a big grin on his face, Preston practically felt like dancing down the dock—and might have if it weren't for his sense of dignity. He hadn't felt this good in months.

Justin Barfield looked at him beaming. "You're pretty damned happy for someone who just had their engine blown to hell. What'd you do, win the lottery?"

"No," he pointed to the rusty derelict of a trawler heading over the horizon, "I just got rid of Lupino."

Justin laughed and shook his head, " 'Fraid not, brother. A bad penny always turns up."

Preston made his way into the fish house to watch his catch spilling off the conveyor into wooden boxes, which were dragged off to be weighed. You had to watch Sam Lawton. He wasn't a crook exactly, it was just that sometimes his arithmetic got a little sloppy, and it was always in favor of Sam. Nevertheless, Preston had done business with him for years because Sam had buying power. No matter how many shrimp came into his house, he always managed to scrape up the cash to buy them. With some of the other fish houses, it was a struggle to get paid, especially in the winter when everyone was broke.

The skipper of the *Lady Mary* stood beside Sam watching attentively as the fish house owner scooped up a five-pound sample of shrimp, and divided it into ten little piles to determine their count. The larger the shrimp, the higher the price.

"Looks like these count out to 60/70's," the old man said thoughtfully, licking his thick lips.

"I would have sworn they'd come out to 40/50's. How about counting 'em again?" Preston insisted.

"We're pretty busy this morning," Sam said. "Like I said, I got several other boats coming in to unload, and some of those Alabama boys..." he stopped in mid-sentence when he saw Preston wasn't going to back down.

A moment later, when Sam counted them out a second time he whistled with surprise. "How about that, Preston. You were right—40/50's. Tell you what, let's count them a third time and settle it." Preston got his price. The shrimpers said you couldn't win with Lawton. If he didn't shit you on the price, he'd get you on the weight or the count.

After Preston's catch was weighed and boxed, Justin towed the *Lady Mary* down to the boat yard and his deckhands helped Charlie hand-line the lifeless hull up to the railway dock. "I sho' hate to leave you in this fix, brother," Justin hollered as he cast off. "But I gotta make a dollar and get back to where you found all them shrimp."

They waved back at him and watched their disabled vessel get pushed onto the railway. When the sixty-five foot trawler floated precisely over the submerged car, the great winches began to turn, drawing the boat up the inclined tracks. Up it came, inch by inch, until it rested firmly on the cradle. Her huge underside, covered with a grisly beard of barnacles and hydroids, became exposed. The sleek lines of the graceful shrimp boat gave way to the enormous red belly that resembled a pregnant whale.

The *Lady Mary* crept along the railway into the industrial complex, where three other shrimp boats and one tug sat on cradles. Men in hard hats with scrub brushes and brooms immediately started work, crawling up the sides of Preston's boat like monkeys, using saw horses and ladders. They blasted away at the fouling growth with pressure hoses and scrapers. Red water laden with poisonous anti-foulant paint spilled down the concrete ramp into the marshes.

Ed Fulcher, owner of the busy complex, and reputed to be the richest man in town, walked up and looked at the fouling growth. "Been a while since you hauled her out, Preston."

"About a year longer than I would have liked, but I just couldn't afford it," Preston admitted. "I was hoping to make the season, but we blew the engine."

The old man nodded, "When it rains it pours, don't it?"

They followed him around as he inspected the hull. Ed pointed to a blackened board, separated slightly and raised up from the smooth flat surface near the keel. "There's your main leak, skipper." He jabbed his pocketknife into the cracks. "All the caulking's rotten. If you want to stop her from leaking you'll have to re-caulk the whole thing." Then he went around jabbing his knife into various boards, and the point went in all too easily. Preston's heart sank when he saw that some of them were honeycombed with wormholes.

"I hate to tell you this," he concluded, "but the worms got to seven boards. They're plum eat up. I got an idea that some of those ribs are rotted, too, and will have to be replaced. I won't know until I get them pried off."

"How long we gonna be down then?" asked Charlie.

"Maybe a month."

"A month?" howled Charlie, standing there with his hands on his hips, "That'll cause us to miss the run. We got to go shrimping."

The old man glowered at him, "You're damn lucky we even found a space for you, Sonny. You see we got a bunch of boats up there already. Lots of fellas in the same fix you are." He had to speak loudly over the scream of powersaws. Nearby, a welder in a heavy hood with opaque glass cut through an outrigger, making a splattering noise and sending up a shower of orange sparks.

"Hush, Charlie, " Preston said, "Ed always treats us right," nodding toward a sign:

THE PRICE YOU ARE CHARGED PARTLY DEPENDS ON
YOUR ATTITUDE. ALL WORK CASH. TO BE PAID BEFORE
WORK LEAVES THE PREMISES. —*The Management*

"Got any idea of what it will cost, Ed?"

"Plenty. Labor's thirty-five an hour now, and I don't have no idea of what we're looking at until we get into it. But even if you don't re-rib it, you're looking at an easy five or six thousand."

"This don't sound sporty a'tall," Preston said as they drove back to Lawton's. "I figure I got to borrow around twenty thousand to rebuild the engine and pay the shipyard bills. And I'm afraid we're gonna miss hopper season."

When they pulled up in front of Lawton's, Preston stopped and faced his deckhand, pained at what he was about to say. "Charlie, I'm afraid you might have to start hunting you another job. Son, reality is reality. I hate losing you, but you gotta look out after yourself."

"I don't want to work with no one else. I'll help you tear down that old motor while she's up in the cradle. We can cut down the time. The more work we can do on her, the less you'll have to pay a diesel mechanic. We can save a bunch."

"It's gonna take a bunch," Preston said gloomily. "And after the fix Lupino's got me into, the bank ain't gonna help."

"You can get it from Sam, can't you? Shoot, he'd be a fool to let you stay broke down with hopper season here. That's when he makes his money. He knows you go out when the rest of them are sitting in the bar bitching about how bad shrimping is. He knows the *Lady Mary* outcatches a lot of them new fiberglass and steel hulls sometimes. It ain't the boat, so much, it's the man who's running it."

"The boat counts a whole lot, too, Charlie. Especially when it's wore out and won't go. But I'll give him a try."

A delicate symbiosis existed between the fish house owner and the fishermen. Without products to sell, the wholesaler is nothing but an empty shell on the waterfront. Sam did whatever it took: lending money for equipment, providing fuel on credit, or even helping with unexpected family crises, like a wife's operation or a sick child, to keep his supply of protein gold coming in.

Sam Lawton's office was typical of fish houses along the Atlantic and Gulf coasts. It was a bleak, rugless back room where raw money was transacted. When shrimpers came in to "share up," his short, fat fingers danced over the calculator as he figured who owed who. Sam looked up from his adding machine tape. "Sit down, Preston," he encouraged cheerfully. "You want a beer? There's some in the refrigerator."

"Thanks," said Preston gratefully, popping one open. The refrigerator was crammed with nothing but beer. Sometimes there was a baked ham or other snacks, but mostly beer. It was a courtesy Sam provided to his fishermen who waited on the plastic couch while he figured their accounts. Some said he did it to soften the blow.

"All right, let me see if I can find your ticket book." He reached into the drawer and began rummaging through the receipts. "It's here somewhere. Ah, here it is." He flipped through the pages. "Let's see, you had eight boxes of 50/60's."

"You mean 40/50's," Preston reminded him.

"Oh yeah," said Sam tearing off his adding machine tape. "I got it right here." He took a puff of his noxious cigar and leaned back. "Comes to $940. They're paying a dollar twenty a pound—price dropped while you were out."

"But, Sam!" Preston yelped.

"I can't help it," Sam shrugged. "They're flooding the market with cheap aquaculture shrimp. Don't blame me, blame the Chinese. They're putting them on the market for three dollars a pound, boxed and frozen. Then you got the Mexicans! What do they pay for diesel, fifty cents a gallon? We have to pay a dollar twenty. They don't use turtle shooters even though they say they do. But we have to, and none of it's fair."

Preston fought hard to control his temper. "You'll have to do better than that, Sam," he said evenly. "I haven't made a dime on this trip, not after I pay my fuel and ice bill and share with my crew."

Lawton shrugged. "Preston, I can't. I'd be losing money, honest. The market's the way it is. Now, how much do you want me to take out on the ice bill and for that new net?"

"None of it. Mary's fixing to have that baby, and I need to hold back some money for it. I'll clear up all these back tickets I owe."

"I know you will," Sam soothed. "What you gonna do about your motor?"

Preston looked straight into Sam's porcine eyes. "I was counting on borrowing about fourteen thousand from you. If the brownies show up in Mississippi, I can pay it off by fall."

The fat man almost swallowed his cigar. "Can't do it, Preston. I'm so doggone overextended right now I can't swing it. You'll have to go to the bank."

"I can't," Preston spat out, trying to control the desperation he was feeling inside. "Not after the *Night Shadow* burned. That little asshole Lupino let the insurance lapse. They're trying to foreclose on my house."

He didn't like the way Sam's little, brown piggy eyes shifted around and refused to meet his. "Well, I got burned too when Lupino's boat went down. He owes me $4,263 in fuel, ice and nets."

"Look, Sam," Preston persisted, "I'm not Lupino. Have I ever not repaid you? You know I'm no deadbeat. How about going to the bank with me and co-signing a note?"

"Even with my signature the bank won't loan you any more on that old boat. And I don't want it." He chuckled, trying to make light of it. He didn't meet Preston's eyes, instead he looked down at the ashtray filled with cigar butts. "The *Lady Mary's* like me, Preston— wore out. Ain't many boats been through what you put that one through, dragging that deep water a hundred miles offshore for royal reds. The rigging is about to fall down. No telling what the hull's like. It's been pounded to death. Shoot, the transmission is bound to tear up sooner or later."

"It already did," Barfield said angrily, annoyed that Sam wouldn't look at him. "I borrowed seven thousand dollars from you the year before last and paid every penny of it back, remember?"

Sam shook his heavy jowls and finally looked up, "It was different then. There was more money floating around."

Preston rose from the hard wooden chair and plopped the beer can on the desk. "I see how it is, Sam!"

The fish house owner pointed to the vacated chair. "Sit back down, Preston, there may be another way." His defensive tone changed to grandfatherly kindness.

As soon as the captain was seated, Sam's voice became low, his porcine gray eyes focused intently on Preston. "How'd you like to make some real money?"

"How?"

Sam licked his thick lips nervously, tapping his fat fingers on the desktop. "Whether you know it or not, you made some good friends the other night..."

"What do you mean?" Preston said in alarm.

"You know what I mean. Your money troubles could be over for life, Preston," Lawton said quietly, watching the other's reaction.

Preston felt like throwing up. Suddenly a lot of things were clear. The rumors about Sam were true. Ten years ago times were hard and people had trouble cashing Sam's checks. Lawton periodically tee- tered on the verge of bankruptcy, and after he'd gone broke on a real estate deal, he had a reputation along the coast for passing "bad paper."

Then overnight it all changed. Sam had his decrepit falling-down docks rebuilt. He bulldozed his rusty icehouse and installed big, new freezers, put in modern ice machines, expanded the processing rooms and installed automated shrimp graders. Then he bought three shrimp boats and several tractor-trailer trucks. He tripled his hiring and credit outlays to local fishermen. The story was that he got a giant Production Credit Association loan, but in retrospect, no loan was big enough to cover all those capital costs. He was laundering money for someone.

"Suppose I decide to meet with 'my friends,' " Preston tested.

"Then you'll get an advance to fix up your boat," Sam replied searching Preston's weathered face for some hint of his thoughts. He found none, but he took the silence as encouragement. "You can slap in a new motor, pay your ways bill, and put in some first-class electronics that you'll need to run south." His voice dropped to a whisper, "And they'll pay you two hundred thousand dollars on top of that! Two hundred thousand dollars, Preston!"

No longer could the captain control the rage and disgust that was building up inside. He bolted up and pointed a finger at Sam accusingly, "Sam, you're a goddamn crook. At least now I know why you won't loan me the money. You figure I'm gonna do it 'cause I'm between a rock and a hard place."

"Now, take it easy, Preston," Sam said nervously. "Really, they're two different things."

Preston took a deep breath, trying to gain control over his temper. "You've shitted me all my life on shrimp. I've seen you steal from those poor tired sons-of-bitches who work day and night out there for two weeks and come in so damn tired they can't see straight. Everyone knows you sneak a box or two off into the cooler if they don't watch you. You cut the price, screw people on the count..."

"That's business," Sam defended, with a little hurt in his tone. "Every dealer cuts corners, most worse'n me, and you know it." He liked to think of himself as the patron, the godfather of seafood. "But have I ever shitted you on a loan, or a deal, or failed to stand by you?" he asked craftily.

"No," Preston admitted. "You've done right by me."

There was a long pause, and no one spoke. Sam's thick lips spread into a smile of satisfaction. He leaned back in his chair, looking up at the boat captain. His girth made the springs squeak and sag. "I'm offering you a chance to get well, my friend. And that offer isn't good forever, but it still stands."

"You're still offering it to me, after what I just said? Why?"

For the fist time, Sam looked him in the eye with sincerity. "Why? Because I need someone I can *trust*. You wouldn't steal the load, or screw up like Lupino, or hang around the bar blowing out your ass. I can't afford any more mistakes now, and you're a good man, Preston. You're honest, and that's hard to find nowadays."

The irony of it made Preston burst out laughing. "I ain't believing this." He shook his head. "Sorry, Sam, but you'd better find yourself another boy. If I can't make it honest, I don't need to make it at all."

Sam shrugged. "That's up to you. But if you change your mind, you'd better let me know in a couple of days. They need someone now. There's plenty of other boys hurting who would jump at the chance."

As Preston got up to leave, Sam added quietly, "Another thing, we ain't never had this conversation, hear?"

Funny, the captain thought as he closed the door and walked into the busy fish house. Sam had made him an offer, and it was all perfectly clear, but he never said what he was offering.

11

The Hopper Run

Spring finally came. The last of the big northern fronts had swept over the continental United States down into the Gulf of Mexico, breaking water pipes and covering the ground with ice. March winds gusted, blowing warmer salty water from the southeast into the frigid estuaries, and each day the sun's rays bore down upon the water. Great banks of fog rose as the sea gained heat.

No one understands the run or why the shrimp do it. But the shrimpers knew when it was about to start. Suddenly the hoppers change from a dull brownish red and become clear. The swimmerets that beat rhythmically beneath their tails rapidly turn a vivid orange red. Then they swarm over the bottom like a plague of locusts, with whiskers touching tails. They get so thick you can see them swimming on top of the water, usually with an armada of sea robins. Their predators go crazy gobbling them. Flounders and trout come up in the nets stuffed with shrimp, with whiskers hanging out of their mouths.

It was ten years since there was really a big run, not just a flurry of pink shrimp, but a real, honest-to-God run. When it happens, hundreds, sometimes thousands of pounds are caught in a single, one-hour tow. The shrimp are so thick you don't have to cull them, just pick out the trash fish and shovel them into the ice hold.

Pink shrimp are nocturnal. When the first rays of morning sunlight penetrate the night sea, they kick their way down into the mud with their swimmerets and walking legs and sleep until dark. But not during the run. They keep moving day and night, and so do the trawlers above them. By the third day captains walk around with glassy eyes. Deckhands think their backs are going to break as they crouch over the piles with sore, rostrum-stuck, waterlogged fingers. Still the shrimp keep coming.

Then, just as suddenly as it starts, the run is over. The nets come up empty, the shrimp have vanished. Tired, happy crews head to the dock with heavily laden vessels to party and enjoy their new wealth.

With his boat out of commission, Preston knew that he was not only missing the run, but he'd miss the rest of the hopper season. And if he didn't get his boat fixed soon, he'd miss that big run of brownies off the Mississippi delta. And if his boat wasn't going by September, the fall run of white shrimp in Louisiana would be gone as well. He sat in the kitchen with his head in his hands. "I don't know whether to shit or go blind," Preston said shaking his head, "shit or go blind..."

"Preston, I've been thinking," Mary eased into the conversation after dinner one night, "maybe we ought to borrow the money from Daddy."

"Not that old son-of-a-bitch," he roared, jumping to his feet from the kitchen table. "That tight-wadded..."

"Preston! Quit your cussing. He's my Daddy, and he's got plenty. And besides, he's the only one we can turn to."

"Are you kidding? He wouldn't loan it to us—not without ten gallons of blood! He got his money by being cheap, living cheap, working his kids to death, and squeezing a nickel until the buffalo suffocated. Any man who would screw his kids the way he did, getting every bit of work out of them and not pay anything for it, I don't have no use for.

"Besides," he said getting hot and pacing the kitchen floor again, "I ain't forgetting what he said when we first got married, that he'd have to feed both of us. We never borrowed a dime from him, and I don't aim to start now, you hear?"

"Well, what else are we gonna do? I'm fresh out of ideas myself," she retorted. "I mean honest ones..."

He looked uneasy, "I just don't know... I've got to do something, that's for sure." He mumbled, watching her move about in her bigness, feeling trapped.

"All right," he said reluctantly, after trying and failing to find more options. "We'll go see your daddy." The words came painfully. "I guess it won't hurt to talk." Preston hadn't spoken to him since their last big argument a year ago.

"Without the *Lady Mary*, I'm nothing," he agonized. "If we get her fixed up, I can make a decent living and have respect. I'll work like the devil to pay him back—with interest. Hell, I'll do whatever it takes."

The next morning, they headed for G.W. Talagera's Oyster House. All the way over Preston was silent and sullen, while Mary chatted cheerfully about the baby and her last visit to the doctor. Even at this last minute, he cast around desperately, hoping an idea would come to him in an illuminating flash.

He pulled into the oyster-shell parking lot and parked among the collection of old cars and trucks. G.W.'s lustrous red Lincoln Town Car was parked alongside the wood frame building. It made the paint-worn, rusty oyster house with the piles of shells outside look even shabbier.

Just then Maggie, Mary's mother, came out of the wooden door, and gave her a big hug. "Why, Mary, Preston...what a surprise! I'm so tickled to see you!" She hugged Preston, and stood back and looked at her daughter with a big smile. "Why, look at you, young'un, you're getting bigger every time I see you." She patted Mary's protruding belly. "I can hardly get used to you. You used to be such a little thing. G.W. and I just can't wait until we have another grandbaby! With Jean, Becky and Rosalie, that'll make us nine grand-young'uns. Think of that. Come over to the house. I've got some lemonade."

To get to their sixty-foot-long, double-wide house trailer, they had to go through the oyster house. Preston and Mary exchanged greetings with the women shuckers and old men who stood around the wet, muddy, concrete stalls, prying the oysters apart, putting the wet gray "meats" into one-gallon cans and pushing the empty shells through portholes where they piled up outside in middens.

Mary's youngest brother Robert was dragging sacks of muddy oysters in, dumping them on the tables and carrying the shucked meats to the cooler. "Hey, Preston," the young man grunted as he dragged a sack past them, "you don't need a deckhand, do you? I'd sure love to get away from this damn work. Besides, oystering is just about over for the year."

A cloud passed over the fish house. Standing in the back doorway was a scowling G.W. Talagera. "No, he don't need a deckhand. His old wreck of a boat's broke down and about to sink. I drink coffee with Ed Fulcher every morning down at the cafe and heard all about it. And you," he said gleefully to Robert, who looked at him blankly, "you ain't going nowhere until you pay for that car you owe me."

"Hello, Daddy," said Mary coming over and kissing him on the cheek.

The wizened old man ignored her and glowered at Preston. Then he crowed triumphantly, "Come to borrow money, didn't you!"

Preston got a grip on his urge to kick the old man's scrawny rear. "Let's go, Mary," Preston snapped back irritably. "I'm not in the mood for a chicken-plucking contest."

There was a hushed silence from the oyster shuckers, waiting for the inevitable explosion to follow. When he saw that production had slowed, G.W. frowned at his workers. "Y'all get back to work. This ain't none of your concern!"

Mary's mother took Preston by the arm. "Let's go into the house and have some lemonade." With Mary looking furiously at him, he allowed Mrs. Talagera to pull him along.

All wiped their muddy feet on the mat outside before they went in. It was comfortable and spacious inside, with rugs and a giant color television. G.W. had done well with his oyster business.

When they sat down, Mary started to talk about her mother's garden and the children when G.W. interrupted gruffly. "You women can talk any time. I ain't got all day. I got a truck coming in this afternoon to pick up two hundred gallons of oysters." He turned impatiently to Preston. "Let's hear your sad, sad story," he said sarcastically. "But let me get a bath towel first so I can soak up my tears and not spoil Mama's sofa."

Preston wondered what his foot would feel like connecting with that bony behind, but he reminded himself that G.W. was, after all, in his late sixties, and he was taught to respect old people. He turned to Mary, "Come on, honey, I knew this wouldn't work, let's go."

Maggie gave the old man a pleading, pained look, but there wasn't much she or anyone else could do with him. "Oh, come on now, G.W. They've just come to pay a friendly visit. Can't I get y'all something to drink? We've got some lemonade and..."

"No, thank you," said Preston shortly. "I wouldn't care for nothing."

The silence continued for a minute, with G.W. looking at them, waiting. His eyes rested on Mary's swollen belly, and his foot began to tap the rug angrily.

Until she had run off with that Barfield boy, Mary had been the center of G.W.'s hopes and dreams. She had been such a pretty and bright little girl, he couldn't stand seeing her stretched out of shape. The rest of his children were workhorses, there to expand the family business and grub out a living in the oyster house, as he had done all his life. Sixty years ago, when his father came over from Italy, the whole family helped with the fishing and farming. They worked from dawn to dusk. That was all they knew—work.

But Mary was different. For the first time in his years of counting money and shucking oysters, brightness had come into G.W.'s life. Mary was certain to better herself, to get a good job as a secretary or even work at the bank. He even talked about sending her to secretarial school. G.W. pampered her—she had to shuck only six gallons a day when she came home from high school.

Then Preston came along, and she got a case of hot pants and ran off with him. And took G.W.'s dream with her. Now she was dirt poor, her hands red from heading shrimp. G.W. looked at Preston with angry resentment. "So you did come for money," the old man jeered triumphantly. "I knew it. I didn't figure we'd see Preston unless he needed something."

On the wall a picture of Jesus painted on black velvet looked down at them, martyred and forgiving.

"All right, that's why I come," he said defiantly. "My engine blew and I need about twenty thousand to overhaul it and fix the bottom. I can make that back easy this year in Mississippi when brownie season starts. You know my credit's good. I pay my debts."

The old man pointed his bony finger at him and crowed with satisfaction, "I told you fifteen years ago when you first bought that boat you were making a mistake. If you'd stayed with me and oystered like you were supposed to, you wouldn't be in this fix now."

"I didn't want to oyster for you. I don't like oystering," stated Preston firmly. "I'm a shrimper."

"Shrimper, hell!" The old man shot him a contemptuous look. "Oystering is hard work, not like sitting on your ass all day pulling a shrimp net. All you shrimpers want is gravy, to get something for nothing. A man who gets out there and uses those hickory sticks builds muscle and character. He doesn't sit on his ass and ride a boat all day, then go off whore-hopping in Key West or Mississippi."

"Preston doesn't do that," defended Mary.

"The hell he don't. All shrimpers do. Just like Lupino. That's all he ever wanted was the good times. That's why he got in trouble—hanging out with Preston."

"Cut the crap," Preston said with finality. "This could go on all day. I need to borrow twenty thousand. Are you going to loan me the money or not?"

The old man looked at him shrewdly, up and down. "No. I won't loan it to you. But I'll make you a better deal, and I ain't doing it for you, I'm doing it for Mary."

He let the silence hang for a minute, then grinned maliciously, showing his yellow teeth. "I'll buy your boat for ten thousand dollars, right where she sits."

"Ten thousand!" cried Preston in disbelief. "It's worth ten times that..."

"Not like she sits, she ain't. Not with no blown motor and a hull eat up with worms. I had coffee with Ed Fulcher. I know what shape she's in. You can go to work oystering for me," he said with a rising voice to drown out his son-in-law's protest. "I'll get you a boat, motor, and a set of tongs, and you can use your truck to haul them back from Apalachicola. And when the weather ain't fitting, you can work here at the house supervising."

Maggie saw her son-in-law bristle with rage, his big chest swelling, as he rose to his feet. "We really do need some help, Preston," the old woman interjected pleadingly. "Someone to run things. G.W.'s health ain't what it used to be. The doctor says he's..."

"I'm fine, goddamn it," snapped G.W. "You just shut your mouth, old woman." Now he looked like a frog with bulging eyes.

"Don't worry, Mama," Mary stormed. "Daddy will be here long after we're all dead and gone, sitting on his money bags like Scrooge McDuck!"

Her brother Robert, who came in during the argument, broke into laughter, and G.W. turned his anger on him. "Get back to work, Robert. This don't concern you!"

"I'm not an oysterman," hissed Preston through gritted teeth, "I'm a shrimper. That's my business." He towered above the wizened old man, his hands shaking. "It's taken me twenty years to learn those bottoms. I'm not gonna throw it down now and let you steal my boat for no ten thousand dollars. Beside, I wouldn't work with you for a million dollars!"

"Please, G.W.," pleaded the old man's wife, taking her husband's arm. "They're fixing to have a baby and they're on hard times. Don't do this!"

"Hush, woman!" he said shaking her off.

"Slavery!" Preston shook his finger in G.W.'s face, "That's all you understand, G. W., is goddamn slavery. You've screwed your kids, worked them for nothing. They could have made twice the money working elsewhere, but you owned them. You made Lupino what he is. Robert's gonna take a walk the first chance he gets. You couldn't stand it 'cause I took Mary away from you. Until now, I've made a good living for her. I'd set a match to the boat and burn it before I'd let you take it over. Come on," he said to his wife.

"Please, Daddy, don't do this," Mary pleaded as she followed Preston to the door. "You owe me that much."

"I don't owe you nothing," G.W. half screamed. "You could have married a goddamn millionaire, a doctor, any-goddamn-body, but you had to get a fire down here." He wildly gesticulated, obscenely jutting his hand toward his crotch. "Now look at you, wearing rags!"

"No, I guess maybe you don't," she said, tears welling up in her eyes. "And you didn't owe Lupino nothing either. That's why he got into all the trouble, Daddy. He wanted to get out from under your hooks. One day you're gonna be all by yourself and miserable. You can't take it with you, you know."

"Come on," Preston snarled, practically pulling Mary out the door, "before I choke the old son-of-a-bitch." As they marched through the oyster house, the workers faced into their stalls. Not a head turned. There wasn't a sound. All had heard the shouting from the mobile home.

Preston helped his wife into the pickup, the tears streaming down her face. He spun the worn tires into the bleached white shells like a teenaged hot-rodder and sped off down the driveway.

Preston dropped his wife at their house and headed for Sam Lawton's at the end of the road.

12

The Conspiracy

It was 4:20 p.m. and Sam Lawton was late. Preston sat in his pickup truck at a truck stop seventy miles from town. He looked at his watch again and glanced around the sprawling asphalt and the acres of tractor-trailers parked with their engines rumbling. The air was acrid with diesel smoke in the afternoon light. I hate this sneaking around, Preston thought. Where the hell is Sam? He wished he'd show, but partly he didn't.

Finally, Sam's shiny Cadillac pulled up to the truck stop's entrance and Preston drove up beside it. "Sorry, I'm late," said Sam hastily through his window. "I had trouble getting away from the plant. Get in, we'll drive around and talk."

It was comfortable in the big, expensive car with its leather upholstery. The ride was smooth, even when they turned off the highway and drove down a rutted road that led to the marshes. "There's been a change in plans. There's no time to get your boat fixed up. They got a boat ready for you in Mississippi, but you have to leave the day after tomorrow."

"I'd just as soon as do it that way, if the boat's any good and it pays enough," Preston said. "If I got caught, the U.S. Customs would confiscate my boat and I'd lose everything."

Sam laughed loudly as they pulled down to the marshy bay. "Not as much as you owe on it, they wouldn't. They'd have to pay it off to confiscate it, and it gets them all tied up in a legal mess forever. And besides, you'll never be able to fix that old boat up; it's a wreck. If you stuck a hundred thousand dollars in it, rebuilt the motor and fiberglassed the entire bottom, all you'd do is make the boat yard rich. It's still gonna be an old boat.

"Besides," he jeered, "I'll bet the *Lady Mary's* under suspicion now. Not only because of Lupino's mess, but because they got a sheet on boats that are behind in their payments. They figure some poor son-of-a bitch with his back to the wall is more likely to make the run."

"It's all I got," Preston said, a little offended.

Sam shook his head impatiently, "Preston, son, I ain't believing the deal they're offering. If you manage to come through with the load, you got a chance to get a boat that you can make a living with from now on. They're gonna give you the title to a near-about brand new ninety-foot steel hull with a 353 turbo-charged Caterpillar engine and a diesel electric winch. She's got all brand-new electronics, and this is the part you're gonna like," he was sounding like a used-car salesman making a pitch. "She's already rigged for royal reds! With enough cable to fish in four hundred fathoms. I ain't never seen them offer no one a deal like that. I think it's their way of saying thank you for saving them from burning up on Lupino's boat."

Preston sat there speechless, trying to fathom what to say. The boat of his dreams was being offered. Sam said in a low whisper, "If you don't like her Preston, after you make the run, bring her back, and I'll give you two hundred thousand for her, cash money. I swear to God I will!"

A great blue heron lighted in the ditch next to the parked Cadillac. It began stalking the green rushes and mud flats for minnows. As it moved, its long snake neck bobbed up and down, its attention focused completely on the fish that darted before it, streaking the shallows.

"Two hundred thousand, huh?" Preston laughed. "Then it must be worth at least three hundred thousand."

"Actually three hundred and fifty thousand because of the royal red rigging."

"It sounds too good to be true. And things that sound that good usually aren't. Maybe we ought to talk cash money. How do they know I won't back out on them, and take the boat and go shrimping and not make the run?"

"They'd kill you and your wife and burn your house down," he said matter-of-factly. "You'll have a free and clear title to the boat before you leave the dock. But do them dirty..." he drew his finger across his throat for dramatic effect.

"Yeah, then what happens if the deal goes sour and we have to dump the load or something like that? They gonna murder us in our sleep?"

"Look, the cartel understands these things," Sam soothed. "As long as you've done your best, they'll let it slide. All you've got to have is a newspaper clipping or some other documentation to show what happened. If you get popped, they'll help with the legal expenses. The reason they're picking you is because you're honest and resourceful. Believe me, they know more about you than you know yourself."

"If the boat's what you say it is, then we got a deal. But if she's some old rust-bucket, you can forget it," Preston said with finality. "When can I see it?"

"When you go to Mississippi. All you have to do is check into the Holiday Inn at Pascagoula, and someone will contact you and take you to it. It used to be over at Bayou La Batre, but after the captain died I don't know where it got moved, exactly."

"The captain died? What happened?" Preston demanded, suddenly remembering his conversation with Officer Miller a few weeks ago.

The owner of the fish house licked his lips nervously, "I don't know. Someone stabbed him in one of those waterfront joints over in Biloxi. They were fighting over some whore, I reckon. You know what a rough place that is."

"You sure he wasn't murdered over running drugs?" Preston demanded. He didn't like the way Sam's eyes shifted around, looking at the steering wheel or out the window.

"No, that's why they're in such a fix. They got a schedule to meet. You got the wrong idea about these people. I told you, if you play straight with them, they'll play straight with you. This fella was a good captain; he'd made several runs for them before. Shit happens. It was just one of those things."

Just then the blue heron in the ditch struck. It shot its neck into the water and came up with a wiggling killifish in its bill. Then it gulped the fish down. "What about the crew?" Preston inquired, watching the heron swallow its prey. "I want someone I can trust."

"They'll provide the crew. But they already figured you'd want to take Charlie along."

"I don't know for certain if Charlie will go. What's his pay?"

"He'll get fifty thousand. Don't worry, he'll go."

Sam knew that when Preston first put Charlie to work ten years ago, he was an anemic fourteen-year-old. His ribs stuck out, and his arms were covered with sores. Charlie's father was a chronic alcoholic who died of cirrhosis. His mother had too many kids to worry much about. The boy was abused and beaten by the old man as well as the stream of "uncles" that came to pay his mother visits.

Charlie came on as a green deckhand, and showed his gratitude by working hard and becoming one of the best deckhands in the fleet. He came to regard Preston as the father he never had. If anyone at the bar ever said anything disparaging about Preston, they'd get Charlie's fist in their eye. Then the police would get involved, and Preston or Mary would have to get him out of jail.

"Yeah, probably he will." Then, changing the subject, Preston said, "Sam, I need some money up front. In case something happens, there's got to be money for Mary and the baby, say ten thousand in advance?"

The fish house owner's heavy jowls settled into a pensive frown and he shook his head. "Sorry, Preston, they won't go for it. I'll loan you some chicken feed, a few hundred to keep the bill collectors away until you get back, but don't tell her nothing. Don't trust anyone, not even your wife. In this business you keep your mouth shut, and don't ask too many questions. The less you or she knows about this operation the better. I try to keep it that way myself."

After Sam dropped him off at the truck stop, Preston didn't go straight home. Instead, he turned left onto a dirt road and drove past a settlement of old shacks and houses until he reached a faded blue-and-white house trailer. The place reeked of poverty. It was shabby even for an impoverished North Florida coastal town. Chickens pecked at the bare, sandy ground beneath the oak trees, and in the yard was Miss Bell, Charlie's mother, making crab traps. That and Social Security were her main source of income. She furnished most of the traps for the crab fishermen.

"You seen Charlie, Miss Bell?" Preston called out.

"No, I haven't, sugar," the old lady drawled as her strong fingers crimped the staples. "You know him, he's probably out running around with some yellah-haired gal."

Preston left Miss Bell's place and tried the bars, but didn't see

Charlie's rusty Chevy with the dented fender. He drove down to the dock and didn't see him. Then he went to the boat yard and looked up at the *Lady Mary* sitting in its cradle. Sometimes his deckhand slept on the boat or entertained his girlfriends there. He always said that added to the romance. But he wasn't there and the boat was dark.

Preston was about to drive off when the wheelhouse door opened and Charlie popped out and waved him in. Then Charlie ducked back inside. Thinking his behavior strange, Preston climbed the ladder and pushed into the dark cabin. "What are you doing here, Charlie? Where's your car?"

There was no answer. Preston switched on the light and saw that his deckhand was wild-eyed and distracted.

"Preston, I messed up bad. I need to get out of town for a while. Can you loan me some money?"

"I ain't got it to loan, Charlie. What's the matter?" Charlie was agitated, sweating. Preston could smell his fear.

"He come home last night and caught us!"

"Who? What?"

"Vonceil's old man. I been messing around with her when he's been away on the tugboat."

"You're crazy, Charlie, messing with her."

"But she was lonely and come on to me! Honest. That goddamn Wilbur's a wild man. No lie, he tore the door off the frame—in one snatch. I jumped out of the window, run down the street buck naked, and him shooting at me. God Almighty, damn, it was close! I *mean* it was *close*."

Preston started laughing. He laughed so hard he had a hard time running water into the coffeepot. He had to put it down.

"It ain't so goddamn funny," Charlie said. "I run all the way down to the boat buck-assed naked, hiding in the bushes. Thank the Lord I had some clothes here. He's gonna kill me, Preston. You got to help me. I got to get out of town."

When the coffee had boiled for a few minutes on the rusty, chipped stove, Preston poured a cup. "Here, have some of this. It'll settle you down." Charlie took a sip.

"How'd you like to take a long boat ride south? I got a job running a boat for someone while mine's getting fixed."

"South? To the Keys? There ain't no shrimp there now."

"No, I mean way, way down south. To Colombia, South America."

"Colombia?" Charlie blinked, beginning to comprehend. "You mean...make...a run?"

"There's fifty thousand dollars in it for you."

Charlie's eyes grew wide, "Fifty thousand dollars! When do we leave?"

"It's risky, Charlie. They got pirates down there, no telling what all. You could get killed. If we get caught, we could go to jail for twenty years."

"Sounds a hell of lot safer than where I am right now. Did the Cubans set this up? How'd you get into it?"

"I ain't gonna say, Charlie. And don't ask. The less you know the better!"

As Preston drove home, he wondered how he was going to break this to Mary. All during supper that night he sat brooding silently. As Mary cleared the dishes away, she watched him nursing his coffee. "Preston," she blurted, "you ain't acting right. You better tell me what's on your mind!"

"Mary, I'm gonna take a trip for a month or two. I'm picking up a boat in Louisiana, while mine's up on the ways."

"What with me fixing to have this young'un, you're gonna go off?" She looked at him piercingly. "You're lying to me, Preston, I can always tell. You're working for those men, ain't you!"

"Look Mary, I missed the hopper run. I'm not gonna lose my boat and our home. And I want a better life for us. Look at this place, it's a dump. We can't afford to fix it up. We're gonna need more room."

Mary's face was drawn, her lips pale, and her eyes welled with tears. "Preston, I hear it's *real* dangerous. People get killed all the time. They find them floating with their heads blown off over dope."

"It's done all the time, Mary," Preston said, staring straight ahead and doing his best to sound convincing, "Most of it goes through without a hitch, and very few gets into trouble. I'll get you a few hundred to tide you over in case I don't get back until after you have the baby. I don't see no other way. The less you know about this the better."

His wife bit her lip and trembled. "I'll go see Mama. She'll help me out, or my sisters will. Don't worry about me," she said with a glance at her big belly. "We'll make do. Lord, I wish there was some other way. I'll pray for you every day, Preston, while you're gone. And so help me, if you come back with a ton of money, I'll tithe it to the church. Honest I will."

When a man goes on a dope run, especially in a small fishing village with a population of two thousand, there are a lot of tracks to be covered. When Preston Barfield wandered into the fish house, there were four other captains waiting to share up. "You just the fella I'm looking for," Sam Lawton said loudly, pointing his finger at him.

"Well, here I am."

"You want to run a boat? I just got a call this morning from a Dubois Fish House in Empire, Louisiana. They need someone to run one of their steel slabs for a while, and I thought about you. Said they were looking for someone who knows how to drag for royal reds. They got a new market for 'em. I told 'em about you and they were tickled to death."

"Yeah, but you know I can't take off for two or three months," Preston said regretfully. "Mary's fixing to have that young'un and all."

"Yeah, I told 'em, and they said you could bring the boat back over here and shrimp it. But they want you to make a shake-out trip for a couple of weeks for those red shrimp, get them up some samples— some special marketing thing. Then you can bring it back around. Later on, after the baby comes, work on back to Mississippi."

"Well, I damn sure need the work." Preston said trying to look relieved, noting the other captains were listening. "I could sure use the work." The whole thing made him feel cheesy. Telling white lies now and then was part of living; like telling the rest of the fleet he wasn't catching shrimp on the radio when he was. Everyone did that. But this was subterfuge: a deep-seated, serious lie, and he despised it.

"That's what I figured," Sam Lawton said knowingly. "I told 'em I know'd a fella that was a good captain, but down on his luck, and he'd probably take it. But they need someone in the next day or so."

"You call 'em right back and tell 'em I'll take it. Charlie's hunting a job, too. Tell them I'm bringing my own crew."

Two days later the captain and his deckhand were speeding down the interstate in a big rented Mercury cruiser, headed west. Charlie was at the wheel.

"You know, I could get used to this real easy. This is smooth as a baby's ass. I know what I'm gonna do when I get my money. I'm gonna buy me a big new car just like this one."

"Well, I'm tired of living poor. It's time we change all that, ain't it?" laughed Preston.

They drove west for five hours through planted pines paralleling both sides of the interstate, cutting across the ancient sand dunes that made up the North Florida hills. In Mobile Bay they sped over a maze of concrete bridges and ramps, and bogged down in the Mobile tunnel. By the time they crossed the Mississippi state line and arrived in Pascagoula, they ran headlong into the five o'clock rush hour as the shipyard disgorged its thousands of workers onto the highway. "What are we supposed to do when we get there, Preston?"

"You know as much about it as I do, Charlie-boy. We check into the Holiday Inn under the name of Moe Portland and wait."

"Moe Portland? That's a dumb name."

Preston filled out the registration card and handed over the eighty dollars.

"Imagine, eighty dollars just to lie in a bed!" Charlie said as they headed to their room. When they opened the door of their room, Charlie exclaimed, "This is the way I like to travel, Skipper. First class."

"Yeah, first class all right," said Preston tersely. "I hope this show gets on the road pretty soon before we have to hitchhike home broke. They said they'd call us." He stretched out on one of the beds and closed his eyes, tired from the drive, but the anticipation of what lay ahead kept him awake. Charlie had the television on, whooping with excitement as speeding automobiles leaped through the air across washed-out ravines, pursued by inept policemen.

Trying to kill time, Preston and Charlie went down to the restaurant on the first floor. It was filled with executives in coats and ties. Snatches of conversation drifted across the room about bonds and debentures, drilling rigs and oil prices.

Charlie looked around in awe. "Look at these guys," he said in a hushed whisper. "You can tell none of 'em ever worked a day in their lives. Look at their hands, soft and flabby. Their skins are white like milk. These are the guys who really make the big money. They're out hunting deals like we hunt shrimp! They're not like us. They sit behind the desk all day and use lawyers and accountants to steal. They're the ones who owns the big, fancy yachts.

"You got to have an education to steal like they do," the deckhand went on ruefully, observing the men in the next table poring over a ledger. "I ain't never had one, but I'm independent, and I've worked hard all my life!" he said proudly. "I know that assholes like that think that working with your hands don't spell squat in this world. But there's one thing good about being a commercial fisherman," Charlie said, warming up to his familiar speech. "You don't have to kiss no man's hind end. Out there you only got one master, and that's the good Lord himself."

"That's true," agreed Preston, warming up to a favorite litany of his own. "But that's why they're trying to get rid of us with all this fisheries management. The reason all these environmentalists and bureaucrats are against us is not because they think we're drowning turtles, tearing up the bottom or catching too many shrimp. It's because they're jealous. Most of them are chained to their desks while we're out in God's country living life. It's just that it's damn hard making a living doing it, or we wouldn't be here." But his words sounded hollow to him. He wasn't working; he wasn't making an honest living. He was here to smuggle, to sneak around and break the law, and to take an extreme risk that wasn't going to provide food for anyone...and that shamed him.

Charlie lost interest in this weighty conversation. "Wow! Will you look at the tits on that gal." He was looking at a waitress across the room. "She makes my tongue get hard."

The deckhand's lewd remark was overheard at the next table, and one of the men looked up and gave him a peculiar look, then stared at them both for a moment before going back to his ledger.

Preston suddenly felt paranoid. "Let's get back to the room, Charlie. A couple of working guys hanging out in a place like this with nothing to do, killing time doesn't look right. It could get a cop suspicious. For all I know one of these guys could be undercover."

"You're just uptight," soothed Charlie. "They're just a bunch of assholes." Then his eyes lit up with excitement. "Damn! You see that? Miss Tits just smiled at me."

"Come on, let's go back to the room and wait. And don't you come back down here, you hear? I don't want to be seen."

Later, just when Preston was thinking that he would go out of his mind if he had to listen to another sitcom or soap opera on the television, or the endless babble of commercials, the telephone rang. He rolled across the bed and grabbed it.

"Moe Portland?" a polished young man's voice asked.

"Yeah, it is."

"There's been a change of plans. We need you and your partner to help unload a freighter tonight. They'll be an extra ten thousand in it for you each. Be down at the flour dock at ten o'clock tonight."

There was a long pause as Preston turned it over in his mind. Obviously these dirt bags were trying to pull something on him, but he said, "Ten o'clock, we'll be there." The phone clicked dead.

"Wait just a goddamn minute," Charlie wailed after Preston relayed the conversation. "We didn't agree to nothing like that. I was just supposed..."

"Look, Charlie, quit being a weenie. We're dopers now. From here on we're criminals. Good cops will shoot at us, and people will think poorly of us if they find out about it. But if we're gonna do it, then let's do it. Ten thousand for one night, that ain't bad. I could use that money bad right now to send back home. And it gives us a chance to check them out and see what kind of people they are."

"Yeah, but it's got real problems," Charlie fretted. "We don't know anything about this unloading. For all we know, it could be some kind of setup. The cops might grab us."

That night Preston and Charlie drove down to the grain elevator and the shrimp boat docks. It was practically abandoned, with run-down wharves rotted through with big holes. A street light illuminated the weeds in the parking lot, heaped with discarded, rusted cables and old shrimp nets and doors.

"This is like a TV show," Preston thought as he walked down the docks, "with crooks getting ready for a heist or something." Large wharf rats scurried; repulsive brown creatures with long pink tails, brazen and unafraid.

A train rattled over the bridge at the head of the harbor, blowing its lonesome horn. Another one pulled out of the factories, loaded with fish oil or pulpwood chips, headed for the mills. They walked the docks looking at deserted, tied-up shrimp boats and slapping mosquitoes. Two more trains rattled by, and still no one showed.

"This is getting old as hell," said Charlie irritably at midnight. He threw a broken brick at a rat and nearly beaned it.

"Just wait," Preston said, but his patience was at an end.

Two hours later he said, "If they don't cut this kind of shit out and get down to business, I'm gonna take that fancy rented car right back to Carrabelle and tell Sam to stick it up his ass!"

"Sam?" said Charlie with sudden interest, his innocent eyes sparkling. "Did you say Sam?"

A sinking feeling overcame Preston. "Forget I ever said that," he snapped, angry with himself for slipping up. Next time, he resolved, he'd be more careful.

Charlie nodded with enlightenment and grinned at Preston. "That makes sense, greedy as he is. It figures."

"We'll stick it out a little longer," Preston went on. "Sometimes these things take time, I reckon." Across, on the other shore of the "Singing River," as the Pascagoula was called, the lights of the grain elevator blazed. The blowers blasting grain into the waiting ships roared steadily through the night.

At two o'clock in the morning the fishermen went back to their hotel. Almost immediately after they entered the room, the telephone rang.

"You checked out fine," said the voice. "Excuse the inconvenience. This was just a test."

"Some test," Preston retorted, trying to control his ire. "Any more little games tonight?"

"No, you'll be contacted in a day or two. Just relax, Skipper. Have a good time. We'll catch up with you. You don't have to wait around the hotel." The phone clicked.

When Preston repeated the message, Charlie beamed.

"Hell, relax. Now that we don't have to stay stuck here, I'm going whore hoppin'. Wow, with a big room like this…"

"You go ahead," Preston said. "But you ain't bringing 'em back here. And don't get into trouble. I don't want to have to bail you out of jail. Remember how mean these head-bustin' Pascagoula cops are. This isn't Key West, and we ain't shrimping."

He started to hand Charlie the keys to the rental car and then quickly changed his mind. Instead he handed him a hundred-dollar bill from Lawton's travel advance.

"Here, take this. Go find a taxi. I'll see you when I see you." He switched off the TV and reached for his novel.

"Can't you give me any more?" pleaded Charlie. "You can't get no cooter, pay a taxi and run around with just that."

"Get gone!" Preston said, pushing him out the door.

13

April

Preston knew lots of people in Pascagoula. Every summer he brought his boat over for brownie season, along with the rest of the North Florida fleet. They sold their shrimp at Wilson's Fish house, and when the season turned, they moved into Louisiana and Texas to fish for white shrimp. But now he stayed away from his usual haunts. He walked down to an abandoned dock near the cat food factory, circumventing friends at the boat yard and the marine hardware store, feeling ashamed.

Preston stood on the wharf, looking across the river at the grain elevators and loading ships. Daddy always taught us to be honest, he ruminated. If we stole so much as a piece of chewing gum, he'd wear our butts out with a hickory switch. "Don't ever bring shame to the Barfield name," he used to say. "There's no need to steal. The sea will provide, if you work at it." So why, Preston wondered, why the hell am I doing this?

But Daddy also ran a moonshine still, Preston considered. He often said the family would have starved to death back in the Depression if it wasn't for the still down by the creek. The old man took great pride in his 'shine and got lots of compliments. Preston and his brothers tended the fire and helped cook the mash. His daddy figured it wasn't any of the government's business if a man wanted a drink of liquor. And look, prohibition was repealed, and no doubt someday marijuana laws would be too. Then, a soft, feminine voice broke into his thoughts.

"You look like a man with the troubles of the world on your back. It isn't all that bad."

Preston whirled around and saw a tall, well-dressed, young woman standing behind him regarding him with friendly green eyes.

"You scared the hell out of me," he snapped, looking her up and down, wondering if she was trying to pick him up. But she didn't look like a waterfront whore. There was a polish about her, and a bold confidence that both confused and upset him. There was also something familiar about her that he couldn't put his finger on.

"You shouldn't let people sneak up on you in your new business, Preston Barfield. That can be very unwise."

He took in her tall, slender body covered smartly with a red dress that tastefully emphasized her curves. She had golden hair that fell softly down her shoulders and around her neck, enveloping her ample, well-rounded breasts.

"Now, don't panic," she said giving him a sexy smile, "but I'm going to give you a hug and feel you up a little."

"What the hell…" he spluttered, as she stepped forward, lightly put her arms around him, and quickly ran her fingers down his barrel chest. She explored his massive shoulders with a fast, soft stroke, then under his arms and down his stomach.

"There, that wasn't so bad," she said stepping back, winking at him. "I had to see if you were wired. You could be a narc. Actually, I kind of enjoyed it. You're quite a hunk of man."

For a moment Preston stood there, red-faced and outraged. "You people are something," he managed. But when he saw that she was embarrassed and a little red-faced herself, he couldn't help laughing. And suddenly feeling excited by her, his eyes pointedly feasted on her bosom, "Can I do it back?"

She laughed heartily and shook her head.

"Well, how do I know *you're* not a narc!"

"Well, now," she said grinning and still blushing, "that's just the chance you'll have to take. I'm April." She assertively extended her hand. "Sorry for the bold introduction, but as I said, we can't be too careful in this business."

He shook it awkwardly, not used to shaking hands with women, especially with one with such a confident, forceful grip. Yet he found the touch to be quite warm, and an electric excitement went through him. Something about this young woman's bold manner attracted him. He tried to judge how old she was, but he couldn't. Somewhere around thirty maybe.

"I wasn't expecting a woman," he said awkwardly, still feeling embarrassed.

She found that amusing. "Women's liberation has come to the smoke industry, although people like your deckhand will never believe it."

"Charlie?"

"Yes, Popcorn Charlie, your trusty, devoted sidekick, and male chauvinist pig. 'Miss Tits' indeed!"

"God, we've been bugged." Preston's eyes again widened in surprise and shock that she'd know such a detail as Charlie's shrimp-culling reputation. "You've been checking us out, listening to everything we were saying?" His voice was incredulous.

"Don't be so outraged," she soothed. "Good security is everything in this business. Either or both of you could be working for the police. Now come on, I'll drive you to the boat. My car's across the street. You'll want to check it out while there's still daylight."

"That's what I'm here for," he said.

Before climbing into her blue Mercedes, April handed him a slip of paper. "If anything goes wrong and you get popped, you need to have this number memorized. It might get you out of jail."

Preston leaned back, enjoying the luxurious ride. It had that new car smell about it. He ran his hand over the leather upholstery and thought about owning a car like this some day. Nice as it was, he had to admit that it really wasn't his style. He looked at the scrap of paper. "Is this a lawyer's number?" he said with loathing.

April shuddered, "Ugh, that tone of voice. They don't have leprosy you know. What's wrong with lawyers?"

"I don't know, I just don't like 'em. They don't produce anything. They don't farm, fish, or mine the earth. All they do is take, take, take."

"You'd better be glad there are such people," April said. "They're useful in this business. With the laws the way they are nowadays, they can't help as much as they used to. Now, it's a matter of luck. The ones who run their mouths get caught," she said tersely. "Think about that with Charlie-boy running around with fifty thousand dollars in his pocket. I don't suppose you could talk him into a trust fund?"

"Uh, no." The complications made him pale. "I'll have to have some long talks with him on the way down."

With the windows open and the wind blowing in April's golden hair, she drove Preston to the far end of town, past the industrial docks, the oil refinery, across the railroad tracks and onto the four-lane highway and the bustling car-scape. Five miles later she turned down a country road that led to a subdivision on the river. As they neared the water Preston could see the black masts of a shrimp boat with its green-webbed nets and bright orange chafing gear looming beside the moss-draped water oaks. The boat was docked at a small private wharf behind a large brick house on the bank of the Singing River.

"There she is," April said, pointing to the majestic trawler at the end of the pier.

"Oh, my God," he breathed. "I was expecting some worn-out wreck. Sam wasn't kidding. That looks like a new steel slab!" He was filled with excitement, like a child seeing a new bicycle at Christmas."

"That's the *Aquarius*," she announced proudly. "I hope you like your new boat. She's all fueled up and ready to go. We've got her docked here so the single side band radios can be installed—ten thousand dollars worth. They'll enable you to talk all the way down to Colombia, but try not to use them. The DEA listens."

He jumped off the dock and walked around the deck of the *Aquarius*, surveying the giant winches with disbelief and pleasure. "It's true," he cried aloud. "She's already rigged for royal reds. She's carrying enough cable to drag the bottom of the Gulf of Mexico, near-about."

April started to say something, but stopped when she saw he was lost to her. The captain was in a trance. He gazed at the nets as if he were looking at stained glass windows in a cathedral. Inspecting the rigging, it was instantly clear that the ninety-foot trawler was well-maintained. The masts and steel rigging were painted—not pitted with rust like the *Lady Mary's*. Her decks were freshly painted and the radio antennas and flood lights were new.

Then he opened the lazarette and noted with satisfaction that it had several spare nets with turtle shooters already installed. But when he hauled back the hatch covers, the smell of washing powders and the residual odor of marijuana almost knocked him down.

"Hey Barfield," he heard April's voice calling impatiently, "help me down, damn it. I've got high heels on."

"Oh, excuse me," he said awkwardly, having forgotten all about her. He dragged his attention away from the boat for a moment. He took her hand. She stepped down lightly, into his arms. For a long second he felt her breasts pressing against him and her long, soft hair brushing his cheek. Preston caught a gentle whiff of perfume, and another surge of electricity went through him. He couldn't remember when he'd held another woman like that.

Preston stepped back, momentarily confused by the mix of inputs: April and the boat. He refocused his attention on the *Aquarius*. She handed him a key and he inserted it, turned the lock, and slid the door back into the spacious foreward wheelhouse. The dark pine paneling glowed softly in the afternoon sun. He climbed into the comfortable pilot seat and spun around, luxuriating in the room. Mounted on the ceiling, following the contour of the rounded cabin, was a mass of electronics, two Loran sets, a radar, a fathometer, a fish-finder, and a barrage of radios.

"Do all the electronics work?" he inquired, switching on the radar. He listened for a moment, noted with satisfaction that it didn't squeak, and turned it off.

"After what we just paid out, they'd better!" said April emphatically. "We're on a tight schedule for this trip. That's why we've had the maintenance crews working on her for the past week. She's got groceries, 25,000 gallons of diesel, and should be ready to go. But you'll want to check her out yourself."

Preston began flipping switches on the panel, checking the Loran, the new depth recorder, lights, pumps, hydraulics and radar. "I better see what this engine will do."

He went out the back door, made his way to the engine room, and crawled down the companionway. What he saw, he liked. A four-thousand horsepower Caterpillar, one of the best, with a fluid-drive transmission. Before firing it off he carefully pulled the dipstick and noted that the oil was clean, with no sign of water or air bubbles that told of blown head gaskets or a cracked block. It cranked without a moment's hesitation: its big cylinders exploding into action, with a good, dependable sound. Not like my boat, he thought. *Lady Mary* was still sitting at the dock back home, waiting for the mechanic to put her back together again.

"What do you think of it?" April wanted to know when he finally came topside. By then the sun had all but disappeared behind the woods across the river, giving the sky an orange glow. The moon was already rising.

"This still sounds too good to be true. Are you sure she isn't hot or something?"

"No," April said in an offended tone. "We go first class in this operation. If we need something we buy it. We paid $350,000 for the *Aquarius*." She took a gold cigarette case out of her purse and lit up.

Preston went into the cabin, found the switch to the overhead lights and turned them on. He grinned with satisfaction at the spacious galley and the bunks. "A boat like this could spoil a man for life!" he said in wonder. "There's not a dozen boats in the Gulf of Mexico that fishes red shrimp. How come..."

"...Because they're the most delicious shrimp in the world. One of my partners likes to serve them when he puts on political fund-raising banquets, but he got tired of trying to get a supply and finally had a boat built that would catch them." She grinned at him. "Part of the deal is you have to keep him supplied."

He tore a paper towel off and wiped oil from his hands. "I'm ready to start right now. If a man hits it lucky off the Desoto Canyon or down off the Tortugas, he can make a fortune. We need to make a check-out trip before we make this run."

"Normally we'd encourage you to shrimp her," said April, watching him wash up. She moved closer. He could feel her warmth, smell her perfume. "We'd like to have the captain run the boat for a month and unload shrimp at the fish house and be seen around the docks so the law gets used to it. But the timing doesn't allow it this trip. You're to take her across to Tampa tomorrow and pick up the crew, and they'll tell you where to go."

"Tampa? I don't understand. Why don't we leave from here? It's a straight run across the Gulf, down to Yucatan and over to Colombia."

"Don't ask too many questions, Preston. Your job is just to drive the boat." Her voice suddenly took on a hard business tone. Preston didn't seem to have noticed any of her advances, and April didn't like being ignored by him.

"Well, you never know," he said slowly, his deep brown eyes getting a far-away look. "Before it's all over I might have a chance to do a little blue-water shrimping out there. I once made a twenty-thousand dollar trip off the Tortugas. A man don't forget a trip like that!"

Suddenly April broke out laughing at the fervor in his voice. "Men and boats! It's instinctive. Maybe it's evolution. I once saw a nature film where monkeys were riding on a log to get across a creek. Probably they were males, and they've been doing it ever since."

She returned to logistics. "You keep to the schedule." Reaching into her purse, she pulled out a great wad of hundred dollar bills and laid it on the galley table. "This is some extra cash in case you need to buy anything for the boat, extra groceries, liquor, restaurants or whatever. Blake will have all the cash you need in case you get stuck down in Colombia, for bribes or whatever."

"Blake?"

"You remember Blake, don't you? Unfortunately, you kept his wretched hide from being roasted. He's going along to troubleshoot. When you pick him up in Tampa, he'll give you the nautical charts and Loran coordinates."

"Oh yeah," Preston nodded, suddenly feeling better. "He probably saved my life that night with those Cuban cutthroats. I'm sure not looking forward to hauling a boat-load of them down to Colombia."

"You may not have to. I'm not sure who will be going. They're a necessary evil, as they control the money," she snapped, lighting her cigarette. "A bunch of macho cowboys. They're okay in Miami, but up in the Florida panhandle with their language and dripping gold jewelry, they've been a disaster. But if you play straight with them, they'll play straight with you. Just don't cross them."

April rose. "How would you like to go out to dinner?" she asked cheerfully. "I know a nice little restaurant not far from here. We can talk without being overheard."

Preston looked at her with surprise. "You take other boat captains out to dinner?"

"Only the strong, silent types," she said effervescently, "but you're the first one like that I've met. Usually I have someone else who handles the contact. From what I've seen of your industry, it has its share of derelict bums and drunks. But I'm fascinated by heroes, and Blake said you were one."

Preston thought about saying no, about going back to the hotel and keeping it all business. But he decided he might learn more about the run from her over dinner, and the more he knew the better. Besides, he was lonely, and there was something intriguing about her.

The tide had fallen, and the dock was above them. She looked up, "Help me up, Preston. I don't want to get this dress dirty."

He stood on the railing, boosted her up, and together they walked down the dock, back to the car. She put her arm through his, and Preston realized that for the first time in days he was enjoying himself.

Once again they sped along the four-lane road, past a neon blur of stores, then across an endless expanse of bridge that led into the old town of Biloxi. April pointed out old southern mansions hidden among the giant water oaks and talked enthusiastically about the history of the area. She pulled up before a spacious frame house that had been converted into a restaurant.

The waiter, a stocky, good-humored black man, was delighted to see her. She introduced him as Steven to Preston, and he directed them to a private room in the back of the restaurant. As they passed through the dining room to get there, Preston felt out of place, since the men all wore suits and ties, and the ladies were impeccable. But Steven did his best to make him feel at ease. Their table, set with white linen and gold-ware had a vase of fresh flowers. On the walls were paintings of the Old South, antebellum houses and trees that once existed before the town was buried in asphalt and burger joints.

When they were seated April turned to Preston and said, "They specialize in Bloody Marys here. Try one."

It seemed to Preston to be more of an order than a suggestion.

"J & B Scotch," he ordered pointedly. "I'm a simple man of simple wants."

"The usual Chardonnay," she said in her sophisticated manner. The image of the woman in the van who gave Raul a tongue-lashing when the *Night Shadow* burned suddenly came to him. He'd only seen her for a few seconds, but he was positive it was April. He decided it was imprudent to ask.

Seeing her in this extravagant setting, he was deeply puzzled. He knew she should not have contacted him directly, but obviously she was impetuous. In the dope trade she was known as a "thoroughbred." He and Charlie were "mules." If they were seized by the Coast Guard or arrested at the loading docks, April knew perfectly well he might turn state's evidence. Often the mules would be offered lighter sentences or even total amnesty if they informed on the higher-ups. So why was she taking this risk, he wondered; it didn't make sense. Unless—a dark shadow passed his mind—he wasn't around to testify.

"Tell me, April," Preston began awkwardly, after the drinks arrived. Her poise and polish made him feel self conscious. "I know why I'm in this business, 'cause I been on hard times. But you..."

She looked at him with amusement. "You want to know why a girl with a great education, from a wealthy, well-connected Mississippi family with every opportunity in the world would be skulking around waterfronts, right?"

Preston cast his eyes around the room nervously, afraid of being overheard. "Er...ah..." his voice dropped, "something like that."

"Don't worry," she said. "Steven takes care of us; no one can hear us. There's no listening devices here. It's checked twice a day.

"The money is important to me just like it is to you. It means independence. But it's also the challenge, the intellectual game of outwitting the cops—although usually that's not much of a challenge."

She didn't tell him that one of her father's companies owned a whole fleet of shrimp boats, as well as a chain of restaurants. Nor did she mention that he was the powerful U.S. Senator Richard Hatchet, chair of the Latin American Relations Committee. "I enjoy putting something over on the power structure," she said with a naughty fervor. "It's an adrenaline high. It's like cheating on your spouse. They'll never make a drug to match it."

She held up her drink in a toast. "Here's to adventure." And with a grin Preston raised his glass. The waiter reappeared carrying leather-bound menus. "The filet of sole is excellent, tonight, Miss April, and so is the shrimp scampi."

"I love shrimp," she said sensuously. "*Shrimmmmp*—the word just rolls off the tongue, doesn't it? Did you know that this is one of the few restaurants that specializes in royal reds? They're one of the most delicious things in the sea. They're almost as good as sex."

"They're good, but not that good!" Preston spluttered, despite himself.

"I said *almost*," she replied.

Was that a hint? Preston wondered. He felt a surge of excitement. Never had he met a woman like her, so confident, capable, self-assured and yet thoroughly feminine.

"You know if you look at it right, there's a lot of similarities between your business and mine," April said sipping her wine. "Both are meaningful and have value to society. It's only natural that they would merge."

Preston almost choked on his drink. "Come on, what in the hell is meaningful about running dope?"

The waiter returned with their drinks and a straw basket of hot rolls. "A lot," she said when he left. "To begin with, people have been using it for thousands of years—same stuff. It's been used for spiritual practice, heals the sick, and if it's not abused, it can improve the quality of life by making you feel better, just like shrimp. And it's environmentally sound. Pot can make three times as much paper as pine, you know."

"Look at it this way," she continued with enthusiasm. "We're in the entertainment business. We distribute God's vegetables, giving a boost to the overworked, the movie actor, the politicians, and the doctors. We make working in cramped-up government offices and putting up with the bullshit of modern life more bearable. Lots of your fishermen smoke it when they're tired and worn out. Our little white powders and our grass are an angel of mercy to the advertising executive or the attorney pushing a deadline. They reduce anxiety and slow things down in this hyped-up, over-stressed world headed for destruction. We alleviate boredom and spread joy and good times. Why do you think we sell so much of it?" She sipped her drink and waited for his reaction.

Preston stared back at her with shock, and shook his head with disbelief, thinking he'd never met anyone who talked like that. "God's vegetables? Entertainment?" He guffawed. "You sure got a funny way of looking at things, April."

"It's not so funny. You're in the entertainment business yourself. You've spent your life catching shrimp."

"What do you mean?" he asked indignantly. "I produce food for people to eat."

"At eighteen dollars a pound in the supermarket? Come on, the only reason people eat shrimp is to get away from the humdrum meals. Shrimp are heavenly," she said, mopping one up in cocktail sauce and popping it in her mouth. "It excites the taste buds. Do you know anyone who lives on eighteen-dollars-a-pound jumbo shrimp? Or lobster, or crab meat, or pompano for that matter? Of course not, they're novelty foods for the rich. Entertainment. And, likewise, our side provides a little piece of paradise also."

Preston's pride was wounded. "I never thought of it that way. It's true; people enjoy eating what I catch. They also get nourishment from it, no matter what they pay." Then he got angry. "Let me tell you something, lady, I *feed* people. I don't entertain them. Nor do I fog up their brains. And until recently, when all this turtle conservation and over-regulation came along, no one would put you in jail for doing it."

She reached across the table and, squeezing his hand, looked into his eyes with warm sincerity and said, "I'm sorry. I didn't mean to denigrate your work. I was trying to say to you that you make a lot of people happy by catching shrimp."

"A man has to have pride in what he does," Preston replied defensively. "You gotta excuse me if I'm a little raw. It's kind of hard to get used to these bleeding-heart environmentalists who don't know a thing about the sea trying to make bad guys out of us." He was feeling the warmth of her touch shoot through him. It started a caldron of chemicals boiling.

The waiter returned bringing a magnificent arrangement of food on silver dishes. When they finished and had coffee, he said, reluctantly, "I suppose I ought to get back to the hotel and see what Charlie's doing. Maybe he's there and not in jail."

"I thought we'd go up to my condo and have a few drinks," April suggested. "There's a few more details we need to talk about and plans to be made. Leave a fifty-dollar tip, will you? Steven's always good to us."

Preston reached into his pocket for her cash, and left it on the table. The bill came to a hundred dollars. He was still amazed when they drove out of the parking lot. April turned to him and asked softly, "Tell me about your Vietnam experience, Preston, it could be important."

"How'd you know I was in 'Nam?"

"It's my business to know."

"There's not much to tell," he shrugged, "I'm pleased to say that I didn't get shot, and I didn't have to kill anyone. Luckily, I was in the Navy, on a little island, miles away from most of the action."

"Well, if you get caught, you can plead post-Vietnam stress syndrome anyway," she said seriously. "Our government did such a great job training our boys in guerilla warfare, teaching them to kill and hide out in jungles, it's only natural they'd run dope. As far as I'm concerned, there wasn't a shred of redeeming value in the whole experience, but it's been great for the dope business.

"Blake's a good example of Vietnam syndrome," she went on. "When we first started dating, we took a sailboat down to Colombia. He woke up one night screaming about his buddy being skinned alive—how they were ripping the flesh off his back. He went crazy. There we were out in the middle of the Atlantic on a thirty-foot sloop with fifty bales aboard, and he turns into a raving madman."

"What did you do?"

"I decked him," she said tersely. "I picked up a Stilton wrench and put his sweet ass to sleep. He said I fractured his skull, but I didn't."

"Damn," Preston said with raised eyebrows. "You're one tough lady. But it's none of my business what's between you and him anyway."

"There's nothing between us anymore except business," she said coldly, and lapsed into silence. Preston felt uneasy, and shifted the conversation back to details of outfitting the boat.

They arrived at the condo on the beach, a twelve-story building that stood above the shoreline next to a row of other similar structures, like a set of teeth. Inside, Preston tried not to gape at its spaciousness, the thick blue carpet, the luxurious drapes and the decorated furnishings. But it seemed like no one lived there—it seemed more like a movie set. April fixed him a drink and ran her finger up his shoulder, stroking the sun-thickened skin on the back of his neck and fondling his curly brown hair. She looked into his eyes softly and whispered, "I think I've finally decided you aren't a narc, but I need more information."

She offered her lips, and he took them, warm and moist against his. He put his arms around her and drew her close. "If you haven't learned this yet," she whispered, "you will before it's all over. You only live for the moment." She pressed against his expansive chest. "Yesterday is forgotten and tomorrow may never come, so let's take advantage of the here-and-now."

For just a moment, he felt a flash of guilt. Mary was home pregnant, for Chrissakes, but she told him once that she wouldn't be terribly upset if he had a fling when he was away on one of those long shrimping trips to Key West or Brownsville. But there were ironclad rules: Don't ever bring it home. Don't catch a disease. And, especially, don't blow any money on her. But until now, it hadn't been a problem, dock-side floozies and prostitutes didn't appeal to him. April was different; there was something exciting and challenging about her.

Preston's big hands tenderly explored her firm breasts, and he exhaled with erotic pleasure, "Now I know *you're* not wired."

April gasped and kissed him fiercely. "Oh, you could be wrong. Keep looking."

He did, until there was no new place to look. "God," he breathed deeply, "I've never taken drugs in my life, but if they made it this good, I'd run that boat to the ends of the earth to find it."

"Believe me," she whispered, now exploring him, "I've tried them all. They don't. Now let's quit talking." She led him to the bedroom. The bed was huge and had silk sheets.

Thoroughly mesmerized, he watched her pulling off her dress, exposing more and more of what he thought must be God's finest creation.

In a moment they were locked together in a sea of pleasure, although right from the start their lovemaking seemed to be a contest for dominance. April strove to stay on top, and he was determined to keep her down. This woman is something else, he thought. Never had he felt anything like her. He pressed his weight on her and she cried, "Don't hold me down, don't!" but he wanted to be deeper inside of her. She dug her nails into his bare back. Then she bit his shoulder— gently at first, then harder.

"Hey, easy, *easy!*" Preston grunted. But April didn't ease up—she was out of control. He felt her teeth biting down as pain shot through him. Preston released his grip on her firm buttocks. He put his hand over her face and pushed her head away, but she was caught up in her own release and kept biting. His shoulder was on fire.

"Stop, goddamn it! That hurts like hell, bitch!"

Preston tried to pull away, but he was coming in an ocean of pleasure and pain. He felt himself pumping into her, pumping out juice as he never had done before, riding a wild bronco.

Finally, his fingers closed over her nose. She couldn't breathe, and want of oxygen forced her to let go. She fell back panting heavily, sobbing. At last she caught her breath and gasped. "Sorry, lover... Sometimes I get carried away."

Preston rose up. "Well, next time I'll put a goddamn muzzle on you. Don't you ever bite me like that again!" He touched his sweat-soaked shoulder gingerly, feeling the indentations, knowing her bite mark would probably show for weeks. He hoped by the time he got home Mary wouldn't see it.

"*Mmmmmmmmm!*" murmured April happily. "You sure are a good lay, Preston."

He looked down at April's glistening body and then tried to get a look at his shoulder, but it was too dark.

"Well, I hope I checked out okay." His voice was heavy with sarcasm.

She sat up and looked at him coldly through her green eyes. "Congratulations! You just passed the last part of our routine check-out. I copulate with all the mules that run dope for us, every seedy, smelly shrimper, deckhand or one-armed waterfront drunk!" Her voice was furious. "Tell your friend Charlie to line up—he's next, you prick!"

Her verbal assault surprised him. "Sorry. I was just making conversation. I was mad at your biting me."

"Pretty stupid conversation," she snapped. Pulling the sheet around her, she slipped out of bed and fetched her cigarettes. She returned to bed and sat rigid, puffing for an interminably long time. Preston wondered what kind of crazy woman he had on his hands.

Finally, staring straight ahead, she said, "I have a friend in Colombia who was raped," she began. "They caught her with a couple ounces of cocaine and told her they were taking her to jail. Only they drove her to some filthy rooming house in Barranquilla and beat her silly and raped the hell out of her. Ten of them, for three weeks, and then threw her in prison to rot." Tears welled in her eyes. "Her parents were so terrified that they'd be removed from the social register that they took their sweet time getting her out. But payback is coming," she said through gritted teeth, fighting back tears. "Oh, yes, it is!"

Preston held her tightly, knowing she was talking about herself, and wondering what he was doing in this insane business. After a moment he kissed her, "I'm sorry about your friend, April."

14

The Tampa Connection

With her great steel masts raised toward heaven, and her handsome, white hull, the trawler *Aquarius* moved down the Pascagoula River past the Gulf Oil docks, shipyards and old fish houses. She was a proud vessel that handled beautifully. Her engine purred as Preston turned the wheel and nosed her into the dock. When he shifted into reverse and shot the power to her, the great trawler responded with ease and dignity.

From time to time, he studied the U.S. Customs documentation papers, which gave a physical description of the *Aquarius*, along with main beam and engine numbers. She was built in the Houston Shipyard, and there was a power of attorney letter from the T & A Corporation out of Delaware transferring ownership to him.

Seeing his name on it, Preston realized how vulnerable he was now. If they got caught, as captain and owner, a great deal of the responsibility for the run would come down on him—a sobering thought. "I don't care what it takes," he said, "I'm gonna come through with this load. And this will be my boat."

Worried as he was about the voyage ahead, and all the risks that beset him, he still bragged happily to his deckhand. "She's some fine boat, Charlie Hansen. It's an honor just to step foot on her. When this run is over, we're gonna make an honest boat out of her. We're gonna shrimp her from Key West to Brownsville. When winter comes and all

the other poor sons-of-bitches are tied to the dock, starving and freezing, we'll steam out to the two-hundred-fathom curve and load up on
royal reds. Listen to that big Cat purr."

Charlie, heaped miserably in the doorway, looked painfully up at
Preston through bloodshot eyes. That wonderful Caterpillar diesel
throbbed in his head. He had no idea how he got back to the Holiday
Inn, but somehow he did, with all his money missing. Now, with a
queasy stomach and a pounding headache, he was wondering if he'd
gotten the clap.

As they left the Pascagoula River, with its industrial shipyards and
docks, Charlie climbed into the co-pilot's seat and sat quietly beside
Preston. He put his head in his hands, groaning in pain. "Oooh, I
think I'm gonna die."

"Go let the outriggers down. Then die," Preston said
unsympathetically. He often began a trip with Charlie hung over. At
least that part of the trip's familiar, he thought. He waited for his
suffering deckhand to lower the great steel arms until they stretched
gracefully from the side off the vessel.

When he reached the ship's channel he pushed the throttle wide
open for the first time, and the engine responded with a high-pitched
steady roar, picking up speed. The prop-wash churned behind, whit-
ening the muddy waters of the Mississippi Sound as they headed for
the Gulf of Mexico. A north wind blustered down, the sky was clear,
and the sea spread out before them. The expanse of sizzling gray-green
water covered with wind-pushed whitecaps rolled away as far as the
eye could see.

When the sea-buoy clanged mournfully behind them, Charlie
watched as Preston spread out a nautical chart of the Gulf of Mexico.
With a pair of dividers, they plotted a course to Tampa. Charlie really
didn't feel like talking about the boat or where they were going or
why. All he wanted to do was crawl into a bunk. His stained, green T-
shirt, with a picture of a foaming glass of beer and PUGIOT'S BAR
AND GRILL in cheerful yellow letters, was draped baggily over his
sagging torso. The beat of the jukebox pulsed in his brain. Vivid memo-
ries festered: a casino sign blinking GOLDEN NUGGET in eye-searing
yellow, and PINK PALACE in god-awful pink, and THE DREAM
ROOM in green. Up and down the strip, from behind closed doors,
music blared and girls—redheads, tall blondes, short, dark Mexicans—
all smiled big smiles, suggestively dropping their glittering costumes

to the floor while shipyard workers, military men, tourists and shrimpers hooted, clapped and whistled.

"I'm going to bed," groaned his deckhand miserably, feeling the ocean swells in his temples. "This hangover is about to kill me. I'm afraid I'm gonna barf all over this floating whorehouse."

"Don't you dare puke on my boat, you hear me! You do and I'll mop it up with your ass." Then seeing his pathetic look and his trembling hands, he said, "Go ahead, but we've got work to do later. I want to get these royal red nets to where they'll fish better. I don't care what she—er, the people said. We'll probably make a drag or two before it's over. I want this boat to look and smell like a working shrimp boat."

All night long Preston stayed at the wheel, listening to the eternal rumblings and throb of the motor like a doctor listening to a beating heart, keyed for fluctuations. But all he heard was steadfast dependability as the estuaries passed far behind them. Ahead was the endless starlit horizon and rolling, dark waves chasing along in rank. Beneath their hull was a thousand fathoms. An occasional freighter passed in the night, all lit up. It was great to be back at sea again. The vastness of the rolling Gulf swells put the hassles of the last few days behind him; he was one with the cosmic ocean and the flow of the Gulf Stream.

His shoulder ached where April sank her teeth into him. He hoped the bruise marks would be gone by the time he got back. He rubbed it and thought of her again. Elation and desire flooded his body. He shook his head, threw open the wheelhouse door, and stepped into the night for a deep breath to cool off.

Then rubbing his shoulder, he thought of his gentle Mary, and then he felt guilty. You really are a bastard, he accused himself. First thing you do when you go off is start tomcatting around worse than Charlie. Here she was, home alone, pregnant and afraid. His passion wilted. "You ought to be ashamed of yourself," he said aloud. "A little snatch gets waved in front of you, and you jump on it like a hound dog after a coon." Then he thought about April, her green eyes, that golden hair, slim figure, firm body, witty conversation, and his passion came back all over again. What could he do: the new woman and new boat blended together in his mind.

When the sun peeked over the horizon, Charlie was feeling better and took the wheel. They had a long, leisurely ride, passing golden rafts of sargassum weed and watching flying fish skipping over the waves. For a while they were joined by a school of spinner porpoises that rode the bow waves.

By dark the next day, their radar began picking up land masses. Preston studied the Loran flashing their position, and he marked the charts.

"We're right where we ought to be, Charlie. Three hours from now we'll be coming in under the Sunshine Skyway Bridge—just like the lady said," Preston said.

"Lady?" said Charlie with sudden interest, feeling immediately better now that he had something on his captain. "Was that the same lady that come by the boat in the little red sports car, the blond that laid a big smooch on you?"

Preston blushed with embarrassment. "Ain't none of your business, Charlie. You don't need to know anything else about her."

His deckhand grinned and said knowingly, "I was drunk when I come into the hotel at four o'clock this morning, but I wasn't that drunk. You weren't nowhere around, and your bunk ain't been slept in. I see you walking around stiff and sore legged—you can hardly go. That's some high class stuff—too rich for my blood. You couldn't touch her kind for less than a thousand a night!"

He quit grinning when he saw his captain's irritated look. "I been working on this boat all night getting her ready, Charlie, for your information. And you just mind your own damn business." But Preston knew they had been together far too long to hide secrets.

"Well, I still want to know why the hell we're coming all the way over to Tampa to pick up some guys to go on down. Why didn't they leave from Pascagoula with us? Must cost 'em a thousand dollars worth of fuel to come over here.

"Hell, I don't know, Charlie. I wish I did, but they don't venture too much information."

Off in the distance they could see the glow of the shoreline and the Sunshine Skyway Bridge. Charlie laughed nervously. "Preston, if you want to know the straight about it, I'm a little jittery about it all myself. We could still turn around and get out of here, and save ourselves a heap of trouble."

"I got nothing to go back to. The bank's gonna take my boat and house away if I don't come up with some money. They wrote me a letter saying they were gonna call the note on my house if I didn't come up with sixty grand for the *Night Shadow*.

"But you don't have to go on, Charlie. You could back out right now. Seriously. I can set you off on the bridge, and you can walk away from this clean."

"No way, Captain! I'm going where you go."

Right on schedule, the bridge loomed up ahead of them, looking like a great string of lights, an emerald-and-gold necklace draped across the bay.

Hesitantly, Preston unhooked the microphone of the citizens band radio and turned the dial to Channel 22. "Well, here goes." He repeated the code April had given him.

"*Miss Trixie* to *Ironsides*. Can you read me?"

There was a long pause before a familiar, Spanish-accented voice came over the speaker box.

"How about it, my friend? Where are you?"

"Coming into the Skyway Bridge."

"Ten-four. See you in a little while. Keep on trucking."

That was all—a short, abrupt communication. The connection had been made.

Preston replaced the microphone. "Ain't no turning back now, Charlie-boy. We just bought the farm."

Charlie sat there dumbly, watching the cars and trucks streaming across the bridge overhead. "It's sure a long way to come just to pick up some passengers," he repeated. They passed through the span and Preston put the *Aquarius* into a circle while they waited.

"I hope to hell these guys know where they're going," Charlie fretted. "I damn sure don't want to end up in some dago jail."

"We're just the taxi drivers, Charlie. They probably do." Preston paused. "Isn't that a boat coming our way?" he asked, looking into the radar screen. As the beam swept the circumference of the grid, a small, bright flash glowed at the outer edge of the concentric circles.

"Goddamn, it sure is, and it's moving like a bullet," declared Charlie. "That must be one of those cigar boats they use for hauling pot. She must be making fifty knots!"

Out from a canal in Boca Ciega Bay, behind a luxurious summer home, came a thirty-foot boat with three men aboard. It moved so fast it hardly touched the rolling waves. In just a few moments the shrimpers could hear the scream of the jet engines as the boat approached with its red-and-green running lights showing in the dark. As it drew nearer against the lights of the bridge, they saw it bucking, leaping upward from the chop, sending explosions of spray in its forward surge.

The cruiser pulled up alongside the *Aquarius*, and another familiar voice cried out, "Hello, Preston! Hey, and here's old Charlie!"

Preston turned on his deck lights, so he could get a better look, and in a moment he recognized Raul amidst two strangers. Then his familiar Cuban voice snapped out a command.

"Turn those lights off! You damned fool!"

Confused, Preston plunged the *Aquarius* into darkness. Why should a departure be so undercover? He soon found out.

Against the starlight-reflecting sea, he saw a short and stocky crewman lash the speed boat to the *Aquarius's* starboard side. And with great muscular power, he heaved the first of two-dozen rectangular wooden crates and a big, heavy steamer trunk on deck. A sickening feeling of uneasiness and fear swept over Preston. Whatever it was, it didn't look good. Then he saw Blake moving with great agility, helping a tiny-boned young man behind him who was having a hard time maneuvering the heavy crates. "Hey fella, quit standing there and give us a hand," his voice shouted up.

"I don't like this," Charlie muttered to Preston as he went forward to help receive the first of the crates. "No one said anything about hauling anything down there."

"What's in the crates?" Preston demanded.

"Supplies," Raul answered evasively, flashing a big, white, toothy grin. "It's for our friends in Colombia. Some things are hard to get down there."

Blake was wearing Bermuda shorts and a tropical plaid shirt, as if he were ready for a vacation. All that was missing were the golf clubs and fishing rods. In the shadows of night, Preston could see his well-muscled form lifting boxes. Charlie jumped down beside them to help and muscled the next crate up on the *Aquarius'* railing. "Damn," he grunted, "these are ball busters. You got rocks in 'em?"

The thin man looked at him with a sullen expression. "No. Guns. AK-47's. Twelve to a case," he said, struggling to lift his end of the next crate.

"Guns!" Preston cried out in shock. He had sworn to himself that he'd keep quiet on this trip and avoid conflict with his new crew, no matter what they were like. But this was too much. "Guns! We didn't agree to run any guns. What kind of crap are you handing us, mister?" he spat out. "Hauling marijuana is one thing, gun-running is another."

Raul's voice turned icy. "It's too late to change now; we have a schedule to keep. You don't have no other choice, Preston. Don't make me spell it out for you."

Then he jumped into his boat and cast off. As he backed away, his voice turned jovial again. "Relax my friends. It's going to be a great trip. You're gonna be rich men when this is over. You're going down to warm weather, plenty of sunshine, tropic seas, coral reefs. I wish I was going with you to that nice warm Caribbean, my friends. Have a good voyage!"

The two younger men then threw their personal suitcases and duffel bags on board, and scrambled up after them. Blake slapped Preston on the back, "Hey, man, it's good to see you again."

Preston said dryly, "Yeah. Delighted.

"Well," he muttered as he followed the new arrivals into the cabin, "now we know why we went to Tampa."

He headed back into the dark wheelhouse. Charlie and their two new crew members followed after him and closed the door. Blake's voice was filled with exuberance. "Look, Preston, this wasn't my idea, but we're stuck with it. If you want to know the truth, this got pulled on me at the last minute, too; and, like you, I'm not in a position to argue."

The shrimper turned on him. Even in the glow of the Loran and radar they could all see his fury. "You're putting us in double jeopardy. What if the Coast Guard boards us on the way down for a routine inspection? We're going to jail flat out."

"Yeah, or what if the Colombian Navy or *Policia* catch us," said Charlie angrily. "We're dead meat!"

The bony little stranger ignored Charlie, but sprang forward and jabbed his finger aggressively in Preston's face. "Look, mistah," he spat in a harsh New York accent, "let's get something straight! You'll haul what the fuck we want you to, when the fuck we want to, and where the fuck we want you to. We're paying you to drive this boat—not to ask questions. I've got a lot of money riding on this trip, and if you give us any shit it won't be healthy. You understand that?"

Preston was taken aback by such crazy effrontery. "Whoa... Are you threatening me?" he growled, his powerful hands clenching into fists. This new guy was something else. He was offensive beyond the pale, and his accent was grating. "Let's get something straight before we go anywhere: I'll drive the boat, but I'm not gonna take crap from a punk like you.

"Easy…easy," Blake urged tactfully, stepping between them. "Just shade your ego, huh, Paul? Preston, relax! I don't want to go to jail either. We have inside information that the Coast Guard's nowhere around, and three of the surveillance satellites are down. That's why the schedule is so tight. Come daylight, we'll rig up a cargo net. Then if we see any sign of the Coast Guard or the Colombian Navy, in two seconds flat we'll winch the guns over the side and deep-six them.

Blake gave the captain a friendly, peace-making smile. "So, now you've met Paul. Sorry about the ruckus. We all want to get along out here, Preston, so just accept it. Like Raul said, there's no turning back."

Preston quietly drummed his fingers on the steering wheel, fighting down his impulse to tell them to take their boat and stick it. But Sam Lawton had made it perfectly clear what would happen if he aborted the trip or caused them problems. Raul and Blake had just confirmed it. The cops couldn't help him now—no one could.

When you lie down with dogs, you're gonna get fleas, and now I'm in flea city, Preston thought, looking at Paul, who blended back into the shadows of the cabin. There was something sneaky and dangerous about him. I'm on my own from here on. I can't rely on anything they say. These dopers are scum, so just keep your mouth shut, Preston Barfield, and maybe, just maybe you'll end up with this boat. The title is, after all, in your name. But I won't ever do this again!

Charlie looked at him questioningly, ready for a fight. He was waiting instructions.

The captain took a deep breath, slowly exhaled, and managed a grin, "Finest kind. It's your charter. If you want us to haul guns, we'll haul guns. I'm the taxi driver. Just tell me where to go."

His deckhand shrugged helplessly then looked relieved when Preston went on. "But let's get one thing straight. I'm the captain. When it comes to running the boat, and to our safety, you'll do what I say, understand?"

The scowling little man with the narrow face and crew-cut hair stepped out of the shadows and started to protest, but Blake cut him off. "That's why we hired you, Preston."

When the Tampa Bay Bridge was far behind them, and there were no tugs or traffic, Preston turned on the lights. Blake pulled a chart of the Gulf of Mexico and lower Caribbean from his duffel bag and spread it on the table. Everyone gathered around, looking at the chart. There was a course plotted that went westward from Tampa Bay around the western tip of Cuba, then twelve hundred miles across the sea, all the way down to the Peninsula la Guajira in Colombia, the northernmost point of South America. It seemed an awesomely long distance. How did I get into this mess? Preston wondered. All I wanted to do was fix up my boat and go shrimping!

15

Voyage to Colombia

Day after day the voyage continued, a solitary shrimp boat on an empty, blue ocean. Preston was alone in the wheelhouse taking Paul's watch. Even if he weren't stoned half the time, Preston didn't trust this city boy to run the boat. And the less interaction he had with him the better. He flipped on the fathometer and watched the spinning stylus etch a line on the moving sheet of graph paper. Down, down, down it went until it ran off the paper. Even the new fish-finder showed no bottom. Here we are, he thought, with nothing but sky above and miles of ocean below, out in the middle of nowhere.

Preston felt isolated, lonesome and, for the first time, no longer in charge of his own ship. It was a unique experience for him. He realized that not since he was in the war did he ever have a boss. After four years in the military, the first thing Preston did was paint a sign at the marina that read, "This is my boat and I'll do as I please." After that, no one told him what to do—especially an untrustworthy sleaze-ball like Paul. Preston wouldn't stand next to him at a bar on the hill, much less have him on his boat.

Blake also troubled him, although the captain couldn't say exactly why. When they first left Tampa, a feeling of uneasiness came over Preston when Blake insisted on learning how to run the boat, taking it off auto-pilot, steering it, learning the controls and electronics. It made perfect sense, considering the long sea voyage ahead, the risks from collision, storms and the dangers that go with smuggling—but it also made him feel expendable.

And he felt even more expendable when he overheard Paul ask Charlie in a joking fashion, "If you had to, youse could run the boat down to Colombia by yourself, couldn't you? I mean, what if our good captain here goes out to take a leak and a *fockin' shaak* grabs his pecker and jerks him overboard?" It appeared in a friendly context, especially since Paul had taken to Charlie and spent a lot of time listening to his stories of the sea, of shrimping, sharks and hurricanes. But Preston worried about the implied threat that he was replaceable. His jaw tightened and his teeth gritted as he thought about it. Just roll with the punches, he said to himself. When this is over and I own this boat for real, no one will ever tell me what to do. In the meantime, I can wade in hocky up to my nose if I have to, if I end up with this boat. Grimly, he watched the bright lights of a ship passing far off in the distance.

Paul's Bronx accent grated on Preston's ears, and so did his profanity. Hardly a sentence passed his lips without him interjecting the F-word. It gave him some pleasure that Paul sunburned himself miserably on the first day out, and hadn't thought to bring sun lotion. While Preston couldn't stand him, with his sallow complexion and hungry look, Charlie thought he was great. He listened avidly to Paul's tales of night clubs, hookers and street gangs. Puffing away on a joint, and passing it to Preston's impressionable deckhand, the city boy bragged about his relationship with the Mafia and how he knew all the angles. Charlie sopped up his tales, and made Paul feel important. He told Preston, that it didn't matter if they were lies or not, they were a lot better than TV. Charlie declared that when the run was over, and he was rich, he was heading up to New York with Paul to see the city life for himself. "After all," Charlie complained, "I've spent my whole fuckin' life in a town so small, it ought to have Entering and Leaving on the same sign."

"Charlie, watch your mouth. You can listen to Paul all you like, but don't be talking that way around me, you hear? I'm sick of it."

"Yes sir," his deckhand said sheepishly, "I won't say it no more."

Preston pushed thoughts of his gullible deckhand and the hoodlum's influence over him out of his mind. To keep awake and get away from the marijuana smoke that saturated the cabin and permeated the bedding and clothing, he walked out on deck. The captain gazed up at the unfamiliar stars of the Southern Cross that looked so very different from the dome of the night sky back home. In two weeks the voyage would be over, and if they didn't get thrown in jail or worse, the *Aquarius* would be his. With a boat like this, a man could be independent for life. Sometimes he dreamed of coming into the dock loaded with shrimp. Mary would be standing there holding their new baby, proudly overseeing the rivers of big royal red shrimp flowing up the conveyor belt, with the other captains watching him with envy.

Then Preston admonished himself, "Now don't go boxing your shrimp until you catch them. There's a whole lot of water you might end up drinking between now and then. Just be careful and get through this."

He thought of Mary, tried to visualize their house, but it all seemed vague and distant. Then he thought about lying beside his wife with his hand on her belly, feeling the unborn life inside and talking with her about the future and what they were going to name the baby. Images flowed through his mind, of holding their baby daughter, listening to her talk about school and friends when she grew up.

But the images faded and changed to April and her passionate kisses. Lust began to tingle through his body. What an endless battle it was. He rebuked himself, angry at letting himself slip, and forced himself to think of her demented attack on him in the name of passion. When he stretched he could still feel her bite.

Fearing an infection, he unbuttoned his shirt, switched on the cabin light and inspected the bruised marks that contrasted against his white skin. She must hate men, he thought. That's not my problem, but it will be if I come home and Mary sees this bite. It was amazing how her imprint lingered even after four days. He was relieved to see that it was getting smaller, healing from purple to yellow.

Preston felt someone staring at him, eyes penetrating into his back, and a chilling sensation ran down his neck. He whipped around and saw Blake looking at him with concern.

"Hey, man, that's a nasty bite. I hate to tell you this, but you'll probably die," he said with a broad grin. "The lady's got cobra venom in her fangs."

"What lady?" Preston demanded guiltily, as embarrassment flooded over him.

"The Lady of the Lake, the Wicked Witch of the North, the Snow Queen. April. It's one of her trademarks."

"I doubt I'll die from her bite," Preston said sullenly, "but I might from the goddamn fix she got me into."

"Bad as the lady is—and she is bad—I'll have to say the guns really weren't up to her. And they weren't my doing, either. There's a war going on in Colombia with feuding cartels competing for the same supply of drugs. They call the shots. If you don't bring guns nowadays, you can't play. Then it gets *really* complicated. There's the Indian nations in the middle of it, and they want guns too. Then there's the U.S. government and the CIA in there monkeying around with Latin American politics. We try to keep everyone happy—that's April's specialty."

Preston shuddered, thinking about the country he was going to. His mind went back to April. "An old flame of yours, huh?"

"Something like that. We're just business partners now. You've got to understand that she uses men the way most men use women. We practically grew up together. We used to live together back in college and developed our contacts together. But after she got manhandled and put in prison in Colombia, she changed. We went our separate ways."

Against the faint blinking lights of the Loran and the luminous green screen of the radar, Preston watched Blake staring off into the waves. Even though he was likable and fun to be around, there was something that made him uneasy about this handsome man with his ponytail and bronze skin. I don't understand these people, Preston thought, and I never will. And it's none of my business anyway. But Blake intrigued him. Why was he out here? The boy has too much polish, too much education to be riding freighters and shrimp boats. He seemed like the kind of guy who should be behind the scenes, away from the direct risks.

Preston noticed that every day Blake exercised, did calisthenics on the fantail, keeping himself fit. He looked like a young movie star.

Every morning, as sun rose up from the sea, Blake was on the fantail, working through Tai-Chi exercises. Sometimes the others went out on the deck to watch. As they laughed, Blake informed them that he was "moving like a dragon rising from hibernation," or a "nimble monkey picking fruit." He informed them that it was all about getting in touch with his "chi" and balancing his body's harmony.

But this flower child also spent a lot of time working with guns, cleaning, and inspecting them. Sometimes, Blake blasted away at the empty pop cans that the thirsty crew tossed overboard, but he refused to shoot at the flying fish that skipped ahead of the bow, which Paul and Charlie loved to do.

Once when Paul trained his gun on the dolphins riding the bow wave, Blake stormed over and angrily snatched the gun away from him. "Don't ever do that again!" he warned, and for the first time his crewmates saw his cheerful disposition turn to cold fury. "Life's too precious to waste," he told them when he had calmed down. "It doesn't matter if it's a fish, a cow, a man, it's bad karma to waste. Dolphins are special. It's really bad to kill one. I don't know if all life's the same, but I've killed more than enough people in my lifetime. I know that life's a vapor. Bang! Like that it goes away. It's a gift for God's sake. Let's not squander any of it."

"All right, all right, I won't shoot Flipper," Paul capitulated, surprised at his partner's reaction. "Jeez, don't make a case out of it, huh, Blake?"

While Blake's argument was lost on Paul, it wasn't on Charlie. "I ain't never hurt a porpoise," the deckhand said. "But as many millions of shrimp and fish as me and Preston have killed, I reckon we'll burn in hell if you're right about this karma stuff. All us fishermen will."

"Are you wasting life and killing for the fun of it, Charlie? No, you're taking it for food. There's a difference," Blake rationalized. "I love to fish, too. I don't know how it all works, I just know what works for me."

Preston avoided getting into that side of things any further, but it tickled him to hear Blake struggling with ethics. He and April made quite a pair. They both loved blathering abstractions. Still, it was a refreshing change from the monotonous conversation of commercial fishermen, seafood dealers and mechanics.

"I'm confused as hell," Preston declared. "The dope runs I always heard about, they get some good ol' boys like me, give them a chart and tell them where to go. If they get caught, they get caught. Most are dumb as stumps anyway. How come you're doing this, Blake? I know why I am, and why Charlie is, and maybe even why Paul is. He's hungry for something. But it seems like you've got more going on and probably enough money."

"Not any more. It's all gone," sighed Blake looking over the horizon, listening to the hiss of the hull hitting the waves. "I've got a lot of debts to pay. The truth is, in this business you get used to a better standard of living, and then you've got to have it. You squander it on women and cocaine. You live in the best hotels, eat hundred-dollar meals, take your friends out, buy gold like this," he said, pulling a gold medallion on a gold chain from under his shirt. "That's two thousand bucks right there."

"If you like necklaces, I guess that's okay," Preston said, trying to hide his disdain.

"Pretty decadent, huh?" Blake said defensively, picking up on the contempt in Preston's tone. "It's an investment. It's hard to invest dope money in anything real. If you buy a new car, or a Winnebago, or a boat or a house, the IRS wants to know where the money came from. About the only thing you can invest in is another dope deal. But after this, I'm going to buy a ranch in Ecuador, way up in the mountains, and breed thoroughbred horses, run cows, grow coffee, kick back and relax."

"So I've been hearing Paul call you 'Wonderman'," Preston said. "Why is that?"

"Because I can do wonderful things with explosives. Like one time blowing out a wall of a Mexican jail to free my friends. It gives you a wonderful sense of power and accomplishment. I'm also good with locks. And I know when to offer bribes and when not to. That kind of thing," Blake said proudly.

Paul stepped through the doorway. "You know, Blake," he said sharply, "I been listening. You talk too fuckin' much. Maybe your buddy Preston here is a good fellow, and maybe he ain't. How'd you like to hear him repeat all this on some witness stand? The judge would love to hear all about your little adventures. I bet Cap here would spill his guts in a second."

"Hold on, Sonny," Preston glared down on him. "I keep my word. I don't roll over for nobody."

The New Yorker gave him a mocking smirk, showing sharp, widely spaced teeth. "Oh yeah, wiseguy? Ya think so? Wait 'til the cops squeeze your balls, you'll make a deal. They got it wired so that if ya don't roll over, you'll rot in some shit hole jail forever." Then he snickered, "Why do you think Blake's stuck on this fuckin' boat? Ask him about his other little sweetie, Leela. Narcs busted her with a pound of coke, wired her up and sent her back to him. They gave her a choice: thirty years or Blake." A smirk came over his pockmarked face, showing his bad teeth. "Guess which one she picked?" He glanced at Blake to gauge his reaction.

He didn't get one. Blake was sitting on the deck propped in a corner with his legs drawn into the lotus position, with his hands in his lap and eyes closed, seemingly lost in meditation. When it was clear that Blake wasn't going to speak, the captain broke his vow not to engage the foul-mouthed New Yorker. "And you, Paul, why are you here?"

"To protect my fuckin' investment, for one thing. But it ain't none of your business. Loose lips sink ships, man. But since ya asked, I'll tell ya. Let's say I want a little adventure. I heard about you cowboys running shit up from Colombia and decided to cut out the middleman and do my own delivery for once."

Paul said he started dealing when he was in junior high, first lids then pounds. Because he never grew much over five feet tall, he became a survivor. He knew the neighborhoods and learned to vanish into alleys and basements when big kids were after him, a skill that later served him well when he started dealing. His father was a street cop in the Bronx, so he knew how cops thought and learned to avoid them.

Even as a youth, he was good at business. He shrewdly invested his money from dope deals in gold shops, real estate and used car lots—anywhere large sums of deposited cash didn't look suspicious. Paul even had an accountant and paid taxes. The money rolled in, but street dealing had lost its edge for him. The idea of voyaging to Colombia on a trawler intrigued him, and so he made his investment contingent on going.

"Well, how do you like it, now that you're here?" Preston asked with interest, looking down at the bony youth.

"Fuckin' great, man," he gave a high-pitched giggle. "Here I am— stuck on a shrimp boat with a couple brain-dead rednecks and Blake the Wonderman. When he ain't drifting off to La-La Land, he thinks he's a bird flapping around doing tai-chi or whatever you call it. Some adventure! Jeez, this is about the most boring thing I've ever done in my life!" He glanced at the clock. "I guess it's my watch, huh?" he said uneasily.

"No, it's Blake's. You missed yours four hours ago," Preston said, "But that's all right. We're coming up on our way point, the Piedro

Banks just southeast of Jamaica. We're in deep water, but it can get shallow fast and we damn sure don't want to run aground out here. You can't trust the Loran too much this far down in the Caribbean. We're too far from the towers to completely trust the numbers. You can both go back to bed. I got it, I'm used to staying up all night."

"No way," Blake said, emerging from his trance and springing to his feet with a cheery grin. "I love running this boat. I get off on watching the waves and stars. I've got it for the next four hours. Get some rest, Skipper. If we come up on a shoal or I see anything, a ship or something in our path, I'll call you."

Paul's good mood instantly faded. "If that was my watch, then why the fuck didn't you wake me up earlier, mister?" he glowered up at Preston. "You tryin' to make me look bad or something, acting like a martyr? Jesus, you remind me of my old man. Was he ever a prick!"

"Well, I'm not your father, thank God," Preston said looking at Paul with disdain. "And I'm no hero either."

"Oh, yes you are! You already saved us once," Blake said with admiration. Then he turned to Paul, "If you were there that night, standing on a burning boat in those heavy seas, waiting for those propane tanks to blow, with no other boats around, you would have thought he was Jesus Christ all right."

"Yeah, yeah, I know, he can walk on water. I heard all about it, a dozen times from you and Raul," Paul sneered. "I also heard that he was afraid to salvage the load and ran off and left it. Some hero."

With that, Paul finally managed to get to Preston. He was fed up with Paul's moods swinging between bragging and hostility. With hands shaking in fury, he swung around on his chair and looked at the punk. "Sonny-boy, I've had just about enough of you."

"Yeah, do shut up, Paul," Blake warned, sliding between the two. "I wouldn't keep screwing with Preston if I were you. I've got a feeling that he'll only take so much before he splatters you all over the deck. What's eating you anyway?"

"Nothing," Paul said sullenly. Actually, he was worried about running out of his diminishing stash of cocaine and was having a harder time managing his high. "Let him try anything! I don't like fuckin' heroes, that's all. My father was a hero in the NYPD. He was a big, ugly, overbearing son-of-a-bitch. But don't you try no tough stuff with me, mister."

The captain gave him a look that bore deep into his petty soul and jabbed his finger at him. "From now on, Paul, for the rest of the trip, I'll see to it that you never miss a single watch. I don't care if we're in a hurricane, you'll be at the wheel. That suit you?"

It didn't suit him at all. Paul hated being on watch. He was just being quarrelsome, but now he'd gotten in over his head. His entire life had been spent in New York City amidst lights, traffic and noise, living in towers of stone. Out here it was all flat. No neon signs, only eerie flashes of light from jellyfish and squid in the water. The dome of glittering, cold stars dimly illuminated the horizon-less sea. You didn't see many stars in New York. Here, out at sea, there were no familiar buildings, no razzle-dazzle, just the wind and the eternal swooshing of waves. He truly despised the idea of taking a watch. He preferred to lie in his bunk listening to the radio. He knew Preston did have power over him and he hated him all the more for it. "Hey, sorry, man," Paul said backing down. "Forget it. I really didn't mean it that way."

"Then watch your lip," Preston snapped. But he was happy to let him retreat. The last thing he wanted was a city boy running his boat. And it was his boat, after all, if all went well. Leaving Blake in charge, Preston went down into the hold and checked the oil. He enjoyed listening to the throb of the engine, thinking about the day when he would own the *Aquarius*. Never again would he have a gangster like Paul aboard.

There was something creepy about the way Paul moved. Even when he laughed, it seemed calculated and phony. His eyes were cold. He was mean, sadistic and petty. Preston tried not to look at his spidery fingers when he sat at the galley expertly rolling joints and passing them around or playing with his pills. He wouldn't have stood next to the little wretch in a bar, but now he had to be confined on a boat with him. It was amazing how small a space ninety feet could become. "Just roll with it," the captain thought, "in a couple weeks this will all be over."

On the morning of the fifth day the sun emerged from the steel-gray waves, rising up to back-light the puffy cumulus clouds on the horizon, making them glow with a majestic golden aura. As the sun rolled overhead, the monotonous blue sea took over again. Charlie went on watch, then it was Preston's turn. As they drew closer to the Equator, their anticipation grew, and the three crewmen talked excitedly about what they'd do with the money they were going to make, of women, and of past exploits. Preston just listened, wishing the journey was over, saying little.

Blake and Charlie were out on deck practicing Tai-Chi. Paul was sitting at the galley, picking seeds from a pan of marijuana. Suddenly Preston heard his deckhand shout, "Cap! Come have a look at this thing!"

The biggest shark that Preston had ever seen was swimming effortlessly alongside the *Aquarius*, keeping pace. "That's a tiger shark," he declared with awe. "What a monster!" He paced off its length along the deck. It was over fifteen feet. He estimated it weighed a ton. Blake's eyes feasted on the creature, with its immense tail fin powerfully sweeping it along. To him the shark immediately became the embodiment of power and spirit, a part of the water itself. A school of black and white pilotfish swam around its great grey head, while remoras clung to its side, mesmerizing him.

The behemoth impressed everyone, but it had the most impact on Paul, who looked down at it in terror, clutching the rail until his fingers were white. "Shoot that fuckin' thing! I want his jaws!" Until now sharks had been theoretical to him, but now here was one that was all too real. Watching its three-foot-tall dorsal cutting surface, he shouted, with a touch of frenzy, "Where's the fuckin' Uzi?" He looked around for the submachine gun, but Blake snatched it first and jerked out the clip. "Let it be, Paul. It would be a sin to shoot a shark like that." He guessed that one that big could easily be a hundred years old. "It would be like cutting down a giant redwood."

"Besides," Preston added, watching Paul's eyes bugging this way and that and trying to keep from laughing, "probably all you'd do is piss him off. Then he might jump up and snatch you overboard. He's probably eaten a man or two in his day. He could swallow a little fellow like you like an anchovy."

"Then get the fuckin' rocket launcher out and blow it to shit! Kill it! *Kill it!*" he shouted hysterically. It was clear that Paul's world had just spun out of control. He controlled the streets, he thrived with junkies, but out here, he controlled nothing. Without firepower, which he knew Blake wasn't going to allow, the shark was now the heavy. Paul shrank back from the railing, defeated, watching it wide-eyed, until Charlie slipped up behind him and said, "*Gotcha!*" and grabbed his ribs.

The city boy screamed and jumped, falling off balance against the rail, then flailing even worse. Then he took a swing at Charlie, who ducked and scurried up the mast like a monkey, howling with laughter. Shrieking like a madman, Paul charged up the ladder after him. He made it halfway up, then stopped and looked at the huge thing cruising below him and froze with fear.

The others were down below roaring with laughter, holding their sides. Paul slowly climbed back down, uttering profanity, and gave them the finger. Then he stomped into the cabin, rolled himself a big joint and puffed away until the shark faded from his mind. When Charlie thought it was safe, he climbed down, knowing that Paul wouldn't stay mad at his only listener.

Hours after the shark merged back into the depths, Blake, Charlie and Preston were still guffawing. That afternoon they sat at the galley eating the steaks, mashed potatoes and collard greens that Charlie cooked up and telling shark stories. Preston told them about seeing a big tiger swoop up from the deep and bite a four hundred pound loggerhead turtle in half. But Blake topped his story.

"I was in Hawaii when this woman got eaten by a tiger shark," he said. "She had a big estate in Maui and used to swim at her private beach every morning. Until one day this ten-foot tiger cruised in and grabbed her. Her butler and friends watched it shaking her out of the water and heard her screaming, but they were afraid to swim out to her. There was nothing they could do. It bit her legs off then came back around and got her arms. All they found was her torso. It created quite a stir, mostly because she was a rich socialite. Sharks aren't supposed to eat the rich, just the scroungy natives."

"I'll stick to loan sharks," Paul shuddered. "You can keep these fuckin' real sharks." That night, the shark came back in his dreams, looked at him with its black eyes, then snatched him off the deck. He saw himself inside its maw being chewed and swallowed and woke up from sweat-drenched sheets yelling. He smoked weed for the rest of the night trying to calm down. The episode broke his nerve. Paul was a control freak, but there was no controlling the monsters of the deep, real or imagined.

From then on Paul had to snort cocaine to work up the courage to go out on deck. Whenever he did, he glanced fearfully at the vastness of the ocean swells expecting the Godzilla-fish to return. He gave up trying to get a tan to brag about. And no matter how much dope he smoked, the image wouldn't go away. As the days passed, life at sea was taking him apart. He was at the mercy of the ocean and the creatures that lived in it. And, as much as he didn't like to admit it, men like Preston knew how to live and thrive in such a world.

"I wish we'd taken an airplane," Paul lamented, taking a deep drag on a joint. "You got no sharks to worry about. Twenty-four hours and you're down there loading up. A day later you're back in Miami drinking gin and tonics at the Holiday Inn. Now there's a real scam. Sneaking onto some jungle runway, taking off with your lights out. My dealers say it's done all the time, but you need these to do it." He held up a bottle of tiny, almost microscopic pills between his thumb and forefinger. "White Crosses," he said enthusiastically. "They'll keep you going when the chips are down."

"Yeah, they'll do that for you," Blake agreed. "But there's a lot of dead heroes hopped up on speed, buried in their planes in those jungles. Be careful with those White Crosses. Too many impair your judgement and you miss the little details that keep you alive. If you're not off the airfield in twenty-four hours, they burn your plane. They also keep a bulldozer handy to shove the overloaded heroes off the runway who crash on take-off. I'll stick to boats myself, thank you. It's a big ocean. At least you have a chance. Even if you sink, you have a lifeboat or maybe can find some wreckage to cling to and stay alive until you float to shore or get rescued."

"Unless that fifteen foot son-of-a-bitch comes across you," Charlie put in with a chuckle. "Then you're shark shit!"

"That's okay," Blake replied. "I can't think of a better way to go. Being part of the food chain would make me feel needed and give some purpose to my life, which, God knows, needs some. I'm sure shark shit helps make more shrimp. That ought to make Preston happy. Right, Cap?"

"You better believe it," Preston chuckled. "If it makes shrimp grow I'm all for it. But, God, you're weird!"

Paul gave them both a dirty look. "You're both full of shit," he said indignantly, stomped off and crawled back into his bunk.

That night, when they were fifty miles off the coast of Nicaragua, Preston checked the Loran then held the pencil with his thick, callused fingers and put another "X" on the chart, showing their slow, steady progress toward the northern hump of South America.

Day after day, the sea was a faceless horizon of blue, with occasional white cumulous clouds boiling high up into the heavens. One mile below the hull of the *Aquarius* passed a hidden submarine landscape of volcanic mountain ranges with steep slopes, and endless soft plains of mud where unknown creatures swam with big, luminous eyes, never seeing the sun. Up above where the sea ended and the blue sky began, churned the bronze propeller of the *Aquarius*, heading closer to the Equator. But on the sixth day they were out of stories and no one was able to sleep or relax.

Everyone looked on the wall where the British Admiralty Chart hung in the wheelhouse. The captain carefully marked their positions against the Loran readings all the way down from Tampa. The trail of small X's led through the Yucatan Strait, paralleling Central America and headed down toward the coast of Colombia. Now they were only inches away from land on paper.

It was three o'clock in the morning on the seventh day when the far-eastern grid of the radar screen began picking up a long, luminous flash.

"I'm picking up land," Preston called out, and minutes later the crew assembled in the wheelhouse and looked at the screen.

"Hallelujah!" whooped Charlie. "We made it. Bring on the *señoritas*!"

"I don't know," Paul's voice was agitated. "With a jake-leg hero like you running the boat we could be in Cuba. You said the Loran ain't worth a shit down here."

"Look at the chart. We've been plotting a steady course all the way down. Here's where we are," Preston said emphatically, stubbing his finger at the tiny numbers on the chart where the continental shelf began to rise near Colombia. "And there's where we should hit landfall. The Guajira Peninsula. We're right on time and in the right place."

"Relax, Paul. That's what we're paying the man for," Blake said with confidence. Hours later the fathometer verified the rise of the continental shelf. For the first time in days, a bottom began to show up from the abyss on the color fish-finder that read down to three thousand feet. The seas were calm as the *Aquarius* approached the mountainous shore of the desert peninsula. Off in the distance they saw the welcoming glow of the Morro Grande Light.

By the time the bottom rose to three hundred feet, the radar screen was displaying an elongated landmass, which Charlie said looked like a hot dog. "And here's the Peninsula just like on the chart," he said proudly. "You see, you didn't have to worry. We made it, just like I told you we would," he slapped Paul on the back, who grinned back weakly.

"As they say in the Bahamas," Blake said cheerfully, "we done reached! Now the fun begins. Let's hope we reach someone. Otherwise we'll have to go touristing up and down this coast, and that *won't* be fun." He reached for the single side band radio, turned the dial, and spoke briefly in Spanish. There was no answer, only empty static, and Blake shrugged. "I hope someone was there listening. I'll try later."

"Yeah, fun," Preston repeated. "I did my part. Now let's see you do yours. I hope you've got the right people lined up so we can get rid of these guns, get the goods, and get the hell out. It would suit the pure fire out of me if we could get loaded up tonight and get back out of here tomorrow. I haven't got the slightest interest in exploring South America, especially with a boat-load of guns."

"You're not the only one, Skipper," said Charlie, pressing the binoculars to his eyes, roving back and forth with them along an island. "There's no telling who or what is waiting for us over there. I'll tell you, if we get thrown in jail for all this, I hope to hell it's an American jail," he said patriotically.

"You better hope so," Blake said dryly. "Down here, they use prisoners for target practice. They put you in one of those little stinkholes about the size of this wheelhouse until you rot...a dirty, black hole where rats and roaches chew on your toes every night. And if you don't pay them off, the guard tells you he feels sorry for you and gives you a chance to run. That's when they blow you to hell."

"Don't you give me that horse shit!" Paul said angrily. "You're supposed to have it all sewed up down here. That's why you're Wonderman, isn't it Blake? We got them all bought off, the *Policia*, the guards, everyone, right? We're a first class operation, we go first class. Our boys don't shit around! Tell 'em!"

"Oh yeah, first class, Paul. We're supposed to have it wired down here, but who knows. Be realistic," Blake retorted as they passed the island and headed for the mainland. "There's no guarantees. Every little village chief or mayor or some other official can delay our plans at the last minute. You buy protection from the army, the navy, the big families, but it seems there's always someone else. For all we know they've changed the government since April set up the deal, and there are new officials that we haven't bought off. Then we've got Raul and Creeper's little sideline with the guns to deal with. If we're caught with guns, well, we won't have to worry about prison.

"I'd better get some things ready," he said, and left for his cabin. He pulled out the steamer trunk, opened it, and extracted several machine guns and clips of bullets. When he was satisfied that they were in working order, he carried them back to the wheelhouse.

When he saw Preston staring coldly and silently at the munitions, Blake said apologetically, "You know, when I hauled my first load twenty years ago, nobody used guns. It was a peaceful business, just a few hippies smoking dope. But the U.S. government and organized crime got into it, and now it's survival. Believe me, with satellites, spy planes and modern technology, nothing gets through unless they want it to. They buy and sell drugs to finance undercover operations. The truth is we're working for someone doing this, it's just that we don't really know who. Maybe April does, but she's not talking. I keep trying to retire, but somehow it just doesn't happen."

"Easy money, huh?" scoffed Charlie, still scanning the countryside with binoculars. "Who's Creeper?"

"Never mind," said Blake ominously. "You don't want to know."

Preston didn't want to know either. He tried to push their doublecross out of his mind. He beheld the dark, brooding peaks among the snow-capped Sierra Nevada mountains rising up from the interior, and the thorn scrub and jungle of the mainland. They resembled the fangs of an enormous alligator, dark and foreboding. Now and then, mysterious wisps of smoke snaked up from the thorn scrub where slash-and-burn agriculture was being practiced, the only sign of human life.

Running parallel to the beach, a mile offshore, they passed a few sparse huts built of cactus stem with thatched roofs, which they spotted with the binoculars. Blake said they belonged to the Wayuu Indians who raised goats and fished for sea turtles, lobster, and shrimp as well, in La Guajira Riohacha, where they were headed.

"If we get a chance, we ought to drop the try net out and maybe catch some of those shrimp for dinner," Charlie said, speaking fast and nervously. Desperate to talk about something familiar and get his mind off the dangers ahead, he went on, "What kind you reckon they got down here, Preston? Whites, Brownies, or what? I bet most likely they'd be like Key West Pinks."

"*Hush!*" snapped Preston, holding up his big paw to cut off their conversation. "I hear something!" Off in the distance they heard a faint hum. Then Blake pointed.

"The plane. Over there, I can see it coming. I must have gotten through. He's right on time."

Their spirits lifted. Blake grabbed the crude cross that April had put on the boat before they left, and climbed up on the wheelhouse. He moved with great agility, almost like a gymnast and held it up to the heavens, signaling. The twin-engine airplane drew near, its hum growing louder.

"I hope he's the one we're supposed to meet," Preston said, feeling the jitters coming again.

"Fuckin'-A, man," cried Paul, putting his hands over his eyes to cut the glare. "It's got to be. If she ain't, we got real troubles."

The aircraft dipped slightly, then passed inshore on the starboard side. Blake held up the cross and hollered, "Hey! Here we are!" Charlie whipped off his soiled T-shirt and waved it, exposing all the tattoos on his muscular, sun-reddened, lean torso. Everyone on board waved, as the plane moved down the coast. They watched it go with apprehensive eyes and worry.

"Son-of-a-bitch," moaned Charlie, "that must have been the wrong plane."

"Yeah, but who was it then?" asked Preston. "The *Policia* ?"

Blake put down the cross and stood there dumbfounded. Their exultation of a moment ago sank into despair as the plane vanished, its engine noise growing fainter and fainter. Then, suddenly, it turned.

"Hey, wait a minute," Blake yelled from the cabin roof. He held his hand over his eyes. "He's coming back!" Preston's heart thumped heavily in his chest, as the engines droned more loudly and the plane came back into sight. It approached, slowed and circled the shrimp boat twice, and once again Blake hoisted the cross, like a cross before a vampire. As they waved, the little plane came in low over the water and dropped an object a hundred yards in front of the *Aquarius*. Then it circled again, and took off up the coast in the direction from which it had come.

Preston hurried into the wheelhouse and steered toward the object at half throttle. A glowing orange bag flamed in the morning sunlight, bobbing gently on the greenish blue sea, until Charlie gaffed it and hauled it aboard. Inside the water proof bag was a neatly typed set of instructions and a nautical chart marking their course down the coast to another big island at the mouth of a river. He scanned the instructions saying nothing, until Paul insisted, "Read the thing, Wonderman! I don't like suspense. What does it say?"

Blake handed it to him. "It says to proceed down the coast until we get there. They'll signal three times with a light from shore at ten o'clock tonight, and we should return same." He tapped a big island at the mouth of the river on the chart. The Loran coordinates were written on the map with a magic marker.

Once again Preston studied the chart, making mental calculations. The island was fifty miles away and there was plenty of time to get there, but they'd be traveling along the coast in broad daylight.

They adjusted course then ambled along, three miles from shore, feeling exposed with their cargo of machine guns packed in grease. Charlie was never far from the winch, ready to jerk on the lever and hoist the crates up in their cargo bag and send them splashing over the side as they ran slowly, trying to look like an innocent fishing vessel, waiting for dark to enshroud them.

16

The Guajira Peninsula

Schools of bait fish rippled in the glassy water, and flocks of sea birds hovered, diving into them. The water erupted into an explosion as a tarpon leaped, flashing its silvery scales. Terrified little fish jumped high into the air, and Preston found himself sympathizing with them. Little fish, with predators lurking, ready to strike for the kill.

As they paralleled the coast, the mountains that rose up from the jungle and flatlands looked inhospitable to the watchers on the boat. The coastline looked bleak and burned. High rock escarpments dropped off into the sea, where waves foamed here and there in the shallow waters over the bones of rusty iron tramp freighters and shrimp boats, wrecked on rocks and shoals. To Preston, everything seemed strange and foreign. The only dependable and familiar thing was the steady chugging of the diesel, taking them ever closer to their rendezvous point. The mountains glowed in the afternoon sunlight, golden and stark, bringing out the barrenness of the shrubby desert landscape. And yet, in places, the land took on a tropical beauty. They passed by expansive beaches, white against a calm green sea.

Ever since the 1600's, the Guajira Peninsula has been a hotbed of smuggling and piracy. Once Spanish galleons sailed along these same empty shores, ravaging the Indian cultures, melting down their golden idols, and working the people to death in emerald mines. They came bearing Christianity and the sword, and left with treasures and blood.

Perhaps today the ancient gods were getting their revenge. Drugs flowed out of Colombia, spreading bloodshed, avarice and corruption into Western Civilization from the wealthiest and most powerful politician to the most humble of fishermen.

Dusk soon took over and the stars came out, displaying the big, speckled Milky Way. Now there was only darkness and stars, with the coastline dimly silhouetted against the sky. The radar screen flashed, showing the land's jagged outlines on the green-grids as they closed into shore. Charlie cooked chicken from the freezer for supper, but without his usual enthusiasm. Preston mumbled hastily through the blessing as he did on all shrimping trips, then grabbed his plate and went back to the wheel. It was proving both awkward and difficult to ask God to bestow grace on a drug smuggling trip. Appetites were poor as they all worried about what lay ahead.

Later that night, after doing push-ups on the deck, and chin-ups on the davit arm for an hour, Blake took a shower, changed clothes, and came into the wheelhouse looking refreshed. "How we doing?"

"We should be there right on schedule," Preston replied, casting a glance at the clock. "The Loran checks out, and the radar shows we're coming up on the next big island. What next?"

"Okay, we go in, and they'll signal us: three flashes and then we return same, remember?"

But the ominous wall of shoreline remained black, and the phosphorescence churned up by the propeller in the wake of the *Aquarius* was the only light.

"We go any further and we'll be past them," said Preston, breaking the throttle back. "We're in twenty feet of water, and this is as shallow as I want to go. They ought to hear us coming, if there's anybody on the island."

"I think I saw a light," said Charlie in a hushed voice, peering hard at the dark shore. "It was just a flicker, like a small fire, maybe. I hope to hell there's no pirates waiting to ambush us like the ones you talked about."

During the trip Blake had been filling them with tales of cutthroats and murders that had taken place down here, among the warring cartels.

"If there were pirates, they wouldn't mess with us now. They'd wait until we were loaded and on our way back. It's probably just a fisherman. Let's not start seeing spooks all over the place."

They waited. The tide was running out, and the *Aquarius* drifted out to sea. Then Preston turned around and motored back to the same position. A half-hour passed. It was half past ten, and still there was nothing. Then it was eleven, then midnight. Out from the mangrove swamps on shore came whining mosquitoes, and the four men waited in bug-bitten misery.

Blake was puzzled. "They're not usually late like this. I wonder what the holdup is...I don't like it."

"Wait a minute, wait a minute." Paul rushed forward, "Blake, this is bullshit. Maybe you think this know-it-all captain is hot shit but I think he's got it all wrong. He probably missed the whole island, and we're way the hell off course. I bet we came in down here, and overshot it," he stabbed his finger at the series of islands up the coast they had passed hours ago. Here's where we should be."

Preston should have been irritated, but he burst out laughing, which made Paul's eyes pop. "He's something else! Never been on a boat before in his life, and he knows all about it. Paul, why don't you stick to navigating the sewers and gutters of New York, and let me run the boat? We're in the right place, whether they call us or not."

Blake smashed a mosquito on his neck, and said wearily, "Yeah, do shut up, Paul. Quit being such an asshole. Preston's the captain—and a good one, that's why we hired him. This is a new landing spot for me, and I think he's right. We're all nervous. Let's calm down. This is where we're supposed to be. Besides, if we go shining lights up and down the coast, we're liable to get into real trouble."

Paul gave them all a dirty look, waved an insect away from his face and stomped out of the wheelhouse.

"Don't pay any attention to him, he's still on the rag," Blake said lightly. "He gets like that." The moment Paul stepped down into the galley, a big light came on at the shoreline and flashed three times from the wall of black vegetation, right where Preston had predicted it.

"There she is," shouted Blake joyously. "Two hours late, but there she is. Turn on channel thirteen on the CB and flash back."

Preston aimed the spotlight at the shore, mashed the button and threw a long beam across the water, once, twice, three times.

"*Buenas noches*, my friends. Welcome to Paradise," came a Spanish-accented voice over the radio. "Did you have a good journey?"

"Paradise, hell," mumbled Charlie, holding onto the back of

Preston's pilot chair, as if it were some kind of security blanket. "This is about as nowhere as you can get! Some joker we got!"

Blake took the microphone. "We were getting worried. Your note said ten o'clock."

"Ah, well, I am sorry," the accented voice said apologetically. "We are having some little problems here bringing your pot out of the mountains. The military is patrolling, and some little towns are holding it up."

"My God!" exclaimed Preston in panic. "Listen to that idiot talking on the air. They're bound to be listening."

"No," Blake said, shaking his head. "Don't worry, the whole coast is wide open here." He spoke into the microphone. "How long do you think it will take?"

"Oh, a couple of days, maybe a week."

"A week!" Paul cried out in outrage, having rushed back into the wheelhouse when he heard the commotion, "Hey, what is this? Tell the bastard we can't wait a week. I got things to do back in New York!"

"Tell him he's got to get the guns off tonight," Preston ordered.

Blake nodded affirmatively, and turned spoke hastily into the microphone, "We have some presents for you from Uncle Raul, two dozen crates of very ripe mangoes, and we'd like very much to get them off the boat tonight before they spoil."

"*Si, senior*, I understand. That is wonderful news. But tonight we have no one to meet you. It's part of the same little problem. Come back tomorrow night, same time. Is there anything we can bring you, any provisions?"

Blake worked his lips silently in disappointed curses, then regaining control of his temper, replied, "Yes, we're running low on food. Our milk is spoiled, and we could use some fresh fruit and bread."

"And tell him to bring some beer and pepsi's," Paul urged. "This pot makes me thirsty as hell."

"And have some good lookin' women in bikinis deliver it," Charlie whooped. "The pot makes me horny!"

"Hush, Charlie! Stop being such a cock-hound," Preston scolded, then added in a whisper, "They might take you up on it. There ain't no telling what kind of diseases you can get down here."

"And bring some beer and pepsi's, if you have any," added Blake, pointedly ignoring Charlie's request.

"Certainly, my friend," returned the voice. "We want to make your stay in Colombia as comfortable as possible. *Buenas noches*, we'll see you tomorrow night." Then he signed off.

Paul stood behind them, listening, the tip of his joint burning like a small hot coal. He laughed bitterly. "He sounds like he's with the Department of Tourism. Now what do we do?"

"Well, I guess we'll get our tails back up the coast and wait," said Preston. "At least we know where to come back to. We'll get off-shore, away from these goddamn, blood-sucking mosquitoes. I wish to hell they'd taken those guns off, though."

It was dawn when the captain got up, feeling the heat and sticky humidity of the tropic air. He opened the cabin door and stepped out on the dew-soaked deck to relieve himself. An east wind blew in his face. Clouds whipped across an angry red sky that silhouetted the over-bearing mountains of the central highlands. The engine beat rhythmically at idle as they drifted in and out with the tide. Blake told him it wasn't a good idea to shut it off. They had to stay poised for flight.

As Preston stood at the rail, adding his stream of nutrients to the ocean, he looked upon a large mangrove island several hundred yards away. In the dim morning light, he made out the form of a small house amidst the bushes and wondered why he hadn't noticed it yesterday when they came past.

Instantly, fear shot through him. Preston jumped back, wetting himself. His hands shook as he zippered his fly and he broke into a cold sweat. That wasn't a house, it was the wheelhouse of a boat, a patrol boat.

He burst into the cabin and shook Blake awake.

"There's a patrol boat out there. And they're flying a flag with yellow, blue and red bars."

"Huh?" mumbled Blake sleepily. "Are you serious?" He jumped to his feet and jammed on his pants, almost in one motion. He bolted out bare-footed onto the cold, damp deck and raised the binoculars. "Holy shit! That's the Colombian flag, all right. It's the Navy, and that's a gunboat."

Behind him came Charlie, looking tense and tight-jawed, and Paul, with wild alarm in his gray eyes.

"Now what are we going to do?" wailed Paul desperately, looking around wild-eyed. Hastily he gulped down three of his White Crosses. "Let's make a run for it."

"Keep your voice down," commanded Preston, "and don't be a fool. They can outrun us in nothing flat. We should drop those guns overboard and ease offshore."

Charlie was almost paralyzed with terror. "Let's do it. I'm ready," he wheezed and started swinging his arms nervously. "I knew this was going too smooth. We gotta get the hell out of here."

"No, wait," ordered Blake softly. "Take it easy. They're too close. If they see us running, dumping things and acting suspicious, they'll come after us for sure. This could be just a chance meeting."

"Who wants to take a chance?" Paul screamed. "Come on, I'm with Charlie. Let's make a run for it! Let's break out the machine guns. We've got enough guns to equip a fuckin' army. Let's use 'em. A good offense is a good defense."

"Calm down. Just sit tight, Paul," said Blake softly, "and for God's sake, keep your voice down. Sound travels far over water."

"No way," Paul said sharply. "I'm not going to let them board us and shoot me without a fight. You can do what you want to, Blake. I'm getting a gun."

Preston grabbed his arm, "Wait a minute..."

"Let go of me, you mother..." Paul snarled and slammed his hard, mean fist into Preston's solar plexus. The captain let out a grunt and staggered a bit. Then, without thought, Preston's big fist sent him sprawling against the wall with one crashing blow. With blood trickling out down the side of his mouth, Paul slid down on his haunches, looking dazed.

"Sit tight, damn you!" Preston hissed. "You'll get us all killed."

With slow, detached thoughtfulness, Blake looked down at his fallen cohort. "Get a hold of yourself, Paul," Blake commanded sharply, in a whisper. "You make any more fuss and I'll deal with you myself. Understand? We don't need a brawl in the middle of this."

Paul staggered to his feet, holding his jaw. "No one lays a hand on me and lives, you big motherfucker," he spat out. "But don't worry, I won't do it now." He stomped off to his cabin, Preston following his every move with apprehension, afraid that any minute, he'd return with a machine gun and turn on him.

"Paul does have a point, though, Preston," he yawned sleepily. "We've got nothing to lose. If they even suspect what's in those crates, they'll kill us." The greater the danger, the slower Blake seemed to become. His eyes became heavy-lidded and thoughtful as he forced time to slow down, while he sorted out the possibilities.

Then he turned to his cohorts. "We can't break open those crates. There's no time, but we've got enough .45's and ammo to go around. If they come over, I'll bullshit them and offer them money. If that doesn't work, I've got a little surprise.

"Charlie, help me get my trunk in here." A moment later they dragged a heavy military surplus steel trunk into the pilot house. Blake pulled out the components of a large weapon. "This is a Heckler & Koch grenade launcher," he said after assembling it. "If we hit them with this, it will be all over but the crying." Reaching again into the trunk, he said, "Here, take this," and handed Preston a .45 automatic pistol, butt first.

Preston grimaced, but took it. Blake's voice became firm. "Don't show your guns until you're ready to start pumping lead, understand?

"Oh, no!" Preston snapped back. "I'm not killing anybody. That's where I draw the line."

"Really? See if you say that when they come in shooting! If you believe in any kind of God, you'd better start praying they move off down the coast. And in the meantime," he said stifling a yawn, "I'm going back to bed. Wake me if they come over."

"What?" cried Charlie, not believing what he'd just heard.

"I said I'm going back to bed." Blake yawned again. "This is too early in the morning for me to go through this kind of a hassle."

To Preston's silent question of utter confusion, the hippie shrugged, "Well, they might not board us. Or they could take half the morning before they do. And if I'm gonna die, I'd rather be rested before I meet my maker to argue my defense." Then he climbed into his bunk, pulled the sheet up around his head, and mumbled, "Remember, wake me if the action starts."

The rest of them looked at each other with disbelief and confusion. They walked back out on deck.

"He's either the gutsiest son-of-a-bitch I've ever seen, or he's totally nuts!" muttered Preston.

"Nuts!" Charlie forced a nervous cackle, but the tension and gut-gripping fear was broken. There was a touch of hero worship in his voice. Now it was only a matter of anxiously waiting and watching the gunboat.

For the next hour Charlie sat in the wheelhouse, binoculars glued to his eyes until they were red, but the boat never moved. Paul sat in the galley, smoking marijuana, machine gun on his lap. Now and then they all cast an unbelieving glance at the sleeping Blake.

"Hey, they're moving," Charlie suddenly cried out.

Paul scrabbled out from behind the galley table, grabbing his machine gun pistol and leaped to his feet. Instantly, Blake burst into the cabin jamming a shell into the grenade launcher. Obviously, he had never been asleep. He stood at the doorway, his hands clasped over his eyes to cut down on the glare of the rising sun. "Stay back," he said to the others. "I've only got one shot with this, and we've got to make it count."

A long tense silence elapsed. Finally, Preston said, "I can't see. Are they headed this way?"

"No, I don't think so," Blake said with a gasp of relief. "They're moving down the coast."

A few minutes later the boat disappeared from sight. Preston turned on the radar and watched the grid as the overhead beacon turned around and around. Suddenly the target disappeared. The screen was empty save for the outline of the shore and the mangrove jungle. No boat.

"They're gone, thank God," said Charlie, at last, breathing a great sigh of relief. "I don't think I could have stood it another minute."

"Yeah," Preston agreed reluctantly. "But they could have disappeared into some cove or creek, and we'd never pick them up. Maybe we got by with the guns, but what I'm worried about is what happens if they're here when we pack out the load. Maybe that's why they didn't pop us...they wanted us to be good and loaded before they made their move."

"Let's not get too paranoid. Maybe they're here to guard the load. There's pirates around, you know."

When they settled down, Paul breathed a big sigh of relief.

"Sorry, guys, guess I lost my cool."

"You sure as hell did," Blake replied flatly. He put his arm around Paul's bony shoulder and explained to the others, "Paul's a little out of his element here. You ought to see him on the street. He's the gutsiest balls-against-the-wall dealer I know. I've seen him talk us out of situations in Little Havana and Harlem that almost made me crap my pants."

Paul grinned appreciatively, and grimaced at the pain it caused. "That was some wallop you gave me," he said with a tone of respect.

"Sorry about that," Preston lied, eyeing the machine gun pistol still clutched in Paul's hand. "Let's put the guns away, huh?"

Paul snickered and said in an almost friendly tone, "Hey, don't worry, man. I admit it, I screwed up and freaked out. No hard feelings, huh?"

Preston nodded, "Sure," but didn't believe him. He shook his finger at Blake. "We'll keep the guns on board until tonight. But if your buddies don't pick them up when we go back, they can go diving for them. Understand?"

Blake looked uneasy, but didn't agree. Instead he side-stepped the issue by saying, "Let's hope it doesn't come to that."

When darkness came, the *Aquarius* moved quietly down the shoreline and made contact with the shore base. Then out from the dark beaches came the canoes—at least that's what Preston thought they were. The four long, flat-bottom boats, twenty and thirty feet long, with pointed bows and flat sterns, called *bongos*, were built from jungle timber and powered by big outboard motors. Two of these craft filled with black men pulled up beside the *Aquarius*.

"These are Indians?" Preston wanted to know, looking at their dark Negro faces. They were dressed in threadbare rags, coated with soil and grease, that obviously had far more wear than fabrics were ever designed to take. Some had on T-shirts that said BUDWEISER, or caps that said, FORD, CHEVY, or CATERPILLAR. Much of their clothing had been brought down by shrimp boats and smugglers as items of goodwill and trade.

"Indians they are. They're Wayuu," came Blake's answer above the murmur of unfamiliar language. "If you were expecting something out of *National Geographic*, with them wearing loincloths and feathers, forget it. That kind of Indian is gone forever.

"It looks like there's also some Mestizos, the Spanish blacks, working with them, which is unusual. They're probably involved with the FARC, the revolutionary group that's trying to overthrow the government, or at least get a voice in it."

"So we're running guns for the Farts?" Charlie hooted aloud, and broke into nervous laughter.

"It's *fark*. F-A-R-C," Blake chuckled. "It stands for Fuerza Armadas Revolucionarias de Colombia. They used to finance their operation by kidnaping wealthy people and holding them ransom. They still do, but lately they're doing more with drug money. They have connections in Cuba and with other revolutionary groups in Nicaragua and El Salvador.

"The people are desperately poor down here," he went on seeing Preston's chagrined expression. "So we try to help them. My friend helped them run electricity down from the mountains," he chuckled, "so they can steal it from the power lines. Nowadays you see huts with television antennas on them."

As the Indians paddled closer, the crew of the *Aquarius* could see groceries stuffed into woven fiber baskets heaped on the bottoms of the boats. And to their disappointment, they could see the baked loaves of bread all crushed, and bananas squashed as they were thrown up on deck.

Charlie was especially angry. "Look at what them sons-of-bitches did to our groceries, Preston. They ain't got bat shit for brains. You say they're Indians, but they look like a buncha coons to me"

"Be quiet, Charlie," Preston ordered. "They might hear you."

"Indians don't understand English," Blake retorted. "Most of them don't even speak Spanish, but just in case one might, I'd be careful what I say. I swear, Charlie, you and Lupino make a good pair—a bunch of racist, redneck assholes!"

After the Indians handed up the groceries, a large cruiser pulled up alongside with an American on board. Even from a distance, he stood out with his hefty red beard, white skin, and a joyous smile of welcome. His good humor contrasted most of all with the sullen and suspicious smaller men around him.

He climbed aboard with his arms spread apart, like Jesus welcoming the fold. Blake rushed forward, and they embraced.

"Bob! Man, it's good to see you again!" cried Blake with great enthusiasm.

The bearded man stood back and looked at his fellow smuggler, "You've come to stay!" His eyes twinkled with happiness.

"No, not yet," said Blake sadly. Then he introduced his friend to everyone on board, and he warmly shook hands all around.

In bits and pieces, Preston gathered that this red-bearded young man, whom he thought acted a bit like a groovy air-head, was the "whip" behind the organization, the man who got things done down there. He supervised the loading of boats, freighters and planes for selected customers. Creating his own brand of Peace Corps, he helped them defend their land rights against the Spanish, and arranged to have smugglers bring in clothing, food and medicine for them when they could. He was wanted in the States—a man without a country, living in perpetual exile. Like Blake he lived everywhere and nowhere.

It wasn't always that way. Bob was in college with Blake and April. They all made friends with a Colombian business major whose family owned a coffee plantation. They smoked grass together, did psychedelic mushrooms, peyote, and laid far-ranging plans for the future. It was illegal to grow marijuana, but from between the cornstalks of the impoverished *fincas*, the mountain farmlands, sprouted the seven-leafed hemp plants. Before long, the smugglers looked with pride at the waving fields of pot that grew on the mountainsides and in the valleys.

They also helped finance the coca fields in the mountains for their burgeoning cocaine trade. The Wayuu and agricultural peasants had a long tradition of chewing coca leaves mixed with lime juice to keep up their energy each day for farming in the high altitudes.

Preston studied this over-ripe hippie of the sixties with his burly red beard and childish simplicity with disgust. He looked at the Indians fingering the crates of guns and thought, "If this is the loving kindness they spread about, I want no part of it."

"Look," he said, "before we do anything else, I want these guns off this boat! I don't want anything to do with your politics or your revolutions, you hear me! We almost got caught by the Colombian Navy this morning."

"Is that true?" Bob asked, looking at Blake doubtfully, stroking his beard and frowning.

"We saw a patrol boat. It was probably paranoia on our part, but it scared the hell out of us. It was definitely *Fuerza Nava*."

"We've got them paid off. But I'll admit it's kind of strange, them hanging around. Normally they run further up the coast when a load's coming through so they won't witness it. I'm sorry we didn't get the weapons off last night. There would have been trouble if they knew about them, but we just couldn't get our act together," the American said with regret. "I know it must have given you a bad time."

In Indian dialect, he ordered the men to take the guns off. A wave of excitement swept over them. Banishing their impassive lethargy, a dozen Indians scrambled on board and began pointing to the twenty-four crates in the cargo bay with happy grins. One wild-eyed young man, with hair that flopped over his eyes, pantomimed shooting a machine gun with a dangerous smile.

Preston was nauseated by the display of would-be murder. The mixture of this erstwhile flower-child and the weaponry was too much for him. Preston persisted, "What I want to know is when we're going to get loaded and get the hell out of here."

"Look, mister," Bob said patiently, looking a little offended, "We're doing our best. But the countryside's crawling with narcotics agents and the DEA. The U.S. government pays the military to help them find smugglers, and we pay the military in turn to lead them on wild goose chases down the coast. Things are a little hot right now—it may take a few days."

Eighteen crates were hauled off, but six remained on deck. Before Preston could ask why they weren't removed, the red-bearded one spoke up, "There's been a last-minute change in plans. We just got orders that after you load up, you are to deliver the rest of these crates up the coast to our friends in Cartegena. We owe them a big favor. It shouldn't slow you down any, or take you much out of your way. A boat will be there to meet you. Just before you leave, I'll give you the Loran numbers and the time."

Preston exploded, and even Blake looked angry, but his friend Bob shrugged, "You know the game down here, Blake. We have to play along to get along."

"We're the taxi drivers," Blake nodded—for the first time, not meeting Preston's eyes. "Just tell us where to go."

Preston said evenly, "If we see any sign of *Policia*, those guns are going over the side, do you understand?"

"Only if there's no other way. This drop is important," the red-bearded smuggler said firmly, as he got back into his boat.

They ran back offshore and waited. Preston had vowed not to ask questions, but his curiosity was getting the better of him. "There's a couple of things that's bothering me about this little operation," he said to Blake when they were alone in the wheelhouse, "and you don't have to tell me..."

"Such as..." Blake said, taking a toke of the marijuana that Bob left them.

"Such as April. If everyone is so buddy-buddy down here and it's all sweetness and light, how come she got raped? And how come she's back messing with them?"

"She's not messing with them. It's a different faction." Blake shook his head sadly, as he drank his coffee. "At the time, April got into trouble because she didn't understand the culture. She was just a twenty-year-old hippie, out to defy her father and get out from under his financial control. She made a few friends down here on her own, but if she just traded on her father's name, she could have been a queen.

"If she'd have stayed with Bob and me, she wouldn't have gotten into trouble. But instead she was flaunting money around, making buys in Cartegena. The whole time she thought she was on a level playing field, investing her grandfather's inheritance buying drugs and successfully building a network of college kids to run drugs through airport customs, she was pissing off the machismo Colombians. They thought she was just a smart-ass bimbo that ran coke through the Miami airport. She screwed up royally by having a fling with a high government official and pissed off his wife, who came from one of the richest and most powerful families down there. The Maiquetia cartel decided they'd humble her and give her some worldly experience. They kidnapped her, passed her around to their friends for a couple of weeks, and beat her up.

"April managed to bribe someone and got word to her father. He's a big muckety-muck in the U.S. Senate and head of the Latin American Relations Committee and could have squelched it right then. But instead of hopping a plane, storming down to the *Policia* and demanding his daughter, he went round about through friends of friends, keeping his name clean. That's why it took so long. She hates him for it, and it changed her."

"But not enough to get out of the business?"

"No, just the opposite, now she's in it with a vengeance. It made her into a very different person, a much more dangerous one. Now she attends dinners and banquets on Latin American Affairs in Colombia and Washington. That's how she and Raul got to know each other. He's the Maiquetia cartel's North American representative who likes to be the only Latino in a crowd of Anglos. He doesn't know anything about what happened to her, and neither do the other Colombians. They don't associate her with that hippie girl, but sometimes April worries me. She's carrying a big grudge."

"How long do you think we'll be waylaid?" Preston asked, wishing he hadn't asked. He decided to curb his curiosity from now on, remembering April's warning, the less he knew the better.

"It better not be too long or it will throw the schedule off, and we could run smack into the Coast Guard coming through the Yucatan Channel. I don't much like the idea of making that second gun drop myself, but there's a lot going on that we can't know about."

Preston stepped down into the galley and fixed himself a cup of coffee. Paul and Charlie were emptying a bag of green, crushed resinous pot buds that the American had given them onto a dinner plate. The green stuff was Sinsemillia. The brown stuff they hadn't opened yet they called Colombian Gold.

The air reeked of the pungent smell of marijuana, and Preston watched Paul's spidery fingers meticulously sorting out the chunks of buds from the hard stems and seeds. He rolled up a bomber, lit and passed it to Charlie, who inhaled deeply and breathed out with pleasure, "This is *goo-ooo-d* shit."

Preston jerked the windows down in the wheelhouse and rejoiced in the hot tropical air that blew in, bringing clarity. When this is over I hope I never smell that stuff again, he thought wearily.

Seeing his deck hand's eyes glazing over, he called him into the wheelhouse for a private talk. "I need you straight, Charlie. Not all doped up. I don't want you to smoke anymore, you hear? At least not until we get the pot loaded, drop off the guns, and get out of here. After that, I don't care what you do."

Charlie took a quick drag and tossed his joint into the sea. "I'll quit, Preston. Whatever you say, you're the captain."

"That's right, Charlie-boy," Paul interrupted sarcastically from the doorway behind them, "Do what the admiral says." He grinned at Preston, "You sure got it made with Charlie, don't you, Skipper. He follows you around like an old shoe."

Charlie's pride was offended. "I ain't no old shoe! But when he's right, he's right! There ain't no telling what can happen." Preston gave the young man a look of contempt, one that said his comments weren't worth answering, to which Paul responded with a derisive laugh, and went back to his dope.

Blake looked at them wearily. "Jesus, I hope we don't get stuck down here, like last time. Not only will it screw up the schedule, but if you assholes go to bickering, it will drive me nuts."

"What happened last time?" asked Preston suspiciously.

"Three years ago, I came down here on a motor schooner to pick up a load. We had to go up a river and wait for the pot to be delivered. The mosquitoes ate us alive, the trip was a bummer. Something overheated, the engine blew, and we were stuck! We stayed there for a month trying to get parts. It was miserable."

"So what happened?" the captain asked.

"Someone finally towed us into Santa Marta and it took three more weeks to have the right parts flown down from Miami. I got a good case of the clap while I was waiting. But finally we got it running, picked up the load and brought it into New Orleans. The whole scam went off slick as a whistle, but late. But this time we've got to come in on schedule. We can't be late."

For two more tedious days they waited, running out, drifting back, but never shutting off the engine, always listening to the radio for the go-ahead. The gentle throbbing of the pistons became part of their existence. Preston tried to banish his worries and went back to re-reading his paperback novels. Charlie brought out his usual stacks of porno magazines, and once again he went back to his old habit of twiddling his thumbs. Meanwhile, between smoking joints, Blake was out on the fan tail, doing his thing—hours of calisthenics, keeping himself in shape for what lay ahead.

17

Packing Out

On the third night, the *Aquarius* chugged slowly back up the coast to the now all-too-familiar black mangrove forest below the burned mountains. After light signals were exchanged, a cheerful Latin voice came on the CB. "Good news, gentlemen. Tonight we are going to pack you out and send you home!"

A cheer went up from the crew of the *Aquarius*. Gloomy spirits climbed—freedom was in sight. "Please stand by," the voice continued. "The trucks will be coming down from the mountains in a few minutes."

Another cheer went up and, with lifted spirits, Charlie and Preston yanked the hatch covers open in anticipation of the load.

With the startling suddenness of a ghostly apparition, lights appeared on the black mountain. The trucks were rolling, casting their beams around the roads that wound down through the barren, burnt hills. Excitement swept through the crew, and the image would be etched forever into Preston's memory.

When the first three boats pulled up to the stern, twelve Indians with long black hair and copper skin charged aboard like pirates with machetes strapped to their sides, and he was once again appalled at their poverty and behavior. They piled on until the back deck was mobbed. Then the first of the pot-loaded boats arrived, their ragged crew formed a human chain, whisking the bales along, throwing them up on deck. There seemed to be no limit to the boats or the bales that kept coming. The work went on through the night.

Up until that moment, the bales of marijuana had always been theoretical to Preston. The closest he'd come to seeing one before was when the *Night Shadow* burned, and they were just cubes bobbing around the sea. Now he was looking at them stacked high on this steel-hull trawler that was registered in his name. One bale alone was enough to send him to prison for years, and still they kept coming.

Blake and Paul supervised the loading to see that the Organization didn't get cheated. Paul put each bale on a portable scale and called out the weight, which Blake recorded. Each bale had a number sprayed on it. They were all tightly compressed, neatly covered with double-wrapped burlap and sealed in plastic. The bales weighed anywhere from fifty to a hundred pounds each.

"This one feels like it's got a rock in it," said Paul, lifting one up and sending it thudding down on the deck.

"Hold it off to the side," Blake ordered. "At twenty bucks a pound, that's a good price for a rock! They sure are getting shoddy down here. You can't trust anyone anymore."

For some reason, perhaps a release of tension, Preston thought that was terribly funny. "Crooks crooking crooks," he laughed aloud.

In a perverse way, it was just like the fish business where "stealage," as the fishermen called it, went on all the time. Fish house owners like Sam Lawton deducted seven pounds of "water" from each hundred-pound box of shrimp they bought, even though they were usually drained and dry. Then retailers always added a scoop of ice to a bag of seafood then weighed it and priced it.

Blake grinned back at him. "It's really a two-way street. Some of the Cuban Mafia have been paying them with counterfeit money down here. But that's life!"

Paul looked at Preston with hostile eyes. "What makes you so high and mighty, mister. You ain't no different from us…or then again maybe you are. This self-righteous bastard pisses me off." Then he tossed off, "Maybe he's a goddamn narc!"

Charlie was helping stack the cubes of compressed marijuana buds and leaves down in the hold. He crawled back out briefly when the first wave of loading was completed and grabbed some air while the canoes went back for more. The deckhand made a futile attempt at brushing away the leaked-out litter of seeds, leaves and bits of stems from his sweat-soaked purple T-shirt.

"Damn, I'm itching all over," he complained. "Soon as we get underway, I'm gonna throw these clothes overboard if I have to ride home buck-naked."

"Don't throw them away," said Blake. "Give it to these guys. Normally we bring clothing down to them from the Salvation Army, but there was no time." There were about twenty natives who stayed on board, but it was hard to tell just how many more were out there in the darkness. One pantomimed lighting up a cigarette and pointed to the Lucky Strikes in Blake's pocket. He offered a cigarette to each native until the pack was empty, and they all happily lit up.

"They won't smoke dope, but they love American cigarettes," explained Blake. "They cost like hell down here and finding a good smoke is hard to do."

"Since when do you smoke?" Preston asked curiously, "I thought you said tobacco was bad for you."

"Oh, I don't, but they do. I always bring some down to make friends. That reminds me..." He produced several cartons of cigarettes from the cabin, opened and passed them around.

Charlie looked at the Indians puffing away, the tips of their cigarettes glowing brightly in the darkness. "I'll say one thing for these guys...they sure know how to pack out a boat!"

"They ought to," agreed Blake, tossing his ponytail back and wiping pot dust out of his eyes. "That's all they do—pack out airplanes, yachts, sailboats, tugboats, shrimpers—anything that floats or flies. We pay them a dollar a day just to sit around and wait. They're on retainer, so to speak."

"A dollar a day!" echoed Charlie with outrage. "I'm glad I don't work around here. I couldn't stand all the loving kindness y'all spread around."

It worried Preston that the boats that had just unloaded hadn't left, and that more Indians were coming aboard. Their empty canoes created quite a traffic jam around the sides and stern of the *Aquarius*. New arrivals crowded into every available space, and were sitting on the railings or propped up against the gunnels as spectators. Some were climbing up on the wheelhouse roof and Preston stormed forward and said gruffly, "Hey, get down from there. You'll break the antennas, and get your butts fried." It was only after he climbed up, and approached two swarthy Wayuu men who were looking at the radar that they turned and jumped to the deck.

"This is getting out of hand," Preston said. "How much more is coming?"

"I don't know," replied Blake. "Get on the radio and call for me. Our people over there speak English. Whatever you do, don't let any of these guys into the cabin. You better watch them. They'll steal electronics off the walls and the engine right out of the boat. Cover the cabin. Things can get out of hand quick, especially at the last minute."

"Wait," he called. Blake grabbed a machine gun pistol, and shoved it into Preston's hands. "This will add a little authority."

Reluctantly, Preston took it from him. He didn't like the idea, but looking at the growing number of men with machetes and knives, he was glad he had it.

The captain guarded the wheelhouse doorway, awkwardly clutching his machine gun pistol as if it were an oversize salami. He pushed through the cabin door, and slid it shut tightly behind him, and keyed the mike. "Hey, out there," he began urgently. "How many more boats you got bringing this...this...*stuff!*" He couldn't make himself say "pot" on the air.

Just then, three Indians yanked back the sliding door and burst into the cabin. Immediately one had the chest of drawers open, rummaged through the clothing, and jerked out a pair of pants and measured it against himself. Another began pulling the sheets off the mattress, and the third stood there like a perplexed shopper, looking at shelves of goods and wondering where to start.

"Hey!" Preston cried, hurrying after the first one. The object of his pursuit was a large, pot-bellied man with wild, bushy black hair and a toothless smile. Preston grabbed him by the shoulder, jerking his thumb back at the open doorway.

"Hey, move it...get out of here. We don't allow visitors in the cabin."

The visitor grinned and ignored him, still clutching the trousers. Preston turned to see the other two going through the silverware in the galley, inspecting the stainless forks and spoons and stuffing them into their pockets.

Preston pushed the three Indians out of his way and yanked open the sliding door just wide enough to expel them. Quickly he slammed it shut, and there was a howl of pain. The door had mashed a young boy's hand, and Preston jerked the door back so he could get loose. He felt sickened and guilty. But that was all it took. First in was the wounded youth, with ribs protruding visibly through his dark skin. He fell in on his hands and knees and looking up accusingly at Preston with large, sullen eyes. Behind him, stepping on and over him into the cabin, were a half dozen others, rummaging, grabbing, and stuffing things into their pockets. Still more were coming.

Preston grabbed the machine gun. "All right, enough is enough!" he bellowed. "Clear out before I blow your freaking brains out!" Standing a good head taller than the human wrecks he pointed the gun at them furiously. His barrel chest, big arms and grim expression made an impression. Slowly they backed out the door, yelling to the rest that Preston had a gun. For a moment that seemed to sober them up—no one moved. They stood there watching him intently as he closed the door behind him, backing the men out on the deck. He pointed the gun at them and told them to get moving.

For a moment it seemed to sober them up. They stood there watching him intently, studying his face, then saw he was bluffing.

The Wayuu broke into contemptuous laughter as they advanced. Preston stood there, looking sheepishly at the weapon. In a second they had surged back into the cabin. "I can't shoot someone over silverware and food," he said disgustedly.

"No, but I can, you fuckin' wimp!" Paul yelled, pushing through the crowd, beating them out of the way with his .45 until he got inside. He aimed his gun at the Indians, snapped off the safety and snapped out a stream of angry street Spanish. For a second, his eyes glittered with a savage light and everyone saw death in them. Brutally Paul pistol-whipped the Indian nearest him and knocked him into the others. Laughing maniacally, he shouted, "Try some of that, bush bunny. Get out or I'll blow your fuckin' brains out!"

In one of the most violent countries in the world, violence was something they understood. They backed out and went back to work.

Meanwhile Charlie climbed out of the hold, panting. He looked with chagrin at the large cruiser that had just pulled up.

The next bales that came aboard were marked differently, each had a blue spot sprayed on the burlap. The red-bearded American was standing on the bow. "Here comes the good stuff," he called out to Blake. "There's some Sinsemillia here that will knock your socks off."

"And the other?" Blake called back anxiously, casting a concerned glance at Paul, who was still aggressively guarding the cabin.

"It's all here," announced the hippie with a joyful grin that split his red beard with white teeth. "Every bit of it!"

Blake grinned back and nodded, and Preston had the distinct impression that something was being discussed, and Paul didn't seem to be a part of it. Maybe it was another part of crooks crooking crooks, but it made him uneasy.

Then he saw four Indians crawl down the ladder of the engine room, and the others started pitching bales down to them.

"Blake, Paul. Tell them to stop," Preston bellowed. "You said we wouldn't put none down into the engine room. Remember what happened to Lupino. The same thing could happen to us. We could have a fire, or spring a leak, anything..."

"We'll keep a corridor open," answered Blake. He looked at Preston guiltily. "There's no choice. I'm sorry. We've got to put it somewhere."

In a short while the *Aquarius* was sitting heavy in the water, the four hundred bales weighing sixteen tons. When Charlie complained again to Preston about their dangerous packing, the captain stormed over to Bob, the whip man, and said flatly, "It can't stay there, tell them to re-pack it. I don't care where else you put it, you can stuff it in the bunks if you have to."

"That's your problem," the red-bearded American said. "You better get moving. By the way, here are some presents for you and your friends."

"More dope? No thanks, I don't smoke the stuff," he said dryly.

"No, it's a gift for your women," he said warmly, pulling out a handful of necklaces. "They're love charms. They'll keep you happy the rest of your life."

Paul cut him off, "Look, asshole, just charm your bush-bunnies off this boat before they steal us blind! And while you're at it, take the rest of these guns with you. No one's paying us to run freight for you." For once Preston agreed with him.

"Too bad," Bob said solemnly, "but that's the new deal. You better deliver the rest of them up the coast. It's a last-minute thing. Take it up with Raul when you get back." Clutching his gun, Paul responded with his usual explicative. The red-bearded hippie spoke to the Indians in Wayuuaike dialect, ordering them to leave but without much conviction.

They looked back, laughed and shook their heads. Then, with the increasing urgency and excitement that always came when boats were packed out and ready to go, everyone reached out his hands and called for pesos.

"Don't give them any money," urged the hippie as he climbed off the shrimp boat and back onto his launch. "It will spoil the economy down here and cause inflation.

"Have a good journey back," he called, waving goodbye. "And watch out for the Great White Shark"—the U.S. Coast Guard. A handful of Indians went back with him. The rest remained behind. "The best way to get them off is to get going," Bob called out as he pulled away.

This seemed to be a signal to the ones who remained, and they went wild. They swarmed over the boat, trying to force their way into the cabin. One was doing his best to unscrew the propane tanks and drag them off. Thirty pairs of hands groped around, fingering everything, trying to tug Blake's bright flower-print shirt off his back. Fingers reached into the wheelhouse windows, taking fruit off the table, canned goods. There were swarthy-looking men on the roof. Two were trying to dismantle the radar, even though it was firmly bolted. One was pulling at the co-axial cable, the other sawing away with a machete.

"Hey, goddamn it, quit that!" Preston shouted. Holding his machine gun pistol awkwardly by the barrel, he scrambled up to the roof, grabbed the one cutting the cable, and shook him like a rat. "What the hell do you think you're doing?" He threw him down onto the deck, an eight-foot drop. "Leave our stuff alone!" The rest scattered before him. When Preston jumped back down, the man, unhurt by the fall, was waiting for him. He was small and evil-looking with a long scar across his throat. He picked up his machete and scowled menacingly as he stepped forward.

Preston stared him down. He made a fist, and the man stood his ground, but just for a moment before he started backing away. Just then, Paul catapulted forward, churning through the crowd, leaving in his wake a chorus of yelps of pain and outrage. He snatched the machine gun pistol by the barrel from Preston's hand and swung it around, battering an Indian in the face, knocking him to his knees. But the pot-bellied, toothless Indian outweighed him. He gave a cry of anger, knocked away the gun and tackled him. They crashed to the deck together, and the Indian groped for his scrawny throat.

"You just messed up bad, asshole," the New Yorker howled, flinging his assailant off with amazing force for someone so small. Before anyone knew what was happening, Paul was on top of the man, savagely beating him. He had him pinned with his knees on his arms and was pummeling his face. The man was half-dead, blood gushed from his lips and broken nose. He was in a pool of blood where the New Yorker was insanely banging his head into the deck, howling like a madman. Preston's big hand reached down and jerked Paul into the air. "That's enough goddamn it."

Paul stared at him with the wild eyes of a maniac, his nose bleeding. "That'll teach those bastards," he cried out, and snatched his gun off the floor.

Just then two Colombian natives, thinner and smaller than the rest, who had kept themselves hidden under the bunks in wheelhouse, burst out of the cabin, their arms filled with goods. One was clutching the boat's big kitchen knife. Paul didn't hesitate. He spun around faster than anyone Preston had ever seen, raised his machine gun pistol and fired. The powerful Uzi shredded the Indian's bare chest. Bullets ripped and tore holes all up and down the scrawny man's neck, stomach and throat. Blood sprayed out of his back as bullets exploded out. Blood splattered on the cabin and everyone around.

The remains of the man fell twitching at their feet. The others started yelling curses and shook their fists, until Paul jumped to his feet and let out a long burst that sent bullets whistling inches above their heads.

When Blake came running and saw the shot man on the deck, lying in pool of blood, he stood in shock. "Oh, my God! What happened?"

"I just wasted one of the bastards," Paul cried victoriously, over the growing shouts of the others. "The little shit was trying to knife me. If any others come near me, I'll kill them, too."

"That wasn't necessary," Preston yelled. "You didn't have to kill him. You didn't give him a chance."

"He was stealing us blind!" Paul said defensively, keeping his gun trained on the crowd. "Anyone who comes after me with a knife is dead meat! I got stabbed once. It'll never happen again!" Paul glanced at Preston coldly, a twisted, satisfied smile on his little rat face. "Take a lesson from it, Mr. Big Man. That's how I stayed alive all these years."

"We've got to get the hell out of here before it really turns bad," Blake cried in alarm. "Preston, get under way. Quick!"

Preston shoved several people out of his way, pushed into the wheelhouse, and sprang for the controls. Charlie was behind him, yelling in a panic. "Kick her ahead, Preston! Paul killed that guy. I ain't believing it. Get us the hell outta here!"

The engine gave a loud, throaty roar and the *Aquarius* lurched forward. Madly, Preston turned the wheel, steering offshore, dragging a big tangle of tethered canoes alongside.

"Let's see if these bastards want to swim back from Florida," Paul cried, firing his machine pistol over their heads, as the Indians scrambled into their ragged boats, slashing and sawing at the lines as the *Aquarius* dragged them out to sea. Several picked up the beaten man and lowered him into a boat. Others that were hanging onto the outriggers dove into the water.

One angry black man stayed on board, right until the last canoe was fifty yards behind, and then he screamed the first English words they had heard from a native. "Son of bitch! You die!"—then he leaped into the sea.

As they left the clutter of boats behind, they threw the dead body overboard. Charlie helped lift the dead weight—blood soaked into his pot-ridden shirt. He started sobbing. "Kill a man over a goddamn pair of pants. I can't believe it. You're something else, Paul."

They headed out into the ocean, leaving the land behind. Blake slumped onto the nearest chair, exhausted. "I hate that, but life's cheap down here. It happens. Stay alert," he said, as Preston steered the *Aquarius* through the darkness. "It's not over yet. We're not friends with everyone down here. And we still have to drop off the rest of these guns."

"Haven't we done enough damage down here?" Preston said wrathfully. "Who else do we have to kill? We did what we were supposed to. Why do we have to deliver those guns? I say let's ditch them! There's no telling what else is waiting for us."

He glanced at the fathometer as he anxiously maneuvered in the shallow waters and saw that the radar screen was blank. After flicking with switches and breakers, he cried out in alarm. "We got problems, Blake. Those guys up on the roof must have tore up the radar! Charlie, hold the wheel, and watch for shoals. We're in shallow water. There's coral reefs all over the place and they pop up quick. I've got to fix that radar or we're in big trouble."

Charlie nodded dumbly, still trembling, and slid into the chair. The captain grabbed a roll of electrical tape from the toolbox and climbed up on the wheelhouse roof. Holding a flashlight, he saw where they had sawed through the plastic coating. They had severed a number of the tiny wires that made up the thick cable.

"Blake," he yelled down, "come up here and help me."

The young man hopped up, grabbed the flashlight and held it, while Preston matched the wires up. "Fortunately they didn't cut too deep, if they did we'd be out of business. It doesn't make a lick of sense," Preston said. "The radar's bolted down, they couldn't hope to steal it."

"It looks like sheer vandalism," Blake agreed. "It's puzzling, they don't do that sort of thing down here much. I don't like this."

"I should have shot more of those fuckers," Paul cried with vindication when he heard the news.

"God, I wish this trip were over," Preston muttered to himself. "I'm still not sure where are we supposed to go, Blake."

"Just offshore from a little village called Calamar outside of Barranquilla, just up the coast. There's an island up there we passed on the way down. That's what we want."

Preston studied the green screen, watching the beam sweep round and round, reassured that it was working again. It made a sweep of the jagged shoreline and the empty Caribbean beyond.

As they approached their destination, a few hours later, Preston couldn't get the killing out of his mind, throwing the body overboard amidst the yelling and caterwauling. It nauseated him. I will never, never, never do this again, if I live through it, dear Lord! He felt sick and numb—his new boat already had a baptism in blood. What good could come of it now?

Just one more drop. Then I can leave this stinking land forever. He checked the fathometer, it was only reading twenty-two feet, a while ago it was thirty, and the *Aquarius* drew twelve. Soon they would be at the drop point.

Suddenly, his eye caught targets on the radar screen appearing out of nowhere. They were zooming around a barrier island, headed for him. He had the radio turned up, on the appointed channel, but there was no traffic.

"Five boats at nine o'clock, coming up fast," he shouted watching them pierce the screen's concentric circles. "Blake, you better get up here and look at this. They're bringing a lot of boats for six little crates of guns, and they're coming fast."

Blake rushed over and stared at the screen. "I don't like this. Bob said there would only be one boat, not five." He turned up the radio on the designated channel, but there was nothing on the air. "They should be making contact."

There was only silence and static. Blake frowned, double-checked the dial, to see if it was on the agreed-upon frequency. He pressed the mike's send button: "Ironsides to Trixie!"

There was no response.

His voice grew tense, "They should have answered." He tried it again. Nothing.

"Man, have we got troubles! Those aren't police boats," he announced, after studying the radar screen. "They're a bunch of low-life pirate scum trying to steal the load. We've been set up!"

"That explains the radar," said Preston. "They were screwing it up so their buddies could jump us in the dark, and we'd never know they were there."

Blake turned to the galley yelling loudly, "Paul, Charlie, break out the guns! Pirates are after us!" The urgency of his voice brought the others scurrying into the cabin.

Paul stood there, tense and alert. Charlie studied the rapidly approaching craft on radar. His eyes grew wide. "From the way they're coming, they're not here to party, that's for sure!" He looked fearfully at Preston. "What in the hell are we gonna do, there's a bunch of them, and they can sure out-run us!"

"Preston. Hold the course," Blake commanded, "keep the lights off. Keep running exactly as you are. We don't want to act like anything's wrong. Don't speed up, or slow down, act like we don't know anything, and we're running blind.

"Charlie, Paul, help me get the guns. This is it, boys and girls. It's been child's-play up to now. Here's where we play for keeps."

As soon as the guns were piled up in the wheelhouse, his voice became quiet, almost singsong. "Charlie, I want you up on top of the wheelhouse." He handed him a machine gun, and showed him how to cock it. Seeing he was trembling, Blake cautioned, "Don't shoot until we do. And don't get excited and shoot us by mistake. Paul, I want you tucked away down by the stern, where they can't see you. I'm betting that's where they'll try to board." He handed him a machine gun. "You know what to do." Next Blake dragged out the rocket-propelled grenade launcher and crammed a long shell with fins into the breech. "When the other boats move in I'll be ready for them with this!"

"Preston, you stay in the wheelhouse and keep us in deep water. Keep running the boat and when I say so, turn on the spotlight and find the boats for us. We'll do the shooting. If they board us, you're on your own. Use this." He handed him an Uzi, and bolted through the door.

Alone now in the wheelhouse, the captain breathed deeply, trying to control his trembling. He set the machine gun down next to him, and focused on navigating, and said to himself, "Lord Jesus, if I get through this, I'll never complain about a thing again!"

He checked the fathometer. They still had plenty of water beneath the hull, but the charts said there were coral reefs near by. It would be all over if they ran aground in the middle of the fighting. He eased open the cabin door in time to hear the screaming of outboard motors closing the distance. And still they ran on through the inky black sea.

The radar showed five boats a couple thousand feet behind them, holding back like a wolf pack following a deer. Then one took the lead, advancing rapidly. Obviously they hoped to sneak up and board the *Aquarius* and kill its occupants before they knew what was happening. Why have a gun battle and risk sinking the boat and losing the load, when they can simply murder everyone.

"Boats five hundred feet away and closing fast," he called out to Blake, who stood outside the doorway staring out at the darkness with only starlight and shining down on the sea, and the fiery wake of the propeller stirring up glowing plankton. Still, it was bright enough out to see the thirty-foot cruiser approaching. Six armed men stood ready to board via the pulpit mounted on its bow, waiting to connect with the *Aquarius's* transom.

Crouched down beneath the transom, almost in a fetal position, was Paul Renaldo, his machine gun pistol cocked and ready. He waited, listening to the motor of the approaching boat. At last he heard a scrape of metal as the pirate's bow-pulpit loomed over the transom. He heard a muffle of voices, over the swish of the sea, the faint sounds of feet tramping over the gangway. He held his breath, his finger closed over the trigger.

Then suddenly he was on his feet killing people, blasting rounds of bullets into the brains and bodies of the shadows. He heard them scream. Panic ensued, and two marauders managed to dive overboard. The attacking boat let out a frantic roar, as the captain tried to back away, while Paul sprayed it with machine gun fire.

There was a brief return of gun-fire from the cruiser, but only for a second. Then there was a fiery *whooosh* that came from the deck of the *Aquarius*, as Blake fired the RPG. The cruiser, which was now a hundred feet behind them, exploded. They felt the heat wave radiate across the water as a huge fireball leapt up. There were agonizing screams, and two burning men were blasted up into the air, like rag dolls and splattered into the sea. The gasoline-soaked waves were instantly on fire in a hellish inferno. A man was out there in the midst of it, screaming and burning but only for a moment before he became silent.

Then the other boats moved in, machine gun bullets whizzing through the air, blasting holes into the metal skin of the *Aquarius*, shattering windows. Preston saw the spits of fire across the water coming from the gun muzzles, and ducked under the dash.

"Turn on the spotlight!" Blake shouted. "Find those boats!"

Preston turned it on, and caught the outline of a boat moving past him. Blake put the RPG to his shoulder, fired and missed. The spotlight, mounted on the wheelhouse roof drew gunfire, until bullets smashed into it. Preston heard a sickening thud on the roof, and remembered in alarm that Charlie was up there. But there was no time to think. Clearly the little boats now had the advantage now over the slow, cumbersome shrimp boat.

There was a lull for a moment, and Preston yelled, "Everyone okay out there? Charlie, Paul!"

Paul called back, breathing heavily in large gasps, "They got Charlie."

Preston felt grief, as he reached for his machine gun, preparing to take a stand. He looked at the radar screen in resignation, watching the four boats circling them. Two more boats were headed their way. And even worse, there was something the size of a freighter rounding the island. He shouted, "There's a whole shit-load of boats coming. What should I do?"

"Run in a tight circle, and hold on."

For a second he wondered if they might be able to cut a deal, let them have the boat and the dope, maybe they'd let them live. But he knew in his guts that no deal was possible. After they shot up the first boat, this bunch would mop up the battlefield, slaying the wounded.

Preston felt lonely and helpless in the wheelhouse by himself. *Well, here's where we all die. Mary, I'm sorry I was unfaithful. I hope the Lord gives you a better life.* Then the guns started firing at them again. He grabbed his machine gun, thinking this was a lousy way to go. It wasn't for God or country, all he was doing was defending the dope, so it could be sold on the streets to kids by a bunch of dirt-bags. God's punishing me, he thought, I should have cut a deal with G.W.!

Next, he saw the bright lights of the freighter rounding the pass. But no freighter moved like that. Preston realized that it was a military ship, at least a hundred-and-twenty feet long, moving into the fray at speed. This is it, he thought, when it gets here, we won't last five minutes.

Suddenly, there was an ear-splitting scream of a missile, followed by a deafening roar. Preston trembled uncontrollably and braced himself, expecting to be blasted to shreds, but it never happened. Instead, one of the attacking cruisers exploded into a huge fireball that lit up the sky. So lethal was the strike that no one even screamed.

The fire was so bright he could see all the other boats around him. At first he thought, they missed him and hit one of their own by mistake. But the blast went off again and he heard horrible screams as a second boat burst into flame, scattering the crew and wreckage into the air.

The four remaining speed boats turned and fled in panic toward the island. But it did them no good. Against the gas-covered, blazing sea filled with bodies, Preston watched the mysterious killer ship coming around. With blast after blast, its cannons met their mark with deadly computer-assisted accuracy. When the pirate fleet was devastated, it turned its guns on the island. There were more explosions as the mangrove forests caught fire, and more shrieks coming from across the water.

All about them was burning wreckage and floating bodies. The ship zigzagged around in a search pattern. Preston watched the gunboat cruising around, stopping now and then. Then came sounds of machine gun fire, as they mopped up the survivors swimming or clinging to wreckage. Then all was quiet.

Preston hurried out on deck, and found Charlie lying in blood. He stepped back shocked—it was coming from his head. He heard him groan, and roll over. He'd only been grazed, and to Preston's delight, was very much alive. He sat up. "Where are they?"

The captain hugged him. "It's a damn good thing you got such a hard head, Charlie, the bullet must have ricocheted off."

Paul and Blake helped Preston drag his deckhand into the wheelhouse. "What happened?" Paul asked. "It looks like they shot each other up by mistake, or something."

"No, they turned on each other. I don't understand why," said Blake, then he thought. "It must have been some kind of double doublecross.

Preston looked out across the water at the ship's blazing lights. "That's some kind of military ship, like one of those escort carriers. It's got to be the Colombian Navy, *Policia* or the Coast Guard. I guess we'll be next. They don't seem to be taking any prisoners."

"They might," said Blake hopefully, "Hurry. Dump the guns before they get here!"

They heard the ship's engines roaring as it approached. When all the crates were overboard, Preston turned on the deck lights, illuminating their nets and rigging, showing they were a civilian shrimp boat. They all stood on the transom, with their hands in the air in surrender. As the gray ship came closer, there was no question of making a stand. It was twice as big as the *Aquarius* and far more powerful. Against the bright lights of the burning sea and half-sunk skeletons of vessels pouring forth clouds of billowing, black, oily smoke, they could see men in uniforms looking them over.

They waited for the attack, the blast that would tear them to bits, but it never came. The gunship never stopped, it passed by a hundred yards away, then faded away into the night. And so did the *Aquarius*.

18

Storm at Sea

Four days after the *Aquarius* left Colombia, she approached the Yucatan Strait and moved closer to the Mexican shore. With guns loaded and ready, they watched the radar screen apprehensively for more pirate boats, but they never came. The seas remained empty save for an occasional passing freighter or sailboat.

Charlie lay in the bunk moaning and puffing a joint to relieve his pain while Preston bathed his head in iodine. "You're a hard-headed hammer-knocker, Charlie," he said. "It's a damn good thing you don't have a brain or you woulda been kilt! But don't worry. No matter what happens from here on, it can't be as bad as what we just went through."

It wasn't long before Charlie was dizzily up and around, and Preston had a great feeling of gratitude to his Maker. He realized how much a part of his life Charlie had become. From here on, the captain thought, every day was a new day. In his mind, all calendars would date from the time they survived both the pirates and the Navy.

Preston stared off in a daze, unable to forget the images of burning bodies, and screams of death. The concussive blasts of the machine guns still rang in his ears. He'd put those images out of his mind once before—he rarely thought about Vietnam anymore. Now if he were going to live with it, he'd have to do it again.

Like any dope run, their trip down had been filled with boisterous plans and schemes by the crew. How they would spend their money was a frequent topic of conversation. But on the trip back, it was no longer theoretical. Reality set in, along with fear and paranoia. And that was increased by smoking pot, day after day, until it permeated the brain and the world became a separate reality. Blake smoked occasionally, but Paul puffed incessantly, one joint after another. Charlie snuck a drag now and then, mostly for medicinal purposes.

Days went by with barely a dozen words exchanged. What conversation there was focused on trying to figure out what happened during the ambush, and why they were still alive.

"It's all very confusing," Blake said as they sat around the galley table. The boat was on auto-pilot as they traveled north a hundred miles off the coast of Belize. "I'm still trying to figure it out. I can understand the pirates; they infiltrated the loading crew and tried to sabotage the radar and jump us."

"Surprise, surprise!" grinned Paul with a murderous light in his eyes.

"Maybe your friend Bob set us up," Charlie said, resting chin in hand, his head bandaged, with a bloody spot seeping through. "Why all that business about us making a second drop of guns?"

"Bob would have too much to lose. Besides, I've known him for years. I think the Maiquetia tried to steal the load," Blake said suspiciously, stretching his muscles, "but there's obviously more to it than that. There was some kind of double doublecross. It's like the pirates knew we were coming and were waiting for us. And the military knew they were coming and were waiting there for *them*. But the Navy didn't know anything about us hauling guns, or we'd have been blown out of the water."

"They didn't even check us," Preston pondered. "That blows my mind."

"I think it's got April's footprints all over it," Blake said. "Maybe she tipped the authorities off somehow, and we were the bait. She cut a deal with them to let us pass. Blowing the Maiquetia cartel off the map would be sweet revenge for her, and no one would ever be able to prove it."

"Sweet revenge for her?" repeated Preston, outraged. "What about us?"

"Us?" Blake laughed hilariously. "Us? We're dog shit to her. But that doesn't make sense either. If things went sour and the cartel stole the load, or if the Navy boarded us and found the guns, April would be out a half million of her own money."

Preston didn't like being used. He thought of his shoulder and the fading marks where she bit him.

"It doesn't matter now. All we've got is the Coast Guard to look forward to. And we've got a boat full of bullet holes to catch their eye. Whoever they are and whoever sent them, they sure messed up my boat."

"I can fix it," Charlie said, happy to have something to do and to get his mind off his troubles. He was feeling better, and hated just lying around the bunk. "We got some paint on board. A little putty and she'll be as good as new."

Charlie, who once had a job at an auto body shop, set to work immediately. He melted a Styrofoam cooler into a molten paste and skillfully packed it into the holes. Then he dabbed white paint over it and made it all blend in. Anything he couldn't patch, he covered with nets. Only the shattered window in the cabin was a problem. All he could do was finish knocking out the glass and tape plastic over it. When he finished, the crew complimented him, and Blake presented him with a big joint as a reward. After that, his energy seemed to drain out of him; and he became listless and tired.

Preston stayed at the helm almost round the clock now, tense and wary. It was here in the Straits of Yucatan, the great Caribbean bottleneck that *El Tiburon Blanco*, the Coast Guard's "Great White Shark" cutter, roamed. The Coast Guard patrolled the narrow stretch—a hundred and thirty miles across from Mexico to Cuba—and it was here that most of the arrests were made. With their powerful radars sweeping over a sixty-mile scan, and with spotter aircraft, any shrimp boat heading north could be intercepted.

Many a great sailboat adventure has ended with men and women being read their rights, chained to a cutter's fantail before heading off to a federal penitentiary. That was one of the main reasons for the schedule—to miss the Coast Guard. April was supposed to have inside information on where they would and wouldn't be, but Preston didn't trust it.

If you were a smuggler, you could pray for bad weather and run the Straits at night. In fact, some captains held back for a few days, waiting for the seas to worsen. But luck held, and Preston didn't have to wait. He was headed right into the middle of a tropical depression building up off Cuba. It was predicted to become a hurricane. He watched the gathering storm clouds hurry across the gray skies as though they were being pursued by a cloud-eating monster. Gone were the fair weather clouds that rose white and puffy into the clear blue. Now the ocean stretched before him, indomitable, immense, with long swells rolling toward them, breaking into white foam.

Charlie sat beside him in the co-pilot's chair, smoking a joint, his eyes glazed.

"It's gonna get sloppy out here, Charlie," Preston said to his deckhand, "and I'm gonna need your help. I want you to stop smoking pot until we get through this. I know it helps the pain, but lately you been letting things slip around here, like keeping the boat clean. I need you a hundred percent, Charlie, not fifty."

Paul came up behind and balanced himself with difficulty. "That's right, Charlie. Do what the Captain tells you," he jeered. "Why don't you stop being his yes-man and make your own decisions. You want to smoke, then smoke!"

Some days Paul tried to be pleasant. For a while, after the grueling experience with the pirates, everyone pulled together. But as the weather deteriorated, his nastiness was coming out again. He was seasick. He smoked dope incessantly to stop it, but that made him even more paranoid and hostile.

Charlie ignored him. "Don't worry 'bout it, Captain. I'm right here." To make a point, he opened the window and tossed his joint into the sea. Paul left the wheelhouse in disgust.

"I ain't listening to Paul no more," Charlie ventured after he was gone. "Not after he shot that Indian like that. I don't like that kind of crap and I don't care whether I piss him off or not."

"He's good at killing people, that's for sure," Preston said. "If he weren't we might all be dead. But I'd watch him."

"Yeah, well so's Blake. Last night he was talking in his sleep about Vietnam, about the smell of burning bodies, blowing up some kid in a village…"

"Yeah," said Preston, "but that was war. I went through some of that, too. This is war, too, of sorts. When Blake blew that boat out of the water, it was something he had to do. But with that little jerk, it's different. I saw the look in his eye when he murdered that Indian. He gets pleasure out of killing people."

"You're right there," Charlie agreed. "He even told me that it was his job to send people to the underworld, and he said he loves the work. He don't know it, but what goes around comes around."

Just then the *Aquarius* came down hard on an ocean swell, jarring the cabin. Cupboards flew open, pots, pans, and dishes tumbled, and Paul fell to the floor. Charlie hurried around tying things down. Preston studied the growing swells, then switched on the VHF radio and fished around the dials until he managed to get the NOAA weather service out of Miami. The signal was weak, spluttering with static, and an impassive, almost mechanical taped monologue recited: "A tropical depression has formed in the northeastern Caribbean. The center of the storm is located at latitude 22 degrees north and 81 degrees west, moving to the west at three miles per hour. Wind speeds are up to forty knots, increasing. Seas are running twelve to fifteen feet..."

He found the coordinates on the chart. The storm was heading right toward them. "We need bad weather coming through the Strait," he fretted to his deckhand, "but we don't need a goddamn hurricane." As the seas worsened over the next twenty-four hours, they made little forward progress. Preston dropped the stabilizers—that helped a little—and lowered his speed. He stayed at the wheel ten and twelve hours at a time making course corrections with the assistance of the Loran and the charts.

It was too rough to leave the wheel, but Preston chanced a quick dash to the galley to fix himself a cup of coffee. He slipped on the deck and spilled it all over himself. "Charlie!" he said furiously to his deckhand who was sitting at the galley table reading a *Playboy.* "I know we had trouble, but ever since we've been headed back, this place is a goddamn stinking hog pen. There's grease all over the deck, dishes piled up—I ain't gonna have it that way. It's dangerous, and I told you to clean it up.

"Well, shoot, Preston, I ain't the only shit-scraper here. The rest of 'em don't do nothin'. Every time I clean it up, they mess it up."

"We'll see about that!" He took the three strides to the stateroom, jerked open the door and found Paul lying in the bottom bunk, for once not smoking a roach, but simply staring at the ceiling. Blake was in the top bunk doing likewise.

"Boys, I want this place cleaned up, and I want it cleaned up *now.* We've got bad weather coming, and someone's gonna get hurt. Blake, you scrub the floor. Paul, you do the dishes. I'll have Charlie batten down the cabinets."

Blake gazed up from his dazed fog, looked pained, and said nothing. Normally he would have been right there, pitching in. But the battles, and puzzling how it all came to happen, seemed to have taken something out of him. Preston noted his soiled shirt, and the three-day growth of beard. That wasn't like Blake and it worried the captain. He could care less about Paul. But without Blake being on top of the situation, giving directions and advice, the trip was doomed. Preston didn't know where to go or what to do when he got there.

"Why don't you go back and play with your boat," Paul snapped from his bunk. "If you want the fuckin' boat cleaned, clean it yourself. That's what we're paying you for. *Ugh!* I'm not feeling so good."

"Look, Sonny," Preston said menacingly, "I'm not asking you, I'm telling you."

Paul rolled against the wall. "Screw you. I'm seasick, goddamn it. Leave me alone."

"Screw you both," Preston said. "Charlie, go hold the wheel, and I'll finish up here."

It was easier to clean up than to whip them. Besides, he thought, when this voyage was over, it was his boat, and they wouldn't be on it. He scrubbed the pots and dishes and locked them in the cupboards. Seeing the captain working, Blake rose to his feet, took a long drag on his joint and went to work. He poured detergent on the floor and started mopping, and the cabin began to take on some semblance of order. Paul lay in his bunk, his intestines rolling with the waves.

Preston watched Blake polishing the floor by hand pushing the rag around and around and around and around as the boat pitched and rolled. "Energy, man…sheer energy. Our whole universe is one big spiral," he mumbled as he worked.

"What are you talking about?" Preston asked, hoping to learn what was going on with Blake.

"The great circular flow of the cosmos. Spirals!" His hand whirled the rag around in circles sudsing the gray fiberglass deck. "The whole universe is one big connected spiral! Snail shells, whirlpools, sea-horse tails, the galaxy, this greasy floor—it's all the same."

"How do you get from a greasy floor to a galaxy?" the captain asked, drying a pot with a paper towel, and trying to follow Blake's reasoning despite his exhaustion. At the same time he was thinking the boy was losing it, and that he'd better watch him. This whole thing will fail if he goes whacko on us.

"You don't scrub a deck sideways, do you? You don't go back and forth in straight lines. If you want to get it clean, you go round and round." Working on his knees in the soapy water, he expanded his work area spiraling around the galley, his swoops getting more grandiose.

Preston chuckled in spite of his worry at Blake's bizarre thinking. He finished the last of the dishes and went to relieve Charlie at the wheel. He found Charlie holding the spokes, looking green. "Skipper, I think you better take the wheel. I ain't sure I can handle it; I ain't feeling too good myself."

"Get some rest then, but stand by. I may need your help pretty soon."

"I'll be okay," Charlie said sliding out of the pilot's chair. He climbed into his co-pilot's seat and sat beside his captain as the boat pitched in the growing seas. "Sorry about me not cleaning up in there a while ago."

The angry black skies continually disgorged rain and blinding flashes of lightning. Preston turned on the pumps every three hours; on the trip down he did it only once a day.

The captain gripped the spokes tightly, throwing all his weight into the wheel, his feet braced firmly on the deck. A huge wave lifted the *Aquarius* and brought her crashing down with such force that paint flew off the hull and windows cracked.

"I'm not afraid of this ocean," Preston said at last, "but I damn sure respect her. I've spent the best days of my life out here. Sometimes when the water's been so slick it looked like someone spilled oil on it. And I've seen it so rough I was praying to get to the hill. But I don't ever recall it being this bad."

Fifteen-foot waves thundered over the bow, and a solid wash of blue ocean roared around the wheelhouse. It flooded the stern and made it look frighteningly like they were going to sink before it finally gushed out of the scupper holes. The *Aquarius* fought the waves and soldiered on. Loaded with thirty-two thousand pounds of pot, she rode heavily. Her outriggers dipped from side to side and the stabilizers sliced the surface.

"Sure is a lot of water to drink," Charlie gulped looking up at the huge swells that were cresting above the wheelhouse. Suddenly they dove off a giant wave and landed with a catastrophic crash. The stove tore away from the wall and flew across the cabin into the opposite wall, knocking chunks off its porcelain. Dishes crashed and broke in the cabinets as water surged through the door, flooding the cabin. Blake was knocked over and had to swim to his knees, cursing, while Preston hung onto the wheel and barely managed to keep the craft from foundering. Paul lay on the floor in a wet, quivering heap, moaning, "Dear God, we're gonna sink." Charlie hurried down to the galley to put things right.

It was dark in the wheelhouse. "Something's not right," Preston said in a low whisper. "She feels loggy. You see the way we're dipping down and not coming up like we ought to. I think we're taking on water. That stuffing box must have come a-loose when we run through that wreckage with those pirates. I hope to God a seam hasn't opened or we got a crack. Better pump her out again and check the engine room."

Charlie flicked the bilge-pump switch, then slipped on his slicker coat and flung the door open, letting in the rain that blasted down. The clouds overhead were ominously black, hurling rain with a vengeance. It stung his face as he worked his way toward the deck hose. To his dismay, he saw that the hose was flaccid and the pump wasn't working.

It's gotta be something simple, he thought desperately. A belt's slipped off the pulley, the pump's intake stopped up. Fear and adrenaline swept through him. Fighting hysteria he repeated aloud, "It's got to be something simple." As he made his way hand over hand toward the engine room entrance and started down the ladder, he glanced nervously at the Zodiac lifeboat lashed to the cabin roof. They might need it.

Charlie jerked the engine room door open, and the diesel screamed shrilly. He switched on the overhead light. What he saw froze him with horror.

The bottom deck and bilge were completely submerged. Just the top of the yellow engine was visible in a sea of oily water sloshing around. Loose bales of marijuana were being pitched wildly, crashing into the immense steel fuel tanks, bouncing off the half-submerged motor.

"Oh my God, we're gonna sink!" he moaned. "Don't panic, goddamn it, just keep calm," he ordered himself. "We've seen tights before like this." But he knew the previous tights weren't at all like *this*. Before, when he'd been on boats in trouble, they were near shore with other boats around. Here they were in the middle of the Yucatan Strait, with no one to call, a boatload of dope, and two miles of water beneath the hull.

Charlie plunged into the waist-deep bilge water and made his way toward the pump, clutching the marijuana bales that were stacked from ceiling to floor. On the surface of this internal sea swirled a thick layer of pot leaves, stems and seeds from ruptured bales.

At last he arrived at the pump and found the trouble. A loose bale had tumbled down and landed on the four-inch diameter spinning shaft coupling, and the bolts had chewed it to pieces. The debris had clogged the pump's intake lines and burned up the impeller.

The deckhand waded to the auxiliary pump on the front of the engine and fired it up. As it sputtered to life, he noted the water being sucked through the pipe with satisfaction. But pot residue was already collecting around its intake screen.

Holding his breath and keeping his eyes shut, he dropped himself into the hot, oily water and scooped a handful of residue from the screen, then another and another. The engine screamed in his ears, and the diesel stench was stifling. He was bleeding from his head wound, and blood trickled into his eye.

Something white floating in the oily black water caught his eye. It was a plastic bag containing a white brick of something like chalk. He picked it up as it bobbed past him and squeezed it suspiciously, then mashed a corner against the motor.

He mashed his finger through the plastic and felt it enter the dry white powder inside. Could it be? Once at a party with Lupino and some girls they picked up on the beach he'd had some. He pulled out a small scoop of the white powder and sniffed it.

"My God!" he exclaimed. "It is!" *Cocaine!*

He held the bag in his hand and shook his head, flabbergasted. There must be twenty-thousand dollars worth right here!

Good ol' Blake, he thought, as he backed out of the crawlway—another surprise. How many of these bales had coke hidden in them? If even a third did, this load was worth millions more than with just the pot. No wonder ol' Blake planned to buy a ranch in Ecuador when this was over.

If he told Preston, there'd be trouble. Preston would go for Blake for sure. And someone might get shot. Charlie decided to keep his mouth shut until it was over.

A smile of malicious joy spread over Charlie's greasy, wet face as he stuffed the plastic bag into his pocket. If we're gonna share the risk, we'll share the profits too, he decided.

But first they had to keep the boat from sinking. Taking the ladder two rungs at a time, he bounded on deck and charged into the wheelhouse.

Preston looked at his oil-soaked deckhand with relief.

"Charlie, you were down there a long time. I was afraid you got washed overboard, but I couldn't leave the wheel."

Just then the bow of the *Aquarius* plunged down into the sea and seemed to disappear. All they could see was water. The captain clutched the wheel and boosted the power, wondering if the *Aquarius* would come back up. As the wave lifted them, he gave the boat full power. The trawler managed to pull itself up. He breathed a sigh of relief.

"A couple more like that and it's gonna be all over. We've got to put out the nets and make a sea anchor. Now what the hell's wrong down there?"

In short, gasping breaths, Charlie explained the problem. Preston listened, quietly, saying nothing. Then he bellowed, "Blake, get your ass up here. You're needed *now!*"

When Blake appeared, Preston said evenly, "We're sinking. We're going down fast. I can't control her. We must have hit something down in Colombia during the fight, and it's getting worse." Suddenly, the *Aquarius* turned sideways, and rocked uncontrollably back and forth, its outriggers slashing deeply into the sea. "Hold the wheel," the captain yelled to Blake above the scream of the wind. Water blew in their faces through the broken, shot-up windows on the side.

"Tell me what to do!" Blake gasped, staring fearfully at the heaving mountains of water, breaking over the bow and washing down the decks.

"Keep trying to quarter into this sea, or she'll broach and go down. Just hold on. We'll be right back. We've got to get the nets out!"

Without further explanation, Preston slipped into his foul weather gear and bolted out of the wheelhouse, his mind racing, sorting out the complex maneuvers that lay before him. The leak had to be stopped quickly, the pump unstopped, and the water pumped out. But first he had to stop the runaway pitching and rolling of the boat.

Charlie was right behind him. Few words were spoken and few

were needed. They had to get the trawls overboard and do it now.
Clutching whatever they could to hold their balance as the trawler
rocked, they snatched ropes off the pin rail until the hanging nets
tumbled to the deck. Then jerking the ironclad doors out of their
brackets, they hoisted them over the side and sent them splashing into
the sea, feeding out cable until they dragged the webbing down behind them. In a few minutes Preston had set a sea anchor. The nets
fluffed out like a parachute, stopping the *Aquarius* from surfing down
the waves, and presented her stern to the seas.

When Preston restored enough stability to work, he raced to his
cabin for a new impeller. He grabbed a screwdriver and some wrenches,
and charged into the crew's quarters.

"Charlie, take the wheel," he commanded. "Blake come with me.
We've got to get your goddamn pot the hell out of the bilge. It stopped
up the pumps. I should have jerked that crap out of there before we
ever left."

Blake sprang to his feet, jerked on his rain suit, and bolted out the
door. Paul just lay in his bunk inertly. Preston shook him, and Paul
rolled over and groaned. "Oh, for Chrissakes, man. I'm dying."

Preston's powerful hand grabbed Paul's arm and dragged him onto
the floor. "Get up or you will die! I'm not kidding you. We're all
gonna drown, and I need your help. Get up!" He pushed him through
the door, and as the rain beat on their faces, Preston tore out two
window screens to use as sieves.

Down the ladder they went, into the stinking brew of diesel fuel
and wet pot. Blake's eyes grew wide with horror when he looked at
the oily mess.

"Good God," he whispered. "We *are* sinking." Pirates he could
handle—guns and attack boats, too—but the brutal forces of nature
terrorized him almost to inaction. Then, forcing himself, he jumped
into the bilge water.

Paul, who had been snarling and complaining, stood in shocked
silence, sweat pouring from his pasty-white skin, whimpering in fear.

"Start seining this pot mess out of the water," the captain commanded as he plunged in. "And keep that auxiliary pump's intake line
open. Whatever you do, don't let it stop up. And watch that shaft—
it'll take your arm off."

Preston waded to the disabled main pump, turned the valve off
and twisted the screws on the housing until the plate came loose. Out

tumbled the old impeller with its burned, broken fins. Doing his best not to be thrown against the hot engine as the boat pitched and rolled, he installed the new impeller. Within fifteen minutes he had it working.

Trepidation and adrenaline kept Blake working in deathly silence. He was on his knees, pulling crud out of the intake lines of the auxiliary pump and praying. Paul carried buckets of it up the ladder, dumped it on deck, and then went back for more. The stench of diesel fuel and the throbbing of the engine made him retch, but there was nothing left to throw up. Finally his adrenaline gave out and he just lay there on the deck filling his lungs with clean, unpolluted air. He was numb with pain, not caring whether he drowned or not.

He clutched the rail and held on, looking up at the waves tall as the boat's masts. The wind blasted spray in his face and stung his skin. Blake and Preston worked below, getting the pumps working. Preston crawled out of the engine room and, seeing Paul sprawled on the deck, shouted, "Get down there and keep that pump clear. We're not out of this yet." Paul pulled himself upright.

"Kiss my ass. I'm not going down there again. We're all gonna drown anyway." Preston started for him, but Paul pulled a vicious-looking little automatic pistol out of his pant leg. "If you push me again, I'll blow you away, and I'm not kidding!"

But he was too slow. Before he could get it out, Preston backhanded him across the face, and knocked him on his back. Still Paul held onto the gun. He leveled it at the captain and laughed viciously. "That's twice you hit me," he spat out, then his voice rose to a scream above the howling wind. "I'm gonna enjoy killing you, you big son-of-a-bitch. I'm gonna shoot you right in the fuckin' guts!" Paul started to aim, but the pitching deck made him lurch. Preston ducked behind the winch an instant before Paul fired. At the same moment there was a deafening roar. They looked up to see a wall of water bearing down on them. Preston heard the shot just as the sea broke over the gunnels. For a moment they were swimming as if in the ocean. Preston was flushed across the deck and thrown against the stern. He managed to grab onto the scupper and held on. Above the roar of water, he heard Blake's yells from below-deck, and Paul's screams as he was swept overboard.

Preston saw Paul only for a second—a dark crew-cut head, arms flailing in panic, fighting to stay up, and then vanishing from sight.

The captain fought his way into the wheelhouse, looking as if he'd seen a ghost.

"We lost Paul," Preston gasped as he took the wheel from Charlie. "He just went overboard. When we get the leak fixed, we'll look for him."

"Well, he's a gone son-of-a-bitch. We'll never find him," Charlie said.

Preston pulled himself together. "The pump's working now, but we got to get that leak fixed before we go to the bottom. Get Blake out of the engine room if he didn't drown down there, and break open the hatches. Jerk that pot out. I think the stuffing box was knocked a-loose."

"I can fix that stuffing box, Skipper. You just keep us afloat," Charlie said and bolted for the door.

Charlie and Blake, who was battered but okay, worked for two exhausting hours to get fifty bales out of the hold so they could make a corridor to the stuffing box in the stern. As the waves broke over the boat, the squares floated around on the deck, back and forth, crashing into the bulkheads, turning into a mush of green and brown leaves. At least twenty bales were swept over the side.

Finally, Charlie tunneled through the crawl space, on his belly, shoving bales out of the way until he felt a steady torrent of water gushing in through the stuffing box's packing gland. This device mounted in the hull enabled the shaft and propeller to turn, and separated the inside of the boat from the outside sea. Under normal circumstances, repairing the gland would not have given Charlie a second thought. But these were far from normal circumstances.

Groaning each time the hull pounded the sea, Popcorn Charlie squeezed his way through the pot to the gland. He tightened the big bronze nut with a wrench. His face was bruised and chafed from being pressed against the burlap in the crawl space, but, at last, the leak was stopped. Within a few minutes the water level in the engine room began to drop.

Windrows of pot seeds and residue began to form along the bulkheads and the sides of the engine. When there was only a little pot residue left, and the boat was under control, Charlie and Blake climbed the ladder and sat on the deck for a moment, breathing deeply, while rain beat on their faces.

Then Charlie dragged himself into the cabin and collapsed in his chair, soaking wet and panting. A bedraggled Blake came in behind him and slumped on the floor with his back against the wall. "You know, this isn't fun anymore!" he managed. "It's too bad about Paul."

"We're gonna find him," the captain said hoarsely. "I've got the Loran numbers wrote down where he went overboard."

"Two hours later in these seas?" scoffed Blake. "Why bother! We must have drifted five miles since then."

" 'Cause I've never lost a man overboard," Preston said, his voice breaking. "And I'm not gonna start now. Charlie, get up on the mast pole and look for him. Blake, you get up on the roof," he commanded. "We're gonna try."

Heading back to the coordinates, he berated himself. I should have jerked the dope out of the engine room, he thought. Then none of this would have happened. The little bastard wouldn't have gone overboard, even though he deserved it. "You know, guys, he went crazy and tried to shoot me out there. But the sea took him first, thank God."

"Well, I guess the sea took him apart," Blake said. "He said he wanted some adventure. He got it. If he had any sense, he would have stayed home."

"Yeah, I wish he had," Preston said ruefully. "I hate that happening. I never lost anyone overboard before. ...Or had anyone flip out on me like that. You know who his family was?"

"No, sure don't. Paul was an investor, that's all. Anonymous in the end like most of us in this trade. He told me he was tired of everyone else taking the risks." Blake and Charlie left the wheelhouse and got to work.

They hunted for four hours, circling amidst huge blue waves, following the drift. "For God's sakes, Preston, give it up," Blake declared. "He went over without a life jacket. He couldn't last ten minutes in these seas. We've got a schedule to keep. The less time we spend in screwing around the Yucatan Straits the better. Face it— Paul's shark shit by now!"

19

The Coast Guard Cometh

Preston switched on the fathometer and saw that for the first time in days, the depth recorder didn't plunge off the bottom of the page. A line marking the sea bottom began to appear at the seven-hundred-fathom mark as the continental shelf rose rapidly from the depth. It was an area that snapper fishermen and royal red shrimpers called the "edge of the earth."

As they approached the coast of Florida, the weather improved and the seas calmed down. Preston made a course correction, put the boat on automatic pilot, and went on deck where his crew sat basking in the sun like turtles on a log. Wearing clean, white shorts and a new T-shirt, a fresh-shaven Blake was stretched out asleep, soaking up the warm rays. "We'll be coming up on royal red bottom in a few hours," Preston called up to Charlie, who was perched on the wheelhouse roof looking at a freighter passing in the distance. "This boat has enough cable to drag the bottom in four hundred fathoms. If we didn't have this daggone schedule to keep, I'd sure like to drop the nets out and see what's on the bottom."

"Not me," Charlie hooted from his roost. "I'm retired from

shrimping, Cap'n. When I get my fifty grand, I'm gonna hit every whorehouse from Key West to New Orleans. I ain't never gonna work that hard as long as I live." He jumped to his feet, cupped his hands to his mouth and hollered across the empty ocean, "I want some cooter! And I want it *now!*"

"Charlie, quit jumping around up there like a scalded ape," Preston said, laughing. "You bump into that antenna and it'll send enough voltage through you to cook you like gumbo."

"Aye-aye, Captain!" he yelled, and gave a mock salute in the sarcastic manner of Paul. He flopped down on his bottom, snatched off his T-shirt and revealed his "Mother" tattoo. He wiggled his toes in the sunshine and drummed his fingers on the rooftop.

Preston squinted up at him, slowly rubbing the thick stubble on his thick jaw, worrying that his deckhand had cracked under the strain. One minute Preston found him withdrawn, moodily depressed, or edgy, the next he'd be elated, booming with confidence, and boasting about what he was going to do with his money. No longer was he the dependable, easy-going, good ol' Charlie-boy he'd known for the past ten years.

Since the storm Preston had to remind him to pump the bilge, to change the fuel filters, or even to go on watch. He spent an inordinate amount of time in the head. Last night when he saw Charlie on watch, pacing around the cramped wheelhouse, snapping his fingers at his side, Preston asked him if anything was wrong.

"You can tell me, Charlie," Preston urged, thinking his deckhand had broken under the tension of the pirate attack, the storm, and Paul going overboard.

"Couldn't be better, Skipper," he beamed, and slapped Preston on the back. "Couldn't be better! We're gonna get rich." Preston noted Charlie's glazed eyes and dilated pupils. It wasn't the pot. He wondered if the bullet had fractured his skull.

Well, it won't be much longer, the captain thought. We'll soon be coming up the coast to the Florida Panhandle, get this crap off-loaded, and be done with it one way or the other. Preston didn't believe for a minute that Popcorn Charlie would ever retire from shrimping, no matter how much money he had. He'd seen times when the shrimp were running good, when he'd paid Charlie two thousand dollars on Friday, and after juking all weekend, he'd be back Monday morning dead broke, wanting to borrow money for cigarettes. When they got back to work, the captain thought, he'd settle down.

The hum of an airplane broke Preston's reflections. He glanced up, wondering if he really had heard anything. But as the drone became louder, all their eyes turned to the sky. More to himself than the others, Preston asked in bewilderment: "What would a plane be doing way out here?"

Blake opened an eye, listened for a moment, and scrambled to his feet with his hands clasped over his eyes. "Don't know," he said nervously. "Could be a seaplane or a charter flight. We're off the usual airways, though."

Then they saw it coming—high up, miles away, and headed straight toward them. It was a big, white plane with a red racing stripe on its tail.

Charlie let out an agonized wail of despair from the roof. "Oh, shit! It's the Coast Guard." He hopped to the deck.

"Pray he keeps right on going and doesn't come back," Preston said.

Charlie's eyes sank deeper into their sockets, and he fixed his gaze on the disappearing plane as if he were looking out from two caves. "I wish they'd go back to cleaning buoys like they used to and leave us alone." He paced the deck, snapping his fingers anxiously. "Maybe it's just a chance meeting."

"Maybe," echoed Blake. He took a deep breath and stifled his fear. His voice was quiet, controlled. "It could be anything. It could be he's looking for a boatload of Haitian refugees or Cubans. We're approaching the coast—we're in the right area for that. Or it could be a search-and-rescue mission."

"Or, more likely he's on reconnaissance," Preston said fatalistically, "looking for boats like us, hauling dope, and April's schedule is off. We're stuck. If they have a cutter nearby, they'll board us. A shrimp boat loaded like we are…"

"Our ass is grass!" Charlie finished for him with a hysterical laugh. "Get it? Our ass is *grass*!"

The other two ignored him. Blake's eyes were cold. "We'll just have to go to Plan B."

"What's that?" Preston asked hopefully. "Dump the load?"

"You kidding?" Blake gave a short, sardonic laugh. "It took forty Indians three hours to get it all loaded. It'd take the four of us a full day to throw it all off. No… At the first sign of a cutter, I'm going to blow her to hell and send her to the bottom."

He produced a black suitcase he had brought with him, but had never opened. He unsnapped the silver locks solemnly, quieting even Charlie. He opened the lid, exposing a number of plastic bags that looked like they were filled with white dough. "We have guns to deal with the pirates. I brought this in case we meet the Coast Guard."

He pulled out one of the soft chunks. "This is C-4, plastic explosives," he said above the wind and creak of the rigging. "If the Coast Guard comes up, we'll open the sea-cocks, set fire to the boat, and blow a hole in the bottom big enough to drive a tractor trailer through. She'll sink like buckshot."

"What?" cried Preston with total disbelief. "Blow the boat? *My boat!* You're crazy!"

"It's not your boat," Blake snapped. "It will be the U.S. Custom's once they confiscate it. It will be tied up at their dock in Miami and sold at auction while we're rotting in prison."

"As soon as they order us to stop," Blake continued, holding up a coil of explosive plastic putty encased in tubing. "I'll set fire to the engine, then I'll light this and the cord will go off in ten minutes. That's long enough for us to launch the Zodiac and go running to them." He patted the suitcase. "There's enough here to level a two-story building. She'll go down in two seconds."

"Man, I like it, *I like it!*" cried Charlie, as if Blake had just revealed a plan for finding buried treasure. "We'll tell those squids we're so glad to see them we could just hug their necks, right?"

"No one will be more surprised than we are when she blows. The boat caught fire and they saved us just in time," Blake concluded. "They'll be heroes."

Preston hooted in derision. "You think they'll believe that? Sheee-it."

Blake's smile faded. He looked at the captain's suntanned face with icy, silencing eyes. "It doesn't matter what they believe," he said. "It's what evidence they have." He laid the packets of C-4 out, one by one. "And the evidence, all four hundred bales, will be sitting on the bottom in two hundred fathoms. That's about as deep as you can get."

"Didn't you learn anything on the *Night Shadow*?" Preston demanded. "You remember when she went down, the bales came to the surface and floated all over the place like crackers in soup? I don't care if you blow the keel slap out of her, with four hundred bales, she'll float like a cork."

Blake's eyes flickered momentarily as he considered this possibility. He paused, uncoiling the cord.

"Then we'll nail the hatch covers shut. The bales can't get out! I'll peel the keel open, and she'll go the bottom. And if she doesn't," he shrugged callously, "what have we got to lose for Christ's sakes? It's for your own goddamn protection, Barfield, not mine. I'm looking at twenty years in the pen. They've got a sheet on me. With you, a first offender, it might go easier, especially if their evidence is sitting two thousand feet on the bottom."

Preston looked anxiously at the empty sky, his heart pounding in his chest. He knew Blake was right, but the idea of blowing up the boat sickened him and he prayed silently, *Please, Lord, let it be a chance meeting. Don't make us have to kill this boat.* There'd been times the Coast Guard had approached the *Lady Mary* for a good look without actually boarding. Maybe they'd be so lucky this time.

The plane vanished, but not for long. Within a few minutes, the distant droning grew louder. Against the glint of the sun they could just see the Coast Guard plane making a wide turn.

With growing despair, they watched it turn 360 degrees, drop altitude and bank. No more than five hundred feet above, they saw the pilot looking down on the *Aquarius*, then watched it zoom by and head back in the direction it had come, steadily gaining altitude. Blake took a deep breath. "That does it," he declared. "Let's get busy. Charlie, get down from there and help me move the bales around. I want to make sure she blows out the bottom instead of the wheelhouse."

"Wait a minute!" Preston cried in protest, watching him unpacking a spool of copper wire and packets of gray explosive clay. "For God's sake, it could still be a chance meeting. Don't you blow us to hell out here in the middle of nowhere!"

"Don't worry," Blake said cheerfully, heading for the engine room. "I'm very good at what I do. They don't call me Wonderman for nothing. If the cutter doesn't come, I won't trigger it."

"Listen, I've got another idea," Preston persisted. "Why don't we go shrimping?"

"Shrimping? The Coast Guard is coming and you want to go shrimping! Have you lost your mind?"

"We're almost to the royal red grounds off the Tortugas," Preston went on. "Let's drop the nets down and start dragging. If the Coast

Guard sees we're just a working boat, they might let us be. They know there's three or four boats that work out here regular."

"Hey, it's not a bad idea," Blake said thoughtfully. "Go for it. But I'm still wiring her up to blow."

Preston turned to Charlie, but saw him vanishing into the head. "Come on, Charlie," he shouted, pounding on the door. "Hurry up! Let's get these nets ready to fish, damn it!"

"Be out in a minute," Charlie called. Hastily he stuffed a finger-full of white powder into his nose and felt the explosive rush surge through him as the cocaine burned into his mucous membranes. Once again his heart pounded, and the noise of the engine and the swish of the sea against the boat magnified as his senses sharpened. A smile of joy spread over his face and he burst out of the head. "I'm ready!"

It took forty-five minutes for the nets to reach the bottom in two hundred fathoms, and by the time they were dragging, Blake emerged from the engine room. "She's all ready." Going into the cabin, he snatched the navigation chart off the wall. It was filled with Preston's Loran scribbles marking their course to Colombia and back. Ripping it up, he handed it to Charlie. "Take this out on deck and burn it."

"Why? I wanted it as a souvenir."

"Forget it. It's evidence that we made the trip. And we've got to protect our money man. If they know where we've been, the DEA might be able to trace it back to our connection down there. The cartel is our ticket out of jail. They'll pay bail."

"Well, maybe we won't have to worry about it," said Preston, collapsing nervously in his chair. "We've been dragging for two hours now. I don't see any sign of a cutter on the radar. You know, that plane could have just checked us out and gone on."

But shortly afterwards, while they were burning the chart, they heard a faint *chop-chop-chop* in the distance.

"Hey!" cried Preston, "I hear something. It sounds like a helicopter." He searched the sky. "Look over there!" He pointed to a dark speck coming over the blue horizon.

They rushed on deck in time to see the helicopter bearing down on them like a dragonfly hovering over a mosquito. And they could see the white body, the big red stripe, and the huge black letters on the fuselage—UNITED STATES COAST GUARD.

The chopper circled them, and they could now make out the form of two men looking down from several hundred feet studying them with binoculars. The blades snapped through the air deafeningly as the machine hovered. After only a minute, it lifted and headed in the direction it had come from.

"They're gone," breathed Charlie with relief.

"Gone? Shit!" Blake said bitterly. "To where? A rock sitting out here in the middle of the Gulf of Mexico? You know they came right off the deck of *El Tiburon Blanco*. It can't be too far away. Right now they're calling our numbers into EPIC to see if we're on the hot sheet."

"Are we?" Preston demanded, ready for the ultimate doublecross, thinking the papers he had were a fraud. "Is this boat stolen?"

"No, we bought it almost brand new," Blake said. "We're not crooks, for God's sake. It shouldn't be listed, Preston. It was a working boat."

And this is what she's been turned into—*a dope barge*—Preston thought as he hurried into the wheelhouse. He flicked on the radar with trembling fingers. On top of the wheelhouse the beacon turned round and round, scanning the open seas, but the screen was empty.

Two hours later, as they dragged their nets over the sea floor, the radar picked up a large luminous flash at its farthest limit, thirty-two miles away. It was the size of a ship and moving fast, headed in their direction.

Preston knew that only one thing could be that big and move like that. It was the U.S. Coast Guard cutter *Dallas*. It was 380-feet long and powered by two tremendous 2500-horsepower engines, and pounded over the waves at a good seventeen knots. It wouldn't be long.

"All right," said Blake wearily. "Let's get that lifeboat ready. Soon as they say, 'Prepare for boarding,' I'll start the fire, set the timer, and then let's get the hell out." For a second his eyes gleamed with madness, his voice hushed. "You know, we could do an *African Queen* number on them. Their gunnels are only three-quarters-of-an-inch-thick steel. If we rammed them right, I could open them up like a sardine can. I love blowing things up!"

"Jesus Christ, you're not serious," cried Preston in alarm.

"No, of course not," Blake grinned. "I'm not ready to die yet." But Preston wasn't so sure. A couple of times on the trip, Blake said he'd rather die than rot in prison.

Preston glanced at the lifeboat. "I just hope to hell that outboard starts. Charlie, go crank it up and see if it works. It would be hell to have to start paddling when this boat blows." Then he checked the radar. The Coast Guard cutter was still approaching, now twenty miles away.

"Come, Charlie," he said tersely, trying not to think about it, "let's wind her up and put some fish on board. That might discourage them. They don't like to get their uniforms all stinky," then he threw the switch.

Round and round turned the winches, hauling back more than a mile of steel cable. All the while, their eyes locked on the horizon of the choppy blue seas. Finally, Charlie, who had good eyes, pointed to a thin vapor of black smoke rising in the distance.

"She's coming."

Standing at the winches, they could smell the stench of diesel fuel emanating from the engine room as Blake unscrewed the copper lines, sending fuel gurgling into the bilge. Beside him was a quart bottle of gasoline with a linen fuse in it. Matches were safely in his pocket.

When Blake emerged, he saw Preston's look of concern.

"Don't worry, I'm not going to do a thing before we have to. Get the life raft ready. And hurry, before we get within range of their Big Eye."

The winch drums fattened with cable and the nets angled down steeply from the outriggers. The cutter was less than two miles away and closing in fast. It was huge, almost the size of a battleship, with smokestacks as big as a steel mill's boiling out black, sooty smoke against the sky. As it drew closer, the earsplitting scream of its two monstrous diesels lowered to a loud spluttering, and abruptly the smoke dissipated into whispering black clouds.

The white ship moved slowly beside them, its huge radar turning. They looked up, intimidated by the fifteen-foot red-slash racing stripe that reached from the gunnel to the waterline and the insignia of two crossed anchors. Tall black letters read COAST GUARD.

At the winch station, Preston looked up at the Guardsmen on the flying bridge that towered above the *Aquarius*. With the chilling interest of wolves sniffing a cornered, frightened deer, four officers stared down at them. Around the fantail, enlisted men stood by next to their battle stations and .50-caliber machine-guns.

Time froze for Preston as the island of steel and armaments loomed closer. He felt the sweat pouring down his neck and drenching his shirt as he wound in the cable. Uniformed officers stared at him through binoculars. Breathe, goddamn it, remember to breathe, he commanded himself, trying to relax. The voice of the female nurse at the Lamaze birthing clinic came back to him: 'Take a deep cleansing breath…hold it…now slowly exhale. Do it again.'

Onto the bridge strode the captain—there was no question of who he was. He radiated authority—from his blue jacket to his white cap with the gilded insignia. His lapel bore a long bar with the colorful decorations of rank. As Preston pulled the cable guide back and forth, evenly distributing the steel wire on the revolving drum, he did his best not to look up at the cutter that towered above them. He didn't want to appear intimidated by all the enlisted men manning machine guns on the fantail, or the giant three-inch-bore cannons mounted on a turntable. Instead, he concentrated on his nets.

When the otter doors finally emerged, they looked funny—the tickler chains and foot lines were matted with hairs, along with a few starfish, pale from living in the icy darkness where no sunlight ever penetrates. Both nets were loaded with something.

"God, she's a heavy mother!" he called out to Charlie, knowing his voice carried across the water. "We must have dug mud or caught a doggone airplane, Charlie."

Suddenly the boat was surrounded by sharks. Great numbers of them appeared, milling about, attracted to the scent. Most of them were six footers, but several were ten feet or greater—great gray shapes. From high above, the Guardsmen could see them circling at different levels, deep into the water.

Preston saw them too. Fearfully, he glanced at Blake standing on the engine room's ladder. Preston prayed he wouldn't panic and detonate the timer prematurely.

As the swollen bags were hoisted out, the heavy ropes pulled taut and vibrated in the blocks, and Charlie threw an extra wrap around the revolving brass cat-hauler. Distracted away from the sharks' menace for a moment, he stared fearfully at the cutter's flying bridge. The rope slipped off the cathead and began to tangle in the winch. Preston shut the winch off.

"Goddamn it, Charlie, pay attention!" he yelled loudly and deliberately so the Coast Guard crew could hear him from the cutter. "Keep your mind on what you're doing! The sharks are about to eat our nets up. We've got to hoist them quick, you hear?" Refocusing, Charlie hastily untangled the rope and started the winches again. The *Aquarius* listed badly as the first net was hoisted over the gunnel. A shark hung on with its teeth snagged in the webbing, thrashing back and forth until it dropped back into the sea. Up above the Guardsmen clustered around the fantail, watching the scene and pointing.

Preston couldn't believe what he saw through the webbing. It was orange-red with the bodies of royal red shrimp. Those weren't worms he saw in the chains, nor hairy brittlestars. They were the whiskers of shrimp.

He gasped, stepped forward, and fought back and forth with the release ropes. Finally, in a monumental *ploosh*, the contents of the net poured onto the deck. Charlie, high on cocaine, and caught up in the moment of the catch, gave a whoop of joy as he hoisted the now-empty net to the boom. They stood looking at each other open-mouthed, standing in a waist-high mountain of shrimp. The whole deck was buried in shrimp, more shrimp than they had ever seen at one time in their lives. For a moment they forgot about the hovering menace.

When Preston glanced up at the cutter, he saw that a number of men were assembled on its deck, talking about the huge load. Obviously, they had never seen such a catch either. "Come on, Charlie," the captain urged. "Act natural. Let's get the other bag."

When the portside net was hauled up and emptied, the deck totally disappeared from view. There was no room to walk. Mounded on the fantail, burying the hatch cover, and piled along the rails were at least four tons of the biggest, prettiest shrimp he'd seen in twenty years of commercial fishing. It was the strike of a lifetime.

Charlie, who had been furiously shoving his secret stash of cocaine into his nose an hour ago to bolster his courage before stepping on deck, suddenly let ring out a joyous *Whaaa-hooo!* He grabbed up four of the big shrimp, completely filling his hand, and turned to his audience on the cutter. "Look at these mothers!" he whooped across the water. The boarding party, wearing life vests and crash helmets, stood by, ready to be lowered. "Come on aboard. Bring your whole damn crew with you. We're gonna put your asses to work!"

Swallowing with fear, Preston looked up at the captain of the cutter, shrugged his big shoulders with a weak smile and shook his head, indicating he couldn't do anything with his crazy deckhand. But he was heartened to see that several men were laughing.

The bossun raised the loud-hailer and barked out, "Please switch to the emergency frequency on your VHF radio."

With his heart pounding, Preston left Charlie on deck, ran through the open door of the wheelhouse, and switched to Channel 16.

"Yeah, go ahead, Coast Guard," he said, clearing his throat. "Can I be of assistance? You see we're kinda busy right now."

"Are you the master of this vessel?" the authoritative voice demanded icily.

"I sure am," Preston drawled back. The microphone was wet from his sweaty palms. He forced himself not to look at the ship but to focus on the oil pressure gauge. He deep-breathed, getting himself under control.

"What is your name?" the voice returned.

"Preston Barfield," he replied calmly, trying to steady his shaking hand.

"Please enunciate more clearly."

"That's Preston Barfield," he repeated, and spelled it. There was a delay; someone was writing it down.

"What was your last port of call?" came the clear, articulate voice.

"Key West. We put into Key West about four days ago and took on ice and fuel," he added, hoping that would help explain the boat's sitting so heavily in the water.

"What is your destination?"

"We're going home after this, back to Port Aransas, Texas.

"Look Captain," he added tersely, "I don't mean to be rude or nothing, but I can't stand here talking. I know your routine, but I've either got to set back out or get these nets up before the sharks tear the hanging out of the wings. Now which is it?"

"Please stand by," came the reply, which told him nothing. If they ordered him to deck the nets, they were going to board. And Preston knew that as soon as he started to do that, they would stand off a ways and Blake would do his thing.

EPIC, the agency that keeps track of suspicious boats and planes, had just radioed that there was no *Aquarius* on the hot sheet. There was silence for a good ten minutes, while sharks feasted on the nets. At last the officer in charge came back on, and spoke in a relaxed voice, "Thank you, Captain. We won't take up any more of your time. That's a mighty fine catch you have there. Good luck with it. Have a nice day."

"Same to you," Preston returned and almost dropped the microphone, his knees weak. He headed out on deck to watch the Coast Guard ship slowly veer off. Black smoke exploded from its stack, and the air thundered as the cutter leaped ahead, growing smaller as it steamed away. The predator had examined its prey and found it wanting.

Unbeknownst to them, the commander had met his quota of smugglers already that trip. Two new marijuana leaves were painted on the mast pole, bringing his total to forty-one busts in the past three years. Any boat they encountered in the Yucatan Strait with a northern bearing, they boarded. Out there it was too deep and too far from any shrimping grounds. But here off the Tortugas, where a few boats shrimped for royal reds, it was hard to separate the good guys from the bad guys. And he had a schedule to keep and a tide to catch in Key West. If they missed it, they'd be stuck outside the harbor.

When the cutter was a mile away, Blake popped out of the engine room, stepping on shrimp, and pounded Preston on the back.

"You've done it! You've done it, by God!" he shouted. His throat was dry and cracked. "You saved the load!"

"I could see myself in the brig..." Charlie said trembling.

But Preston didn't feel like a hero. He looked at the enormous pile of shrimp—big jumbos that would go sixteen-twenties to the pound. His heart was breaking. He sank to his knees and scooped up a double handful. His face was tortured.

"All my life, I've wanted a deck-load like this. And now it happens." He started to laugh hysterically. "And we can't do a goddamn thing with them! The only ice we got on board is what's in the refrigerator's ice-cube trays. It's all going to spoil, every bit of it. I wish we could throw the goddamn pot overboard and keep the shrimp. That's twenty-thousand dollars worth, right here!"

"You're crazy," laughed Blake. "Eight million dollars worth of pot for a few shrimp? Money's money, isn't it?"

"You don't understand," Preston struggled to explain. "This is different. When you come into the dock with a load like this, it's something special. You're top dog. People come from all over town to see what you done, and there ain't no better feeling in the whole wide world. A man can hold his head up and be proud of hisself. This, what I have to do now, is a bad, bad thing."

The captain grabbed a shovel and bitterly started pushing the big red jumbo shrimp through the scupper holes. He turned to Blake and said savagely, "I'll tell you the difference! The shrimp are honest and the dope is filth, that's the difference! And so is anyone who hauls it. A man can be proud when he comes into the dock with a catch like this. He doesn't have to sneak around like a low-life criminal dirt bag."

Blake fumed to himself, he didn't see it that way. He saw himself as a businessman, working against a hypocritical society that wanted mind-enhancing potions. Millions of people wanted his wares. His self-image was important, but after seeing the wild look in Preston's eyes he wasn't about to argue.

Charlie had never seen his captain so upset. He picked up a shovel to help clear off the deck, and put the haul behind them.

"Don't touch it, Charlie. This is mine to do," Preston growled between gritted teeth. "Go run the boat." Then his voice thundered, "Both of you get in the wheelhouse and leave me the hell alone!" Fearfully, they obeyed.

It took him four solid hours to clear the decks. Preston shoveled hard as penitence, pushing load after load into the sea. Finally, he gave out. His nervous energy expended, he collapsed on the rail, panting heavily, with tears running down his beard-stubbled cheeks, watching the beautiful reddish shrimp sink down, down, down into the depths. Most didn't get that far. The sea was boiling with sharks, circling by the hundreds, tails splashing, dorsal fins cleaving the water, mouths open, snapping, gulping.

"What a waste!" Preston moaned, watching their frenzied dark shapes and the yellow flashes of jacks zooming in for the feast. "What a goddamn sickening, useless waste. I deserve to burn in hell for this!" With the deck hose, he blasted away every bit of shell, every whisker, every trace of the royal reds, wishing he could wash the catch of a lifetime from his mind.

20

The Return of Lupino

Mary Barfield's strong fingers rapidly pinched off the heads of the shrimp that lay before her on the stainless steel table. Even though her fingers were sore from shrimp acid, and stuck from their rostrums, she enjoyed working at Lawton's fish house. It was a chance to catch up on community news, hear the gossip, and be with her friends. Now in her ninth month of pregnancy, just moving around was hot and bothersome. Some days it was a chore to drag herself down to work. But it was better to keep busy than stay home and worry.

Her friends, cousins and her sister asked her repeatedly when Preston was coming back. Her mother's questioning at the dinner times made her nervous. "Times are hard," she said at work, as her flying fingers parted heads from bodies. "He called the other night," she lied, "said they were having breakdowns and all kinds of trouble bringing that boat around from Louisiana. He'll be back before the baby comes."

Mary wasn't comfortable lying, although she was better at it than her husband. She worried that she would never see Preston again. There was no one to turn to, no one to confide in. So when she came home from work one day and found her brother sitting on the couch looking like a wreck, she cried in joy. "Oh Lupino, I'm so glad to see you. In spite of all the mess you've put us through, I am!"

"Hello, big sister," he said emotionally, and jumped to his feet to hug her. "You are the prettiest sight I've seen in a long, long time. Look at you! You look like you're fixing to pop any minute."

Of all her family, she was closest to him. They were the only ones who had managed to get away from the clutches of G. W. Talagera.

Mary stepped back, looking at him with shock. "Oh, you're a mess!" His hair was matted, his clothing ragged, and he reeked of fish. It was so totally unlike Lupino, who spent hours combing his hair and looking in the mirror to see if he looked like a Nashville singer. He spent days at the stores selecting brightly-colored sports shirts that had to be tapered just so.

If Lupino had a low opinion of shrimping before he left town a month ago on the *Judy C*, he had an even lower one now. The obese skipper and derelict deckhand who had picked him up at Lawton's dock brought him to the low point of his life. The work wasn't hard. Usually the captain and his mate were too drunk to do much out there.

By day they lay around the filthy cabin like hogs, getting drunk. Grease was caked on the walls. Dirt and slime were everywhere. Roaches scurried over the bunks and crawled on him as he lay in his bunk at night. His crewmates snored and farted. Frankie, the first mate, would wake up screaming about imaginary rats gnawing his feet. Sleep was difficult.

The captain had a habit of urinating in a jelly jar when he was too drunk to get up and go to the rail. The glasses of yellow liquid accumulated on the table until he or Lupino threw them out. One day as Lupino walked past the cabin door the captain tossed a piss jar, accidently dousing him. That was the final straw.

That afternoon they anchored in Galveston Bay. Lupino tearfully left his guitar on his bunk and dove overboard. With determined strokes he fought the current and, utterly exhausted, reached the shore. He crawled up the beach and hitchhiked back to Florida, seeking shelter at a Salvation Army along the way.

Listening to the story, Mary's temper rose. Lupino cringed, knowing it was coming. "Why in the hell don't you quit dreaming about Nashville and dope and get a job, Lupino? Learn to be a carpenter, or a plumber, anything. Your dreaming gets us all into trouble. If it weren't for you, Preston wouldn't be..."

She stopped herself short, stammered and continued, "...over in Louisiana, having to run someone else's boat."

Lupino looked at her suspiciously. "Over in Louisiana, huh? And you nine months pregnant? Not the way he talks about how proud he will be to have that young'un, him going to those Lamaze classes with you, and how he's gonna be there to help deliver it." He stood back looking her up and down with a jeering, appraising scrutiny. "Bullshit, big sister. Bullshit, I say. Now where is he?"

She said huffily, "In Louisiana, like I told you."

Lupino gave her a long, knowing nod, smirking at having the upper hand for once. "Something don't smell right. Something's going down, isn't it? I think I need to stir around and find out what's going on. Sounds like it could be profitable."

Tears came to his sister's eyes. She had to talk to someone. What if Preston disappeared and was never seen again? What if he were in jail down in South America somewhere? Where else could she turn? She broke down and told Lupino all she knew.

He listened, nodding, and then said, giving her a sympathetic hug, "Don't worry. Loads get through all the time. I'll see what I can find out.

"Mary," he said as he held her.

"Yes, Lupino?"

"Can you loan me a couple hundred?"

"Loan *you* money!" she cried out with disbelief, shoving him away. "You've gotta be kidding, after all the debt you put us in, you little rat."

"But I've got to have something to wear," he shrieked dramatically. "All my clothes burned up on the boat. I didn't have any in my apartment up in town, and if these get any worse, they'll arrest me for indecent exposure. You gotta help me."

He saw her temper beginning to boil over, and stood back waiting for the inevitable eruption. And judging from her expression, it was going to be high on the Richter scale. "Your little love nest in town!" she screamed. Her voice rose in fury, "Did you know Eloise and the kids had their lights turned off? The church had to raise money for her to get them turned back on. And you're paying rent up in town to keep some whore."

But in the end she reached into her purse, took out the shrimp money she'd earned, and gave him half. Lupino tried not to grin triumphantly. "By the way, John Henry's been hunting you. He said it was real important."

"Oh, he did?" Lupino cried joyfully, his eyes bright again. "The Lord is at work here. I came back just in time. Mary, please let me borrow your truck. I'll put gas in it and have it back in a couple of hours, honest."

That brought more argument, but in the end he prevailed. As he skipped out the door, he sang out, "I knew it, I knew it, I knew it. Something was bringing me back from hell in Texas, and now I know what it was. And Captain Goody-Two-Shoes Barfield is square in the middle of it," he chortled.

Mary yelled after him, "Don't go near the bar. And don't go whore hoppin', goddamn you, Lupino."

Whether or not it was the Lord or the Devil that helped Lupino's situation improve was often the object of conjecture. But his nemesis, Raul, who would have liked to dice Lupino into small cubes and roast him over a fire, had mysteriously vanished, putting the operation into disarray. Instead of being in the Florida Panhandle to honcho the forthcoming off-loading operation, he and two other Cubans were found brutally murdered in their Tampa beach condominium.

The *Aquarius* was en route from Colombia loaded with pot, and there was no time to shed tears. Millions were at stake, and like any well-run organization, nobody was irreplaceable. The show had to go on.

Even so, it was only with the greatest of reluctance, and out of respect for Preston, that Sam Lawton agreed to let Lupino in on the operation. Dope smuggling is marked by a need for fresh talent and plagued by a high turnover rate. Even those who have made past mistakes may find themselves forgiven and pressed into service if conditions warrant.

For five long days Lupino paced the floor of his little Tallahassee apartment, anxiously waiting for the telephone to ring. All over the state, other "mules" were doing the same thing, killing time until the shrimp boat neared the coast. When it finally rang, Lupino caught the seven a.m. flight to Orlando, under the name of Jim Henderson, as he was told. Parked in the airport lot in a sea of other vehicles was a red-and-white Ford pickup, with a new twenty-four-foot tunnel boat on a trailer, with a new five-hundred-foot "legal"-sized net piled on the transom. The keys were hidden in a small magnetic box stuck under the hood, exactly as the voice on the telephone had said they would be.

At a designated address in a subdivision, Lupino picked up a young man, about twenty, who climbed into the truck with his hand thrust forward. "My name's Mike. I'm sure glad I can ride with you. I'll tell you, I've been cooped up with those Cubans the past couple of days, and to tell you the truth, they give me the creeps. They'd cut your throat for a nickel."

"I know what you mean," Lupino muttered. He introduced himself as "Will," pressed the gas pedal, and pulled onto the highway. Outside of town they met two other trucks with camper shells. A big motor home fell in behind them. "How'd you get this job?" Mike asked as they headed down the four-lane.

"Oh, I got connections," Lupino answered mysteriously. "I know the area, so they made me lead mule."

"You done this before?"

"Yeah, lots. But you never get used to it," he tossed off casually. He pressed hard on the gas pedal, pulling out with the big boat and passing a car that was dawdling in front of him.

"This is the first time I ever did anything like this," the young man went on anxiously, tapping his finger on the dashboard. "I need to make some money bad. One night's work, this buddy of mine at the Ford dealership said, and you can make twenty-thousand bucks. Well, we just got a new baby, and he's growing up fast, and me and my old lady were already crowded. We got a girl five years old, and the kids will need rooms of their own. You know how it is these days—you work and you work and you work, and still don't get nowhere. My paycheck—by the time I get it cashed and pay the bills, there's nothing left over."

By the time they approached North Florida, they were chatting and having a good time. Lupino told him all about his life of shrimping and working on oyster boats.

"I'm getting hungry," Lupino announced to his passenger. "We're coming into Foley in a little bit. There's a place up ahead where we can get some good burgers." Lupino spoke into the CB radio and told the other members of the caravan of his plans, and all agreed.

The town of Foley was distinguished only by its tall, steel water tower, a few houses, a truck stop, and a grocery store.

The waitress's name was Mabel. She was too plain to be noticeable, except in the small world of the truck stop, with dim lights and red-and-white-checkered oilskin tablecloths. She knew all who came and went: the pulpwood haulers, truck farmers, the workers at the phosphate plant. Now and then a lost tourist stopped at the drab little cafe and took a chance with the burgers or fried mullet.

"Well, well, if it ain't Lying Lupino!" she scoffed when he came in the front door. "A bad penny always turns up. Don't you know the Grouper Troopers were in here asking about you a few weeks ago?"

"Ah, shoot, there ain't nothing to them," he said grinning weakly, and made a beeline for a table in the rear. Mabel looked suspiciously at the camper trucks and motor home that had pulled into the parking lot. They didn't act like weekend fishermen just back from the Suwannee River. They had the mannerisms of men with a job to do. Contractors, she thought at first, yet they looked like weekend tourists. And they seemed to be traveling with Lupino in some way.

Her ear caught heavily-accented voices and snatches of Spanish as they came through the door. As she led them to Lupino's table and told them about the mullet special, the waitress noted their diamond rings sparkling in the afternoon sunlight filtering through the dirty windows. Everything about these men looked expensive, from their gold medallions to their shiny, alligator shoes.

Mabel retreated to the kitchen to give the cook their orders. Later, as she poured coffee, she overheard them mumbling something about "loads," and once the word "pot" caught her ears. When it was time to pay, one of the Cubans opened a pigskin wallet, flashing a hefty stack of crisp hundred-dollar bills that made Mabel's eyes bug. He fished out a crisp new bill and paid for everyone.

Mabel collected the ten-dollar tip as the campers pulled out. She peeked from behind the curtain, scribbling down the letters and numbers of each license plate, and with fingers trembling excitedly she dialed her husband at the sheriff's department.

Under the watchful eyes of the police, the small caravan proceeded up the coast, along the winding North Florida roads. None of the riders paid any attention to the unmarked Plymouth sedan that followed at a discreet distance. Nor did they see the helicopter that passed high overhead as they turned off the main highway onto the road to Scallop Bay.

As they headed down to the coast, a cold front was turning the air misty. The sheriff saw no reason to call the U.S. Drug Enforcement Agency or even the Florida Department of Law Enforcement. It couldn't be much of an operation, he thought, if Lupino Talagera was involved. Yet the caravan was too big of an operation for a simple air drop, though big planes had landed on remote local roads. In all likelihood a boat was bringing in the load. He thought about calling the Florida Marine Patrol and the U.S. Coast Guard, but he was in no rush to share the glory, or worse yet, have the sting operation taken away from him. Elections were, after all, coming up in a few months.

So the sheriff and his undercover officers, wearing blue jeans, plaid shirts, and carrying fishing poles, drove along in unmarked cars and trucks. Over the years the sheriff had fattened the county's coffers seizing boats, trucks, motor homes, and other equipment and selling it at auction. They were able to build a new jailhouse with it and buy radio equipment. The dope itself was booked as evidence then trucked off to the incinerator under heavy guard. But there was some suspicion that while all the pot was reduced to smoking ash, a good amount did so inside rolling papers.

* * *

Although there wasn't a speck of land in sight, Preston Barfield knew he was home. As they headed up the Florida peninsula into the Panhandle, he watched the water change from a deep oceanic blue to a murky estuarine green. He flicked on the depth-recorder and studied the familiar sloughs and gullies on the moving sheet of graph paper. The events of the past three weeks had taken their toll. They were etched into his life like growth-rings on a tree. As they began picking up shrimp boats on the radar, a wave of homesickness swept over him and he worried about Mary and whether she had the baby yet. Time and again he wanted to call Mary on the landline through the marine operator, but he didn't dare.

He sat at the wheel listening to his buddies talk about their catches, torn up gear, and mechanical breakdowns. The hopper run had played out and the boats were talking about heading to Mississippi for opening day.

Hearing the familiar voices, and just thinking about shrimping made him feel better. While those turkeys are tied to the dock this winter and starving, he thought, I'll be back down in the Tortugas catching royal reds in blue water. Maybe I can hit them again like we did.

Preston fought the desire to grab the mike and start talking, to get news of Mary and his family. Standing beside him listening, Charlie chortled, "Boy, oh boy, if they just knew what we were doing out here." He slapped his thigh and laughed.

"I hope to hell they never find out," Preston said dryly. "But it would be a good story," he chuckled. It felt good to laugh. His taut facial muscles had relaxed for just a moment.

"That's the trouble with this business," Blake quipped. "There's lots of good stories but damn few people you can tell them to. You can't write to mom back home." Then he looked Preston hard in the eyes, "It's the ones who keep their mouths shut that stay out of jail—and live a long time."

"What does that mean?" Preston demanded, sensing a threat.

A buzzer sounded on the Loran, and the red digital numbers blinked out their arrival at the fourteen-forty line, ten hours from shore. They had reached the point of the first radio contact.

Blake switched on the big single side band. "*Lady Sue*, this is the *Lady Sue* calling the *Miss Trixie*. Can you read me?" He repeated the pre-arranged coded greeting twice.

Only empty static answered them. It was a tense time, more than one shrimp boat had to dump the load and flee when they missed their connection. If the shore crew had been arrested, or something went wrong, they were sitting ducks out there loaded with dope. Four hours later, Blake paced the deck in worry. "This isn't right," he said. "We should be able to reach someone." Just as they were beginning to give up a voice roused them, "Go ahead *Lady Sue*, this is the *Miss Trixie*. I'm reading you loud and clear at Force One. You catching anything down your way?"

Blake grinned at the rest of them and made an okay sign with his fingers. His boyish demeanor returned, but only for a moment. A short while later Blake turned moody, and Preston didn't like it. Blake had started acting strangely right after the pirates attacked in Colombia. With each day his instability worsened. Some days he was fine, on others he was nutty, retreating to sit cross-legged on deck in meditation, withdrawn and lost to them. The captain wanted to talk to Charlie about it, but his deckhand was acting hyper. Preston wondered what was up with everyone. Nevertheless, two main points were established. First, everyone was standing by and waiting; and second, of three possible alternative off-loading sites, the first, the most preferred, "Force One," was still viable. No cops had been spotted; everything looked ordinary.

Blake remained deeply troubled, although he wasn't about to share his concerns. The voice on the radio was Rick's, the gun-toting thug from the *Night Shadow*. It should have been Raul. "Something stinks here," Blake muttered to himself. "First pirates, and some kind of doublecross; and now Raul's not sitting the radio."

Blake's instincts were good. They had kept him alive all these years and mostly out of jail. Without Paul, he felt desperately alone. He couldn't rely on Preston or Charlie to kill anyone if the need arose, it was all up to him.

The captain kept an eye on him, noting how exhausted and worried he looked. Gone was his relaxed and friendly manner. Blake was feeling vulnerable and looked like he might explode any minute. Jesus, I'm ready for this trip from hell to end, Preston thought. I love this boat, and I hope I end up with her, but this ain't worth it.

Hours later, as they approached the shore, Preston gazed at the barrier islands and sand dunes. Wind-sculpted slash pines were silhouetted against the glowing orange afternoon sun. He was home at last. All about them in the lee shore were shrimp boats, scattered about with their nets hanging from outstretched outriggers, like a young girl's curtsy.

Preston felt numb listening to John Henry Robins on the *Angela F* complaining, "I wish these environmentalists had these TEDS in their ass. I could have caught double the shrimp today if I wasn't shooting them all out. I'm damn tempted to tie them up and go on fishing."

"You better not or the booger man will get you," D.O. Wilson of the *Miss Randal* drawled back. "They was two of them out here the night before last making sure we had them and that we were dragging behind the closed line."

Preston panicked. He had forgotten to change the nets. Even from the distance he saw the round metal frames of TEDs in everyone's nets. All shrimp fishermen were forced to use them by the Endangered Species Act to keep sea turtles from drowning in their nets unless they were fishing far offshore in deep water. When the law went into effect the shrimpers blockaded ports, went on strike and caused a big stink, but in the end they lost. Now the law was heavily enforced.

"Charlie, Blake," Preston yelled. "Hurry! Get those turtle shooters off the roof. We got to pull these royal red nets off and put those other nets on or we'll draw the marine patrol like flies to shit."

"That's for sure," his deckhand joked. "Messing with an old turtle is a heap worse offense than having a boat full of dope these days."

Moments later the chains rattled and the anchor splashed into the sea. Without a word, Preston went down to the engine room and shut off the breather.

For want of air, the great motor spluttered, rumbled, and died. And for the first time in three weeks, the boat was silent.

As Preston climbed back on deck, the *Aquarius* strained against her anchor line. Only the creak of the rigging and the swish of the waves against the hull could be heard as they changed fishing gear.

Then Charlie checked the fuel. "We've done burned fifteen thousand gallons going down there and back," he reported. "And we still got four or five thousand gallons left. She damn sure don't burn much for all that running. You're lucky as hell, ending up with this boat, Captain."

As the sun went down, sea fog started blowing in on a gentle south wind. Blake was ecstatic. "If this fog holds, it will work in our favor—if the off-loading boats can find us. The cops won't be able to see us from the air. Except for losing Paul, our luck's held so far. Maybe it will go on."

Preston's feelings about losing Paul were mixed. Partly he was relieved at getting the murderous little bastard off the boat, but he also felt a surprising and numbing sense of loss. The hateful and dangerous little man was there one minute, the next he was eaten by the sea. Preston was also concerned about Blake. There was a terseness about him, an unfamiliar edginess in his voice.

As darkness descended, the shrimp trawlers around them pulled anchor, turned on their lights and set out their nets. "We'd better get moving or we'll look suspicious sitting here," Preston said tensely. "Let's just ease down the coast and blend in."

Three hours later, as the *Aquarius* moved closer to the sea buoy, the rendezvous point, their sleepless bodies were tensed and ready to spring. Charlie and Blake covered the name *Aquarius* with a white water-based paint and turned out the lights. Now she was a ghost ship moving through the evening fog and darkness.

Blake switched to Channel 22 on the CB and twanged into the microphone, "How about it, *Mary Jane*. This is the *Lady Sue*. Can you read me?"

"This is the *Mary Jane*, reading you loud and clear."

"Finest kind," Blake drawled in a southern accent, sounding like any other good ol' boy. "Just calling for a radio check. Appreciate it."

"Standing by."

"Well, this is it, boys," Blake declared with relief. He took a deep breath to dispel his tension. "In a little while it'll all be over with. Now, let's get the hatches pried loose and start stacking the bales on deck."

21

The Off-Loaders

The hum of a motor broke the heavy, wet silence of the night, slamming hard on the surface of the misty sea. The shuttle boat slowed to an idle, and its occupant skipper gazed at the wall of mist with an infrared scope and caught the flash of the sea buoy. The off-loaders had located the dark shape of the *Aquarius*. A man's voice called out from the fog, "You got something for me?"

"Who wants to know?" Blake yelled back, his hand never far from the .45 strapped to his side. Anything could happen.

"Potluck," the voice barked back.

"Come on then."

The two crews handled the heavy bales with amazing speed. Charlie un-stacked them in the hold and whipped them along to Preston's waiting hands, then to Blake, and on to the man in the pilot boat. One after the other. The task wasn't made any easier by worsening seas. It took about twenty minutes to pack out the first boat with sixty bales. Then another arrived.

Piloted by a fair-haired man in his early twenties, the bird-dog boat pulled up portside to the *Aquarius*. Charlie told the pilot to pull up to the starboard side. Judging by the granny knot the skipper tied onto the line, Charlie knew he was inexperienced and flustered.

Thud! The first bale landed in the bottom of the bird dog. *Thud, thud, thud,* again and again. *Crack!* The little boat was lifted by a wave and smashed against the *Aquarius*. "Hey!" the off-loader cried, "take it easy. Slow down a little, will ya?"

"Goddamn amateur," muttered Charlie, as he tossed bales rapidly. If the lines had been tied properly, the smaller craft wouldn't be slamming. He was sweating in spite of the damp cold. He cleared his throat, dry with nervousness. "Come on fella," he said to the off-loader, "this is no picnic, hurry up."

Another wave sent the boat bouncing into the crash bumper and one of the loaded bales slipped over and tumbled into the sea.

Blake was breathing hard as he watched the current carry it away. "Hey, you goddamn shit," he snarled, "you just lost us twenty thousand bucks. I ought to blow your empty head off."

"Hey, man, don't do that!" the young man, Mike, begged, "I'm sorry, I'll get it."

"Ease up Blake," Preston warned. "We don't need trouble now. What happened to your cool? Don't get riled up on me the last minute, for Heaven's sake!"

"We lost twenty or thirty bales in that storm already," Blake snarled angrily. "I'm already going to have to do some heavy explaining, and now we've got idiots throwing the rest overboard!" Then he got a grip on himself and he spoke to Mike in a monotone, "I'll tell them we're one short, so they won't kill you when you get to the hill. That is, maybe they won't."

"Hey..." the other begged, "I'll find it."

"Just get out of here!" bellowed Blake, and cut the granny knot loose. Two more boats arrived, and each left heavily loaded, groping through the mist to the Scallop Bay channel.

When the next one came, Charlie shouted joyfully, "Hey Cap'n, you ain't gonna believe what's just crawled up on our boat. It's Captain Lu-Penis!"

"Man! You went all the way down to Colombia and back in this?" Preston hurried out from the wheelhouse and stopped at the sound of that familiar boisterous voice. "Charlie-boy," Lupino bellowed, "I gotta say one thing, you boys go first-class. This is a floating whorehouse."

"Good God," breathed Preston. A flood of mixed feelings—anger, fear, and relief—came over him as he saw his brother-in-law standing before him, his hands braced on his hips against the roll of the little boat.

"Who in the hell hired you?" Blake stormed. "Raul said you'd never work for him again."

"Never you mind," Lupino snapped nastily. "I hear they found your buddy so full of lead down in Tampa a couple of days ago that you could melt him down and make an anchor. Now what I wanna know is who ripped off my goddamn money! You and that truck driver were the only ones who knew I got paid off, and that man in Orlando who gave me the cash..."

"Raul's dead?" Blake said in shock.

"Yeah, like the mean, son-of-a-bitch deserved. Now gimme my money, Blake!"

"Here's your goddamn money," Blake snapped with fury, whipping out his pistol and slamming its butt against Lupino's head, knocking him to the deck. Blake leveled his arm and took aim.

Preston yelled and grabbed his arm. "Hey, don't shoot him! He's my brother-in-law." At the same moment, Charlie grabbed Blake in a headlock. "He's my friend, goddamn it."

With a quick, hard punch to the solar plexus, Blake effortlessly knocked Charlie to the floor, where he doubled up, gasping in agony. In the same moment he wrenched the gun away from Preston and shoved it into its holster, and backed away. "All right, all right," he breathed, the insanity fading from his eyes, "I won't shoot the aggravating little son-of-a bitch. Not now. But I don't like people calling me a thief."

The bushy-haired youth crawled to his feet and spat out, "Now I know it was you that stole me blind." He reeled dizzily, and turned apologetically to Preston, "I was gonna pay you back every dime I owed you. I had forty-thousand dollars in cash and this son-of-a-bitch ripped me off!"

Preston's gruff voice shook the night. "Get off this boat, Lupino, before I shoot you myself. Don't you know when to quit, you little asshole?"

Preston muscled him back to the rail and shoved him into his tunnel boat. Blake picked up a bale and sent it thundering down into Lupino's boat, hitting him squarely in the chest. More bales rained down, and between calling them vile names, Lupino deftly stacked them. He can work when he needs to, Preston thought. He was hump-ing steadily, dodging Blake's assault, stacking bales, and lashing them down expertly.

Charlie popped his head up from the ice hold. "Those were the last ones. We'd better start getting those bales out of the engine room."

"No! Hell no. I'm not trusting those bales to Lupino," Blake said. "Raul's supposed to be here in the cabin-cruiser to take them."

"Raul's dead," Preston said. "Remember? Give them to Lupino. He's the last boat. This trip is finished. Now get those bales off my boat!"

"No," Blake yelled through gritted teeth. "Not yet. Not those. They're special. There's a launch coming for those. It was agreed from the beginning. Someone will be here in a few minutes. Check the radar, they should be coming from the east."

Preston followed him into the cabin; he was fed up. "Special? What's special about them," he demanded suspiciously. "Why are they painted blue. What in the hell's going on?"

Charlie grinned at him. "Blake, why don't you tell the captain about your other little surprise—the one we're not supposed to know about."

A mean grin spread over Blake's face. "Good old Charlie," he said slowly. "He's not near as stupid as he looks. When did you find out?" Against the blinking red numbers of the Loran and the sweep of the radar, Blake, with his hair pulled into a ponytail looked more like a pirate than ever.

Charlie pulled a plastic bag of white powder out of his pocket. "I should have told you," he said to Preston contritely, "but I was afraid how you'd act. When the bale got caught in the shaft coupling and tore it open, I found this floating in the bilge. It's cocaine."

Preston looked at it like it was a cobra. "*Cocaine!*" he gasped. "First guns, now coke," his eyes were wide with disbelief and terror. "How much are we hauling? Is it in all those bales down there?"

"So you thought you'd have a little fun on the side, huh, Charlie?" chuckled Blake, avoiding the question. "I should have known that's why you were acting so funky! Well, it doesn't matter."

"Give me a break," scoffed Charlie, "you been snortin' that shit all along and acting mighty weird yourself."

"Hey!" yelled Lupino. "I'm still waiting. What's the hold-up? I still got room for more."

"Look, Preston," Blake said, ignoring Lupino, "nobody said you were going to be told everything. You're going to get paid and you're going to end up with this boat. You just do your job and do what I say. There should be a boat here in a minute..."

A hysterical voice screamed out over the radio, "It's a bust! Cops all over the place! Run for it!" then the line went dead.

* * * *

On shore, sheriff's deputies watched the shuttle boats coming and going. Some hid in the bushes, others in nearby houses. They watched the off-loaders nervously pacing beside their camper trailers and Winnebagos. They observed one of the motor homes back down the boat ramp without lights. No faces could be seen, only the forms of six men madly passing bales from hand to hand.

When a shuttle boat was empty, the next moved into place. And when the vehicle could hold no more, it crawled up the boat ramp and bounced away over the dirt roads of the subdivision. When it hit the paved road, the driver turned his headlights on and picked up speed, and the next camper truck moved into place.

The police did not use radios, rightly figuring that the smugglers had police radio scanners and other electronic detection devices in their command cottage. The cops had lost out on busts before, storming in to find scanners and overflowing ashtrays with fresh-burning joints but no people. It wasn't going to happen this time. Three miles up the road, sheriff's deputies and highway patrolmen armed with shotguns and rifles waited at a roadblock. The jaws of the trap were spread wide, waiting to snap shut.

The first vehicle to leave the ramp, a Winnebago was blocked at the highway, by a man with a flashlight. The Winnebago slowed. A car sped up behind with flashing blue lights. Suddenly there were cops all over the place, pointing guns, shouting, "Hold it. You're under arrest for importation of narcotics. Get out! Put your hands behind your back!"

Minutes later the next vehicle was caught and then the next. One driver managed to shriek over the radio, "There's cops all over the place. It's a bust. Run for it!"

"All right! Let's get 'em!" another voice barked over the police walkie-talkies.

At the launch ramp, a voice bellowed over a bullhorn, "This is a bust! Police! Hands up! You're under arrest!" A flare went off and a blinding white light lit up the night sky.

A half-loaded camper truck spun its tires as it zoomed up the ramp and charged down the sandy road, only to be blocked at the highway. The terrified off-loaders scattered, diving into bushes, climbing trees. Squad cars with flashing blue lights and sirens screamed from all directions. Officers stormed out of cottages with pistols drawn.

They chased one man into the canal and tackled him in the water. They pulled others from beneath the stilted floors of seaside cottages.

Shots were fired in the air. When it looked safe, weekenders and cottage-dwellers came out to watch the police lining up the suspects, handcuffing them, reading them their rights, and putting them into squad cars. The smugglers were dripping with sweat and coated with flakes of leaves and seeds from the evil weed. Their shirts were impounded at the jailhouse as evidence.

* * *

Panic and confusion swept over the *Aquarius* like a windswept fire through a dry pine forest. "You heard 'em," Charlie shrilled. "It's a bust! We've got to get out of here."

He bolted for the wheelhouse and threw the boat in gear, heading out to sea as fast as they could go, dragging Lupino's boat with him. Waves splashed into the tunnel boat. "Hey, goddamn it!" screamed Lupino. "You'll sink me!" The boat rolled and crashed into the side of the *Aquarius*, sending him sprawling. "Stop it, goddamn it!" his voice squealed over the throaty roar of the engine. With knife in hand, Lupino crawled over the bales, toward the bow rope that held him fast.

Preston rushed into the wheelhouse bellowing over the screaming diesel, "Slow her down, Charlie. Slow her down! You'll drown him."

But when he saw his deckhand's rigid death-grip on the throttle, he pushed him aside. Charlie held on. Preston's powerful hand closed on Charlie's wrist. "Let go, Charlie, damn it," and wrestled the throttle back.

The *Aquarius* slowed just as Lupino cut through the tether. But not in time to keep him afloat. A big wave rolled over the bow and submerged him in cold sea water up to his knees. Water surged into the stern, washing bales overboard, and in a second the boat sank beneath him. He felt the icy water close over his head. He swam desperately upward. To his horror he felt something snag him, pulling him down as he fought to get to the surface. It was the gill net that had been piled in the back of the tunnel boat, now adrift with its corks, lines, and webbing bunched together, floating beside him.

Lupino kicked his way up, screaming for help, and swallowing salt water. In the distance he could hear the rumblings of the *Aquarius* fading into the black mist. Then he went down again. He flailed in the inky void. Suddenly, deep in his soul, he knew he would die if he didn't stop panicking. So he stopped, and lay still, fighting his icy fear. Calmer, he kicked his way up again, took a breath, then felt for his knife. There it was, in his pocket. He managed to get it out, pull it open, and begin cutting through mesh after mesh after mesh.

At last he was free, swimming in the open water, swept along by a swift tidal current. Exhaustion and cold swept over him. He cast around for something to cling to, but there was nothing.

Then something bumped into his back. Hard. *Shark!* leaped through his mind. In gut-wrenching fear he spun around to beat off his attacker. His fists struck something solid, cloth-covered—it was the all-too-familiar feeling of burlap. Like an octopus seizing a crab, Lupino grabbed onto the block of marijuana and held on as the current carried him away.

Had it been a north wind, Lupino would have been swept out to sea. But the southeast wind carried him toward shore, and before long he felt his feet dragging on sand. He sat hopelessly on the emerging sand bar—shivering, teeth chattering—waiting for daylight and a marine patrol helicopter to spot him. It was all over. Then, against the mist, he saw a dark shape floating. It was his boat.

Lupino waded as fast as he could go. When he got there, mercifully an inch or two of freeboard managed to stay above the waves. He found the five gallon bail bucket wedged in the bow and, standing in waist-deep water beside the boat, he bailed as he had never bailed before.

When the gunnels were high enough to keep out the waves, and the boat could support his weight, he climbed in. Shivering in the cold wind, he finished bailing. A grin spread across his wide face as he discovered the lumpish shape of two dozen bales still in the boat. He turned the key on his motor, praying out loud, "Please start, motor. Please start! You been a good motor to me, help me out now!" The starter spluttered and whined—a good sign. It whined and whined, but the battery grew weaker. Just when Lupino was about to despair, it coughed, spluttered, and amazingly cranked up. If he had been a comic book character, Lucky Little Lupino would have had dollar signs flashing in his eyes.

22

The Fight

Preston expected to hear any minute the powerful engines of police boats bearing down on them with flashing blue lights. *Aquarius* plowed through the rolling waves at a pathetically slow twelve knots. He could feel the engine's vibration running through the boat, tortured machinery heating up, the pistons pounding in their cylinders, throbbing in his brain, *SURVIVE...SURVIVE...SURVIVE!*

He could picture sheriff's deputies with guns drawn scrambling aboard, shoving him against the wall, jerking his hands behind his back and slapping handcuffs on his wrists. No, he thought, no. Not after we escaped from the pirates, the storms, from Paul. Not now! My boat, my boat! I must save it.

Charlie stood beside him, frightened and bewildered at the fear he saw in the eyes of the man he looked up to. "Where are we going, Preston? What are we going to do now?" he wailed over the scream of the engine and the noise of the radio.

Blake pushed through the cabin door and shut out the chill of the foggy night. He'd been on deck listening for approaching boats, trying to formulate an escape. He was breathing heavily, desperate and cornered. If Raul was dead, there were others who knew the plan, who would come and take him and the dope off the boat. And he could escape into the night. But the reality impinged upon him: they heard about the bust and vanished. They may even have been caught.

He pushed Charlie aside to get to the radar and pressed his face against the rubber light-shield, studying the grid on the screen the way a scientist examines bacteria through a microscope.

Although there were at least 50 blips of larger shrimp boats ahead, there was no rescue boat. But nor were there police boats pursuing them, cutting rapidly through the concentric lines of the screen. He snatched the single side band radio and twisted the dial, trying to reach someone on one of the designated channels. There was only empty static.

Preston turned to his deckhand. "We'll be coming up on the fleet in a little bit. Get the forepeak open, bring the rest of these coke bales up from the engine and start pitching them. The way the current's running and these south winds, there will be bales scattered from hell to breakfast. By morning, everyone will have a bale or two and that'll drive the cops nuts!"

"Oh no!" said Blake shaking his head and backing away. "We're not gonna do that. There's still a chance we can get by with it and salvage what's left of the load. My contact's out there somewhere; if it's not Raul it's someone else. We've gone this far, we're not quitting now."

Preston turned on him furiously, "Forget it, Mister. It's over. I've had enough doublecrossing. And if you think we can still get away with it, you're out of your mind. This coast will be buzzing with cops by daylight. Charlie, get those bales topside and start pitching them."

"Right," said Charlie, and thrust open the sliding door.

"Just a goddamn minute," Blake snapped icily, "You move, Charlie-boy, and I'll blow your addled brains out all over the cabin."

The captain and deckhand looked with disbelief at the pistol pointing toward them. "Close the door," Blake snapped. "Now, let's just settle down and talk this over."

Until now the marijuana had been ethereal in Blake's mind, always apt to be snatched away like fairy gold. But now, with millions of dollars worth of cocaine-loaded pot still on board, Blake could taste the coffee on his ranch in Ecuador. He could feel the horse beneath his rump. There was no more Navy, no more pirates or Coast Guard. It was a foggy night, and escape was completely possible. All that stood between him and his dreams were two stubborn shrimpers.

Preston moved forward. "Put that gun away, Blake, before I stick it up your ass."

Blake thrust the .45 in his face. "I've got no choice, Preston. That's eighteen million dollars worth of toot down there, and it's my only chance to get away. It's not going overboard." He shoved the gun hard against Preston's face. Charlie froze against the door, but his eyes darted frantically, looking for a way to attack.

Blake grinned at him, "I'd hate to waste either of you, especially after all you've done for us. But one thing they taught me in Vietnam was how to kill people. Don't either of you try to cross me or forget who's in charge here, or the only thing that will go overboard tonight will be your dead asses."

Preston cleared his throat, and tried to put stability into the trembling knees that threatened to buckle. "Tell you what, Blake. Just set Charlie and me off on the nearest buoy. She's all yours. You don't owe us a dime."

An ugly grin came to Blake's lips. "Just like that, huh? Not on your life, fella. You can't walk away from this one. If I get caught, you get caught. And you're gonna get the main rap."

"Me?" choked Preston.

"Yes, you! You're the captain, the boat's leased to you. It's in your name. *You* ran the boat down to Colombia and picked up the load. *You're* the Master of the Vessel. *You* evaded the Coast Guard and brought in the shuttle boats in the fog. For all we know, the cops have your voice on tape right now."

"Put the gun down, Blake," Preston said, with fists clenched.

Blake's thumb slipped the safety off with a click and pointed the pistol between his eyes. A different Blake stood there, one Preston had imagined might be there from the start, hiding beneath an encouraging grin and an easy-going and reasonable disposition. He was terrifying to see, like a cornered jaguar. "You wouldn't be the first captain that's gone overboard in this business," he said with a snarl. "So just shut your goddamn mouth, Preston, and run this boat." He backed up a step, the gun steady in his hand.

"Hey," Charlie cried in alarm, raising his hands, "take it easy, Blake." He did his best to muster a laugh. "We're all in this together. We've been through too much to have it come to this."

Blake ignored him. "Get out there and drop the nets out. We're going shrimping. It worked before with the Coast Guard, maybe it will work again."

"Yeah, right," scoffed Preston, "only the Coast Guard didn't know we were carrying a load of dope. By morning, they'll be crawling all over these boats.

"Shut up and do as I say!"

With growing fury at having to work with a gun pointed at him, Preston set out the nets. Meanwhile, with the auto-pilot steering the boat, the wheel turned all by itself, as if it were being run by a ghost. And the *Aquarius* strained ahead, pulling her two 45-foot nets and 2,000-pound doors.

"Looks like I'll have to stay awake," Blake said wearily when they were back in the cabin. "Charlie, get me some strong black coffee. I can watch you from right here," he said, looking down the three steps into the galley, "so don't you try any shit while you're making it."

"Coming right up!" the deckhand replied obediently. "Now just don't shoot anybody."

"Stand where I can watch you," Blake called down after him. Then he positioned himself behind Preston and gestured with his pistol. "You just run the boat."

The captain swallowed hard, doing his best to control the fear and rage boiling inside him, and looking for an opportunity to jump him. Blake read his thoughts and gave an unpleasant laugh. "Don't try it, baby."

"Now I see why you brought those explosives," Preston said accusingly. "Too bad, Blake. I liked you. But it was your plan to kill us all along, wasn't it? Now I know why you signed the boat over to me so easily. When the run was over, you were going to kill us and take her out to deep water and blow her up, right?"

"You shit, that's what you think I'd do?" His voice rose incredulously.

"Why not, you made us haul guns down there. That was never part of the deal. Neither was running cocaine; we thought it was just pot. You're a bunch of lying cutthroats!"

"Just shut up," Blake said furiously. "I'm not going to argue with you, Preston." He had to sort this out, to figure a way to unload, and failing that, a way to escape.

Charlie returned with the coffee, and sat beside Preston in his co-pilot's chair. Blake lapsed into silence. Once or twice Preston tried to make conversation to ease things, but his words died in cold silence. Blake just stood there, drinking his coffee with one hand, the gun in the other, and watched through deadly alert eyes, giving no hint of what he was thinking.

Preston sat silently at the wheel, watching the hazy auras of the shrimp boat lights ahead of him. He could feel Blake's cold, blue eyes boring into his back, knowing he was watching his every move like a calculating computer. He cringed in anticipation of a bullet smashing into his spine. I've got to do something, he thought, or this crazy son-of-a-bitch will kill us.

Preston cast his eyes around the wheelhouse for a way out. His eyes landed on the Loran. It blinked their position in red digits. He knew the gullies, the sleighs, and the sea bottom by heart. He also knew that just one gridline away lay a sunken barge sixty feet down. He made a slight course change and sat back, waiting tensely. Again Blake reached for the single side band radio. "Come in, *Miss Trixie*."

And again there was empty static, silence.

Suddenly the *Aquarius* lurched violently, the starboard outrigger tilting sharply into the waves as the cable snatched backwards like a dog jerked on a leash. The great funnel-shaped net, sixty feet down and three hundred feet behind, had tangled with the barge. Preston jumped for the control and, instead of breaking back the throttle, rammed it full speed ahead.

Blake let out a cry of alarm as he lost his balance and hot coffee hit his belly. In a flash, Preston spun around and flung himself across the room. He landed a smashing hook into Blake's jaw and grabbed the gun with both hands. "Get him, Charlie!" he bellowed

Preston tested his opponent's strength and found it unbelievably strong. Blake's long hours of calisthenics on the boat kept him in top-notch shape. The gun exploded, there was a spit of flame, and Preston felt a numbing shock. For a moment, he thought the bullet had passed through him, but then realized that Blake's unbelievably fast kick to his solar plexus had knocked the breath out of him. Blake held onto the gun, and would have regained the advantage, but Charlie sank his teeth into Blake's hand and held on like a bulldog.

Blake let out an bellow, and his gun clattered to the deck. His free hand sent a vicious chop to Charlie's throat that left him choking. Next he delivered a rattling kick to his groin; and Charlie bent over in agony, grunting. Then he kneed Charlie's jaw, cracking it and throwing him on his back. Even in his agony, Charlie's fingers groped for the gun. Letting out a ferocious battle roar, the blond pirate stomped on his hand. The deckhand wailed in agony and rolled over, as the gun went sliding across the deck.

Before Blake could grab it, Preston slammed him in the stomach, and Blake's wind escaped with a hiss. He whipped around to face Preston, but not in time to avoid a well-aimed, shattering roundhouse punch. Then another. At that moment, Charlie rolled over, wrapping his muscular arms around Blake's legs, and down he went.

The captain was on top of him. He ripped the gun from Blake's hand, grabbed him by his long, yellow hair and banged his head hard on the deck. He sat down hard on Blake's chest, and jammed the barrel into his eyeball and pressed down, breathing in shuddering gasps.

The cold steel bore painfully into Blake's eyeball, almost squashing it. He lay still, immobile, like a sheep waiting to be slaughtered. Meanwhile the *Aquarius* was running round and round in a tight circle, her starboard net tethered to the sunken barge.

Charlie struggled to his feet, leaning on the pilot's chair. "The son-of-a-bitch broke my hand," he sobbed. "Let me, Preston. I'll blow his brains out his asshole."

Barfield's mouth was open in a deep guttural snarl, his teeth bared like a wolf's. He pressed his finger against the chilly steel of the trigger, testing the tension in the spring. He felt sick. The taste of bile churned in his stomach; he wanted to vomit. Another tiny unit of force and this man's head, brain, and hair would be all over the place.

The fight had gone out of Blake. He took a deep breath and forced a painful grin at the man who jammed a gun in his eye. "You're not going to kill me, Preston. It's not in you. Right now Charlie might, but you won't." His words came out slowly, almost casually.

There was silence. "No," Preston finally spat out, "you're right. You're not worth it. And not over a bunch of stinking white powder, I won't."

"He's right," shrilled Charlie. "Give me the gun. I'll shoot the son-of-a-bitch. What was your last surprise, to blow us away when the trip was over?"

Blake took another deep breath. "I never planned to hurt you. We had to keep some things secret for security. We had a deal, and a deal is a deal. Preston, can't you take that thing out of my eye, it hurts like hell."

Preston pulled the muzzle back an inch from Blake's bruised and watering eye. "Thanks," Blake gasped, and went on. "Look, we're businessmen, we need people like you to get our products through. If word got around the waterfront that we shot people or doublecrossed them, how would we ever get anyone to haul a load?"

"Go find a rope and tie his hands, Charlie," Preston ordered in disgust, still pressing his weight on Blake's chest.

"I can't," Charlie replied painfully. "The son-of-a-bitch has ruined me! I think he broke my fingers too."

The captain released him, and Blake propped himself against the corner and wiped his bloody mouth. He mustered a painful grin. "Hey, that won't be necessary," he said thickly. "I give you my word. I won't give you any more trouble."

Preston laughed nastily. "After all the lies you've told us, your word's not worth much."

Blake wiped the blood from his mouth again. "I've never lied to you. I've omitted telling you some details, but tell me when I've told a lie."

"Go search his bunk and bring back any guns you find," Preston said, ignoring him.

Keeping Blake covered, he stood up slowly, reached for the controls, and pulled back the throttle, taking the pressure off the cables and snared nets on the hang below. The tilted boat righted itself.

"There's a pistol under my mattress, and there's one in my footlocker. The machine gun's under my bed," Blake volunteered, looking at Preston earnestly. "Look, if I were trying to screw you, would I tell you that?"

"Maybe you've got some stashed around where we can't find them. It's easy to hide a gun on a boat this size."

A few minutes later, Charlie dragged the rocket and grenade launchers, machine gun pistols and other firearms on deck.

"Throw them overboard," Preston ordered.

"You think we ought to?"

Preston gave a firm nod and Charlie obediently sent the weapons splashing into the sea. "I've been wanting to do that the whole trip," he said with relief and satisfaction. "No one's gonna find them, unless they're stupid enough to drag around this barge."

Preston threw Blake's .45 overboard. "Now we're on a level playing field. It's two to one, and we're in charge. You can't whip us, so you better behave!"

Charlie gasped, and Blake grinned appreciatively. "I've never seen anyone who gets such jollies tossing guns overboard."

"Shut up! Stand where I can watch you," the captain ordered Blake.

The wind had changed and the fog was blowing; it was starting to lift. In the distance he saw the glow of working shrimp boats. They looked brighter than a few minutes ago. He knew that as soon as the sun came up in a couple of hours, the shroud would burn away.

"We've got to get these bales before the U.S. Customs comes looking for us. I want to get every bit of pot off my boat, scrub the bilge, and get the deck loaded with fish before they come snooping around."

High above, they heard the hum of an airplane flying the coast. "Go ahead, dump it," Blake jeered. "Those bales will leave a trail bobbing right over to us. They're probably using color infra-red photography and night scopes right now. I can just see the video footage being shown in court."

As the engine noise became louder and passed over, Preston had to agree. "Let's get the nets up, Charlie. Then we'll run from here and dump it."

"Screw up again, why don't you, Preston," Blake needled. "Get to the very end, then chicken out, just like you did on the *Night Shadow*."

"Damn you. Shut up before I kick your ass all over this deck again."

"Go ahead, beat my brains out. I have nothing else to lose," Blake tossed off. "Look, you're the man in charge now, Preston, I'm not going to fight you. Hear me out. I'll help you dump the load, but for Christ's sakes, let's dump it where I can turn it into money, and you can keep the boat."

Doing his best to ignore what Blake had said, Preston pushed him out the door. Then he turned on the red-and-green running lights mounted on the cabin roof, the white bulb on the top mast, and the four 200-watt deck lights. Once on they banished the darkness with an eerie glow visible in the fog. Preston was startled by the litter of marijuana residue strewn over the deck. Bales, torn in the rapid handling, left leaves, stems, and flakes all over like shredded tobacco.

Charlie turned on the deck pump and blasted the litter through the scupper holes, while Preston manned the scrub broom.

"You'll never get it all off," Blake forewarned, leaning against the railing, gently rubbing his jaw. "And all it takes is a little bit of residue to get a conviction. They can match it up to the bales. I don't care how you scrub it. One seed will do it. And when, not if, they find the cocaine in the bales, we're all going to be charged with trafficking a Class-A narcotic. That means twenty years. You've got a better chance if we go through with it.

"He's got a point there, Skipper," Charlie shouted hoarsely over the winch's noise, keeping his eye on the port-side otter doors of the un-tethered net that was rising up out of the water. Using his good hand, he threw the brake just before the chains collided with the block. "We ain't got nothing to come back to, Preston. He's right. Even if we get away with it, which we ain't likely to do now, we'll still be poor as owl shit. You still won't have a boat that runs and you'll still be in trouble with the banks."

"Just shut up both of you," Preston snapped. "I don't want to hear it. If we don't get off this sunken barge, we can all end up figuring out what to do in the jailhouse."

"Sunk barge?" Blake's voice was incredulous. "Then getting hung up was no accident?" He broke into laughter, and looked at Preston with respect. "You snagged that barge deliberately! God damn, you're *good*, Barfield."

23

The Marine Patrol

As the sun rose higher, the sky turned a foggy orange, and the lights of the other shrimp boats blinked against the lightening horizon. The *Aquarius* was still hung up. The boats around it were leaving, heading into the sound to anchor in protected waters.

Charlie looked at the big orange globe and the thinning fog. "We can't pitch the bales now. If we were gonna do it, we should have done it last night."

Preston looked at the cable hanging straight into the water, "We've got to get that net unhung and go behind the reef with the rest of the boats or we'll be a sitting duck out here. Charlie, I'm fixing to snatch her off. Stand clear of the rigging. She's gonna bleed, shit, or blister, but I'm gonna get her loose. Let off on the brake, and let the cable out. When I holler, lock her down."

The *Aquarius* surged ahead, with the freewheeling winch spewing out a thousand feet of cable. Charlie jammed on the brake. There was a violent snatch as the stubborn net tore loose, and they quickly pulled the tattered remains on deck and followed the rest of the fleet into the bay. While Preston ran, Charlie hoisted up the net bag, opened it, and a half ton of scaly, dead creatures spilled on deck.

By the time they anchored behind the barrier islands with the rest of the fleet, the sun had burned through the fog, warming the creatures on deck. Blue crabs feeling the rays on their shells bubbled and frothed, and croakers fighting to stay alive, wiggled and thrashed. Here and there a shrimp feebly flexed its spidery legs and twitched its wind-dried antennas forlornly. An early morning fly sampled the fish and squid.

Charlie started shoveling the catch overboard, but it was painful to grasp the shovel with his bruised and possibly broken fingers. Preston stopped him, "Leave it. We may need that stuff on deck."

Passing seagulls watched from above, and headed their way. One after the other they appeared. One would grab a fish in its mouth and six others would follow in hot pursuit, shrilling angrily with repetitive calls. They fought airborne battles for the fish, as they sank into the depths.

The *Aquarius* anchored in the midst of the fleet, next to the Alabama boats that were hooked together in chains of as many as four boats. There were dozens of local boats as well as some from Texas, from Louisiana, and a few from South Carolina. Some crews were still culling off before going to bed.

They had barely set the hook when Blake suddenly stood erect. "Listen. There's a speedboat coming this way."

Moments later two Marine Patrol boats with blue rotary lights roared in from opposite directions. Their fiberglass hulls pounded violently, battering the metallic waves, sending up explosions of white spray. They cruised to a stop in the middle of fifty-odd anchored boats.

The officers tied their boats up side by side and compared notes, laying out a strategy. They looked like hungry lions surveying a herd of wildebeest on the African plains, making their presence felt to the guilty and not-guilty alike.

Preston watched them move apart and begin their search. It was a difficult job. There were shrimp boats scattered for ten miles. They cruised past the local boats tied up stern to stern. Sweat beaded on his forehead and trickled down his neck. His knuckles whitened on the handle of the deck shovel. He watched one approach an old Mississippi bow-lugger with its rounded belly and square cabin mounted on the stern. The gray-uniformed officers climbed aboard, carrying shotguns. The other boat roared off to the trawlers silhouetted against the morning sun on the horizon.

"Keep right on going boys," Charlie said softly as he culled the shrimp. "Go check those boats over yonder and leave us alone."

"We got one thing working for us," Preston managed grimly, the sound of his heart starting to pound in his ears. "I don't think they have the first damn idea who they're looking for." The patrolmen were at least ten boats away now. Blake said nothing, but slowly picked away the catch. He seemed to be praying.

With his aching hand, it was a chore for Charlie to cull—even slowly. He fought his nervous energy to scrape the deck clean. He worked slowly, dragging out one shrimp at a time and throwing them into a basket. "One thing is for sure—if they had any idea which boat it was, they'd be after us like ugly off an ape. Lord, let them pass us by!"

But they didn't. Preston's heart sank as the gray patrol boat drew near. Then he brightened. "Hey, I know one of the boys running that boat. It's Teddy Miller. He was my blocking buddy in football. Back in high school we used to date the same girls. He was sweet on Mary. Just keep your mouth shut and let me do the talking."

As he watched them approach, Preston had visions of the two of them in their younger days. He recalled how they hunted squirrels in the oak hammocks and fished on lazy rivers in long-past innocent days. He fought the desire to bare his soul to Ted, to come clean and get it over with. If anyone would be sympathetic, he would. But it was too late. The lines were drawn. He was outside the law and couldn't turn back.

Ted Miller sat at the controls, while his partner looked with binoculars from boat to boat, watching for waterlines too low in the water or damage from tying up boats or extra crash bumpers. Preston was thankful he had remembered to cut the crash bumpers loose, and that he had Charlie wash off the water-based paint that covered the boat's name.

Praying to remain calm, Preston grabbed the aluminum shovel, dug deep into the mound of culled fish, and shoved it through the scupper holes. The fish splattered into the water like coal raining down a chute, the water turning milky with juices and scales. The wind-dried, semi-dehydrated bodies of hundreds of small fish floated away in the current. With shrill cries of delight, the gulls flocked, hovered, and screamed in greedy anticipation.

Pretending to look sleepy and indifferent after a hard night of shrimping, Preston leaned on the rail, watching the two trim officers in their gray uniforms approach. They wore patches of officialdom on their shoulders, and their gray boats bore the seal of the Great State of Florida.

"Hello, Teddy," Preston called down, taking in their broad gray hats, shiny black belts bristling with silvery bullets and holsters with .38 service revolvers. The other officer was tightly holding a sawed-off shotgun.

"Preston!" Officer Miller said in surprise. "I didn't recognize the boat."

The captain yawned sleepily and rubbed his three-day growth of stubbled beard. "I'm running this for Sam. Picked her up in Morgan City a few weeks ago. My boat tore up so I thought I'd try to make a few dollars until I could get caught up, but we ain't had nothing more than breakdowns. Then this happened." He gestured to the tattered remains of the webbing hanging on the doors.

"Ugh, that is a mess!" shuddered Miller. "I see you found the rocks all right."

"It could be worse," Preston agreed. "Didn't have to cut no cables. But that's shrimping!"

Miller put the patrol boat into reverse to keep it from being carried away with the tide. "Preston, this is Lieutenant Blakemore. He's up from Key West to help us with some trouble."

"Pleased to meet ya," drawled the captain. The lieutenant returned a curt, unfriendly nod. The officer had no love for shrimpers. He was fastidious and took pride in his uniform and his polished black shoes. Fishermen smelled bad, and climbing aboard their fishy vessels measuring nets and counting shrimp was messy and distasteful. He much preferred to be back in the Keys, looking at the girls on the sailboats while he checked boat licenses. He'd already been cursed out three times that morning by other North Florida crackers when he boarded their boats and woke them up.

"I saw Mary at the post office the other day," Ted Miller ventured casually. "Looks like she's about to have that baby any time now."

"Yeah," said Preston guiltily, "we figure it'll be on this next moon. You know how women do, I figured we'd get this boat on around before she popped. I wouldn'a gone, but I owe everyone in town, and we haven't got a dime of hospital insurance." He yawned, feigning sleepiness.

Miller's eyes turned to Preston's crew, and Charlie nodded at him and grinned. His yellow Caterpillar hat stained with black engine grease was pressed down hard over his bushy hair, hiding the bandage and bullet wound. Ted Miller had arrested him last year for tonging undersized oysters in closed waters, but there were never hard feelings. Charlie simply accepted that Miller was doing his job and was more careful the next time he poached.

The marine patrolman watched the other one, the strange deckhand delicately picking out the shrimp, trying to keep from getting stuck by the sharp spines of mantis shrimp and little catfish that had already hit him.

"Got a green boy there?" he asked.

"Yeah," Preston answered, trying to keep the butterflies, shrimp and other creatures in his stomach quiet. "Picked him up in Louisiana. He ain't worth a flip. But he's trying."

Blake grinned back at him and went on working.

Meanwhile the Marine Patrol lieutenant's eyes roved over the *Aquarius*. His eyes stayed on the long whip antennas on the wheelhouse. "Those are pretty big radios you're carrying," he said.

"Oh them, yeah," Preston tossed off. "That's the AM set. This is one of them royal red boats. We fish in two or three hundred fathoms, about a 150 miles offshore." He pointed to the winches fattened with cable, far more than other boats had. "That's a lot of water to drink out there, so we need something that will carry better than the VHF. We worked the Desoto Canyon off Pensacola coming around in two-hundred fathoms, but didn't catch anything. So we come on in here, put the turtle shooters back on and been catching rocks."

Miller looked at the splintered doors, the tattered webbing and the stretched chains encrusted with limestone mud. That part of his story sounded authentic enough, but there was something that bothered him. He had never seen Preston Barfield looking so haggard and worn, usually even in the midst of the grueling work, he managed to shave now and then.

And then there was that hippie deckhand with the ponytail. He was too polished, suntanned, his body muscular and athletic, his jeans weren't faded and eaten with shrimp acid enough. Not like the rags good ol' Charlie wore.

"Oh crap," Miller thought with a sinking feeling. "We got our mother ship." And it wasn't being run by some mangy low-life with a gold earring and an eye-patch who would slit someone's throat. It was his friend.

But the idea of storming on board, finding a load of pot or residue, drawing his gun and handcuffing Preston Barfield made him physically sick. There was no prestige in making a bust like that, and Ted Miller liked to feel good about himself. His neighbors would despise him for it, his wife would be upset, and for what?

Right now, if he were on a jury, he'd have a hard time convicting *any* commercial fisherman and sending him up for years under Florida's mandatory drug sentencing law. The new fisheries regulations made it almost impossible for fishermen to scratch out a living now. Shrimpers were a dying breed and would soon be replaced by retirees in condominiums and yachts. Ted Miller thought the new laws were garbage.

Every day he'd have to look at Mary Barfield, struggling along with a child to feed, living on food stamps. He'd heard about the cussing match Preston had with G.W. at the oyster house a month ago. Barfield was a proud man, and so was his wife. He'd have to watch their kid growing up in rags.

Screw it, he thought bitterly. Goddamn it, screw it. I'm not gonna do it. If this authoritarian piss-wad next to me doesn't have the sense to bust him, why should I?

The lieutenant sniffed the air, thinking he'd caught a whiff of something else besides fish. "You say you picked this boat up in Louisiana? How come it says Port Aransas, Texas, on the transom?"

Preston answered cautiously, not liking his tone or him. "Because that's her port of registry. Like I said, I picked her up in Morgan City, where Sam Lawton told me to. She belongs to the A & B Fish House," and remembering the title was now in his name, he added, "and she's leased to me. If you want, I'll go get the papers for you. Come on aboard."

Preston turned to his deckhand. "Charlie, shovel this trash overboard so they don't get fish scales over their pretty shined-up shoes," he said sarcastically. Ted grinned, and began to doubt whether he had the right boat or not.

Charlie leaped into action, madly shoveling the catch off the deck. Throwing all his pent-up anxiety into it, he pushed hundreds of pounds of moribund fish with glazed eyes and dried scales through the scuppers. There was an explosion of bird life. Gulls that had been sitting on the water took to the air screaming. Others that had been circling, uttering impatient cries, dive-bombed wildly, grabbing fish and fighting with each other.

The officers had to shout to each other above the shrieks and screams of two hundred birds as they discussed whether to board or not. A seagull swooped overhead, and with a vengeful, shrill cry bombed the patrol boat's deck, rotary light, and windshield with white liquid droppings. But the lawmen got the worst of it. The lieutenant's wide brim hat was covered. The fetid liquid dripped down his impeccably pressed shirt and onto his neatly pressed pants.

Preston and Charlie erupted in belly laughs. Blake joined in, but his eyes weren't laughing. Charlie leaned on his shovel and guffawed. "Damn seagulls don't have no respect for the law!"

Ted grinned back, wiping the bird droppings away. "Don't feel bad fellas," Preston chuckled. "Leastways you were wearing hats. One time I had one shit on me and it run all down my nose and into my mouth. But it's against the law to shoot the nasty buzzards."

The lieutenant's dignity was shattered. Spluttering and cursing, he glared at the shrimpers grinning at him like gargoyles. He thought about arresting them. Surely there'd be a fire extinguisher out of date, an oil leak, or an undersized net aboard. But how could he maintain the dignity of the law with bird excrement dripping off his nose?

If he arrested them on a technicality, he'd have to escort them to the station and the real smugglers would get away. Then he'd look bad. He turned on his subordinate. That good ol' boy, that local yokel from North Florida Hicksville was shamelessly laughing at him with the rest. "Think it's funny, do you Miller?"

"No sir," Miller said, trying not to laugh.

The officer furiously scrubbed the white blotches from his uniform. But all he succeeded in doing was grinding it in and making the wet spot spread. That made him angrier. He dipped his handkerchief in seawater and wiped his face, trying to rinse away the guano smell. Blakemore glared angrily at his fellow officer. "Well," he hissed, "do you think we should board them or not?" Each word was enunciated through gritted teeth.

Ted took a deep breath, and pursing his lips to keep from laughing, and said solemnly, "That's your decision. I've known Preston all my life, but..."

"Then let's get the hell out of here," Lieutenant Blakemore barked.

After they'd zoomed off, Charlie let out a whoop of laughter and threw a handful of shrimp high into the air for the gulls, giving thanks.

"You did it again!" breathed Blake with genuine admiration. "I didn't think it was possible, but you managed to save our asses."

"Oh, no, I didn't," Preston said, white and trembling now that the moment of hilarity had passed. "Ted knew. I didn't fool him one bit. He isn't stupid. He knew, and he let us go. I could see it in his eyes."

"Well, we're home free. Most likely, they won't bother us anymore," Blake said hopefully.

Preston was pacing the deck now, watching Charlie clear it off. He was the only one taking the culling seriously, picking out the shrimp with aching fingers, tossing them into the fish basket, and pushing the dead croakers and catfish behind him. "At first dark," he said, "when the fog comes back, we're gonna pitch the dope overboard, clean her up good, and run back to port."

Blake looked into his blue eyes with contempt. "Why not dump it now? Go ahead, make it easier for your friends," he said sweeping his hand around at the boats anchored nearby. "Make it easier for them to pick them up. Maybe some day the town will build a bronze statue to you, ol' "Tossing Bales" Preston. You're sure improving the economic well-being of the community for everyone."

Charlie guffawed and Preston silenced him with a dirty look. Still chuckling, Charlie went back to work.

"Why quit now, Preston?" Blake reasoned quietly. "You'd be crazy. You'll end up with nothing. I'll see to it that you won't have this boat. You haven't fulfilled your contract. There's no one after us now, not the Marine Patrol, the Coast Guard, or the sheriff. If you dump the load now, it's because you're mad, and I'm going to tell my friends, and you'll have nothing.

"Not only that," he went on in a quiet, rational monotone "the Cubans took a big hit when Lupino lost that load. They might kill you, your wife, and your kid if it happens again."

He watched Preston tense and tighten his fists, and went on calmly, "What are you going to do, kill me to keep my mouth shut? It's not you, Preston." Blake laughed with pleasure. "And even if you might end up with a $350,000 boat, what's Charlie get beside screwed after getting shot in the head?"

Charlie strode forward and looked Preston hard in the eye. "Yeah, what do I get, Captain? Please, don't do me this a-way. If we dump it now, I won't have jake-legged shit! When you're broke and out on the street, the cops have a way of finding you."

"Not if you've got fifty thousand dollars in your pocket in cold, green cash," Blake put in. "You can hide out in luxury until it all blows over, Charlie."

Preston began to waver, "I don't know. What if someone else talks. What if they catch Lupino? What good will money do then?"

"Lupino?" Charlie howled. "They won't catch him. He can fall into a bucket of shit, swim around in it, and come out clean and smelling like a rose. We ain't that lucky."

"He's the only one who knows who we are. And we've been damn lucky so far," retorted Blake, "or we'd be in cuffs by now. Look, if we get through, and it starts getting hot, I'll make you both a promise. We'll fly you and your family to South America, get you phony passports and everything. You can live like a king down there, Preston."

Barfield paced around the deck again. "It guess it's too late. You're right. If I turned myself in, they wouldn't give me any breaks, not with cocaine in the bales.

"To the contrary," said Blake. "You're the captain. You'd take the biggest hit—twenty years."

Preston leaned wearily against the rail, watching the dead fish and trash sink into the depths. It reminded him of dumping the royal reds. It seemed like an eternity ago, even though it was only three days. "If you're gonna be a rotten, low-life drug smuggler, then be a rotten, low-life drug smuggler," he said to himself bitterly.

He looked Blake in the eyes. "Just tell me where to go. Maybe our luck will hold. Tonight we'll make a run for it.

24

Reunion

It took nearly a week before Blake managed to make contact with April and set up a new drop site. There was no question that the police were glued to the air waves, listening for clues. But it did them no good. Even though Preston knew Blake and April were talking in code, he could discern nothing from their chatter about good times, mutual friends, great restaurants and old fishing spots. They sounded like young lovers, excited about a big party in Ocean Springs, Mississippi, and the upcoming Blessing of the Fleet.

All the while the *Aquarius* headed west, along with the rest of the fleet. Hour after hour Preston held the wheel, churning the ocean, with the bales still stashed in the engine room. There were roughly four thousand shrimp boats in the Southeastern United States, and it seemed like they were all headed to Pascagoula for the opening day of brown shrimp season.

Each year the Mississippi River carries the rich, eroded soil of America's farmlands down to the Gulf of Mexico, making the sea bloom with protein. The bays and sounds are closed to shrimping along most of the central Gulf Coast in the late spring so the shrimp can grow large enough to harvest.

On opening day, shipyards and oil refineries practically shut down from men calling in sick as an epidemic of shrimp-fever breaks out. The fleet moves in from all over the Gulf of Mexico, poised and waiting. At twelve o'clock on the official day, sirens sound across Pascagoula Bay, and hundreds of otter doors and nets splash down. Boats run over each other as tons and tons of small shrimp are caught until there are no more. Days later, comes the Blessing of the Fleet. Into this madhouse came the *Aquarius*, pulling her trawls along with the rest of the fleet, flocked about with seagulls.

Preston listened to the shrimpers on the radio, wishing he could borrow some groceries from his friends, but they had to make do. The long trip down to Colombia and back had exhausted their resources. They ran out of groceries and were forced to eat shrimp.

Then unexpectedly, but to everyone's relief, a voice blurted over the radio speakers. "How about it, *Aquarius*? This is the old *Potluck* calling the *Aquarius*. You over this side?"

Blake scrambled into the wheelhouse and grabbed the microphone. "Yeah, how about it, *Potluck*? The steaks are on the fire, the beer's getting warm, and we're ready to party."

Then another voice broke in on the same frequency, "This is the *Sea Island*, the *Sea Island*, calling the *Four Sisters*, come in, Chip."

They waited impatiently for the other hailer to leave the channel. Normally they would have switched frequencies, but Blake was afraid it might expose them to detection by the authorities. When the channel finally was clear, he started in again and the smugglers quickly worked out a rendezvous point. Preston listened to the unfamiliar Cajun voice talking in code. "Oh yeah, right," the voice from the *Potluck* concluded. "Might see you down that way. We're going in to Cat Island. Okee-dokey, the missus just put some food on the table, so we'll talk at you later. *Potluck* clear," the voice drawled and signed off.

"*Potluck*?" Preston demanded incredulously after Blake turned down the radio, "Ain't that a little much to talk about on the air?"

"No," answered Blake, looking pleased. "There's boats in every port named *Potluck*. It's become a joke around the coast."

By the time they reached Cat Island, the foggy days were over. Preston backed the *Aquarius* up hard to make her anchor bite deep into the soft mud and shut the engine off. In bright sunshine they waited and watched flotillas of boats moving into the Mississippi Sound. It looked like a veritable city at sea. "I bet if you tied all these boats up from bow to stern," Charlie said, "they'd reach from here clear into Biloxi Harbor. I don't know how anybody's going to find anybody."

"If we don't get some fuel soon," Preston said, "it'll be easy to find us. We'll be drifting. We're just about running on fumes. Soon as we get this load off, I've got just about enough diesel to run into Bayou LaBatre and get some."

Noises from parties drifted across the water, joyful laughter, celebration. With a mixture of paranoia and envy, they watched the good times going on around them.

"We got anything left to eat besides shrimp?" Preston asked hopefully, after looking through their exhausted larder. The smell of frying steak was carried across from the next boat, making him hungry.

"No, Cap'n, just a can of sauerkraut and some other junk. I can cook some flounder, but I'm out of grease. I reckon I can steam 'em," he said with resignation.

They had eaten shrimp and seafood until they were sick of it. "Just say the word," Charlie said, "and I'll swim over to that boat over there and ask that gal with the little red bikini if I can trade her some shrimp or dope for some pussy or food."

"Forget it," snapped Preston, remembering an incident in Louisiana. Charlie wanted a beer, and Preston wouldn't let him go get one, so he swam half a mile to a party boat and came back with two quarts. "Just fix supper best you can."

Preston lay down, wishing he were at home having one of Mary's home-cooked meals of rice and gravy, creamed corn, turnip greens, and her famous fried chicken. No wonder old G.W. Talagera pitched such a fit when she ran off with him. He lost the best cook in his house, Preston thought with satisfaction. He loved his wife dearly, but at the moment, he loved the idea of her home cooking even more. Thinking again about the penurious old cuss, he realized at least one good thing came out of the trip: if he got through it without going to jail or worse, he wouldn't have to go to him for money.

Through the open cabin windows he heard the delighted squeals of children as they dove off outriggers into the water, and the warning call of their parents. That made him think of children. He wondered if Mary had had the baby yet, and if it went okay.

Four hours later they spotted a sleek white yacht, almost as big as the *Aquarius*, headed right for them. Like many of the others, it was decorated with brightly colored flags, ornate bunting, and glitter. *Potluck* was emblazoned on its sides. Its twin engines slowed to a crawl, and the crew of the *Aquarius* stood dumbfounded as several gorgeous women waved a cheerful hello.

Charlie's eyes were popping at the generously displayed feminine pulchritude. He was almost speechless as the yacht backed up. There was a flaming redhead in a black bikini. Her skin was pink from the sun and she looked to be in her late twenties. The other girl looked younger, with dark glowing hair and dark skin. She wore a white thong.

Then April stepped on deck. Her long, blond hair flowed, and she wore a white evening dress that fit her slim figure impeccably. She stood apart from the bimbos, in style and manner. Remember, Preston warned himself, I'm the fish and she's the bait. Remember how this fish was gutted, filleted and eaten before. He tried to recall her savage bite, but it seemed far away now. In spite of his admonitions to himself, he had a hard time taking his eyes off her.

"Here comes the Snow Queen herself," Blake said chuckling. He turned to Preston, "April always did have style."

In the calm, sheltered bay, the yacht backed up easily to the stern of the *Aquarius*, mashing the rubber crash bumper between them. A man with a familiar face emerged from the yacht's cabin wearing a big white toothy grin. He wore cut-offs and a nondescript blue T-shirt stretched across his muscular chest. It was Rick. The thug didn't have his machine gun in hand, as he did when the *Night Shadow* burned, but Preston knew it couldn't be far away.

Whatever tingling desires he might have had for April vanished, replaced with fear. Rick's grin went to his spine. Be ready for anything, he commanded himself. These people don't play straight. Remember the guns, the coke. They don't need me now; I'm expendable. It's pay-off time, and I'm in more danger now than on any part of the trip. Just play it cool, keep your mouth shut, and roll with it.

Behind Rick, hanging back as if he didn't want to be seen, was an older man dressed in a white outfit, wearing lots of gold jewelry. His face was hidden behind sunglasses, and from beneath his yachting cap, which bore a Commodore insignia, puffed a cloud of well-groomed silver hair. He remained on his boat, in the shadows. Blake's eyes bugged when he saw him.

"Who is that guy?" Preston asked him.

Blake shook his head but looked frightened. Clearly this was someone high up in the echelon.

April was the first to hop aboard, followed by the two other attractive women and Rick. She gave Blake a hug, then squeezed the captain's big, callused hand and introduced him to the younger women. "Everyone, this is Preston, the superstar who saved our dope. Man, it's great to see you guys!" Then looking around the boat, she asked, puzzled, "Where's Paul?"

Blake shook his head. "Fish food. He didn't make it. We lost him about halfway back. He went overboard. We had trouble. I'll tell you about it later."

Her gaze focused hard on the blond pirate. "That's too bad. How much of the good stuff did we end up with? As far as we know the police didn't end up with any of it."

"We have nearly all of it," Blake cried exuberantly, "about a hundred kilos, give or take a couple." He grinned at Charlie. "We lost some in the storm coming through the Yucatan."

"Oh, that's tremendous," April cried effervescently. "You are indeed a superstar, Preston." She gave him a warm hug, exciting his groin. He took a deep breath and pulled away. April grinned at him, enjoying watching him wrestle with his instincts. "Come on, before we all start having too much fun, let's test it."

Blake produced a brick he had hidden under his bunk, and April laid it out on the galley table. Everyone crowded in and watched in anticipation, especially Blake. With a golden razor blade she slicked off one corner, and crushed it into a powder with a butter knife. Then she sprinkled it on a mirror and expertly cut the powder into two lines.

Preston's disgust was heightened as he watched April roll a crisp hundred-dollar bill into a little tube and put it into her left nostril, plugging the right nostril with her finger. Then she leaned over the glass and inhaled. She vacuumed the powder into her nose. It wasn't a pretty sight.

The others watched her expectantly. Her eyes watered as the energy went to her brain. "Oh, gee! If it's all like this, we'll get fourteen million easy. We need to move it to the yacht now!"

Preston watched a delegation climb into the engine room. As if in

a surrealistic dream, he gazed at the burlap-covered bales of marijuana stacked from floor to ceiling. During the trip, he had moved,
rearranged, and stashed them in a safer position than before. There
was a soft chipping sound as hatchets split through the compacted
bales. The white two-kilo bricks were removed and wrapped in plastic bags and piled into a mound. The engine room was a mess. There
seemed to be no limit to the tiny seeds, flakes and resinous buds scattered over the floor. Charlie, Blake, and Rick busily repackaged the
open bales, taping up the gashes with silver duct tape, putting the
bales into new green plastic garbage bags. They were covered with
pot residue. It was on their skins, in their hair, and on their faces.
While April supervised, Toni and Roberta toted the white bricks over
to the *Potluck* yacht, cradling them with reverence, as if they were
handling the crown jewels.

Wanting no part of it, Preston went to the wheelhouse and waited.
It was none of his business, he figured, and the less he knew the better.
An hour later, Blake came into the wheelhouse, pulled his pot-cov-
ered T-shirt off, and wadded it up. He looked over the new shirts
April brought along, deciding which one would look best. "Nice going, Blake," April called coming in after him. "This is high grade,
primo stuff." She dismissed Toni and Roberta, and sent them over to
the yacht. "Now," she said to Blake, Preston and Charlie, "I want to
know what happened. Tell me everything, and don't spare any details!" she said enthusiastically.

As Blake related the events, April listened with glowing eyes. Preston
hung back, saying little, noticing how she smiled with pleasure when
Blake and Charlie told her about the pirates. "We still can't figure out
why they didn't blow us out of the water, or even board us. It doesn't
make sense," Blake said, puzzled, looking into her green eyes for clues.

"Shit happens in this business!" she said, sounding sincere. "Thank
God you made it through and the Navy didn't shoot you. We have a
lot to be thankful for at the Blessing tomorrow, don't we?" She then
gave Blake an evil smile that sent chills up Preston's back.

Blake looked uneasy for a moment, then went on. He described
the storm at sea, how they almost sank, and how Preston had saved
them. Then she gave Preston a hug and shook her head sorrowfully
when she heard how Paul was swept overboard after losing it and
shooting at Preston. When Charlie boasted how they skunked the

Coast Guard with the royal red shrimp and how they slipped into the fleet and evaded the Florida Marine Patrol, April was positively delighted. Then she asked for a full accounting of how and why twenty-two bales were lost.

Preston watched her closely. Maybe the hilarity was from the coke she was snorting, but he didn't think so. The way she breathed in short gasps and slowly ran her tongue over her lips seemed calculatedly sexual. April reached over and squeezed his hand affectionately, but Preston didn't squeeze back. Whatever passions he felt before they sat down had wilted. The bitch knows too much, he thought. She laughs too loud and enjoys these details too much. "What happened with Raul?" Blake asked when he got to the off-loading part. "We heard he got shot."

"It's true," she said regretfully. "Either he was holding out on the cartel or he had a bunch of enemies. I don't know the details, but we sure had to scramble to get ready for you. I have no idea how the cops got wind of it; probably just dumb luck. Anyway, that's over," said April with finality.

She changed the subject abruptly. "Now here's the plan. Tomorrow morning we're going in with the Blessing of the Fleet, and will tie up to Galtin's dock. There'll be a crew down there to unload and haul it off."

"What?" cried Preston incredulously. "Unload in broad daylight? Are you out of your minds!"

"Sugar, don't worry about it. We're about to pull off the ultimate scam. This year the Blessing and the Seafood Festival are going to be the largest in history. The Chamber of Commerce says there'll be over fifty thousand people in town. Every cop for a hundred miles around will be directing traffic during the parade," she said jubilantly, her green eyes flashing with pleasure. "We couldn't pick a better time!"

She stepped out on deck and called out to the others on the yacht, "Okay, everyone, time's wasting. Rick, Toni, Roberta, bring out the decorations. Let's get started!" April was exuberant, like a girl on a high school cheerleading team. "I want this boat cleaned until it sparkles."

Then she turned back to Preston with a glowing smile and added, "Really Preston, your boat is a frightful mess. If I owned a boat like this—and incidentally we have all the papers transferring title to you

—I wouldn't let it get into such a fright. Here you've taken a perfectly respectable pot boat and made it into a horrible, smelly shrimper.

"All right, Charlie," the captain said wearily, "you heard the lady. Let's get busy."

Roberta, wearing her thong, came to the railing, and beamed Charlie a sexy smile as he helped her aboard. He almost fell down the ladder on his way to crank the engine and switch on the deck pump.

He returned in a minute with scrub-brushes and washing powders and scoured away. Rivers of suds spilled overboard until every bit of grime was removed. He blasted away all the remaining sea life and mud, but he had trouble focusing on what he was doing. He couldn't take his gaze away from Toni. The voluptuous redhead perched on the railing dabbing suntan oil on her legs, gently and sensuously rubbing them their whole length. He feasted his eyes on her bouncing buttocks as she moved around the deck wrapping the rigging with bunting.

A speedboat whipped by with a pack of college boys whooping and shouting at the women. Watching them wave and smile back Preston got Blake off to the side and asked in a low voice, "Who are these girls?"

"They're a couple of coke whores," Blake said uneasily. "Window dressing. They belong to Creeper. They're his mules. Long as they've got coke to keep them up, and pot and Quaaludes to bring them down, they're okay."

Creeper, Preston learned, was the strange man with all the gold jewelry. He was the one who financed the operation and controlled marketing. Blake explained that Creeper kept the girls around as pets, having them run errands, including occasional trips to Colombia to pick up cocaine, which they smuggled back in their underwear.

"I don't feel too great about them being here myself," Blake said, acknowledging Preston's discomfort. They watched Rick gluing a cut-out porpoise covered with glitter to the wheelhouse wall. Blake gave the girls a look of contempt. "If they got caught, they'd spill their guts."

The girls brought out box after pasteboard box of bunting and tinsel from the yacht, while Rick climbed the mast, fastening red, green, and yellow pennants to the stay cables. Blake gazed at the flags, flapping in the breeze.

"How's it look?" April called from the wheelhouse roof. Red, white, and blue crepe paper was wrapped around the masts and boom, and orange, and purple bunting covered the wheelhouse.

"Like a used car lot grand opening," Preston said caustically, "only tackier."

"The tackier the better!" April crowed triumphantly, thoroughly high on cocaine. "We want to look like everyone else." She was all over the boat, supervising, ordering, embellishing and then standing back like an artist to see that it was done right.

By the time the sun set, the *Aquarius* was transformed into a giant pom-pom, festooned with banners, pennants, and tinsel running up and down the stays.

Satisfied at last, April pulled Preston into the cabin and poured him a drink from a new bottle of scotch. "Here, this will make you feel good. See, I remembered—J&B," she said putting her arms around him. "I've missed you, baby. I've been thinking about you every minute you were gone."

He pulled away. "Look April, after this I'm going home to my wife. I want this whole thing behind me. Our little fling..."

"Oh, Preston, stop being so uptight. Blake told me all about the fight. I know you're angry about the coke and the guns, and you think we're a bunch of crooks, but it's not true. We're business people, and sometimes we have to do things that aren't kosher, but we're honest. You've got your boat title, and you'll see, we're going to pay Charlie off as soon as we get to the dock and unload the pot."

Preston swallowed his drink. "What do you know about my wife? Is Mary...okay? he asked.

"Yes, Daddy," April said warmly. "Congratulations, you had an eight-pound eight-ounce boy last week. Mary's fine. That was part of the deal, remember? She'd be taken care of. Sam Lawton saw that she hasn't wanted for a thing, except you, maybe. But she couldn't want you any more than I do right now."

"Really, you've got a funny way of showing it, trying to get us killed down there."

April's green eyes widened. "No, honey, I never tried to kill you. You've got to believe that."

"Oh come on, you mean to tell me we just blundered into those pirates, that they weren't set up and waiting for us?" His voice rose in anger, "And why didn't the Colombian Navy grab us?" He pointed an accusing finger at her. "It's because you set us up, didn't you?"

"No," she said firmly, her anger mirroring his. "I just used you as bait to destroy the Maiqueita cartel. Why would I turn this boat and load over to my enemies? My contacts told the Navy that the Maiqueita had been behind some recent massacres against them and then gave them evidence from my spies, including all the Loran coordinates and times where their men had been attacked. They told them when and where the Maiqueita was waiting to hijack an American fishing boat. Well, they couldn't wait to get even. It was the perfect set-up, one that I'd been building toward a long time. The Navy readily agreed to let you pass. They had no interest in us this time. But communications broke down, and the timing got all screwed up.

"The military should have wiped them out a day before you reached Calamar, but you had been loaded a day ahead of schedule. Their spies in the off-loading crew must have radioed ahead that you were coming." April put her arms around him and kissed him on the cheek, "I'm sorry you walked into the middle of it, Preston. You weren't supposed to. But those bastards got what they deserved. Now we've got to get over to the yacht. I've got some party clothes for you."

Preston felt her warmth. He fought the urges that swept through him. He took a deep breath to clear his head, and thought, *To hell with her!* But don't get mad or show your hand. Just play along. It's almost over.

Preston pulled away from her. "I got work to do on my boat, April. I've got to change oil and fuel filters and doublecheck the stuffing box. We don't want to sink in the middle of the channel or break down do we? When I get cleaned up, I'll come over."

She gave him a lascivious smile. "I see the only way I'm going to get you in the sack is to get you off this boat and back over to my condo. ...And I promise I won't bite."

It was almost midnight when he showered, shaved, and dressed in clean pants and shirt. He vaulted over the transom to the deck of the *Potluck*, and a voice commanded from the shadows. "Hold it, mister." Preston froze, looking into the bore of a submachine gun with a silencer on it. Rick's cold blue eyes were tense and ready. "Oh, sorry," said the hit-man apologetically, raising the barrel and slipping the safety back on. "I forgot you were on the other boat. Can't be too careful."

"Yeah," said Preston shortly, wondering if good ol' Rick might get trigger happy and blow some cop away if they were boarded. Then I'd be up for murder as well as running dope, he thought. The words of his Marine Patrol friend came back to him, *Once these people get their hooks into you, they never let go. Don't play in the big leagues when you belong in the little leagues.*

He stepped down into a luxurious cabin, with thick carpets and leather couches, and saw the man called Creeper, wearing his commodore hat and too much jewelry. April went to the bar and fixed Preston a drink. She and Blake were thoroughly stoned on cocaine. Sitting in the corner, with bourbon in hand, Preston watched Roberta move over to Charlie and run her long, sun-tanned fingers with manicured pink nails down his shoulder. "Charlie-boy," she said seductively, "it's getting late. You're going to be paid tomorrow. Are you getting ready to party with me? Creeper said you can stay on the yacht."

"You betcha," Charlie crowed boisterously. "Before I take another boat back down to Colombia, I'm gonna have all the fun I can."

"What!" cried Preston incredulously. "You're kidding, aren't you? You're not going back down there!"

Roberta wiggled up to Charlie and said in a baby voice, "Tell him you can run a boat all the way down to Colombia all by yourself."

"He knows that," Charlie boasted. "I been working on boats all my life, and running them too."

"Charlie," Preston stormed, "you ain't got bat shit for brains. You saw what we just went through!"

"Far as I'm concerned, I've shrimped my last," Charlie declared in a drunken slur. "A man could get used to this kind of life. These are good people, 'specially Toni here," he said as she came and joined the two on the couch. His callused hand stroked Toni's bare back, and pulled at her bikini strap.

"You tell 'im," Toni said with a wink. Then she shot Preston a sly smile.

Captain Barfield rose and headed for the door. "I'm going back to my boat. Have a good evening, folks. Thanks for the drink. Like you say, it's your life, Charlie. Go for it. I wish you luck!"

25

Blessing of the Fleet

Loud, raucous music was coming from someplace nearby and getting louder. Preston flung open the cabin door and stepped into the bright morning sunlight. Steaming past was a sixty-foot yacht with twenty musicians playing clarinets, horns, bass drums and guitars. Jittering, wiggling girls were keeping beat to the music on board. Ahead of them was a decorated shrimp trawler, the *Miss Sarah Dell*, that out-glittered the *Aquarius* and swarmed with people. There were hundreds on board. People were standing on the cabin roof, crowded against the rails, the bow, hanging out of the wheelhouse, hollering and waving. "Wake up!" they shouted as they moved past the *Aquarius*.

Preston watched the procession of boats, including a speedboat zigzagging in open water pulling two water-skiers. The women from the *Potluck* waved gaily. Charlie came aboard with a drink in his hand looking pleased with himself. "I been fed, I been bred, and I'm ready to party!"

His greeting was interrupted by a sudden burst of screams and sirens coming from every direction. Preston, Charlie and Blake jumped in fright. With wild eyes they cast about for a place to run. "That's not the cops, you idiots," April giggled. "Come on everybody. The Blessing is about to begin. And we're about to pull off one of the greatest scams in the history of dope smuggling!"

"Lady, I think you're out of your mind. We're going to get caught, sure as hell," Preston said.

Toni and Roberta hurried aboard the shrimp boat. "They're coming with us?" Preston asked April in surprise.

"We have to look like we're partying, don't we? And they're party creatures. Remember, during the Blessing, anything goes!"

Rick untied lines and Creeper ignited the twin engines, spluttering hot, gaseous waste through the exhaust pipes into the green waters of the Mississippi Sound. The yacht took off, too, creating distance from the *Aquarius*, and fell in beside the others headed for the Blessing. Preston watched it go, wishing the remaining pot and the two bimbos and everyone else on board were on the yacht with Rick and Creeper so he could be alone with his boat. He wondered where the yacht was headed and worried that it was being watched through police binoculars. In a moment he thought he had his answer.

He heard the flapping shock of chopper blades and looked up to see a U.S. Coast Guard helicopter. Preston felt terror not unlike that of chickens being dived-bombed by a hawk. Blake and Charlie were ready to dive overboard and flee. Someone aboard the chopper pitched a large object overboard. It plummeted through the air. It was a floral wreath, and it splashed in the water next to the *Aquarius*.

The women pealed with laughter at the men's panic. "Really, boys," said April, "there's nothing to worry about. The wreath's a memorial to the sailors and fishermen who have been lost at sea."

"...And to all the good smugglers like Paul who have gone down between here and Colombia," Blake added shakily, "including a few with concrete blocks on their feet."

Bundles of helium-filled balloons were released. One nearly hit a low-flying airplane dragging a beer banner. The shores that were ringed by tall condominiums, grandstands and marina docks were mobbed with people. As the *Aquarius* drew near, Roberta and Toni were greeted with catcalls, whistles, whoops and amorous propositions shouted across the water by drunks in the grandstands. The girls stood by the railing waving at the crowd, blowing kisses and looking beautiful. Cameras clicked, horns blew and Preston gazed with disbelief at the sea of faces.

Moving down the four-mile-long channel that funneled into Biloxi Harbor, the boats were almost gunnel to gunnel. Positioned in the middle of the harbor, creating a bottleneck, was a hundred-foot yacht, the *Petroleum Queen*, with a silk banner running her length: BLESS-ING BOAT. Aboard it was the Archbishop, looking stately in his ceremonial red robe, velvet cap, and gold cross around his neck. As the boats passed, he sprinkled holy water and boomed his blessings over a loudspeaker.

They watched a little shrimper receive its blessing. It had been scrubbed and lavished with decorations. The captain, an old Cajun, stood proudly at the helm with his head bowed in prayer. *God bless the* Miss Wanda Star *and all who sail upon her on the high seas. In the name of the Father, the Son and the Holy Ghost.* The captain's wife and young children kneeled on the bow crossing themselves, and the stern was filled with a cluster of praying relatives and friends. Then came a thundering round of applause and cheers from the reviewing stands, drowning out the hymns of the six choir boys dressed in white robes singing behind the Archbishop.

"Move in closer," April shouted over the cacophony of rock bands playing near the stands. "I want the Bishop to bless us!"

Preston steered the *Aquarius* toward the Blessing Boat, and April crossed herself. Then she came back into the wheelhouse, and Preston asked, "Don't you think it's a bit sacrilegious bringing a boat-load of dope into the middle of a Blessing?"

"Not at all," she replied. "When I was a little girl growing up around old Biloxi, the Blessing meant something to fishermen like my grandfather. But now it's turned to bullshit. It's all a monstrous tourist rip-off. In America there is only one thing that counts, and that's money. And with that stash of coke we just sent off, and the load we've got down below, we're worshiping at its altar. Besides, I intend to tithe my share. There's only one problem with this," she added with a shade of melancholy.

"And what would that be?" Blake asked.

"No one will ever know!"

And so the *Aquarius*, with its crew of lawbreakers and cargo of marijuana, waited for its benediction. Preston prayed for forgiveness, and asked God to wash away the blood that had been spilled on his boat. He swore that if he returned home safely he would never mess with drugs again. After being blessed, the boats passed the cheering spectators, made a circle into the bay, and dropped anchor to party into the night. Some headed to various marinas and wharves around the city, and a few took off up the river to exclusive residential sites and canals behind expensive waterfront homes.

One of the faces in the reviewing stands stared at them with utter disbelief.

A fat little blonde snuggled against a lean young man in a bright blue and red Hawaiian shirt. "What's the matter, Lupino, baby? You look like you seen a ghost."

Lupino took his arm off Lucille's chunky shoulder. He removed the other arm which had been draped over the bony shoulder of a brunette with a missing front tooth. After nearly drowning and getting stranded on a sandbar, he'd run back up a river, hid the dope in the woods and sold the twenty bales at firesale prices.

With fifty thousand dollars in cash, Lupino was having the party of his life. He'd flown to Nashville and bought a ten-thousand-dollar electric guitar and a rhinestone coat that would put most country singers to shame. After banging around for a few weeks, trying to get auditions, he decided the gatekeepers of country music didn't have the good sense to appreciate his talent. To console himself he bought a used baby-blue Lincoln Continental convertible and drove to Biloxi, hoping to double his money at the casinos. He picked up two hookers who thought his music was absolutely wonderful, and they'd been having a hell of a good time ever since.

Lupino stood and clasped his hands over his eyes to cut the glare off the water. "It's Charlie!" he cried. "That's my old buddy, Charlie! Hot damn!" His eyes grew wider and wider as he took in the garish shrimp boat and the beautiful women. He shook his head in disbelief. "I ain't believing *this*!"

Then he caught a glimpse of Preston. Unmistakably it was him—tall, weathered, sunburned—there was no question about it. And there was only one explanation, they had unloaded the dope somewhere, or maybe they had jettisoned it. But in any case, they were now having a celebration.

And Lupino was in a party mood. He had women; he had hundreds of hundred-dollar bills sewn into the lining of his jacket; and he couldn't have been happier.

"Look yonder, that's my brother-in-law," he said, pointing to Preston. "And that boy over there with the short yellah hair, that's

Charlie, my best friend, I been knowing him all my life. He and I have had some good times together. Come on, we'll meet them at the dock!"

"I don't know that I want my Snuggles to be around those other women," the brunette said. She blew coquettishly in his ear, "Lupino honey, you been *sooo* good to us!" She smiled, but her eyes were granite.

Lupino grinned proudly. "Baby, I'm gonna show y'all a time! Let's get the car. Somehow we gotta catch up with them. We're gonna have the best party of our lives!"

They pushed through the crowds to the parking lot and got in the convertible, but they ran into a parade on the way out. Police cars with sirens wailing and lights flashing moved slowly, four-abreast. The dignified looking officers waved to the cheering crowd. Then came the National Guard tanks rumbling mightily and shaking the ground with their great steel treads. Following were politicians in limousines, or standing in the backs of pickup trucks, waving and smiling, throwing candy, hopping out to shake hands with the crowd. A high school band played "Stars and Stripes Forever," and a troupe of teenage baton twirlers, marched behind.

Sitting in their car, Lupino and his lady friends watched the Festival Queen, enthroned on her float, wearing a white chiffon dress. Bountifully, she tossed packets of candy, and children ran from behind the barriers to retrieve them. "Keep back. Keep back!" the motorcycle cops shouted as they rolled by.

The Navy band passed next playing "Victory at Sea." Eight more squad cars brought up the rear. The happy threesome was able, at last, to get out of the parking lot.

Meanwhile the *Aquarius* crept alone down the long, industrial canal, away from the other boats and parties. Silence closed over them as they left the Blessing behind. Preston gripped the wheel tightly, taking breaths only as his body demanded oxygen. "Your little plan ain't so sporty right now," he snapped at April. "We're out of place over here." His skin felt clammy, and he fought the panic in his voice.

"It's no worse than the time we unloaded a boat on the Sunshine Skyway Bridge at two-o'clock in the afternoon," Blake said, trying to put everyone at ease. But he was uneasy as well, his face drawn and pale. "I guess I'm getting too old for his," he said, letting his breath out heavily. "But this is my last trip!"

"Relax, I've got it all covered," April said encouragingly. "Come on, keep up the party," she said to Toni and Roberta, who were looking solemn and scared.

"There's no one here," Toni said and smiled weakly.

They moved slowly, parallel to the long waterfront wharf that led to Galtin's Seafoods. The silence grew. They passed the docks of Pretty Kitty where, on a business day, croakers and trash fish by the ton were ground into cat food. Then the glittering *Aquarius* passed the porgy plant, where menhaden were sucked from the bellies of three-hundred-foot fishing trawlers and rendered into oil and fertilizers. Normally, at any one time, there were hundreds of people working around the dock, but on this day of the seafood festival, it was like a ghost town. Yet, five blocks away, where the town's tourist center was concentrated—with fudge, T-shirt, and trinket stores lining the street—30,000 people pushed and shoved against barricades watching for the festival parade.

With its engine rumbling softly, moving along at half speed, the *Aquarius* ran parallel to the rusty iron corrugated buildings at the end of the canal. From the deck they could see the old railroad spur line that ran along the waterfront street, past the piles of discarded iron cables, fish nets, and rusted junk that grew amidst the weeds. Five blocks away, through the alley-way corridors, they could see the main highway, lined by a wall of humanity waiting for the parade.

Ahead, at the end of the canal, was a faded white-on-black sign on pilings reading Galtin's Seafoods. A crowd of run-down and unloved shrimp boats clogged the docks, leaving a gap only at the entrance to the company.

As soon as Preston had backed into the space and tied off the boat, old man Pierre Galtin stepped out of the side door of the tin building, while his Vietnamese workers opened the big sliding metal doors. Preston recognized him. He'd seen Galtin at Sam Lawton's place once or twice. He spoke with a thick Cajun accent, had a bald head and a small mustache. His trucks were all over the southeast, buying and selling seafood. When he saw the garnished *Aquarius* and April and her crew in their party clothes, he began to chuckle, then laughed until his whole body shook. "You sure brought the fat out of the fire..." he managed to get out between belly laughs. "My God, this is something—right in the middle of the Blessing." April gave the old man her sexiest smile and winked. That brought on another outburst of hilarity.

Charlie looked suspiciously at the dozen Vietnamese workers with their impassive oriental faces, in their denims, and T-shirts, coming out of the opened doors and waiting for orders. "What about these gooks? Can you trust 'em?" he said loudly.

Galtin was indignant. "I'd rather have them than a dozen white guys. They don't have no big mouths. They're the best seafood workers I've ever had. They don't speak much English, so they don't hang around bars blowing their asses and bragging like some dumb rednecks do," he said pointedly. "You got any other questions, Sonny?"

Charlie huffed with indignation, but Preston shot him a menacing look. "Come on, we've got to get out of here," April said, cutting him off sharply. "The band's coming. Let's get into the crowd."

A sixteen-wheeled tractor-trailer was parked in front of the warehouse blocking the entrance and any view of the Vietnamese off-loading the boat. The driver was sitting in the cab, with the engine running, nervously smoking a cigarette while he waited for the loading to be completed, his eyes hidden beneath sunglasses.

From a distance, blocks away, came the beat of drums and the shrill of music amid a wail of sirens. Charlie Hanson didn't notice. Never in his life had he seen so much money as April and Pierre Galtin were now giving him. His money—hundreds, fifties, twenties and tens, some new, some old and ratty—was being stacked on the galley table. He tried to follow the old man as he counted aloud, but he soon lost track. The girls stood by smiling, their eyes gleaming with delight, as they poured him another drink and cooed in his ear.

Finally, when the last dollar was stowed away in Charlie's duffel bag, and Preston received the notarized title, Mr. Galtin hurried back into the fish house, where Blake was on the telephone, making his flight arrangements to Ecuador. "Come with me, Charlie," Preston urged. "You know how you blow money. You won't have a dime left in a few days. Soon as we're unloaded, I'm headed home to Florida."

"No, stay with us, Charlie," Roberta cooed. "We'll give you all the pussy you want, honey," Toni pleaded in her little-girl voice. "We've got a condominium on the beach..." She threw her arms around him and gave him a deep tongue-thrusting kiss, pressing her breasts against his chest. "Let's go to the condo and fuck our brains out!"

"Yeah, and they'll rob you blind," Preston insisted. "Come on, Charlie, get real!"

April beckoned Preston outside to the deck. "He'll be all right," she assured him. "You can come with us and look after him. Don't be a party-pooper. Pierre will take care of your boat. You can trust him. He's the one that fitted it out for the trip. I'll have it steam-cleaned for you. He'll have his army of Viet Cong scrub it and get rid of all the residue."

"I appreciate it, but..."

"Look, Preston, the whole time you were gone, I could think of nothing but you. Come with me, we'll have the time of our lives. I know how to spend money, Preston," she said urgently. "We'll have a ball. I'll show you Europe, the old castles, the museums, we'll go to horseraces in Monte Carlo and sights you've never seen..."

"Hey, lady," Preston laughed, "I'm just a commercial fisherman. Don't paint any illusions about me. I smell like fish, I've got fish scales all over my ratty old clothes and grease on my fingers, and I like it that way. I'm going home!"

A police car turned the corner and moved slowly toward the boat. Preston froze. Charlie turned pale. Blake stared at April in alarm. "Relax," she said confidently, but in a hush, "he's one of ours."

The big, red-faced officer got out of the squad car, sweating profusely, nervously wiping his face with a white handkerchief as he watched the bales being off-loaded. He stole furtive glances at the smugglers, but mostly he stared straight ahead. The whole thing made Preston feel dirty. He had his beefs with fisheries management issues, but he was basically a law-and-order man. A cop on the take made him feel sick. True, his friend Teddy Miller had looked the other way when confronted with Preston's marijuana smuggling, but he wasn't on the take.

"You know, if dope were legalized and taxed," April said, sensing his thoughts, "there wouldn't be any of this. It's the money that corrupts, not the dope."

Pierre Galtin hurried to the boat. "Y'all better move this boat from here and get back to the Blessing. We're finished loading, the truck's pulling out."

Blake hopped aboard and extended his hand to Preston. "It's been a real pleasure working with you, man, it really has. I'll never forget you." He turned to Charlie, "You coming with us?"

From below, Charlie looked at Preston guiltily, lost for words. Finally, above the roar of the tractor trailer hauling away the load and the grind of gears as it shifted up to the highway speed, he blurted out, "Preston, I reckon I'll be goin'..."

"Go on," the captain said angrily. "Go ahead and die for snatch, you damn fool. It sure ain't for money, 'cause you won't have any in a day or two. Charlie, I love you like a brother, but you ain't cut out for this. You don't need to be running a boat down to Colombia." He shook his hand, and said painfully, "Watch your self, Charlie. If you ever need anything and I can help, you know where to find me."

Preston realized Charlie was twenty-three and had to make his own mistakes.

Charlie sniffled, moved to tears at the parting. He forced himself to look away, clutched his duffel bag of money, and hustled down the dock after Blake, Toni, and Roberta. They hurried down the long wharf paralleling the canal and headed toward town, the men swaying on their sea legs, feeling terra firma for the first time in weeks.

"You better go with them," Preston said to April, who stood by his side. The afternoon sunlight made her diamond earrings gleam like stars, her hair looked like glowing fire. But her hold on him had vanished. "I'm outta here!" he said. "Nice knowin' ya."

"What do you mean, 'Nice knowin' ya'?" she said in surprise. "We had a nice thing going. I don't want to lose you. At least not for a while."

"Well, *I* want to lose *you*. Among other things, you murder people, April. You killed Raul, didn't you?"

"Yes. Well, not exactly. I had him killed." Her tone was open, straight-forward. "I had to. When he learned what happened down there in Calamar, he started putting two and two together. But it was revenge, Preston. I'm no random killer. Those people hurt me bad. I hope I killed every one of those mangy bastards down there. I found out that Raul worked with the Maiqueitas, the ones who raped me and beat me. There was no one in my family to take revenge for what they did to me. My father wouldn't do it. I had to do it myself. But it's finished, it's over now. I'll never do anything like this again. Preston, forget the past."

"Sorry, April," he said, thinking of the burning bodies, blood, and murder on his boat. "I'm going home to my wife and kid. I'm going shrimping, and you're getting off my boat. Now, please leave!"

He lifted her over the railing and deposited her on the wharf.

"Go ahead, go back to your mousy little wife and shitty diapers in your inbred village," she spat at him as he cast off. "If you think you can go back to shrimping after this, you're dead wrong. You never get out of this business once you're in. Never. You'll get bored, you'll blow your money and you'll be back. When you do, I'll make you crawl, you bastard!" She hurried to a red sports car and drove off in a squeal of tires.

Preston backed away from the dock, turned the wheel, shoved down the throttle, and the *Aquarius* moved majestically down the canal, parallel to the sea-wall and boardwalk. The afternoon sun was beginning to set and the orange light made the old shrimp boats and corrugated buildings glow softly. With April behind him, and the sea ahead, he was wondered how he was going to get fuel. He had only a couple hundred dollars on him.

It was hard to see against the glare, but he spotted Blake and Charlie hurrying along the sea-wall with the two coke whores behind them. A shiny blue convertible pulled up next to them. Preston's heart leaped into his mouth—undercover agents! A short, bushy-haired young man got out of the car, glittering and flickering in the sunlight like a revolving disco light. He was followed by two coarse-looking women in heels and gaudy tight-fitting dresses, weaving drunkenly. These weren't cops, just intoxicated tourists. But there was something familiar about the boisterous young man. "My God, it's Lupino!" Preston gasped, as the *Aquarius* drew nearer.

"Charlie! Hey, Charlie!" Lupino shouted joyfully. "Oh Jesus," Charlie groaned. "Not him! Not now!"

"Who are those people?" Roberta said, staring at the approaching threesome. Toni glared at Lupino's women disapprovingly. Blake's jaw dropped.

"Hey Charlie!" Lupino slurred as he rushed toward them. "I want you to meet these gals. Lucille, Kathy, this is Charlie, my best friend in the whole world."

Charlie forced a smile and put his arm around Lupino's shoulder. "This is my good friend, Lupino, who was just leaving," he explained to the two women. Then he whispered, "Look, you asshole, we're in the middle of some business."

"Get out of here, Lupino," Blake said, "and I mean now."

"*You!* I ain't forgetting what you did to me on that boat, you son-of-a bitch," Lupino shouted, drawing his scrawny fingers into a fist. He stepped forward like an angry polecat. "You ripped me off and almost drowned me! And now you're gonna give me back what you stole, and I'm gonna whip your ass! That money was for Preston!"

"Come on, Lupino," his two hookers cajoled. "Let's not stick around. Come on back and play some music for us."

Lupino dug into his pocket and pulled out a wad of bills. "Look, Lucille, Kathy, why don't you go find something pretty, do a little shopping. I'll catch up with you at the hotel. I got business here."

Mixed among the fives and tens were a number of hundred-dollar bills. He gulped and tried to pull them back, but it was too late. The gal with the missing front tooth kissed him on the cheek, stuffing the cash between her breasts. "Oh, you're so generous, Lupino!" That made him even angrier at Blake. He snatched off his rhinestone jacket and handed it to Lucille. "Here hold this. I'm gonna whip his ass!"

Toni and Roberta stared at the other women with disdain. "You know these people?" Toni asked Charlie dubiously.

Ignoring her, the pudgy blonde clung to Lupino like a wisteria vine. "Oh, Lupino," she cried with disappointment, "don't fight. You said we was going to party. After you run us all this way down here, don't make us go away, honey-lamb. Let's go have some fun."

"Yeah," the other one whined, "forget about these jerks. Come back with us and play more of your beautiful music."

Ignoring them, he stomped over to Blake. "Now, you low-life, son-of-a-bitch. You mother-son-of-a-whore," he bellowed. "This ain't night, on a boat when I ain't onto you. Hand it over!"

From the wheelhouse of the *Aquarius*, Preston watched his brother-in-law swinging his fists at Blake. He saw Lupino's attempted round-house punch, and Blake's deft step to the side as the punch swung past him. Then, almost as an after-thought, Blake delivered a single punch behind Lupino's ear that sent him sprawling on the dock. Charlie's hookers wailed, but Lupino's women watched the brawl with detachment, looking slightly bored.

Lupino pulled himself up groaning, and with an outraged roar, butted Blake in the stomach. Blake, to his great surprise, hadn't expected such an explosive movement and was caught off balance. But as he went down, he managed to deliver another smashing punch behind Lupino's ear. The two men crashed in a heap, but the blond man extricated himself and was on his feet again. Lupino lay groaning on the wharf. Charlie dropped his duffel bag and squatted beside his best friend. "You better quit now, Lupino. I mean it," he begged. "Blake's a bad son-of-a-bitch." Lupino crawled to his knees. "Help me up, I'm gonna kill him!" he groaned. Blake alternated glances at Lupino and the approaching shrimp trawler.

Preston took the boat out of gear, hurried out of the wheelhouse, and grabbed the bow line. Blake stepped past his fallen adversary to catch it, tied the boat off, and turned in time to duck another clumsy punch from Lupino. Blake sent him crashing to the deck with another blow. "Lupino, I've got a plane to catch," Blake said impatiently. "Can't we stop this?"

The bushy-haired youth struggled to his feet. His pupils were dilated. He ignored Charlie's pleas to quit and charged again. Again, Lupino's swing went wild, and again Blake sent him sprawling. This time Lupino lay unconscious on the wharf. His best friend crouched down beside him, fearing he was dead. Meanwhile plump little Lucille, clutching Lupino's rhinestone jacket, fingered the bulges inside the lining. "He's got a bunch of money sewed into the lining," she whispered to her friend excitedly.

No words were spoken among the women. No words were needed. Toni and Roberta, the two high-class prostitutes, were focused on Charlie's unattended duffel bag. Their eyes met the low-class hookers, and together they glanced at the baby blue Lincoln with the understanding of sisters under the skin.

Charlie, who was trying to rouse Lupino, heard the engine start. He heard Preston yelling from the boat, "Stop them! Stop them! Charlie, they got your money!" Charlie's eyes widened in shock as the women backed the car up. By the time he could move, the girls were speeding down the alley with his duffle bag. "Shit," he shrieked. "I'll kill those bitches!" He took off running after the car, hoarsely screaming curses and threats. Charlie returned minutes later, panting, out of breath, looking desperate and hopeless.

The captain jumped to the dock and grabbed Lupino. "Come on, Charlie. Help me get him on the boat. Let's go shrimping."

"My money! I can't go," he gasped. "I've got to find them!"

"Good luck! Forget those whores," Blake said with certainty. "You'll never see them or your money again. They're halfway to New Orleans or Mobile by now."

Preston dumped the unconscious Lupino on the deck like a sack of potatoes. "What are you going to do?" he said to his distraught deckhand. "You can't exactly go to the police." Charlie was still bawling and cussing when he came aboard. Preston turned to the hippie. "Blake, cast us off. We're outta here! From now on, we're gonna earn our money the honest way!"

Blake jerked the loop off the piling, grinned, and gave a slow, respectful salute as Preston pulled away from the dock. He watched the sparkling *Aquarius* move down the canal, her masts and nets silhouetted against the setting sun as she headed out to sea.

The End

Author Biography

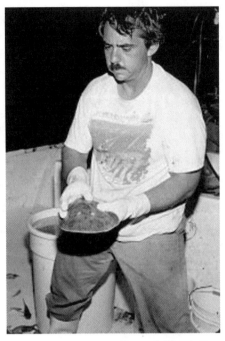

Rudloe with Electric Ray.

Jack Rudloe was born on February 17, 1943 in New York and has lived in the Florida panhandle since 1958. He is married to Anne Rudloe, and they have two sons, Sky and Cypress. His six non-fiction books, *Search for the Great Turtle Mother, The Wilderness Coast, Time of the Turtle, The Living Dock, The Erotic Ocean* and *The Sea Brings Forth* have been widely reviewed, circulated, and are presently being reprinted. He and his wife have published articles in *Audubon, National Geographic, National Wildlife, Natural History, Scientific American* and *Smithsonian*.

Mr. Rudloe has participated in a number of scientific collecting expeditions, including the International Indian Ocean Expedition to Madagascar. Aboard a deep sea royal red shrimp trawler, he brought up giant sea roaches from the Gulf of Mexico and brought them back alive to the New York Aquarium. Mr. Rudloe has worked closely with the commercial fishing industry, helping to develop the markets for rock shrimp and slipper lobsters in Florida. He has traveled to Malaysia, Thailand and China to learn how to harvest and process jellyfish to help commercial fishermen put out of work by the Florida net ban.

Through Gulf Specimen Marine Laboratory (gulfspecimen.org), which Mr. Rudloe established in 1964 as the only independent marine institute on the north Gulf Coast, he provides specimens to thousands of universities and research institutions. His colorful life has been written up in book chapters (*A Border of Blue, The Florida Handbook,* and *Twentieth-Century Florida Authors*) and other publications such as the *New York Times, Audubon, Sports Illustrated, Southern Living, National Fisherman* and the *Wall Street Journal*. His work has been the subject of a number of television documentaries aired on public radio and television programs. In conjunction with his books and environmental activism, Mr. Rudloe has appeared on the NBC Today Show, Good Morning America, PBS, the Fox Network and others.

Out Your Backdoor Press Catalog of Books

Topics

- **Outdoor Culture:**
    - *Momentum: Chasing the Olympic Dream*—Pete Vordenberg
    - *A Dirt Road Rider's Trek Epic*—Victor Vincente of America
    - *The Cross Country Look, Cook & Pleasure Book*—Hal Painter
    - *The Captain Nemo Cookbook Papers*—Hal Painter

- **Fiction**—*Jack Saunders and Potluck by Jack Rudloe*

- **Philosophy (Fifth Way Press)**—*Ronald E. Puhek, Vince L. Lombardi*

- **Local Culture Ruminations**—*Jeff Potter*

- **OYB Anthologies Vols. I/II**—*The Magazine of Cultural Rescue, Modern Folkways and Homemade Adventure (OYB #1-8; #9)*

How to Order

Publisher: Jeff Potter
Mail: OYB Press, 4686 Meridian Rd., Williamston MI 48895
Email: jp@outyourbackdoor.com
Most books $15. Send cash, check, or MO. Shipping included.
Order with a credit card from the OYB Bookstore at OutYourBackdoor.com
All titles available via Amazon, Barnes&Noble, and Borders, who take more than half the proceeds. Best to order from me directly! All titles in 'Books In Print.'

What is OYB?

What is OYB? It's a resource for otherwise unobtainable books which are at a high level of cultural development. These titles have an integrity which is hard to find these days. As a result, perhaps you'll be inspired to set aside any subject biases. If you don't like bike books, novels, or religion books, don't fret. These ain't like that. OYB books are cross-training for the brain, often in multi-genre format. Even when they're about specific topics, they're general interest because they build from the roots of life, working against fragmentation and alienation. I've read most of what's been done in these areas, found something lacking, backtracked to the writer who fills that need (often unknown or out-of-print)...and now publish them for you. A few years ago this could *not* have happened. Thank you, Internet, for breaking down barriers set up by the bookstore and publishing establishment. Thank you, DocuTec and recent short-run printing innovations. Get your hands on an OYB First Edition and you know you have something worth reading. Be the first on your block. And if you know of similar topics or books that need help, feel free to let me know. —*Jeff Potter*

Outdoor Culture

Momentum: Chasing the Olympic Dream

AUTHOR: Pete Vordenberg ISBN:1-892590-56-5 PAGES: 200 LISTPRICE: $17.95 DESCRIPTION: An inside look into life as an elite XC skier. Vordenberg is a 2X-Olympian, Natl Champ and a current US Team Coach. The most interesting picture to date on what it's like to ski...and live...really fast. (With dozens of black&white photos.) Vordenberg says: "We have seen the Olympics through the filter of mass media. But at the edge of the screen there is another figure. When the camera zooms out you can see him, almost too small to recognize. This is the story of the figure at the edge of your screen. It's a voyage following the pursuit of my dream to win an Olympic gold medal. It travels the world, crossing from childhood to the precipitous edge of adulthood. It shares the quixotic humor, excitement, and poignancy inherent in the pursuit of dreams. It is not a retelling of the little engine that could. Rather, it is about why the little engine even tried." REVIEW: "The marvel of Vordenberg's book is that it appeals to the non-skier as well as to ski racers past and present. Healthy doses of self-revelation, touches of *On The Road*, and remarkable insights make this a unique book. It's supposedly about skiing—but it's more about life and seizing it." —Bob Woodward, veteran XC ski journalist.

The Recumbent Bicycle

AUTHOR: Gunnar Fehlau ISBN:1-892590-53-0 PAGES: 180 LISTPRICE: $22.95 DESCRIPTION: There haven't been any general books about a whole amazing, creative side of bicycling: recumbents and HPVs. Finally, here's one! Enjoy. This book covers History, Racing, Touring, Construction and much more, as regards the colorful, diverse world of recumbents and HPVs. Many great black&white photos, full color 12-pg center spread. REVIEWS: 5-star ratings at Amazon.com. "A most informative Recumbenteer's handbook. Its coverage from grass roots right up to current standards is a "must" for anyone interested in building or improving a recumbent."—L. Morse. "This is a fantastic history of recumbents, along with lots of technical information. It has everything you need to know to get started, if you're thinking about buying a recumbent. If you're experienced with recumbents, it has a lot to offer as well."—a reader "No other book that I know of deals with recumbent bicycles in this breadth and depth. It also helps that it is extremely readable and full of cool pictures. Lots of interesting stuff here, from the history of these odd vehicles to the latest speed records and excellent tips on how to get one for yourself. Very well written and well-suited to anyone who might be interested in these bikes, even if they have no previous knowledge. A bargain at twice the price."—P. Pancella.

A Dirt Road Rider's Trek Epic

AUTHOR: Victor Vicente of America ISBN:1-892590-50-6 PAGES: 100 LISTPRICE: $15 DESCRIPTION: If you're a bike buff, you know how rare bike literature is. Here's a bit of story-telling to savor, *A Dirt Road Rider's Trek Epic* by Victor Vincente of America, a bike cult guru hero. This book presents the many media offerings of a unique *victor*. The *Epic* is showcased in this volume along with media reprints from VVA's heyday as first US road racing champion, first modern-era Euro winner, first ultra-distance record holder, and early mountain-bike innovator, dirt guru, events host and then some. Illustrated with his own art from many projects, including bike-making, coin art, posters, and stamps. Sports today seem one-dimensional: why? Here's a fantastically different take: the world of a champ who explores widely. Among many surprises, you'll find that offroad riding offers a treasure of lore and insight. Our author has mined a wondrous chunk of life. His notorious So. Calif. newsletter was the first home of his prose-poem about days and nights in the natural and cultural outback.

Fold-It! —The World of the Folding Bicycle

AUTHOR: Gunnar Fehlau ISBN:1-892590-57-3 PAGES: 150 LISTPRICE: $21.95 DESCRIPTION: The world's only book with everything you need to know about folding bikes. Covers history, development, features and the various models offered, with pro's and con's. With so much new technology readily available, the scene is booming, and the future of the folding bike never looked better! Elegant established models are still inspiring and holding their own, while gorgeous new models are coming out to challenge rigid bikes in every way—but especially in convenience! Find out for yourself. *(Due to be released April, 2003.)*

The Cross Country Ski, Cook, Look & Pleasure Book

(Out of Print: some dealer copies available.) AUTHOR: Hal Painter ISBN:1892590514 EDITION: 2 PAGES: 154 LISTPRICE: $20 DESCRIPTION: Reprints and originals available of this 60's-style classic. A unique literary art book on cross country skiing capturing the spirit of the outdoor culture heyday in the US. Zen and the art of skiing. An antidote to consumerism in skiing and an energetic attempt to reconnect skiing with its roots in fluidity, friendship and just plain fun.

The Captain Nemo Cookbook Papers

Everyone's Guide to Zen and the Art of Boating in Hard Times Illustrated, A Nautical Fantasy *(Out of Print: some dealer copies available.)* AUTHOR: Hal Painter ISBN:18925905522 PAGES: 135 LISTPRICE: $20 DESCRIPTION: Reprints and originals available of this comic 60's look at boating through the eyes of a variety of escapees from the rat race. Zen nuggets, marina etiquette, boat fixer-uppers and an appearance by a wildly mythic hero of boating all combine for a rare literary addition to the boating bookshelf. A great period piece that offers wit and antidotes to the consumerism that's overwhelming modern boating.

Fiction: The Novels of Jack Saunders

General Description of Jack's Style...

In no-holds-barred "Florida writer" tradition, Jack Saunders writes stories about publishing, academia and everyday life, about what it's like to work and succeed while being true to oneself and one's family and culture. He writes honestly and creatively, and that's the understatement of the year--yet it's accessible, fits like a shoe. Tastes like coffee (being an acquired taste, a step up). He writes with encyclopedic insight about how this effort relates to the world around him, other authors, books, movies, music, Florida, cooking, his life, work, business, progress. In folk vernacular with local color that won't quit. Jack names names, uses cultural artifacts in his poetry so superbly you'll be spurred to rent movies, read books, listen to music that you never would've otherwise. Heck, you'll get new appreciation for boxing and baseball..and everything else. (Sailing? Farming?) Folky yet also a linguistic eye-opener. It's that big. It's all about someone trying to do their best in the modern world, to write honestly. Give it a try and see where it gets you, is one of his motifs. Each book is a slice of a larger ouevre (ahem, can you say forklift pallet?)--with letters, memoir, poetry and essay all playing off each other. In the end, though, "it's just stories." Jazz and the blues. In the mainstream of American outsiders: Whitman, Melville, Faulkner, Kerouac, Miller, Algren, Thompson, Bukowski, MacDonald, Willeford, Burke, Hiassen and Finster. As he says, the Cracker spirit lives on and a country boy will make do. Except for insiders, he is entirely unknown. But he's been working close, prolific and giving it his all for 25 years now. Why haven't you heard of him? Find out...

General Reviews of Jack's Books...

In Jack Saunders our generation is extremely lucky to have a powerful and determined writer, an honest writer. A Diogenes not merely of words, but of provocative thoughts. From his hideaway in Florida, like a super-energized lobster, Saunders lashes out at the sickening hypocrisy which is deadening our senses and rotting our souls. It is Saunders' adamant, boneheaded, determined persistence that is his great strength, his great gift to a society staggering in its own materialistic greed. Saunders is America at its best. He spells out what spirit is all about. And humanity. How do we live? When do we really come ALIVE? As we should? And deserve? America needs writers with such strength and ferocity and independence and integrity, not all those greedy little wordmongers contemplating their private parts on every supermarket shelf. Saunders is more than a literary volcano. He is a live, writhing, crackling wire. Spewing sparks in all directions. Creating and developing a brighter, newer world. *--Raymond Barrio*

As exasperating and slippery a "read" as they come. This work is totally unpretentious (and thus honest) and yet its theme is the total unrelenting pretension of a life. That life is excruciating and unavoidable, unedited and ambiguous, squalling and scrawling, elegant and vulgar, ordinary and completely out of the ordinary. Read it; you'll never forget it. *--John M. Bennett*

I have a hunch your stuff is wild and terrific and keeps going off the rails. I have no better explanation for why you don't find publishers, since you certainly write well enough sentence for sentence and paragraph for paragraph. *--Norman Mailer*

This is some very clever writing...rings true to my own wars with the publishers--good luck! *--Theodore Roszak*

All fine hard hitting work. The works of Jack Saunders give us hope. Hope that our lives won't be horrible wasted foolishness. Even when it seems that hope is all we have left, if you feel you can live a fuller life and spend your days in a more profitable way for yourself AND MANKIND you should read Jack Saunders for a ray of hope and a great deal of enjoyment and amusement. OK it rings so true that you'll forget you're reading & think you're talking to yourself. *--Larry Schlueter*

Hey it broke me up--I imagined someone calling here and asking what I was crying about. I was not crying, kid. I was laughing at Jack Saunders' new movie. *--David Zack*

Nothing studied about this one. He just knows. And does. It hangs together, flows together, makes a lot of sense. Cooking like a Tasmanian Dervish. All I can do is tip my hat. *--Carl Weissner*

Jack Saunders is an American original and his life is an open book. His dedication and commitment are evident throughout, and his abundant energy enlivens every page. *--Lawrence Block*

Screed

AUTHOR:Saunders,Jack,L ISBN: 0912824247 LISTPRICE: $15 DESCRIPTION: Stories about life and dealings with the fine arts scene, as world literature. REVIEWS: Thanks for the copy of Screed. I liked it very much. In fact, I've been reading it aloud to my wife in bed at night. You write in a kind of natural, organic, free-flowing and perfectly lucid style that I much admire. *--Edward Abbey* Dear Jack: Thanks for Screed. It's good diatribe. The reason I know is that diatribe makes me feel better. And I felt better reading it. *--Walker Percy* Thanks for Screed. Nicely done. He rolls on. *--Charles Bukowski*

Evil Genius

AUTHOR: Saunders, Jack L. ISBN: 1892590298 PAGES: 277 LISTPRICE: $15 DESCRIPTION: Mortgages house and gives self Evil Genius Award, first prize ever won. Many cultural reviews. Stories of his days in archeology and grad school, fun with The System, as world literature. REVIEWS: In my library the novels of Jack Saunders go right next to MOBY DICK, ISLANDIA, and THE RECOGNITIONS. EVIL GENIUS is an astonishing feat--like watching a man lay eight hundred miles of track single-handed, without ever once stopping, or faltering, or resorting to adjectives. *--Dr. Al Ackerman* Thank you for sending me EVIL GENIUS, which I read last night. I didn't really want to stay up so late, but the book moved forward with a momentum that was overpowering and almost tragic. Your fiction can also be very annoying--which is a virtue, I think. *--Richard Grayson* I am very pleased at the way you handled the tale of your life in EVIL GENIUS. It owes something to Henry Miller, but every writer owes a debt to those before them and those in turn were helped by their predecessors. No one is an absolute original, but you come close. *--William Eastlake* Words for Evil Genius? I took nearly a year out of my own writing time to work on SCREED, on its production, what more need to be said for how I feel about your worth? You're a diamond in the rough, Jack. You've got an intrinsic worth worth more than the realized worth of about 99% of the writers in this country lumped together. If you feel in your heart of hearts that what you're doing is what you must do, then that's settled. Settled with nothing further implied. I'd say your chances of being treated with any sort of kindness, your chances of being recognized for your intrinsic worth, are worse than mine, and mine are Virginia slim. *--John Bennett*

Open Book

AUTHOR: Saunders, Jack L. ISBN: 1892590301 PAGES: 250 LISTPRICE: $15 DE-SCRIPTION: Covers what happened to Evil Genius, how he goes from bad to worse: who would follow up EG with another book? None but a blockhead. Stories about working life after college, as world literature. REVIEW: Thanks for Evil Genius and Open Book; I enjoyed both of them, and asked my publisher to send you my new book, Sideswipe, when it comes out in Feb. In 1957, Theodore Pratt told me that Delray Beach was a better town than N. Y. for a writer. "If you stay in Florida," he told me, "you'll never run out of things to write about." He was right, of course; I never have, and you won't either. My most productive years were from age 50 to 55, and I'm sure that yours will be too. *--Charles Willeford*

Forty

AUTHOR:Saunders,Jack,L ISBN: 0945209010 LISTPRICE: $15 DESCRIPTION: Stories about Jack's efforts to enter "Stage 4" of writing, to give it up, then see what happens. Plenty of culture and bluegrass reviews and overview of life on the edge, with kids, as world literature.

Common Sense

AUTHOR: Saunders, Jack L. ISBN: 1892590263 PAGES: 137 LISTPRICE: $15 DE-SCRIPTION: Part 1 of a 2-part series, Jack Saunders writes stories about his efforts to acculturize IBM during the early days of the PC so they wouldn't get left behind by a competitor more in tune with the times...it didn't work. ("Full Plate", book 2.) An open discussion with his superiors asking how a committee system which rewards buck-passing could ever recognize innovation. "This is the only treaty I will make." World literature.

Full Plate

AUTHOR: Saunders, Jack L. ISBN: 1892590271 PAGES: 76 LISTPRICE: $15 DESCRIP-TION: Part 2 of a 2-part series, Jack Saunders writes stories about his efforts to acculturize IBM during the early days of the PC so they wouldn't get left behind by a competitor more in tune with the times...it didn't work. ("Common Sense", book 1.) "A Contract between Dem and I'Ashola." World literature.

Blue Darter

AUTHOR: Saunders, Jack L. ISBN: 1892590255 PAGES: 85 LISTPRICE: $15 DESCRIP-TION: An aggressive, tricky fast pitch: "Rare back and hurl your blue darter at their ear." Stories from Jack's youth. World literature.

Lost Writings

AUTHOR: Saunders, Jack L. ISBN: 189259028X PAGES: 158 LISTPRICE: $15 DE-SCRIPTION: "Minor chord: Bigfoot sidles into the shadows." Fiesty writings, as world literature.

Other Fiction

Potluck

AUTHOR: Rudloe, Jack ISBN: 1892590375 PAGES: 264 LISTPRICE: $14.95
DESCRIPTION: Hard times and opportunity collide on the high seas. *Potluck* is a page-turning thriller about a decent captain who decides, in extremity, to take a big risk. It's the only realistic picture of small family commercial fishing on the Gulf Coast of Florida and the problems and temptations that confront it. Corrupt forces on all sides are pushing this stalwart breed of Americans into desperation or extinction. But they still do their best to feed us. If you've ever wondered what the lives are like behind the few fishing boats you still see along the coast, look no further. A rare look at the broad and surprising impacts of drug smuggling, misguided regulation and realtor greed along the coast. Author Rudloe is the pre-eminent conservationist of the Florida Gulf Coast, author of highly regarded naturalist books, and operator of the only independent (and thus frequently bureaucratically besieged) marine institute in the region. REVIEW: "Jack Rudloe's non-fiction account of living on the Gulf Coast, *The Living Dock at Panacea*, is a Florida classic that ranks with *Cross Creek*. In *Potluck*, Rudloe proves he can handle fiction with the same energy and insightful style."—Randy Wayne White (*Shark River, Sanibel Flats*)

Tales From the Texas Gang

AUTHOR: Blackolive, Bill ISBN: 1892590387 PAGES: 339 LISTPRICE: $19.95
DESCRIPTION: Wild Bill's writing is in the tradition of Melville...and Keroauc and Castenada and Abbey. It's a bit like Cormac McCarthy as well, only more realistic, authentic and candid. If you like the thrust of those other writers, you'll be thankful for *Tales From the Texas Gang*. It's one of the rare significant additions to American literature. And it's based on real life, and a real life gang. It's set in the late 1800's. It's an outlaw gang gunfighter novel...but so much more. (*Due out Fall, 2003.*)

The Emeryville War

AUTHOR: Blackolive, Bill ISBN: 1892590395 PAGES: 109 LISTPRICE: $12.95
DESCRIPTION: If you liked *Confederacy of Dunces*, you'll like this. Only, remember, it's real. Life in the fringey, unhip edge of Berkeley in the 60's. You've never seen neighbors, cops and city officials like these, nor an observer like Wild Bill—dogs, barbels, wrecked cars and all. (*Due out Fall, 2003.*)

Philosophy: Fifth Way Press

Author: Ron Puhek

Fifth Way Press is an imprint of OYB. It is sponsored by the MIEM, the Michigan Institute of Educational Metapsychology—a fancy way to say "workable religion, philosophy and psychology for living today, inspired by the best of the past". The institute has been represented for 30 years by weekly meetings of quiet, polite folk. Typically these have been people from the 'helping' professions who themselves see that their ways need help. Are in desparate straits. Due to modernism. The 'Fifth Way' concept comes from 'the fourth way' of Ouspensky and Gurdjieff. The previous three ways to attain contact with reality were: the emotional way of the monk, the intellectual way of the yogi, and the physical way of the fakir. These were unified and superceded by the fourth way of the householder, who lives normally in everyday life. The Fifth Way takes the best of all ways without leaving any behind, transcending them all: count your fingers: thumbs up!

If you like Simone Weil, St. Theresa and St. John of the Cross, you'll like Puhek. It's plainly written but maximumly intense philosophy for a modern age. His reflections integrate and build on many works, especially Plato, Sartre, Jung and Freud.

Analects of Wisdom

SERIES: The Art of Living, Book 1 AUTHOR: Puhek, Ronald E. ISBN: 1892590123 PAGES: 118 LISTPRICE: $15 DESCRIPTION: Analects are, literally, "cut readings." In this collection of verses and commentaries, not just the verses but even the commentaries are brief. They all use two devices of higher knowledge: *paradoxical logic* and experiential thinking. Representing the first phase of the soul's transformation in this life, the *Analects* provide instruction in how to live. They establish "rules" whose truth can be tested even by the mind still held captive by the senses. Anyone can understand them without a great development of faith. These stirrings of other-worldly wisdom can work effectively in guiding life in this world. We are of the opinion that the verses themselves may have had more than one author. This is almost certainly true of the commentaries. *Analects of Wisdom* is the first volume of the trilogy, *The Art of Living*. This trilogy is companion to its predecessor, *The Science of Life*, and it is recommended that each volume be read in tandem with its parallel in the other trilogy.

Descent into the World

SERIES: The Art of Living, Book 2 AUTHOR: Puhek, Ronald E. ISBN: 189259014X PAGES: 175 LISTPRICE: $15 DESCRIPTION: As the middle book of the *Art of Living* trilogy, the *Descent into the World* deals with the second phase of development. It is the one hardest to pass through. In the first phase as we launch on our inner journey, hope sustains our spirits. In the third phase, as we draw closer to our destination, we see it distinctly ahead and the joy of anticipation arises. The second phase, however, requires that we return to face the world where we will do our final work. The *Descent* describes this harshest and driest time. Now the comforts of inward meditation leave us. We meditate but return to the world where we must overcome severe tests and avoid deep traps if we are to find in the end the redemption of love.

The Redemption of Love

SERIES: The Art of Living, Book 3 AUTHOR: Puhek, Ronald E. ISBN: 1892590123 PAGES: 118 LISTPRICE: $15 DESCRIPTION: The Redemption of Love is the final book of the six books composing a double trilogy. Each of the three volumes in the two trilogies describes development in qualities of soul called hope, faith, and love. The first volume in each trilogy focuses on the inner and outer growth of hope; the second in each, on faith; and the third in each, on love. The twin trilogies are distinct in as much as one (*The Science of Life*) deals with the three-step movement to integrity in life by means of an upward and inward journey to knowledge of the integrating good that alone makes a life of integrity possible while the other *(The Art of Living)* deals with how actually to live in the world with integrity and meaning. Each volume in the "Science" trilogy parallels its like number in the "Art" trilogy. This is because the first volume in each represents the principle of *hope*. Hope is the virtue of memory. The first volume of each trilogy represents how human, not individual, memory stimulates and guides hope's development first upward through group study under rules where the group represents human or universal wisdom and then downward through insightful sayings of inherited wisdom guiding life. The second volume in each trilogy represents the subsequent movement of *faith*. Similarly, this involves first an upward direction by losing illusory beliefs in the realm of visible goods and attending to the timeless or eternal good and then a downward direction the practical world. Finally, the two third volumes represent the movement in *love* upward to the ultimately indefinable Good and downward to living divine love in the world. While each volume stands on its own and can be read independently from the others, the six volumes also permit of two additional reading strategies. First, the reader might follow the movement of understanding from one book to the next in the "Science" trilogy and then the movement of life in the world in the "Art" trilogy. Alternatively, the reader might even better follow the path of hope upward in the first book of the "Science" and downward in the first book of the "Art," then the path of faith upward and downward in the second books of each trilogy, and finally the path of love upward and downward in the two trilogies.

A Guide to the Nature & Practice of Seminars in Integrative Studies

SERIES: The Science of Life: Book 1 AUTHOR: Puhek, Ronald E. ISBN: 1892590093 PAGES: 145 LISTPRICE: $15 DESCRIPTION:"Seminars in Integrative Studies" is written to serve a distinct and special kind of learning. Integrative studies focus on searching for a principle of unity or integrity to hold together our knowledge and our life. These studies concern themselves with consciousness and conscience. Consciousness and conscience are different from mere knowledge and value judgments. Consciousness and conscience are comprehensive and integrating instead of single, narrow and analytical. Consciousness integrates your understanding and conscience integrates your sense of the good. We concentrate here not on offering a preliminary and superficial "exposure" to the concept and practice of integrated knowledge. Instead, we address those with a serious commitment to integrative research and to those working together as a permanent community dedicated to integrative studies. Thus, the idea of "seminars" in integrative studies refers not to classes in any ordinary sense of external enrollment but to personal intention, interest, and involvement. Seminars are regular gatherings of those devoted to pursuing integration in knowledge and life. These seminars have formal and informal rules. They require an inner commitment and a desire to grow to knowledge of life through investigating the nature of life using the only concrete and direct perspective we have: our own existence.

Spiritual Meditations

SERIES: The Science of Life: Book 2 AUTHOR: Puhek, Ronald E. ISBN: 1892590107 PAGES: 166 LISTPRICE: $15 DESCRIPTION: Spiritual Meditations, the second book in the trilogy The Science of Life, is an excursion into the second stage of human spiritual development. Its primary focus is on the practices that will allow us to elevate our understanding so we might better perceive the standard of value that can inwardly bring us peace and outwardly guide us to the best life possible. Integrative knowledge is essential to both and methods of pursuing such knowledge are essential if we are to gain it and live fuller, less violent, and more harmonious lives. None of the methods prevailing today is adequate to the task of arriving at integrative knowledge. This book presents part of the process of an effective response to life.

The Spirit of Contemplation

SERIES: The Science of Life: Book 3 AUTHOR: Puhek, Ronald E. ISBN: 1892590115 PAGES: 175 LISTPRICE: $15 DESCRIPTION: *The Spirit of Contemplation* is the final book in the trilogy *The Science of Life*. It explores the culminating phase of spiritual development and what needs to happen after the completion of the spiritual exercises associated with meditation. Meditation takes us out of the world; contemplation returns us to it. Meditation renders us unable to live in reality; contemplation realizes the redemption of reality. It is the highest peak of the mountain of sprical growth. The entire trilogy, however, is only the first of two. *The Science of Life* concentrates on the development of spiritual understanding; the second trilogy, *The Art of Living*, will focus on the transformation of life.

Meaning & Creativity

SERIES: Blue Trilogy, Book 1 AUTHOR: Puhek, Ronald E. ISBN: 1892590069 PAGES: 118 LISTPRICE: $15 DESCRIPTION: Meaning and Creativity, first book of the Blue Trilogy, explores the illusions of meaning that dominate life today and how to break out of their chains-a vital first step in the process of reality. Life is not worth living if it is not meaningful. Most of the strategies for living today are, however, merely methods of enabling us to endure frightful meaninglessness. They are all mechanical and operate by encouraging us to flee from one meaningless activity as soon as we catch the scent of its decaying character and race to another, equally meaningless. Life becomes a continuous merry-go-round. We move in circles, getting nowhere, but are lost in the illusion that we are moving along a straight path to greater good-even when we try to use methods that are thought to counteract this. So long have we lived like this that if we would wake up and see our true state, we would be shattered. Nihilism would be our fate. To avoid this catastrophe, we need to prepare ourselves with some understanding of how to live a life of meaning. The only meaningful life is a creative life. This is easy to see once we realize what "creativity" consists of.

The Abyss Absolute

The Autobiography of a Suicide SERIES: Blue Trilogy, Book 2 AUTHOR: Puhek, Ronald E. ISBN: 1892590077 PAGES: 146 LISTPRICE: $15 DESCRIPTION: The Abyss Absolute is the second book of the Blue Trilogy. It is the heart and soul of this series. Realizing the meaning-lessness of most of contemporary life and even understanding how we must live if we are to find meaning are not enough. By themselves, these achievements may end in nothing but disillusion-disillusion of the meaninglessness and disillusion with the prospects of finding an alternative-even among those approaches typically thought to bring hope. This is because before we can find a way upward we must first allow ourselves to fall into an abyss so profound that it feels as if it will annihilate us. Courage to enter this abyss is the only hope of escaping the emptiness of contemporary life, but there are dangerous traps along the way.

Killer Competitiveness

SERIES: Blue Trilogy, Book 3 AUTHOR: Puhek, Ronald E. ISBN: 1892590085 PAGES: 130 LISTPRICE: $15 DESCRIPTION:Killer Competitiveness is the third and last book of the Blue Trilogy. We explored the meaninglessness that dominates life today in Meaning and Creativity, the first book of the series. Then we face a great challenge when we take up a path to meaning in the second book, The Abyss Absolute. This last book accounts for how it is possible for us today to exist so long under meaningless conditions without realizing it. So empty is life without meaning that it could continue only with the help of an extremely powerful illusion. This compelling illusion is generated by competitiveness in nearly everything we do-even in our supposed efforts to cooperate or function independently. Competitiveness generates the illusion of value. Therefore, we do not see the valuelessness of our lives even as we suffer from it.

Mind, Soul & Spirit

An Inquiry into the Spiritual Derailments of Modern Life AUTHOR: Puhek, Ronald E. ISBN: 1892590026 PAGES: 148 LISTPRICE: $15 DESCRIP-TION:The prevailing styles of living today require the "derailment" of our energies. The spirit or energy that life grants us to fulfill our destiny is seized, imprisoned, and then turned away from its natural direction, usually to be amplified for ulterior motives. The various derailments of spirit operate unconsciously upon their victims. We today are particularly vulnerable to blindness here because of our ignorance of the dynamics of spiritual life-even as many of us pretend to spirituality and feel energy which we trust to be helpful. Spiritual knowledge is almost completely absent in all contemporary education, and, as a society, we are nearly bankrupt spiritually. This book maps out the many ways our spirit gets diverted without our knowing it. We must take back our spiritual birthright.

The Powers of Knowledge

SERIES: The Crisis in Modern Culture: Book 1 AUTHOR: Puhek, Ronald E. ISBN: 1892590042 PAGES: 83 LISTPRICE: $15 DESCRIPTION: Modern culture is the source of a crisis in civilization. This now world-wide culture is generating increasingly intolerable conditions of human life mostly because of the faulty assumptions built into it that concern our powers of knowledge. Because of these assumptions, we fail today to develop and use the whole range of our powers. Consequently, we find ourselves increasingly unable to perceive, let alone understand, the forces flowing into and out of our lives. We can see that things are bad but not why they are so. We do not see this because the very tools of perception we use are the flawed victims of a culture that renders them inadequate. The Powers of Knowledge (Book I of The Crisis of Modern Culture) explores our powers of knowledge-both those we only partly or wrongly develop and those we entirely neglect. It shows how we may expand our awareness by actualizing all of them in a more integrated way. It illustrates how we can turn aside the forces of destruction that today are reaching critical mass everywhere, even in places we thought were protected.

Violence

SERIES: The Crisis in Modern Culture: Book 2 AUTHOR: Puhek, Ronald E. ISBN: 1892590050 PAGES: 82 LISTPRICE: $15 DESCRIPTION:This book (Book II of The Crisis of Modern Culture) presents an approach to understanding the specific forms of violence particularly appropriate to contemporary life. It illustrates that most violence today is completely invisible both to those who do it and to those who suffer it. This is because the prevailing concept of violence is inadequate. If our concept of violence encompasses only its physical or sensible forms, we will not see it when it operates even when we think we fight against it in its emotional and especially in spiritual forms. Today the dominant form of violence is spiritual. Today we can even love violence because we suffer from it in ways we do not see. Today there is violence in our acts of love. We must be concerned, therefore, both about our love of violence and the violence of our love.

Stephen of the Holy Mountain

AUTHOR: Puhek, Ronald E. ISBN: 1892590018 PAGES: 94 LISTPRICE: $15 DESCRIPTION: An inner journey, outwardly masking itself as a sojourn up the side of a high mountain, Stephen of the Holy Mountain seeks answers to the most perplexing questions that come to those who have awakened from the sleep of ordinary existence. The mysterious figure of Stephen acts as a guide both to the author and to many others who climb Stephen's mountain to find him. His advice is often too harsh for many who think they seek it. Unfailingly kind, however, Stephen does his best to aid all who come to him.

The Metaphysical Imperative

A Critique of the Modern Approach to Science AUTHOR: Puhek, Ronald E. ISBN: 1892590034 PAGES: 135 LISTPRICE: $15 DESCRIPTION: Metaphysical assumptions are and have always been a necessary and unavoidable part of human life. Unfortunately, today we have fallen into the catastrophic belief that our basic perceptions of reality do not rest on metaphysical judgments but are purely "physical." If we use the term "metaphysics" at all, it is only to refer to abstract philosophical ideas or, worse, to half-crazed religious attitudes. Consequently, we have rendered ourselves unable to distinguish between the metaphysical and non-metaphysical aspects of any knowledge and are still less able to judge whether our hidden or flaunted metaphysical assumptions are faulty and, if so, how they might be corrected. The Metaphysical Imperative explores the nature of metaphysical assumptions, how they are all-pervasive, which ones dominate our attitudes today, what their flaws are, and how we might improve them.

Social Consciousness

Renewed Theory in the Social Sciences AUTHOR: Puhek, Ronald E. ISBN: 189259000X PAGES: 202 LISTPRICE: $15 DESCRIPTION:This is a unique study of the theoretical foundations of social science. In particular, it criticizes the practice of applying the methods of the physical sciences to the study of human life. Methods very appropriate to the study of "things" or objects are not appropriate to the study of the human self. When we use such inappropriate methods, we end in making the human self into a thing, and all the knowledge we gain affords us only more power to dominate and suppress the human. These methods violate human freedom and dignity in any use, let alone in their application in fields like psychology, advertising and politics. This study concludes by developing an alternative approach to explanation.

Matricide

AUTHOR: Lombardi, Vincent L. ISBN: 189259031X PAGES: 287 LISTPRICE: $15 DESCRIPTION: A novel about a crime that shook a small town and hurled a 12-year-old girl into the bizarre world of court-appointed professionals. As she grows up, she's driven to madness, torn between cultures, struggling at the crossroads of what comes next—will it be Brave New World or a new Renaissance?

Local Culture Ruminations

Making Somewhere from Nowhere: Growing Up in Freeway Exitville

AUTHOR: Potter, Jeff PAGES: 100 LISTPRICE: $15 DESCRIPTION: Contemporary essays written about the author's hometown—a faceless suburb of professors, professionals, mall-rats, and mini-malls. A rare look at 'here,' but perhaps it's important to break the aversion to looking at what's closest to home since everywhere is starting to look like 'here.' —It's a traffic-packed sector smashed out of the rural countryside in the last 30 years. But it's also a place with hidden natural and cultural distinctions. How can it survive the onslaught of speculation? That's the drama of it. Potter writes about Place versus Noplace and offers practical methods which can be used to rebuild somewhere out of the nowhere created by our best and brightest. A candid, polite, unpublishable point of view unseen before (the average view) intended to raise the level of discussion by taking it away from experts, specialists and those who hope to separate people from each other for their advantage.

"Out Your Backdoor" Zine Anthology, Vols. 1 & 2

OYB: the Magazine of Cultural Rescue, Modern Folkways and Homemade Adventure (*OYB* Issues #1-8 & #9)

OYB has been covering the neglected aspects of modern folk culture since 1990. The latest issue is the Vol. 2 anthology; earlier issues form Vol.1.

OYB is the back porch of culture, where people hang out helping each other find the nifty things that people really do. (The front door being for salesmen and authorities.) *OYB* revives the jaded, helps those who've 'been there, done that' to get to the next level. *OYB* is for all-rounders and generalists, like most people are. It works against the alienating specialties that society uses to split us from ourselves and each other. It creatively explores all sorts of things, including: biking, books, boats, movies, zines, religion, skiing, fishing, hunting, garage sales, getting by, making do. Get the picture? (Big website at www.outyourbackdoor.com.)